A Fire in Paradise

'Rana Safvi choses the most turbulent and torturous period of Indian history to tell a touching story through the young daughter of the Emperor Bahadur Shah Zafar [who he has had] from a concubine. The endearing presence and poetry reflecting the anguish of Zafar makes one feel the vulnerability of the times, making his touching verse both timeless and relevant.

'The novel is studded with gems describing a culture and a way of life that was soon to vanish with the victory of an ugly, exploitative colonial might'—Muzaffar Ali

A Firestorm in Paradise

A novel on the 1857 Uprising

RANA SAFVI

PENGUIN BOOKS

An imprint of Penguin Random House

PENGUIN BOOKS

Penguin Books is an imprint of the Penguin Random House group of companies whose addresses can be found at global.penguinrandomhouse.com

Published by Penguin Books India Pvt. Ltd
4th Floor, Capital Tower 1, MG Road,
Gurugram 122 002, Haryana, India

Penguin
Random House
India

First published in Penguin Books by Penguin Random House India 2024

Copyright © Rana Safvi 2024

All rights reserved

10 9 8 7 6 5 4 3 2 1

ISBN 9780143466048

Typeset in Adobe Garamond Pro by Manipal Technologies Limited, Manipal
Printed at Gopsons Papers Pvt. Ltd., Noida

www.penguin.co.in

MIX
Paper from
responsible sources
FSC
www.fsc.org
FSC® C191020

This book is dedicated to and inspired by:

Prof. Shamsur Rahman Faruqi sahib.
With my utmost respect and much love for who you were and
your support and faith in me.
I have learnt so much from you. You continue to guide
me even now.

Agar firdaus bar ru-ye zamin ast
Hamin ast-o hamin ast-o hamin ast
If there is Paradise on earth
It is this, it is this, it is this . . .

(A verse inscribed on the top of the arches in Diwan-e Khas in the
Red Fort.)

Contents

Introduction

The Story of Falak Ara

In 2014, I took up the task of translating Zahir Dehlvi's witness account of the Uprising of 1857. As it turned out, *Dastan-e-Ghadar* (Penguin Random House India, 2017) was a transformational book for me, opening up as it did, the world of the later Mughal emperors and the city of Shahjahanabad where harmony and peace had prevailed amongst the citizens for so long. I was very impressed by the character traits of Emperor Bahadur Shah Zafar, whom one knows only in reference to his ghazals or his exile. This led me to explore more accounts from that era, and I came upon Munshi Faizuddin's *Bazm-e Aakhir* and Wazir Hasan Dehlvi's *Dilli ka Aakhri Deedar*. These two books described a Delhi that people had long forgotten. Further reading, of course, revealed to me a city marked by poetry, songs, festivities and celebrations—the emperor may have lost political power, but cultural activities flourished, and the flame of civilization burned bright, unaware of the tragedy that waited on the horizon.

It wasn't only cultural activities that were thriving. In Delhi, education had always been considered important under the Mughal rule, and there were several madrasas teaching religious and even secular subjects such as logic, philosophy, mathematics and astronomy. Delhi College, opened in 1825 by the British, had established a 'Society for the Promotion of Knowledge in India through the Medium of Vernacular Languages' in 1840 to translate scientific books and treatises from English into Urdu, Bengali and Hindi.

The people of Delhi lived in communal harmony and despite occasional friction, there was no evidence of deep-rooted distrust between them. This is symbolized by the *Sair-e-Gul Faroshan* or *Phoolwaalon ki Sair*, started in the reign of Akbar Shah II in the 1820s, wherein a procession of the flower-sellers would offer *pankha*s both at Qutub Saheb's dargah and at the Jogmaya temple in Mehrauli. The writer Farhatullah Baig recounts an incident in his book, *Phoolwaalon ki Sair*, that when Bahadur Shah Zafar was unable to go to the temple to offer a pankha due to ill-health, then, in a spirit of fairness, he also declined to visit the dargah subsequently, so as to not hurt the feelings of his Hindu subjects.

Baig also records that when Zafar was exiled to Rangoon (now Yangon, Myanmar) after the fall of Delhi, there was a palpable sense of loss amongst Hindus and Muslims alike, who felt as if they had lost their father.

This was also a city where Hindus and Muslims lived and celebrated together, where the emperor treated all as his children. In fact, before leaving the Red Fort on 17 September 1857, his last prayer—as recorded by his daughter and later documented by Khwaja Hasan Nizami in *Begumat ke Aansoo*—was: 'The entire Hindu and Muslim population of Hindustan are my children and trouble surrounds them all. Don't let them suffer because of my actions. Safeguard them from all trouble.'

Inspired by this long-forgotten world and curious to fill the lingering gaps in our history, I felt compelled to explore further. This was how I ended up translating Munshi Faizuddin's *Bazm-e Aakhir* and Wazir Hasan Dehlvi's *Dilli ka Aakhri Deedar* and Arsh Taimuri's *Qila Moalla ki jhalkiyan* as well as a few stories from *Begumat ke Aansoo* by Khwaja Hasan Nizami—all of which were collated in *City of My Heart* (Hachette India, 2018). This, in turn, spurred me to translate the complete set of stories in *Begumat ke Aansoo* as *Tears of the Begums* (Hachette India, 2022).

However, I still felt I had not done justice to this city that was so close to my heart because there were so many other accounts that needed to be brought to public notice, but remained buried in archives, untranslated, if not lost to history altogether. This made me think in terms of writing a novel where I could incorporate all this wealth of detail—the stories, the chronicles, the trivia, the poetry—and present it entertainingly for contemporary readers who, I hope, will share my love and curiosity for this dramatic, distinctive epoch. And, in doing so, if I happen to succeed in bringing new readers into the fold of Delhi *dil-walas*, then I will consider myself truly blessed.

The story of Falak Ara is fictitious, as is her character, but the background, customs and events are real. Emperor Bahadur Shah II had many children and since I wanted to draw on royal protocol, I took the liberty of making her the Emperor's daughter.

I named her Falak, sky, to show the expanse of that world.

While all the characters, real or imagined, have a religious affiliation, I have purposely withheld assigning any kind of religion to two very important characters: Hira and Hariyali. It was important for me that readers view these characters essentially as human beings, irrespective of faith. The word 'Hariyali' signifies fertility and prosperity and is a common dua given to girls: '*Hari bhari raho.*' The story starts and ends with her. Hira, 'diamond', signifies someone who is unyielding and stubborn, as much as it symbolizes greed.

The customs and festivities inside the Red Fort as well as the details of how the food was prepared and served have all been based on Munshi Faizuddin's *Bazm-e Aakhir*, Wazir Hasan Dehlvi's *Dilli ka Aakhri Deedar* and Syed Nasir Nazir Firaq's *Lal Qile ki Ek Jhalak*. The political turbulence inside the Red Fort is drawn from information found in Arsh Taimuri's *Qila Moalla ki Jhalkiyan.*

Khwaja Hasan Nizami's account of the daily activities of Emperor Bahadur Shah Zafar, described in *Bahadur Shah Ka Roznamcha*, have been incorporated in a few court scenes and in the particulars of certain financial transactions described in the novel.

The Uprising of 1857 and the Siege of Delhi are real, and I have used the accounts from Zahir Dehlvi's *Dastan-e Ghadar* as well as Munshi Jeevan Lal and Kotwal Muinuddin Hasan Khan's accounts as translated by Charles Metcalfe into *Two Native Narratives of the Mutiny in Delhi*. I have shown Zahir Dehlvi saying some of the dialogues that he has recorded in *Dastan-e Ghadar*.

Khwaja Hasan Nizami's accounts were very useful for presenting a picture of the 'haram' in the palace before and after the Uprising. In this context, I should mention that I have intentionally used the word 'haram' and not the westernized 'harem' throughout the novel. The word means 'sanctuary'. When used in the context of palaces, it meant the area reserved for the royal ladies which was out of bounds for all men except the emperor and a few royal princes. But the haram not only offered the royal women protection from prying eyes; it was a space of thriving activity which had to be run very efficiently, in accordance with a strict hierarchy, by the women themselves. Mughal women, especially those at the very top of the hierarchy, had control of financial resources and, after the reign of Akbar the Great, were known to commission buildings and even play a role in business and trade—all from the secured confines of the haram, with eunuchs being engaged as agents to interact with the outside world. On the other hand, the term 'harem' in popular imagination has a negative connotation and has come to denote some kind of exotic sexual playground of Muslim rulers and nobles. This is because, over time and under a colonial lens, the rich and layered Mughal haram found in Persian sources came to be twisted and morphed into a caricature of a decadent Mughal society. Likewise, the women were reduced to unflattering stereotypes—often just seen as faceless ladies, whether submissive or licentious or scheming, without humanity or depth. It is this caricatured and reductive image that I wish to avoid in my novel.

The two editions of Sir Syed Ahmad Khan's *Asar-us Sanadid*, which pay loving tribute to the monuments of Delhi, are the main source for my descriptions of the magnificent Red Fort, which forms the background for the novel.

I have also relied on S. Mahdi Hasan's book, *Bahadur Shah Zafar and the War of 1857 in Delhi*, for details of the '*ghadar*' and the character of the emperor.

A full list of sources and books has been provided in the bibliography at the end of the book. I have also included, for reference, a separate historical note on the Mughal empire in the nineteenth century.

I have added some subaltern characters to show the other side of the city, representative of the many stoic and resilient denizens of the city, all of whom perhaps suffered the most in the cataclysm and whose voices have largely been left out of the historical record. I have added a commentary in their words on how they perceived the ways of the rich.

The Uprising of 1857 brought to an end not just an empire but a way of life. I wanted to bring that memory back into public consciousness.

Most of the chapters in my novel begin and end with fragments of verse and song that represent the mood and culture of that time. And in order to stay true to the spirit of that era, I have ensured that each of these verses is taken from the period before 1857. However, readers will notice that I have not included any verses or songs after 16 May 1857. I have done this deliberately—to symbolize the destruction of this way of life after that fateful date.

I have used the formal court language for the dialogues spoken by the royalty and aristocracy, as was the norm, peppered with verses and *Begumati* zabaan for members of the *zenana*. While Persianized Urdu was used by the elite, the common folks of Shahjahanabad used a dialect called *karkhandari zaban*. Conversations between women, particularly the attendants and serving maids, were filled with expletives and curses since they were in female gatherings away from men. This was highly idiomatic, drawing from daily life, earthy and often bawdy and in complete contrast to the flowery, polite language spoken by the elite. Due to infant mortality, epidemics and seasonal diseases taking their toll, conversations were peppered with references to evil eye, hexes and prayers for longevity of their charges.

The city that was once Shahjahanabad—a '*Shahr Panah*', or city of shelter, for its residents—now exists in people's memories as a legend of sorts, a lived reality from a forgotten time. In fact, I was told by Ashok Mathur, a resident of Shahjahanabad, that his family and community most of whom have shifted out of it to New Delhi still refer to it as 'shahr'.

Despite increasing polarization in the country today, I find that the depleted city of Shahjahanabad still clutches on to its age-old syncretic customs. It is that enduring spirit that I wish to honour through my novel.

Historical Note

The Mughal Empire in the Nineteenth Century

The first half of the nineteenth century brought about far-reaching changes in the history of Delhi. But the historical context that made these changes possible began a century earlier.

The Mughal capital was beset with political intrigues after the death of Emperor Aurangzeb Alamgir in 1707. Within a decade of his death, a power vacuum followed, and Abdullah Khan and Hussain Ali Khan—popularly known as the Saiyad brothers— became a formidable force and were instrumental in determining which emperor ascended the throne.

Emperor Bahadur Shah I (r. 1707–12) was succeeded by Emperor Jahandar Shah. The latter was assassinated on the orders of the Saiyad brothers in 1713 and succeeded by his nephew Farrukhsiyar (r. 1713–19) with the brothers' help. The Saiyad brothers were now virtually in control of the Mughal empire. In 1719, they handpicked three princes one after the other from the closely guarded quarters where the *salatin*—descendants of previous emperors—lived and crowned them emperors. While Rafi-ud-Darajat (r. February–June 1719) and his brother Shah Jahan II (r. June–September 1719) each died within a few months of ascending the throne, the third emperor, Muhammad Shah, had a long reign (r. 1719–48). Early on, Emperor Muhammad Shah had realized the danger posed by the Saiyad brothers' concentration of power. And so, he schemed to have them killed in 1722, after which he came into his own.

However, his luck did not last very long. Persian Emperor Nadir Shah invaded the Mughal empire in 1738, and sacked the Mughal capital in 1739, consequently decimating not only the emperor's powers but also the might and wealth of his empire. By the second quarter of the eighteenth century, the Mughal empire had started losing its territories to regional powers such as the Marathas, Jats and Sikhs. The governors of provinces such as Awadh, Bengal and Hyderabad had more or less established themselves as independent rulers, though officially they accepted Mughal suzerainty.

This decline was further compounded by the invasion of Afghan ruler Ahmed Shah Abdali and the imprisonment of the Mughal Emperor Alamgir II (r. 1754–59). Though Ahmed Shah Abdali reinstated Alamgir II to the throne before returning to his capital of Kandhar, power rested in the hands of Najib-ud Daulah, who had joined Abdali. In due course, the Mughal wazir, Imad-ul Mulk ousted Najib-ud Daulah from this position with the help of the Marathas. The balance of political power shifted into the hands of the Marathas—Imad-ul Mulk continued to wield some influence in the court and, in 1759, was instrumental in organizing the assassination of the emperor.

Alamgir II's eldest son, Ali Gauhar, who had already fled Delhi to escape Imad-ul Mulk's intrigues, had to crown himself in Bihar, away from Delhi, in 1760 as Emperor Shah Alam II.

In 1764, the combined armies of Mughal Emperor Shah Alam II, Nawab Shuja-ud Daulah, and the nawab of Bengal fought the armies of the British East India Company in Buxar, west of Patna. The East India armies under Major Hector Munro prevailed. This was a watershed moment in the history of political power in India and the rise of the fortunes of the British East India Company.

The following year saw Emperor Shah Alam II sign the treaty of Allahabad with Robert Clive, giving away the revenues of the Mughal empire's richest provinces—Bengal, Bihar and Orissa—to the British East India Company. The Company was to collect the revenue from these states and pay an annual tribute to the Mughal emperor of twenty-six lakh rupees to maintain the Mughal court in Allahabad.

Shah Alam II could only return to Delhi in 1772 with the help of the powerful Marathas and lived under their protection. Intrigues and power struggles continued in Delhi and in 1787, Ghulam Qadir Rohilla, grandson of the ousted wazir Najib-ud Daulah, demanded to be made the Mir Bakshi—head of the emperor's army throughout the Mughal empire. He left the Mughal court a few months later, but in 1788, he tricked the emperor into granting him an audience and used this ruse to successfully capture the emperor and the fort.

Then started the ravaging of the Red Fort in search of the hidden treasures said to be worth millions. In relentless pursuit of this fabled treasure, the Mughal emperor was tortured while the modesty of the Mughal ladies was brutally violated. And when torture yielded no results, the aged emperor was blinded by Ghulam Qadir with an Afghan knife on 10 August 1788.

Thereafter, the combined armies of the Marathas, under Mahadji Scindia alongwith Begum Samru and her army, succeeded in defeating Ghulam Qadir Rohilla and reinstating the blind emperor on the throne, under the Maratha protection.

This state of affairs continued till 1803, when the Marathas were defeated by the British East India Company led by General Gerard Lake in the Battle of Delhi.

The proclamation in the city was now, '*khilqat khuda ki, mulk Badshah ka, hukm Company ka* [the Lord's creation, the emperor's territory and the British East India Company's rule].'

The British were de facto rulers of Delhi and the tribute that was to be given to the Mughal emperor, as per the treaty of Allahabad, was now a pension, though nowhere close to the amount that had been promised as per that treaty

Both emperors Akbar Shah II (r. 1806–28) and later Bahadur Shah II (r. 1828–57) had sent emissaries to Britain to plead their case for increasing the pensions with the directors of the East India Company. In 1830, Akbar Shah II had sent Ram Mohan Roy, who had been given the title 'Raja'. Subsequently, in 1843, Bahadur Shah II—popularly known today as Bahadur Shah Zafar after his pen name 'Zafar'—had appointed the anti-slavery activist George Thompson to represent him. Both the emissaries failed to get any concessions and thus the pensions continued.

The Emperor had been receiving a stipend of twelve lakh rupees per annum in 1813; this was increased to fifteen lakh rupees per annum in 1833. Eventually, the emperor was also divested of his command over the Red Fort, and nothing could happen without the British Resident's consent.

That was not all. The Mughal custom of *nazr* being offered to the emperor by visitors was stopped and he could no longer mint coins in the imperial mint. By 1835, the emperor's name was removed from the coins.

By 1845, it was an established practice that British officers did not need to dismount if the emperor's procession passed by. In 1846, orders were given by the British officers that all Hindustani nobles should be informed that if they saw any Englishman's carriage coming in the market when they were on their elephants, they should take their mount to a corner so that the Englishmen did not face any inconvenience.

Despite all this, the Mughal emperor continued to be revered by his subjects, who would ritually assemble every day under the balcony of the Musamman Burj, known as *zer-e jharokha*, for a glimpse of the much-loved emperor.

Dramatis Personae

Names in bold refer to real historical personages.

<small></small>CHARACTERS IN THE RED FORT

- Falak Ara, a daughter of Bahadur Shah Zafar from a concubine
- Dil Ruba, a concubine and mother of Falak Ara
- Mirza Qaiser, a salatin, living in the Red Fort
- Mirza Aftab, Mirza Qaiser's father and cousin of the emperor
- **Emperor Bahadur Shah Zafar** (also referred to as the Badshah, the Emperor, Huzur Badshah, Badshah Salamat, Majesty, Jahanpanah, Huzur Purnur, Huzur Mahabali, Huzur Jahanpanah, Alampanah Badshah)
- **Nawab Zeenat Mahal Begum**, wife of Bahadur Shah Zafar, (also referred to as the Malika-e Dauran, Empress, Badshah Begum)
- Mubarak, Falak Ara's foster mother
- Naseeban, a seamstress employed in the Fort
- Sikandar Ara Begum, Emperor Bahadur Shah Zafar's great aunt
- Zohrun Nisa Begum, cousin of the Emperor
- Rashid Ara Begum, cousin of the Emperor
- Afroz uz-Zamani Begum, a Mughal relative living in the Red Fort haram
- Zeenatun Nisa, a thirteen-year-old cousin of Falak Ara
- Zebunnisa Begum, a ten-year-old cousin of Falak Ara
- **Sharafat ul-Mahal Begum**, wife of Emperor Bahadur Shah Zafar, mother of Mirza Mughal

- **Mirza Mughal**, son of the Emperor
- **Amani Khanum**, wife of Mirza Mughal
- **Mirza Qadiruddin Mohammad Bahadur**, son of Mirza Mughal
- **Mirza Abu Bakr**, son of Mirza Fakhru
- Khwajasara Agha Jan, the *darogha* of the *zenana*

CHARACTERS LIVING IN THE CITY OF SHAHJAHANABAD

- Hariyali, the bangle-seller
- Hira, a trader
- Rahim, Naseeban's husband
- Miyan Nabbu, son of a *jagirdar*
- Kunwar Mohammed Ibrahim, a student
- Mirza Abu Bakr, a Mughal descendant
- Zoravar Singh, son of a Rajput chieftain, Sangram Singh
- Thakur Sangram Singh, Zoravar's father
- Hamid Ali Khan, a student of Mir Panjakash
- Nawabzada Shahrukh Beg, a noble's son
- Santosh Lal, son of Munshi Subhash Lal, a student at Delhi College
- Brijnath Zutshi, a Kashmiri Brahmin scholar studying at Delhi College
- Imamuddin Khan, a student of Master Ramchandra at Delhi College
- Dr Bishambar Nath Kaul, a childhood friend of Mirza Aftab
- Thakur Madhav Singh, a landlord involved in the plotting against the British
- Imam sahib, co-conspirator of Thakur sahib
- Mir sahib, co-conspirator of Thakur sahib
- Bhooray Khan, a disaffected sepoy from Awadh
- Mushtari bai, a *derawali tawaif*
- Daaran bai, Bahadur Shah Zafar's favourite singer
- Mahtab Ara Begum, sister of Mirza Aftab

- Chand Kunwar, mother of Zoravar Singh
- Thakurain, wife of Thakur Madhav Singh

OFFICIALS OF THE MUGHAL COURT

- **Nawab Mahboob Ali Khan Khwajasara**, the Mughal wazir till his death in June 1857
- **Hakim Ahsanullah Khan**, a physician who became wazir in June 1857, after the death of Mahboob Ali Khan

LUMINARIES OF SHAHJAHANABAD

- **Mirza Ghalib**, a renowned poet, known popularly as Mirza Naushah
- **Mufti Sadruddin Khan Sahib Azurda**, appointed the Mufti of Shahjahanabad by the British
- **Syed Zahir Dehlvi**, courtier and poet
- **Mirza Nawab 'Dagh' Dehlvi**, a poet
- **Mir Panjakash**, an ace calligrapher

MISCELLANEOUS

- **Gami Khan**, a British spy employed by the East India Company
- **Kulsum Zamani Begum**, daughter of Emperor Bahadur Shah Zafar
- **Bakht Khan**, a celebrated officer in the British Army who joined the emperor's forces in 1857 and was appointed its commander-in-chief

Prologue

1857

Shahr Panah. Shahjahanabad. Dilli.

City of kings, the domain of splendour and beauty. This was where poetry and music, silks and spices, rare jewels and fine horses—all could be sampled and savoured. For centuries it had shone as the crown jewel of a magnificent empire. But now its days of bounty seemed numbered.

Falak Ara stared into the cloudless sky, hoping for rain and relief. It pained her that the city she and her ancestors had called home now stood on the brink of peril—if not already engulfed in its fiery jaws. Violence stalked the avenues of the city; cries of anguish echoed in the air. The agitated glances of those around her carried the ever-present fear that carnage on the streets could just as easily find its way into the sanctity of their home. Survival, therefore, would depend on abandoning this city to its fate.

When men behave like beasts, all one can do is run and hide. But when there are no hiding places left, what then? Falak knew that leaving her beloved Dilli had become imperative. And this broke her heart. Even though the rules of the palace had forbidden her from wandering the city's streets, she had always felt at one with Delhi, seeking strength in its timeless glory, its ancient history, its syncretic culture. It was also the city in which she had found love—a love she was in danger of losing, it seemed if she lingered here much longer.

It was impossible to imagine that after seeing and enduring so much, Shahr Panah would be destined to witness its own doom. Falak could not bear it.

How, she wondered, *could a glorious capital such as this descend into utter madness?*

1

Falak Goes to the Jharokha Fair

1856

Namaz e sham e ghareeban chu girya aghaazam
Ba muyaha e ghareebana qissa pardazam

I commence the prayers of the Night of the Exiled
like weeping,
With estranged laments, I narrate the story.

—Hafez

The summer night was coming to an end. Bells could be heard chiming in the temples of Shahr Panah, or the city of refuge, the imams of various mosques were performing their *wuzu* in preparation to give the *azan*, the faithful were stirring in their homes. While some would flock to the Jamuna River for their ritual bath, others would rush to the mosque for dawn prayers. And all of them would converge under the *jharokha* of the Qila-e Mubarak for a *darshan* of their beloved Jahanpanah Badshah.

The sleeping ladies in the *mahal* of the Qila were woken by the melodious sounds of a ghazal by Mirza Naushah, being sung in Raga Bhairavi by a pre-pubescent boy on his *ektara*:

1

wo baada-e-shabana ki sarmastiyan kahan
uthiye bas ab ki lazzat-e-khwab-e-sahar gayi

Where are the intoxications of the nocturnal wine?
Wake up! Enough now! For the dream of dawn has gone.

The maids and female attendants were silently setting ewers and jugs for the morning's ablutions. The *maalans,* or female gardeners, were quietly putting baskets full of fresh flowers like jasmine and roses next to the sleeping forms of the ladies and young girls so that the royal ladies woke up to a fragrant morning.

Falak Ara stirred. She was covered in a white Dhaka muslin dupatta—her long hair and dusky cheeks resting on a silk cushion, her right hand nestled under her face.

Mubarak, who had nursed and raised Falak since she was born, had come to wake her up. The older woman thought to herself:

Baras sathrah ya solah ka sin
Jawaani ki raatein, muraadon ke din

Aged seventeen or was it sixteen
These were the nights of adolescence and days of dreams.

Today was one of those special days when the ladies of the haram, or *mahalsara,* as the area where the ladies lived was known, went out of the palace onto the sandy banks of the River Jamuna, which flowed under the Qila.

Hariyali, the bangle-seller, came in with her basket on her head, swaying in tune to the immortal words of Hazrat Amir Khusaru that she was singing:

Ghar naari ganwari chaahe jo kahe
Main Nijam se naina laga aayi re

Let the women say whatever they want;
I have stolen a glance from Nijam's eyes.

Since glass bangles were considered a sign of a *suhagan*, or wedded woman, she was a fixture in every event in the palace as well as in the city. Young girls would wear glass bangles hoping that the tinkling sounds would attract the man of their dreams.

She continued singing as she put down her basket and took out red and green bangles to entice the residents of this part of the royal palace:

Sohani soorat, mohani moorat,
mein to hirday beech samaa, aaii re

His darling face and charming form
Have I hidden in the depths of my heart.

The Qila was no longer the paradise that Badshah Shah Jahan had planned. The years had been cruel to it, but it was still the heart of Dilli, as Shahjahanabad was now called. For its denizens, of course, Dilli was the dil, the very beating heart, of the world.

Hariyali was familiar with this world of underground rooms, intricate passages, enclosed courtyards, mysterious corners, secret doors and outlets which communicated from house to house, and she negotiated her way through them daily. There was a maze of houses in the compound—some grand, some lowly—to house the ever-expanding royal family and entourage that lived here.

Some 2000 residents in the Fort depended on Huzur Alampanah, who provided for them from his pension. There were a few who lived outside the Qila with permission. Huzur bestowed a monthly salary from the Royal Treasury upon all of them and also disbursed the salaries of the ministers, clerks, other officers and menial workers. Apart from this, he gave gifts and grants on festivals, marriages, tonsure of babies, circumcisions, births and even death proceedings.

Seeing Falak Ara getting ready, Hariyali called out, '*Shahzadi,* I have just the bangles for you! Wear my bangles and see how you charm the darling one hidden in your heart.'

All the ladies were used to Hariyali's blandishments and ignored her. Hariyali didn't mind as it gave her ample time to observe everything around and carry gossip and news to various parts of the walled city. Given the intrigues that abounded in the city, news was at a premium. Nowadays, with the *angrez* in control, it was even more important to know what was being planned and where.

Meanwhile, the princess herself was in a state of excited panic. This was the first time she had been invited to the jharokha fair by the Malika-e Dauran herself.

As the daughter of one of the many concubines who had caught the royal gaze for a few fleeting moments of ecstasy, she wasn't sure if the Badshah knew about her existence but yearned to be known. Maybe today was the day.

Today was the *Jharokhon ka Zanana,* a day when the ladies of the mahalsara came out of the palace to enjoy the fair that was held especially for them under the jharokha, as the balcony jutting out over the Jamuna was called, on the river's sandy bank. It was here that crowds gathered at dawn, every morning to pay their respects to the Badshah, and Falak Ara had often studied them from her small room in one corner of the *mahal,* as she sketched scenes. There was a young man who came every day and stood under that balcony, resplendent in his *jama,* with pearls around his neck and a dagger tied in a sash on his waist. Like her, his jama was made of chintz, and it would have beautiful damask roses or designs of the opium poppy, iris and lily. Sometimes his jama would be almost plain while his silk sash was profusely decorated with floral patterns. She had seen the same motifs on the floral borders that framed the miniature paintings in the *kutubkhana.*

This man would vociferously praise the Badshah Huzur's verses and she had even observed him writing them down. Was he a soldier or a poet?

She hadn't seen many men up close as only the Badshah, baby boys and the *khwajasaras* or eunuchs could come into the part of the haram where she lived, but she'd heard stories from the other women. The khwajasaras loved to gossip, and their exaggerated accounts of passionate, praiseworthy men—often handsome or heroic or romantic or selfless—often drove the ladies wild. Of course, even though the khwajasaras were supposed to perform guard duties in the passages and outside the haram, they had their ways of sneaking in and undoubtedly, they knew where some of the women would turn to satisfy their desires.

The colour code for the day was orange. The slight dusky tinge of Falak's skin glowed in orange clothes. She knew she was looking the best she had in her sixteen years, her beauty enhanced by the pearls and emeralds she had chosen to wear that day. She fiddled with the silver locket around her neck. It had been put on her neck by her mother before she had died, and to Falak's knowledge, had never been taken off. While bathing she just held it up; and in any case, amulets were sealed and the paper with Quranic verses in them was protected by waxed paper.

'Oh, my princess, may I be sacrificed over you,' said Mubarak applying kohl to her almond-shaped eyes, 'you can slay with your eyes today.' Mubarak was Falak Ara's *anga,* or milk mother, having nursed the child after her mother's death in childbirth. Since there had been no one else to take care of the baby, she had become her nursemaid and now was her attendant.

Falak Ara was getting impatient as she could hear other girls getting ready and knew that their clothes and jewellery would be far more expensive and of better quality.

Mubarak was dressing her and completing her toilette as carefully as her artist mistress painted beautiful portraits and landscapes.

'Stop fidgeting, my shahzadi,' remonstrated Mubarak. 'Or else my finger will go into your eye.'

'Applying kajal is an art, Mubarak and you've been doing it since I was born. I know you can't hurt me.'

'Oh, my precious, may a thousand blossoms be sacrificed over your budding beauty. Of course not, but what chance does my art have against a young excitable girl whose eyes never stop flicking this way and that? Whom are you looking out for?' she teased.

'No one,' replied Falak Ara with a blush staining her cheeks. 'No one,' she repeated, this time with a tinge of sadness.

The haram in the Lal Haveli, as the Qila was increasingly called, had very strict rules. Eunuchs and female Tartar warriors guarded the haram, and men weren't allowed in. All rules of comportment laid down during the reign of Akbar Badshah *arsh ashiyani*—he whose nest is on the divine throne—were not just followed but carefully enforced by the daroghas and *mahaldars*, who comprised married matrons or khwajasaras. Of late, since the Lal Qila had been reduced to a shadow of itself under the Company rule, and was being called the Lal Haveli, some laxity had crept in, and a few royal princes would come to meet their mothers or sisters in the haram and perhaps flirt with some cousins. But Falak Ara lived in the area of the mahalsara near Khurd Jahan, which was occupied by old Mughal princesses, and no one dared to breach protocol by venturing there. This was just behind the beautiful European-style mansion that Mirza Babur, Huzur Alampanah's brother, who had copied the way of the *firangis*, had built. It was now occupied by Sahib-e Alam Mirza Fakhru, Huzur's eldest surviving son and *wali ahad* or heir.

Since it was important to know what was always happening to prevent rebellion and overturning, spies were employed everywhere, and the espionage in the women's quarters was carried out by eunuchs and serving maids. And so, one had to be careful.

Princesses could marry but marriages were carefully arranged with men of royal blood. If no suitable match was found, they spent their days alone. In the back quarters of the haram, there were ways of dealing with pent-up frustrations, but all this was done with a great deal of secrecy. If the princesses gave in to temptation and were discovered, there were some drastic punishments in store. Examples would be made of them.

There were rumours of a *phansi ghar*, or gallows, in the bowels of the fort. It hadn't been used in Falak Ara's memory but there were stories of ill-fated lovers who had somehow managed to meet in secret—thanks to the attendants or maids who smuggled the men in—only to end up meeting an untimely death in the rumoured phansi ghar, and then tossed into the river through a trap door. She must remember to ask Mubarak about it. Shaking her head to get these morbid thoughts out of her head, she returned to the present.

A great deal of attention had been paid to the toilette before this. Early morning, Mubarak had first massaged her body with an unguent of saffron and sandalwood paste, then prepared a perfumed bath for her and gave her *dhungari* of sandalwood, a brazier of coal on which sandalwood and other perfumed ingredients were added. As soon as Falak came out of her bath, she sat on a stool covered by a sheet and the brazier was put underneath so that the perfume could be imbued by her body. *Missi*, considered an essential part of the toilette, was used for tinging the lips and teeth with a black hue. This along with *kajal* were the only embellishments used by unmarried girls.

Her long, black, curly hair had been plaited with flowers. Falak Ara was dressed in a beautifully embroidered orange brocade *angiya*. Her muslin *peshvaz* was fitted at the top and flowed from the waist till her ankles; flared panelled silk *pajamas* and a diaphanous organza dupatta completed the ensemble. She was fidgeting, blissfully unaware of the impact she had on those who beheld her; her every movement emphasized her youth and the swell of her breasts suggested a voluptuousness that contrasted tantalizingly with her beguiling innocence.

The angiya *kurti* or bodice shirt, such an essential part of dressing nowadays, had been modified by Zebunnisa Begum, daughter of Aurangzeb Alamgir Badshah, for the Mughal ladies and it seemed to have been made for Falak. She filled it with her soft curves and seductive contours.

As the daughter of a deceased, minor concubine, her access to jewellery was limited, and all she had were a small *teeka* on her forehead, some earrings dangling from her ears, a necklace around her long swan-like throat and flowers on her wrists and hair. She didn't need anything else except her youth but even though she looked radiant, having seen the other women, she felt something was not right.

'Mubarak, do you think I should wear a *nath*?'

'*Ai oooi*, Shahzadi, young girls don't wear nath. That's to be worn only on your wedding day, and the next day it's taken off,' replied a scandalized Mubarak.

'But why?'

'Oh, how do I explain it to you, a *nath* is only worn by a bride and taken off after she has—well,' she hesitated here, before continuing, 'after she has spent the night with her husband. You will understand when you are one.'

'When will I be a bride, Mubarak?' she asked immediately, followed by a wistful, 'Will I ever be one?'

'Come on, stop fidgeting, or I will never finish putting the *kajal*. Today is a day of celebration, and you are looking like a fairy princess, today is not a day to fret. Of course, you will be a bride soon. Sooner than later, I should think, seeing the way your bodice is ready to burst. I don't know what that wretched woman, Dulari, was doing when she measured you for it.'

'I told her to make it very fitted,' said Falak, smiling impishly. 'I hate those loose bodices with creases. One is never sure whether what's underneath is real, or handkerchiefs stuffed in.'

'I don't think that is a worry you need to have, my princess. These peaches are ripe and ready for the taking and I am quite sure Mallika-e Dauran has someone in mind,' said Gulab Jan, a young and saucy attendant of Shahzadi Zebunnisa, with a knowing smile.

'That is if she even knows I exist,' retorted Falak.

'Stay still, my lady. You display so much patience when painting, just remember today I am the artist, and you are my subject,' said Mubarak. Then, turning to Gulab Jan, she added, 'As for *you*, please learn to hold your tongue if all it can produce are bawdy remarks!

That is not the way to speak to a princess.' But she immediately thought of a conversation she had had with another serving lady in the Fort who was in the Empress's inner circle. Falak's luscious beauty was evidently being noticed.

'They say that no other girl dares enter adulthood this year for fear of being overshadowed by Shahzadi Falak. This girl seems to have burst out from adolescence into youth like a rose in full bloom, spreading her fragrance everywhere.'

'When I am painting, I know that it is for posterity, but who cares how I look except you and me? I need to get ready now!' Falak was getting impatient and stamped her foot, sending her anklets ringing in wild abandon.

'*Arre* shahzadi, have some patience. Just let me add a black dot to ward off the evil eye. There are plenty out there waiting to hex you. And mind you, don't eat any food offered by the maids or nannies, or even the other shahzadis. Only eat what I bring or the Mallika and Alampanah give you. These evil wretches go to that old *faqir* in the bazaar and buy magic potions to cast spells,' Mubarak muttered darkly.

Falak was too busy admiring herself to heed such warnings. With a twirl of the organza dupatta and a pout of her missi-coloured lips, she bounced out of her room towards the jharokha, Mubarak huffing and puffing behind her, blowing air after reciting *duas* and spells to ward off the evil eye from her precious ward.

The *Jharokha Darshan* was an old Rajput custom of kings appearing before their subjects on a balcony built for the purpose. It had been adopted by Emperor Akbar arsh ashiyani and since then, barring Aurangzeb Alamgir, all the other emperors had followed it.

Access for the women was through the Khizri Darwaza in the Musamman Burj, where the Badshah sat in the mornings giving darshan to his subjects after his *fajr* prayers.

It was the missing of a couple of these Jharokha Darshans that had led to rumours about the death of Badshah Shah Jahan and a war of succession between his sons. People with old memories and

long tongues often spoke about it but in hushed tones. The wars
of succession had left a huge toll on the empire and people talked
of the machinations of the Sayyid brothers who kept propping and
deposing their favourites from among the salatins, the offspring
of previous emperors, kept in confinement in the Salimgarh Fort
adjoining the Qila.

And of course, the atrocities of Ghulam Qadir Rohilla. The
Rohilla had tortured the emperor and the *begums* for days to extract
the location of the treasure that he believed Badshah Shah Alam
had inherited from his ancestors and which was said to be hidden
somewhere in the Qila.

To date, there were many seekers of that treasure and there were
hints of a map or clue in the possession of someone in the zenana,
but no one had succeeded in finding it. Yet.

If only there had been a law of primogeniture in the Mughal
dynasty, it might still have been intact instead of becoming a
pensioner of the Company bahadur.

But all that is for another day. Mubarak came back to the
present with a jolt as she followed her charge running merrily along
the marble channels with silver and gold fountains laid out for the
nahr-e bahisht in the various mahals. The word 'mahal', attached to
a building denoted the fact that it was a part of the private palace-
complex, where the ladies lived. Since Mubarak was not part of
the haram and only worked there, she had seen the world beyond
the beautiful mahals too. Each part of the Qila was envisaged and
adorned as a piece of paradise. Although the gilding had long started
fading, it still had the power to enchant and captivate the viewer. The
gurgling of the nahr-e bahisht added to that heightened sensibility.

The Malika-e Dauran was sitting on a settee with beautiful gold
and silver embroidered bolsters and cushions around her. The legs of
the settee and the poles holding the embroidered canopy were golden
and encrusted with gems.

She was a vision of beauty, with a classical oval face and almond-
shaped, kohl-lined eyes that one could drown in—and obviously,

the Emperor had! She was much younger than the Emperor, but her beauty, charm and presence of mind had soon made her his favourite and the Chief Consort. With the birth of a son, her place in his life was sealed.

Her power was reflected through her clothes and jewellery— she was wearing a silk and organza ensemble in various shades of orange, rust and earthy tones, which cast a hue on her creamy skin, making it glow like sunlight on marble at dawn; kundan earrings dangled from her ears and a diamond and emerald necklace hugged her swan-like throat. Her *solah shringar*, an age-old Hindustani tradition of sixteen steps that completed a woman's toilette, was paid special attention to.

The ladies wore necklaces, bracelets, bangles, *bazubands,* payals or pazebs and a *jhoomar.* Married women wore a nose pin which exemplified the rite of passage of losing their virginity. Henna or *mehndi* was applied on the hands and feet, its rich colour signifying the essence of love. It completed the shringar. The Malika's shringar was all this and more! A diaphanous dupatta covered her head with all its ornaments, adding to the mystery and lure of her classical beauty. No wonder, the Emperor besotted with her, and she, fifty years younger than him, had him entwined around her little finger. This was the thought in the minds of the women sitting in that room.

All the girls and ladies sat as per their rank in the zenana around her. They were looking like fairies, with their dresses embroidered with *zardozi* and *zari* work, heavily embellished by gold decorations such as *salma, kora, dabka, chikna, gizai, zik, chalak, tikora, kangri, champa, kinari* and *khichcha.*

As the daughter of a junior, deceased courtesan, Falak sat on the edge of the circle, head covered and respectfully bowed. There had been a moment of hushed silence as she had come in, looking radiant, bursting with youth and an innocent charm, but now attention was back to the Malika, who was smoking a gold and silver huqqah, the pipe enclosed in a silver filigree cover, a jewelled mouthpiece attached to it.

Falak had never come here and was trying hard to see everything around her.

A sweet smell emanated from the tobacco, and the *gulqand* or sweetened rose petals from the pans. A beautiful gold filigree *khasdan* was kept on a silver table next to the Malika's settee, with a silver spittoon under it. Prepared betel leaves called *giloris* with *gulqand* were kept inside it.

On one side, Falak could see the golden-canopied, conjugal bed, with an exquisite bedcover and fragrant flowers scattered all over it. The maidservants, eunuchs, personal attendants and female guards—all stood with folded hands in the courtyards waiting for their orders.

The *urdabegni*, an armed female guard, entered and presented a *kornish*—a special bow that entailed bending from the waist and placing one's hand to forehead in greeting. Once she received the royal nod of acknowledgement, she said, '*Aali janab Malika ko salam*. If this miserable servant has the royal permission to utter a few words,' and waited to receive another royal nod before she proceeded to say, 'The darogha of the zenana, Khwajasara Agha Jan, says that the area is ready to be illuminated by your royal presence.'

A wave of excitement ran through the room. Some of the ladies and girls present here had not stepped out of the cloistered mahalsara for months. It was only on occasions like these when the area had been sequestered from male presence that they could go out.

Despite the throbbing excitement, no one could stand or step out till the Malika had given a sign for everyone. Falak Ara was storing everything in her mind to sketch it on paper later.

A nod to her chief lady-in-waiting indicated permission to let them go out and enter the gateway that led to the Khizri gate in the Musamman Burj. This was a small gate in the tower below the Musamman Burj which opened onto the sandy banks of the River Yamuna or Dariya-e Jun as it was called by them.

The chattering ayahs, *mughlanis*, nursemaids, wet nurses, servants and slave girls were all walking alongside the ladies, each attendant or nursemaid jealously guarded her charge, covering them with parasols and exclaiming over their beauty and willing to be sacrificed over their particular ladies or charges.

Of course, the harsh sun or elements weren't the only danger hovering over their fair ones, so dark warnings were given to stay away from the attendants of their peers, as these wicked creatures would go to any length of sorcery to jinx their beautiful ones. Then there were the spirits and the *jinns* who haunted the flowering trees and bushes in the evening and of course, their darling had to make sure she covered her head with a white *chador* as soon as dusk approached. There was no end to the dangers that these delicate darlings were about to face if one was to believe their attendants, but the girls were oblivious to anything except the day's freedom they were about to experience.

The servants and attendants, of course, were oblivious to anything except the danger that their charges faced in a hostile world where it was the survival of the prettiest ones, the ones with the most wiles. If anyone commented on the ladies, then the servants and attendants would pounce on them and curse them for casting an evil eye. All kinds of antidotes would be prescribed to counter the evil eye.

There are many underground rooms in the Fort but they didn't have access to the sandy banks. The two gates, Khizri Gate and Water Gate in Asad Burj, were closely guarded by the khwajasaras and Tartar women soldiers so that no stranger could enter the haram complex. The flowers of the Timurid Empire were well nourished but closely guarded so that their fragrance remained within and didn't spill out into the open.

As soon as the ladies appeared, the guards stood attentively all around to ensure no stranger could come near it. The royal princes were of course exceptions.

The area was beautifully decorated with tents, festoons, flowers and stalls. Children and serving women from the Fort had put up shops here. Hariyali was also sitting in one corner with her basket of bangles.

Small, covered boats were waiting for the royal ladies' pleasure so that they could enjoy boating in the small area that had been cordoned off for them. The boatmen were the khwajasaras and female guards and attendants who knew swimming.

Near the mahalsara was a small area known as Nau Muhalla or new locality. This is where some of the princes, whose direct ancestors were monarchs, but had been passed for the throne, lived. They were known as salatin. Today, these princes along with their begums and princesses came out of the Khizri Darwaza and collected here.

The salatins had been closely guarded till the start of the century, as there was always the fear of a coup d'état. There were tragic stories of many salatins living in miserable conditions in the Salimgarh Fort, which was joined to the Lal Qila by a bridge because either they or their ancestors had once challenged the reigning monarch's authority. The ones who could be a potential threat to the reigning monarch or his heir apparent were kept in prison. But now that the British company decided who would be the heir apparent, they had complete freedom to move around.

Anyway, those were stories for another day. Today Falak Ara was going to enjoy herself. Would that handsome young man be there? If he was a salatin, and her luck held, perhaps she could see him again.

Soon the banks of the Yamuna were full of young girls prancing about, their chaperones and attendants clucking behind them, begums walking about staidly inspecting the stalls, instructing their attendants to buy anything that caught their fancy. Seeing their colourful dresses and beauty, the nursemaids said to the others, '*Ek tave ki roti, kya choti kya moti* [they are all cast in the same mould, and it is hard to decide who is prettier].'

Falak Ara was beside herself with excitement as she ran out of the Khizri Darwaza onto the sandy banks. Bar a few times she was able to stroll in the small garden inside the *zenana* this was her first outing in the open air in months. With Mubarak tut-tutting behind her she darted around, her face raised to the breeze, hair ruffled, dupatta streaming behind her like a kite's tail, anklets tinkling.

May I be sacrificed over my darling, but she is like a kite, soaring high with so many waiting to bring her crashing down to earth.

This thought came unbidden into Mubarak's mind and then she determinedly shrugged it away as today wasn't the day to be thinking of such things.

Suddenly a hush came upon the gathered crowd as the Badshah's personal bodyguards came out and announced the arrival of Alampanah. He was accompanied by *jasolinis* whose job was to relay royal messages between the mahalsara and the outside world.

A spiritual radiance emanated from Huzur Badshah's face for he was an ordained Sufi of the Chishti *silsilah* and much of his time went in prayers. Once he emerged from the mahalsara, he was ceremoniously seated in the *hawadar*, or sedan chair, and lifted by female porters. Abyssinian and Turkish female warriors dressed in male attire, with green turbans on their heads and red sashes on their waists, accompanied the hawadar, walking beside it with spears in their hands. The khwajasaras walked by the side, waving the royal whisk, while the jasolini called out: 'Attention everyone, stand still, the Huzur Alampanah, Refuge of the World, arrives. May God keep him safe and grant him a long life.'

Everyone stood up in attention as the Badshah Huzur emerged from the Khizri Gate. Khwajasaras walked beside the flywhisk made of yak tail and carrying the royal huqqah.

They set the sedan down. The jasolinis and attendants helped him alight, and he went inside his tent known as *jahannuma*, or reflection of the world. He was wearing a *charqub*, a turban with a *goshwara*, *jigha*, *sarpech* and the royal crown with a *turra* of pearls. On his neck, he had a short necklace of pearls, another of alternating pearl and emerald beads with a ruby clasp after every ten beads and other necklaces of emeralds and diamonds. On his arms, he wore a diamond and nine-gem armlet, and on his wrists seven bracelets of precious gemstones.

When the emperor entered the richly embroidered tent, the empress was already seated on a gilded and decorated settee with brocade bolsters and embroidered cushions. She got up in respect and sat down only when he was comfortably seated on the *shahnasheen* or throne chair, his feet on a brocaded stool and attendants all around him.

Jade huqqahs with jewel-tipped pipes for the imperial couple, a jade arm stand near the shahnasheen for the emperor to rest his hand, silver spittoons, basins for washing hands and jade and silver trays with cardamom and cloves and an exquisite silver filigree *khasdan* were kept in readiness.

The announcement was made that the Emperor was ready to receive and everyone came in one by one or in groups and presented their salutations and a small *nazar*, or gift, as befitted their ranks. The kornish was an elaborate affair for the Emperor with everyone bending waist downwards and bringing the palm of their hands from the floor to their forehead thrice.

When the last salutation had been presented, the Badshah Salamat signalled the start of the festivities. To the delight of the children and youngsters, he announced that they may raid the fruit trees that were growing there.

In the twinkling of an eye not only the children but also the ladies were running around.

There were sounds of rejoicing and merriment and it almost seemed to Mubarak that birds of paradise had been let out from their gilded cage. Thank God, she was an ordinary sparrow and could return home to her mate in the city every night and smell the free air outside the cage.

She was broken out of her reverie as Falak called out, 'Mubarak please help me break these bananas.' Falak was standing under a banana tree trying to catch the swinging cluster and grab one. Her dupatta was awry, her *angiya* had ridden up her firm breasts under the *kurti* and she was jumping up and down, oblivious to the attention that had suddenly focused on her. Horrified, Mubarak ran towards her, mumbling under her breath, 'O God, please protect her from the evil gaze, there are enemies everywhere, keep my precious one safe.'

Mubarak wasn't the only one, there were clucking, muttering and disapproving sounds from many of the attendants, accompanying their beautiful charges. Their voices could be heard cautioning the young princesses, but no one was paying heed as all were busy having fun.

When such fun and freedom were available rarely, who would listen to these old muttering attendants? There were mango trees to climb, lemons to loot and suck with salt. Those who couldn't climb the mango trees sent their agile maids scampering up the trees, while others threw stones at the fruit.

And lo and behold, the expected happened. A young princess fell off the tree with a thud.

While the attendants gathered around in sympathy to check her bruises, her sisters and cousins laughed merrily.

A thorn had pierced someone; another had scraped herself and was howling loudly: 'I got nothing except a few injuries!'

Finally, with bags full of fruits, they decided to go boating. There was much splashing of water at each other, pushing and jostling.

The boat that Falak and Mubarak were in was full of laughing, giggling girls. Falak sat quietly in the rear, but she had attracted attention. Three young princesses, her contemporaries, were whispering with their maids. Suddenly they all got up as if to come towards Falak, tilting the boat dangerously.

'Oh, be careful,' cried out Mubarak but by then it was too late. Falak had fallen into the river.

Mubarak was ready to jump in to save her floundering charge, but she was stopped by the other maids. There was pin-drop silence. Falak did not know how to swim, unlike some of the other girls, and was thrashing around wildly.

'Help, help!' Mubarak screamed at the top of her voice, helpless as she feared a certain death for her charge. Suddenly, there was a splash from the bank and young, powerful arms could be seen swimming strongly towards the now sinking girl.

In what seemed like a miracle, Falak had been pulled up, other swimmers had also come to the young man's help and were taking Falak out of the water. Mubarak's boat, with everyone sitting in stunned silence, also turned towards the bank.

Soon Mubarak was running towards her darling, weeping, saying prayers of gratitude to the Almighty and running as fast as her legs could carry her. There were some attendants, some khwajasaras trying to revive Falak. The young man who rescued her was leading it, pumping her chest. He seemed to be one of the salatin princes who had been invited to be a part of the celebrations.

Falak was spluttering out water and struggling to regain consciousness.

Mubarak tried to gently slap the princess to open her eyes.

'Am I in heaven?' she said as her dazed eyes fell on that same young man she had seen from her window in the Jharokha Darshan.

'God is great, my precious, you are here in my arms and safe. I knew nothing could happen to you, my Allah is very benevolent and merciful. He could never take you away from me or harm you!' Mubarak was weeping uncontrollably as she literally snatched Falak out of the young man's arms and into hers. Falak was still staring at him when their gaze was interrupted by the arrival of the shamefaced princesses who had caused the accident.

'We never meant to do anything but scare you a bit. It was just a game. We are truly repentant, and you can give us any punishment you want,' said one.

Mubarak was quiet since she could not say anything to a shahzadi but just then the *anna* of the shahzadi came to ask Mubarak if Shahzadi Falak was all right. It was just the opportunity Mubarak had been waiting for, and she let go of her anger. She couldn't say much to the royal girls but pounced on the maids.

'Stay away from my little one, o you of evil intentions. Don't I know that you are jealous of my beautiful one and want to harm her!' The weeping had now turned into anger, and Mubarak was in full form.

'Don't you dare come near us again. May the blight of the Almighty fall on you, you filthy pieces of leftover vomit. How dare you push my child? How dare you? The curse of Allah be on you. I hope you fall flat on your faces and smash your noses and then go around the palace

with a disgraced face. May insects crawl all over you in your grave.'
Mubarak's eloquence was increasing when suddenly she felt Falak
wriggle in her arms and turned her attention to more important things.
Falak was trying to sit, looking furiously around, for with the entry
of the girls and their maids, the young man had discreetly withdrawn
and was nowhere to be seen.

The gathered attendants helped Falak stand up and head towards
her tent. Instead of looking bedraggled and like a drowned rat, the
young girl was radiating a luminosity, her young figure in the wet
clothes clearly visible, walking as if in a dream.

Someone thrust a glass of cooled milk in her hand, someone
wiped her face and wrung out her clothes; but she was somewhere
else. Had she really been held in his arms? Had he seen her or was
she just someone he had rescued? Thoughts were jostling in her
mind, threatening to burst out, but even in her restless state, she
knew she couldn't let anyone know. She silently fiddled with her
locket, feeling a connection with the mother she had never known;
her mother must have known passion to have given birth to her.

Young girls were sheltered, kept cloistered in the mahalsara,
only allowed to meet a man once he became her husband and then
too on their wedding night. The Emperor and princes of the royal
blood were the only ones who ever came inside. He was a salatin,
kept in the Fort but segregated from the other royals. Though
now there was no fear of a violent takeover, memories of mischief
or evil play from the salatin, who were descended from emperors
and could at any time stake their claim to the throne with the
help of pliable and sympathetic nobles, were still fresh. Everyone
knew how the Sayyid brothers had played kingmakers, blinding
and deposing Farrukhsiyar Badshah and pulling his unknown
cousin Rafi-ud Darajat out of the salatin quarters and crowning
him emperor.

As things settled down, the other girls decided to return to their
tents for a quick toilette, after which they were ready to hear the
music and dance performance.

Falak had changed into another dress, which was always reserved for emergencies by Mubarak, and was lying quietly on a carpet piled high with bolsters and cushions. Mubarak was fussing around loudly, chanting prayers to ward off the evil eye, to keep Falak safe and of course a curse on the blighted ones who were jealous of her little one.

Unknown to these two, the news had reached Jahannuma, the royal tent, and while the Emperor was curious, the Chief Consort didn't know whether to be curious or furious.

Leta nahin mere dil-e awaara ki khabar
Ab tak woh jaanta hai ki mere paas hi hai

[S]he doesn't bother about my restless heart
For [s]he thinks it beats for me.

—Mirza Ghalib

2

A Royal Summons

Sar-e atish jo ashk rezaan thaa
kisi aashiq ki thi kabab mein jaan

No doubt this kebab has a lover's mind
Fire and tears together where else would you find!

—Ghulam Hamadan Mushafi

Huzur Badshah was a slim man of medium height, with a long neck, oval face, dusky skin, aquiline nose, high cheekbones and a white beard. He was reclining against the bolsters on his shahnasheen, the huqqah pipe in his hand, a faint smile on his lips and a spiritual radiance emanating from his face. The jewels in his crown and around his neck were twinkling and dazzling his attendants.

The whisk bearer stood behind him with the yak tail *morchal,* and the attendants were standing at attention. The Malika was sitting on the settee with a jewel-studded huqqah pipe in her hand too.

There was a sense of peace when the sounds of screaming came floating in. The Badshah indicated with a wave of his hand and the jasolinis and khwajasaras went out to find out who was the impertinent person daring to make a ruckus so close to the imperial tent.

Even the Malika sat up a little straighter, listening attentively. 'Huzur Jahanpanah, may your glory and dignity last forever, it is

21

nothing to worry about,' said the khwajasara after presenting his kornish. 'Just one of the young girls, who fell into the river. She's been rescued and is now resting.'

'Hmm,' came the royal response but the Malika was more curious. 'Who was it?'

'Her name is Shahzadi Falak Ara, Alampanah,' said the khwajasara.

The Malika had heard the name but couldn't immediately place it and said sharply, 'Who is she?'

'She is a shahzadi. Her mother was the concubine Dil Ruba, who died in childbirth. The shahzadi has been brought up by her milk mother and attendant Mubarak, in the mahal,' came the khwajasara's reply. 'They say she's very pretty, but anyone who has seen you, Your Highness, has much higher standards of beauty. These buds blossom for a day or so and fade away, not like the lasting beauty of my Queen,' the khwajasara added in a bid to keep the Empress's temper sweetened. She was known to be short-tempered.

'Send her my summons to come for the morning meal in the mahal tomorrow,' came the commands from the Badshah. He had remembered the strong, musky fragrance and taste of Dil Ruba, whose name literally meant 'one who attracts the heart', or 'sweetheart'. He had forgotten all about her. After he had married the extremely beautiful, seventeen-year-old Zeenat Mahal, he had had no eyes for anyone else. Of course, orders had been given for the daughter to be looked after, an allowance fixed as was his wont with his concubines and their offspring. Though the *darogha-e mahal* or mahaldar would give him a daily report on the welfare, actions and movements of the various relatives and inmates of the mahal, he had never specifically asked about Falak Ara, but he would now.

This was not unusual, for the mid-morning meal eaten in the Badi Baithak was a well-attended affair. The Badshah would invite the current favourite sons, daughters and women in the haram. However, this was the first time that he had invited someone he had never met before.

The khwajasara turned to one of the jasolinis and quietly told her to convey the Badshah's summons to Falak Ara.

Brimming with excitement and anticipation not just to convey the message to the tent where Falak Ara was resting but to others as this was too juicy a morsel to not be chewed on thoroughly and regurgitated in gossip, she presented her salutations to the imperial couple and backed out of the tent.

There are rows and rows of tents along the eastern wall of the Fort, on the *reti,* for the royal ladies to rest in, offer prayers, eat and gossip. Many young children and girls were still running around but the ladies had retired to their tent for the afternoon meal. They would reappear after sundown when it became a little cooler.

The jasolini enquired and was directed to the tent which Falak Ara was sharing with some other young princesses. The tent was quiet as the girls and their attendants were still shaken by the near-death experience of their peer, and Falak Ara was lost in contemplation of those hands on her chest and the look in her rescuer's eyes. *Who was he, where is he now?* were questions jostling in her mind.

She was woken out of her reverie as the jasolini entered.

'Salam Shahzadi *sahiba*, wake up, for your destiny definitely has woken up,' she said breathlessly.

'Are you in your senses, what gibberish are you spouting, and can't you see the shahzadi is resting? You jasolinis are too much, you think you are important just because you wear a uniform,' an exasperated Mubarak started muttering.

'*Ai* Mubarak, get up, you will surely give me that ring on your finger when you hear the news I have brought.'

Now alert, Mubarak replied, 'May God prevent all troubles, quickly tell me what is it? And this ring was given to me by my late mistress, it's never coming off my finger.'

The jasolini and Mubarak were old friends and so she could take liberties with her, that she wouldn't otherwise when she went to convey royal messages.

'First, you give me that ring, then I will tell you,' she teased Mubarak.

'Oh yes! I am a newborn babe to fall for your tricks. I know you have been eyeing this ring forever but it's not coming off my finger. You are a good-for-nothing wretch who is just trying to take advantage of a poor woman's moment of weakness and gratitude at her darling's rescue,' said an emotional Mubarak.

'*Arre* Mubarak today your name is truly *blessed*,' said the jasolini, playing on the meaning of the term 'mubarak'. 'I will never tease you at such a time. You and I have been friends since we were knee-high. I bring you glad tidings. Huzur Alampanah has requested the presence of Shahzadi Falak Ara for tomorrow morning's meal in the Badi Baithak.'

'Am I dead or dreaming?' Mubarak was excited, astonished, dumbfounded, incredulous and above all, supremely happy, as she could see her dreams coming true, but still had no idea if this was reality or still a dream. She was jumping up and down in excitement and blabbering, tears flowing down her cheek, hugging the jasolini and kissing her hands and face and blessing her, 'May Allah bless you with such plenty that you forget where you have stored it all.'

'What is the commotion about?' asked a tired Falak Ara.

'Oh, my precious, my baby, my darling, may I be sacrificed for you. May Allah give all my happiness to you. This is what I have been waiting for forever. My shahzadi, the Badshah has invited you for the morning meal tomorrow. Finally, you will come out of your obscurity and get what you deserve. My mistress Dil Ruba's spirit must be so happy today. I am sure it is her blessings and good deeds that have made the Badshah aware of your presence.'

Though there were rumours that the British, who were living in and around Shahjahanabad, had an early morning meal called breakfast, the people in the Fort and city followed the age-old custom of a substantial meal served at 10 or 11 a.m. and a second meal which was after the evening or *maghrib* prayers. Before and between them, only betel leaf and huqqah were enjoyed. Eating four times a day seemed like gluttony to the residents of the Qila and the city: nourishing the soul was far more important than unnecessarily feeding the stomach.

'Oh! Oh!' This was something that Falak Ara herself had longed for ever since she was a child: to be acknowledged by her father. But languishing in a corner of the mahalsara, she had long since abandoned the dream and reconciled herself to living and dying in complete obscurity there.

There were so many women whose fate was exactly this. They just lived and died in some forsaken corner of the mahalsara. At least, as a daughter of the reigning Badshah, Falak Ara had a few more privileges than the extended family of relatives and children of maids-in-waiting who rarely went out of the rooms that they shared with many others. Subject to jealousies, backbiting, envy, frustration and loneliness, they lived in darkness, finding enjoyment either in gossip, black magic or religion.

It was an interesting place for any student of life, and Mubarak was the one who closely studied it. She could afford to, as she wasn't confined to it, and could go home every evening. While some corners would crackle with gossip and laughter, the others reverberated with the sounds of the Quran or some other religious texts being recited, since the harams were full of women of many faiths. The emperors married and had begotten children by Rajput women who came with their entourage of attendants and serving women. Since the days of Akbar Badshah, who married the Rajput princess Harkha Bai of Amber, none of the Hindu wives were ever asked to change their religion. Harkha Bai, who was given the title of Maryam uz-Zamani—Mary of Her Age—was not only a very respected queen of Akbar Badshah but also had great respect as the mother of Jahangir Badshah. Huzur Badshah's Rajput mother, Lal bai, had been given the title of Qudsia Begum.

Tonight, I will stay in the Qila, said Mubarak to herself. *I have to get my darling ready for tomorrow and be on the guard for all the hexes and evil eye that will be cast on my little one as news of this invitation spreads.*

The gossip and the evil eye would be in full swing as the nurse maids and attendants of the other girls in the tent had also heard the jasolini's message. Was the imperial invitation a sign of the importance that Falak Ara was about to get? How would it affect the chances of the other young princesses waiting for imperial favour? Resources were limited and everyone had to vie for them. Even though there were tales of buried treasure in the Qila, no one knew if they were true; and if the ladies neglected to look out for themselves and further their own prospects, then, like the hidden treasure of legend, they too could merely end up forgotten.

Falak Ara was sitting stupefied, as the message still hadn't sunk in, and she was lost in dreams of the young salatin who had saved her. Her eyes brightened, wondering if he would be there too, then slowly dimmed, for just as the daughters of forgotten wives and concubines of royalty languished in the mahalsara, the sons languished in a compound in the Salimgarh Fort or the Nau Muhalla. It was unlikely that the Emperor would invite him. She would have to think of other ways to see him.

She woke up from her reverie, startled as the smell of burning coals reached her nostril. Mubarak had got hold of a small brazier and after waving red chilis round her face seven times, burning them in it while chanting *aaltu jalaltu, aayi bala ko taal tu*—a corruption of the chant '*Allah, jalle jalal tu aai bala ko taal tu*' which implored the Almighty to remove any evil omens.

'See,' said Mubarak rubbing her hands with satisfaction, 'not an iota of the smell of burning chilis has come from this. I knew it, the envious ones are eyeing you. I will have to repeat this regularly now.'

There was chattering going on in the room from the other young royal princesses and their maids in the tent.

'God forbid that we eye your charge, you evil-mouthed old woman, Mubarak. Isn't my charge as beautiful, if not more? And further, she is born from a legally wedded wife of the Emperor' brother. Stop this nonsense of yours,' said the nursemaid of one of the young royal girls.

Insults were being traded among the maids and Mubarak, arms akimbo, had come into her own.

'Oh! May the curse of the gods be upon anyone who tries to harm my baby! Don't I know that the strumpets, witches and whores who inhabit the lower levels of the mahalsara have lost their sense of decency and have become shameless and disgraceful! All of them are out of control! No shame left in their eyes! Ready to open their drawstrings for anyone!'

'Oho! The pot calling the kettle black! Don't we know how many times your drawstrings have opened and your pants have fallen? Just because you are old and ugly now and no one looks at you, you are calling us names. One always thinks the worst of others if they have committed the same crimes. Drawstrings my foot!'

Mubarak's strident voice letting out years of pent-up frustration, and the retaliatory insults from the other attendants in the tents soon had a few young girls crying.

'Mubarak, behave yourself!' shouted Falak Ara, snapping out of her dreams and melancholy. 'Stop this at once. What is wrong with you, that you have forgotten all decorum? Do you want the Malika's jasolini to come and punish you for this commotion? See you have made these little ones cry.'

Suddenly Mubarak came to her senses. What if news of her misbehaviour reached the Empress and she got the invitation cancelled? The Empress was known to be quick-tempered and temperamental. Thankfully she only had a son and no daughter, otherwise, all other girls would have been cast in the shadow of obscurity for fear that they may outshine her daughter. Though by and large there was a sense of harmony, and on the surface, camaraderie among all the women sequestered in the mahalsara, there were always underlying tensions of rivalry and vying for the Emperor's attention.

Anyway, she had to think of tomorrow, and she might need the help of these very attendants in assembling her little one's ensemble for the event.

The night had passed in a daze for Falak Ara. Mubarak, of course, had been quite the busybody, running around getting the princess's ensemble ready. But not before she had applied every kind of unguent and cream on Falak's face, limbs and hair. Bangles had been bought from Hariyali. The bath water had been warmed and just before dawn prayers, Falak was given a bath in rose-scented water. Finally, she was happy. She had sewn an angiya from a piece of light pink silk that she had been saving for just such an occasion, to go with the kurti. A white muslin peshvaz on top of the kurti, a green gauze dupatta and tight green silk pyjamas, green glass bangles and Falak was ready. The nursemaids of the young ones, who had no reason to fear Falak's growing prominence and every reason to feel that her patronage might help them when their charge grew up, were all working with her throughout the night. In the absence of jewellery, floral jewellery had been made and all that Falak Ara wore was a pair of gold and ruby earrings. Jasmine attar had been applied on the wrists and pressure points.

'She looks like a *harsinghar* bud,' said one attendant, referring to the night jasmine. It was a flower very popular in the mahal and had been used to make a decoration for Falak's braided hair.

Oh yes! The nazar teeka to ward off the evil eye . . . a weeping Mubarak took some kajal from her eyes and put it on Falak's forehead under her bangs.

Finally, Falak Ara was ready, and it was time to go.

The young girl walked diffidently and shyly, quaking on the inside. She had been tutored in the etiquette she had to follow there but was still unsure if she would be able to remember and follow it.

Falak Ara was escorted by a khwajasara from her quarters near the erstwhile palace of Mirza Jahangir, through the Khurd Jahan, the beauteous Imtiaz Mahal and across the fragrant gardens to the Baithak which adjoined the *khas* mahal where the Huzur Badshah lived when he visited the mahalsara.

The Baithak was beautifully decorated, and a long, white *dastarkhwan* spread out on a piece of leather on a very low wooden table. When the jasolini announced that Falak Ara needed permission to enter, the Malika, who was seated on her settee, nodded her head. Falak entered and immediately presented her kornish. A wave of the royal hand told her where to take her place and she sat down decorously.

A jasolini came as advance guard and announced that the Emperor was about to arrive. The urdabegni entered and announced that his eminence was about to enter. Everyone present, including the Malika and other wives, princes and princesses stood up.

The sedan entered the Baithak, where the Emperor alighted and sat on his royal chair. Each person there presented their kornish.

Falak watched in fascination as the daroghas, khwajasaras, and mahaldar came and presented their daily report on the happenings outside and inside the haram. The haram, like its name, was a sanctuary or protected space, inhabited by the ladies of the royal family and their attendants and was very efficiently run. Falak had heard that there was a system of daily reporting but living in a corner of the palace, had never seen it herself.

The *tehwildar,* or female accountants, gave their account of the expenditures separately. Of course, with resources severely curtailed due to these *firangis*, there wasn't much money available, but even then, the Badshah and *munshis* managed beautifully.

The uncharitable of course wondered where the Malika was getting all the money for her fancy jewellery! Rumours of her being in touch with the accursed firangi, just so she could secure her beloved son's claim to the throne, were rife. God alone knew what she did when she went to stay in the Zeenat Mahal haveli in Lal Kuan, gifted to her by the doting Huzur Purnur.

Everyone in the room was sitting in hushed silence as the daily report of the mahalsara was given. No one wanted to be on the wrong side of the Badshah or Malika so early in the morning.

Orders were given and petitions were signed.

Lo, it was mid-morning, and the royal kitchen superintendent now asked respectfully for his orders. Huzur-e Anwar ordered the food to be served. The *dastarkhwan* was laid out.

The food was brought and the female attendants relayed it down the line, 'Ladies, get the *nimatkhana* ready. Bring the royal food.' The food was brought in a relay system for smooth delivery, with the women holding the baskets of food on their heads.

All the sealed dishes were brought in a covered tray to prevent flies from touching the food and served in individual silver and porcelain bowls. The entire room was fragrant with the smell of musk, kewra and saffron. The tablecloth shimmered from the reflection of the pure silver foil that covered every dish. Attendants stood in a corner holding silver basins, ewers and soap dishes containing gram flower, jasmine and sandal scrub to wash the royal hands after the meal. Another set of attendants stood with separate handkerchiefs for wiping the hands, nose and mouth.

The jasolini announced, 'Huzur, the food has been laid.'

They say that even if dead, an elephant is worth a lakh and quarter! Though the empire had long since ceased to exist except nominally, and invaders like Nader Shah and Ahmad Shah and power brokers like the Rohillas and Marathas had looted it, there was still enough left to give royalty a worthy, regal frame.

The Emperor sat on a soft, padded cushion at the head of the dastarkhwan; on his right was his Chief Consort on a quilted coverlet, while the other wives sat according to their status to his right. The many princes and princesses, and the ladies of the haram, sat to his left.

The attendants in charge of handkerchiefs put the napkins on the royal knees. It was time to eat. Finger bowls were kept on the table in case they were required. The kitchen darogha broke the seal and tasted from each dish. Poisoning was an ever-present danger and while food tasters would taste the food before the darogha sealed it, she would be the first to taste to show that it had not been tampered with in her custody.

Huzur Badshah had once been the target of poisoning by his son, Mirza Kaykumars, who had been foolish and evil enough to believe that he could poison the Badshah and succeed in his place. He had given his father a tiger's whisker in a paan. The occasion had been a musical soiree where everyone was enjoying themselves. Engrossed in the ragas, the Badshah had taken the paan offered by his son little suspecting that there was mischief afoot on that magical evening. He immediately took ill and the royal physicians, suspecting foul play, gave him emetics to induce vomit. He vomited blood and eventually the whisker came out in one of these purges. Of course, reprisal had been swift, and Mirza Kaykumars was given a cup of poisoned sherbet. Knowing he had been found out, the prince drank it and passed on to the next world to await eternal hellfire for his evil deed. Since then, Huzur was very careful and ate frugally as his digestive system had been affected.

The Emperor sat cross-legged, as did the others. The begums, princes and princesses kept their gazes respectfully lowered.

It was the Emperor's custom to call upon someone and give him or her a morsel with his own hands—this was called the *ulash*. The person so honoured would stand up and bend low to present his or her salutations and deferentially take the morsel.

This was an occasion that most excitedly waited for. The Jahanpanah gave morsels of food to his sons, Mirza Mughal, Mirza Fakhru and Mirza Jawan Bakht, who stood up and presented their salutations before taking it from him. Next it was the turn of the Malika-e-Dauran, Nawab Zeenat Mahal sahiba, and after that the daughters.

Falak Ara had been sitting with her eyes lowered and pecking at the food that was put in front of her. Though the food served to the various residents of the mahalsara was plenty, she had never seen such a repast in her young life.

Lost in reflection, she suddenly heard her name called. Jahanpanah had called her for the ulash! Was there some place she could sink in and bury herself? Everyone was looking at her . . . her entire body was frozen . . . she couldn't move.

The daroghas came towards her and firmly helped her up. For the rest of her life, Falak Ara couldn't remember how she managed to reach the head of the dastarkhwan, present her kornish and take the morsel.

Everyone's eyes were on her and she somehow managed to walk backwards, as no one could present their back to Huzur-e Anwar, without falling. Reaching her place, she tried to sink into the dastarkhwan but eyes were still on her.

Mahabali Badshah was a very frugal eater, but he waited for everyone to finish before he offered his formal thanks to God for the food and got up. The attendants were ready with oil cakes, pieces of sandalwood and gram flour to help everyone wash their hands.

It was only as the Emperor got up to go and everyone's attention was on him, bidding him farewell, that Falak dared to raise her eyes and see who all were present. As she anxiously and furtively scanned the gathering she realized with a pang that the one she was looking for wasn't there.

The meal over, everyone started to leave, but a jasolini came to her and asked her to stay back.

The Malika had commanded her presence.

Quaking in her slippers, Falak wondered if she had done anything wrong. She followed the jasolini to the low settee where the Malika had returned.

'Girl, what was your mother's name?' came the imperious question.

The question took Falak back into the past—into the stories she had heard about her mother from Mubarak and others in the haram. Instinctively, her hand went to her locket—as it always did whenever she thought about the mother she had never met—and she replied humbly, 'Dil Ruba Begum.'

Aalam kisu hakim ka baandha tilism hai
Kuch ho to aitbaar bhi ho kaainat ka

This world is a spell cast by some wise man
There should be something to invoke trust in the universe

—Mir Taqi Mir

3

A Bud that Never Bloomed

Gor kis diljale ki hai ye falak
Shola ik subh yaan se uthtaa hai

The sky is the grave of which burning heart?
A flame rises from it every morn

—Mir Taqi Mir

Falak's mother, Dil Ruba, had been fourteen years old when she had entered the haram.

The mahalsara had many inmates and a very complex system of maintaining law and order in it. The mahaldar, usually the wife of a prominent noble, was in charge of its smooth functioning. The tehwildar was in charge of the accounts and not only gave money as and when required for expenses but also gave a fixed stipend for each woman living there. The khwajasaras and jasolinis acted as the information network.

This was needed as so many women lived in there: the wives of the emperors, his mother, aunts, foster mothers other relatives, and of course the concubines.

A large number of women worked in the service of these women. Some held highly respectable posts of teachers, while some did the menial work. Some were paid menials, and many were slave girls, captured in battle or gifted by subordinate rulers. There were singers and dancers too, kept for the entertainment of the begums and princesses.

Except for the high-ranking officers and some attendants who could go to their homes at night, most of the women had to stay confined to the mahalsara.

The most guarded, of course, were the concubines. Many of the concubines were gifts from vassal states, spoils of war, or rose from the rank of slaves. Concubines had no will of their own and were at the whim and fancy of their employer. They could be gifted to others, kept as slaves by their owners, and generally led a charmed life only for as long as they commanded their patron's sexual interests. Once over their prime, they stayed on in the haram as attendants to the begums and current favourite concubines, teaching them tricks to please their patron, helping prepare unguents, pastes and aphrodisiacs. If they had skills, they even became entertainers. Of course, if they were lucky enough to bear a child, they lived the rest of their life in the haram as a much more favoured inmate.

Dil Ruba's parents had been in the service of Mirza Salim Shah Bahadur, the brother of the present emperor. They had died in 1836 under mysterious circumstances shortly after Mirza Salim's death. There had been much speculation about the death. It had seemed like a particularly cruel murder. But why? What did the poor couple have that anyone would want to murder them for? Their neighbour was also employed in the mahal's *bhinda-khana*, and when she heard the distraught screams of the daughter, she and her husband rushed there to investigate. They had found the girl traumatized, sitting beside her parents' bodies, beating her clenched fists against her head. While the husband called the police, the wife took the girl into her own house. Throughout this ordeal, she had kept her fist closed as though holding on to a secret of some kind. Only when she was alone, and her sobs had subsided, did she unclench her hand to contemplate a silver locket nestled in her palm. This amulet was all that remained of her mother, and she wore it solemnly, vowing to treasure it.

The police never did find the culprits. Nor could they fathom the reason for the murders. The girl's parents had been administered poison and died a horrible death. The daughter could shed no light on the matter. All she recalled was that her parents had gone out, and by the time they staggered back in after an hour or so, they were in a state of palpable discomfort, and vomiting and had died soon after.

The lady started taking the girl with her to work and soon everyone forgot about the mysterious circumstances of her parents' death.

The old timers remembered her entry and the envy she had generated.

The orphan girl was employed in the bhinda-khana, and no one remembered her original name. Dil Ruba was the name the Badshah gave her. Before she caught the Emperor's fancy, her job had been to accompany the darogha of the huqqah department, carrying a bag of coal and a box of tobacco. She would sit in a corner and light the coals with a firelock and put them on the *chillum* wherever the Jahanpanah decided to sit down at any given time. As soon as the Huzur gave a signal, the daroghaji would present the chillum and arrange the fresh huqqah in front of him. Other servants would remove the stale huqqah.

One day, Huzur Badshah had come to the palace and gone for a round of the gardens there in his sedan chair. It was Diwali day, and he had been weighed against gold and silver, which was distributed among the poor. Once gold would have been more in proportion, but nowadays it was vastly overshadowed by silver. He had held a special durbar in Diwan-e Aam and was pleasantly tired.

The Diwan-e Aam, with its multi-foliated symmetrical arches, was plastered and gilded. Though the paint was fading, and the exquisite and sumptuous brocade and Kashmiri carpets were a little frayed at the edges, just like the empire itself, it still struck awe in the hearts of visitors.

And nothing was more awe-inspiring than the Nasheman-e Zill-e Ilahi or 'seat of the Shadow of God on Earth' that was ensconced in the centre of the back wall. Built entirely of marble, with lustrous *pietra dura*, it was very high. The attendant or visitor had to stand on a low marble table to look up to Alampanah. This was inspired by the multi-columned halls and throne of Prophet Sulaiman, to inspire the Badshah to emulate the Prophet's acclaimed justice to every creature on earth. Further reference to Prophet Sulaiman's famed justice was found in a panel behind the throne depicting a firangi story of a shepherd boy Orpheus whose lute could charm birds, animals and humans.

Prophet Sulaiman, gave equal justice to everyone, be it the lowly ant or the mighty Queen of Saba or Sheba.

For the Diwali durbar, carriage drivers had decorated their bulls' hooves with henna, gilded their horns, tied bells around their necks and placed gold-and-silver embroidered cloth on their backs and then paraded them in front of the Jahanpanah in the Diwan-e Aam.

A buffalo, a black blanket, mustard oil, a mix of seven cereals and grains, and gold and silver were distributed as alms to avert any misfortune that may befall the Emperor. The Qila was illuminated on all sides. Puffed rice, candy, toys made from clay, sugarcane, and lemon and small clay houses were distributed to everyone by the jasolinis and the maidservants. At night, mud houses made by the royal children were filled with puffed rice and *batashe* sugar candy, and lamps were lit in front of them. The *naubat* was playing.

In the morning, sugarcane plants had been placed in all four corners of the mahal, with lemons strung up on them. These canes were to be distributed amongst the maidservants the following morning.

Huzur was now looking for a few moments of relaxation with his huqqah in the Khurd Jahan garden. There was a group of female dancers performing to the music of male musicians seated behind tents so as to keep the sanctity of the haram. They had been brought in blindfolded by the khwajasara and would leave in the same way. Tanras Khan was also expected to regale the Badshah with his mellifluous singing. Huzur was particularly fond of *dhrupad*.

Along with the diyas illuminating the fort and city, the wondrous colours of the twilit sky had made the Jamuna look radiantly beautiful. Birds were coming back to nest in the branches of trees and seemed to be blessing Jahanpanah with good fortune. Jahanpanah read his evening prayers in a *baradari* there and asked for his huqqah.

The garden was no longer as beautiful as it had been for Mirza Jahangir, the Emperor's brother who had built his mansion there. Mirza Jahangir had long since died, and the mansion was now used by the ladies.

The darogha started looking hither and thither but the girl who carried the coals and tobacco was nowhere to be found. By now she was frantic and fearful of Jahanpanah's wrath if his wishes weren't fulfilled on time. Her eyes were silently darting all over the garden when she heard that girl call out softly, 'Daroghaji, here am I. The chillum is ready too.'

Daroghaji went up to her angrily and said, 'O wretched woman, where were you? Why are you staring at me like a ghost? Why don't you tell me where you had gone to die?'

The girl replied, 'I was looking for you everywhere in the garden when I found myself amongst the gular trees. Perchance my gaze went up and what do I see! On top of the tree something as big and round as a grinding stone was burning as brightly as coal. My eyes were bedazzled by it. My heart started pumping, and I ran like crazy from there till I reached here and found you. God knows what the secret behind it is?'

The darogha immediately replied, 'Oh! That's no secret. Today is the night of Diwali and everyone knows that the flower of the gular blooms on this night only. Anyone who sees it becomes a king and if a woman sees it, she becomes a queen or a king's consort. Now that you have seen this flower, your luck has turned, and you too will enter Huzur Jahanpanah's palace. You will get a title too. Oh! You foolish wench, you have no idea how lucky you are.'

No one had any idea if there was any truth to the story of the gular flower but in a few days Huzur Jahanpanah's gaze fell on her, and he showered his favour on her. She entered his haram soon after.

Truly, when fate conspires, no one can stop an ordinary girl from becoming a Badshah's beloved. She was given the title of Dil Ruba.

The uncharitable speculated on the addition of another concubine to the haram, and the showering of gifts on her. Some gossiped that there was no gular flower at all, for who had ever heard of flowers deciding a woman's fate? Others pettily insinuated that she wasn't even that pretty, so she must have deployed black magic to somehow beguile the Badshah Salamat's discerning eye.

In truth, the Emperor was living on an already very stretched pension from the British. There had once been plenty of treasures in the palace, but they had all since been looted or—if rumours were to be believed—hidden in some secret location of which no one seemed to know the whereabouts. It was well-known that Ghulam Qadir Rohilla had tortured Badshah Shah Alam, eventually blinding him, in an attempt to find out where this treasure was hidden. He had even humiliated the Badshah Begum and other shahzadis after entering the haramsara. The begums and shahzadis had been dragged out of the apartment and paraded naked before the Rohilla chief and his men, before being violated. Consequently, wracked with shame and anguish, many of these ladies had taken their own lives.

The palace was scoured, and its grounds dug up a few days later to hunt for this treasure but nothing was ever found. Even if Shah Alam Badshah had known of its location, surely the secret must have passed away with him. That did not stop subsequent emperors from hoping to find and claim that hidden wealth for themselves. After all, some sort of bounty was needed to shore up the Timurid Empire, bereft as it was of revenue after the treaty of Allahabad. Conspiracy theories abounded—including one about a possible map, but efforts to locate it had been in vain.

But all talk of hidden treasures suddenly seemed tired and stale, overturned by the new gossip about Dil Ruba, whose evident beauty had clearly caught the Emperor's eye against all odds. And then came the news that she had been summoned by the Badshah Salamat.

Dil Ruba had only been in the haram a few months when the Emperor asked the daroghas and attendants to get her ready and bring her to the *khwaabgah*.

Dil Ruba had been working in the haram and knew what was required of her. She let herself be prepared for the night submissively. She was oiled, bathed and perfumed; dressed and bejewelled. She had refused to take off her simple silver locket, even though the attendants showed her the tray with jewels that had been sent for her. She was taught a few moves by some of the other women in the haram so that she could please the Emperor. One of the older concubines, seeing her youth and very slim frame, gave her an opium-laced sweet to eat. Dil Ruba obediently ate it and after a while, started feeling her limbs and mind relaxing.

She was led to the heavily perfumed, beautifully decorated royal khwaabgah in the Khas Mahal. The room, glowing from the gilding which shone in the luminous candlelight, was exquisite with *parchinkari* or inlay work decorating each inch of it with red flowers and green vines intertwined to heighten the sensuous pleasures of the inmates. Bowls of rose petals, *itrdaans,* added to it. Just outside the carved copper door, female musicians played music on their instruments, while singers sang. Under the gaze of the attendants who were there to guide, she performed her duty in a daze. The opium helped in dulling the pain, even though the Emperor was gentle. Why had no one told her that the pain wasn't only once but happened every time she was taken?

The Emperor, enchanted by the musky smell and taste of the young girl, was also taken up by her innocence. He spent time talking to her. He had even asked her what was in the locket.

'Huzur Alampanah, this was given to me by my mother on her death bed,' she prevaricated. 'I don't know what lies inside, but it must be a supplication to Allah to keep me safe from the evil eye.'

'Where was your mother from?' he enquired.

'Huzur, she worked in this palace. My father had been the darogha of Sahib-e Alam Mirza Salim Bahadur's household, and she served in his zenana as a milk mother after my birth. Both my parents died after the sainted Sahib-e Alam's demise. As I had no one to look after me and no means of sustenance, the darogha of the bhinda-khana, who was my neighbour, brought me here and put me to work alongside herself. Then of course, my stars shone, and your blessed gaze fell on me.'

'You will definitely need protection from the evil eye, Dil Ruba. You have truly enchanted me and will live like a queen in the haram and never need anything,' he said, gently stroking her neck and breast.

Soon the strokes grew longer and culminated in another bout of lovemaking.

Languorously, she yawned and sang a Farsi song in a melodious voice:

> *Within my bosom stirs once more tonight*
> *A voice of song. Love, erewhile slumbering,*
> *Intones his mystery, and the flowers of spring*
> *Relive and bloom. Winter, forbear to smite*
> *My heart's late flowers. Listen! From left and right*
> *Through the green boughs, the bulbul's note is heard,*
> *And, wing-clipt and imprisoned, my heart's bird*
> *Flutters against his barriers, wild for flight.*[1]

'Subhan Allah!' exclaimed the emperor. 'Where did you learn this from?'

'Huzur, I am an unlettered woman. I had heard this from my mother's mistress, the sainted Nawab Malika Sultan uz-Zamani Begum sahiba. She would read out from a book of poems that she had. My mother made me learn this one by heart and sing it for her, after Sabib-e Alam's death.' Lulled into a feeling of languor and sensuousness by their tender lovemaking, she revealed something she had promised her mother she would not. 'I think this song is from a book that Nawab Begum sahiba possessed. I was very young when my parents died, but I remember that my mother regarded this book as very special. I never thought to ask her why. There was something about this book that made my mother very sad—she always cried when she saw it. And I cannot remember precisely how I know this, but there is some connection between the *taveez* in my locket and that song . . . I had forgotten all about this book. It was your magical touch that suddenly made this lowly woman remember those beautiful words.'

Fortunately for Dil Ruba, the Emperor was so taken by her beauty and the sensual pleasure that her youthful body gave him that he didn't probe further. There were far more exciting discoveries waiting to be probed in her taut body.

In the morning, the attendants escorted her back to her corner of the mahalsara, fawning over her as they helped her take the ritual bath that was stipulated by *sharia* after every bout of lovemaking, for they had seen the gleam in the royal eye and knew that Dil Ruba would be called often from now on.

The young girl had visited the royal apartment only for a few months when she found out she was pregnant. The visits to the royal bedchamber stopped. By then the Emperor had also married Nawab Zeenat Mahal Begum and was oblivious to everyone else.

A lady was employed to look after Dil Ruba when she went into confinement. At the time, Mubarak had just given birth to her own son, and was filled with compassion for the heavily pregnant concubine with whom she had begun to feel a closer sense of solidarity. *It would be good to have a close friend in the haram*, she thought; and there was always the welcoming notion that their children would be close enough in age to play with each other as they grew older. Mubarak was also pragmatic to realize that, since she was still feeding her son, she could also later act as milk mother to Dil Ruba's baby, if necessary.

And so, a great friendship blossomed between Mubarak and the gentle Dil Ruba. Mubarak would tell her stories of the city that Dil Ruba had once lived in but was now destined never to revisit.

The older women in the haram had been quick to perceive that Dil Ruba's tiny frame might not fortify her against the challenges of childbirth, and so she had given her some opium earlier. But when the midwife came to attend to Dil Ruba, it was surmised that even more opium would be required: this was going to be a difficult birth.

Mubarak was wise enough to understand the gravity of the situation while making sure that nothing was said or done to alarm Dil Ruba. As predicted, the birth was prolonged and extremely painful. Ultimately, there were cries of relief as a tiny girl was pulled out. The baby's cord was cut, and she was handed over to the nursemaids to bathe. But Dil Ruba's bleeding refused to stop. Mubarak's brief spurt of joy quickly turned to grief as the haemorrhaging Dil Ruba caught Mubarak's hand and weakly begged her to take the locket from her neck and put it around the baby's. 'Mubarak, please look after my baby. I have given my life for her, now she's yours. And let this locket be my legacy to her. It will keep her safe and come to her help in times of need. Name her Falak, and may the sky be hers.'

Mubarak's infant son had passed away a few days before—a tragedy that she would never fully recover from. She had at first refused to let Dil Ruba learn of this because she was concerned that such talk of death would only agitate an already anxious Dil Ruba further. But it is impossible to quell bad news within the zenana, and it was Dil Ruba who broached the subject sympathetically with her friend, gently admonishing Mubarak for suffering in silence when she could have shared her grief and, in doing so, alleviated it. Mubarak was tearfully grateful for Dil Ruba's compassion, and this strengthened their friendship.

Now, faced with the twin losses of her own child as well as her close friend, Mubarak was beyond distraught. With nobody to turn to for solace, it was not surprising then that she found unexpected comfort in caring for Dil Ruba's baby. Mubarak was still lactating, and it made pragmatic sense to relieve the pain in her full breasts by feeding the orphaned infant. This gave the older woman a sense of purpose as well as a channel for her reserves of affection. And so, it was not long before she became fiercely devoted to the motherless girl.

*

Falak Ara waited respectfully after answering the Empress's question.

'Oh yes! I remember now,' said Nawab Zeenat Mahal Begum sahiba. She died very young. That was just before I got married and came to the mahal. I hope you are comfortable and looked after.'

'Yes, Malika Hazrat. Mubarak looks after me, and everyone is very nice to me,' replied Falak Ara.

Dismissing her with a wave of the hand, the Malika said, 'If you need anything, let me know.'

Presenting her salam, Falak exited backwards, careful not to turn her back on the Empress since that would be considered an insult. Suddenly, she felt a weight lift off her shoulders. She could go back to the safety of her own corner and her paints. Her anonymity had offered her refuge, and she didn't want to exchange that for anything.

But that was not to be, for now, her beauty had been noticed, and this would no doubt catapult her into the Badshah Huzur's ambit. Tongues and minds were busy.

Falak had none of these concerns for her heart was busy. She had hoped to meet her soldier here, hoped against hope that he was also a prince and one of the favoured ones invited.

She reached her room in a daze. Mubarak was waiting for her there. 'What happened, my child? Please tell me everything.'

The other ladies and their attendants who also shared the room were all agog to hear what had transpired. Gulab Jan was also hanging on to every word. She knew it would be worth a pretty penny and some romance for her.

Looking at her, Saeedan, jealous of her youth, said to her, 'Look at Gulab Jan—always showing off under false pretences.'

'Arre, look out for yourself, dry as dust by age! As long as there's oil in my lamp I will burn,' said Gulab Jan with a pout and flounce.

One old attendant was excitedly asking, 'What did you eat?'

'Sshh, quiet!' admonished Mubarak. 'Can't you think of anything but food? This is not the time to worry about food. May I be sacrificed over my Alampanah's generosity? What did the Badshah Salamat say?' Mubarak's only interest was in any attention her charge may have received.

'What was the Nawab Malika sahiba wearing?' asked Zebunnisa.

Falak Ara sat down on her bed and started talking as if she was a mechanical toy that had been wound up. 'The Nawab Malika sahiba is very beautiful. She was bejewelled from top to toe and was wearing a green silk peshwaz and a magenta dupatta. She was very nice to me. The other begums were also very well turned out. Kulsum Zamani Begum was the prettiest,' referring to her stepsister, the Badshah Salamat's daughter. 'She looks like a fairy. The table was laden with food, and I couldn't count the number of naans, rotis, qormas, kababs, qaliya, nuqti and halwa that were served.'

'Forget the qorma, my precious,' said a frustrated Mubarak. 'Did Huzur Purnur notice you or not?'

'Yes, he called me and offered me the ulash. I could have died of mortification. I don't think I have ever felt so embarrassed or naked. I was exposed to everyone's eyes,' said a blushing Falak.

'Bajijan were there some handsome princes there?' said another young girl.

'I don't know, I didn't lift up my eyes,' Falak replied. All she knew was that *he* hadn't been there.

As usual when she was agitated, she started fiddling with her locket. Mubarak started stroking her arms and soon she calmed down.

Unknown to her, her poet was also trying to break out of the locks binding him down.

Dekhna, ai Zauq honge phir wahi laakhon ke khoon
Phir jamaaya uss ne laal-e lab mein laakha ka paan

Zauq, you watch! The blood of those same lacs will be shed once again—
once again she's made the rubies of her lips lac-red with paan.[2]

—Shaikh Ibrahim Zauq

4

The Lock and the Locked

Ham-sar-e-zulf qad-e-huur-e-shamaail thahraa
Laam kaa khoob alif madd-e-muqaabil thahraa

Like the vertical 'laam',
a worthy rival
to the rising stroke of 'alif',
my beloved's tresses billow
like a shamal, rising
to the stature of houris of heaven.[3]

—Ameer Minai

In one corner of the one-hundred-and-twenty-five-acre fort was a huge compound known as Nau Muhalla, home to the descendants of previous emperors. This is where Mirza Qaiser lived with his father.

His father was the Emperor's cousin and as such had been considered a threat in the previous emperor's lifetime. Now he was old, and so he and his son enjoyed considerably more freedom than *his* father had. Also, as there were no Sayyid brothers or Imad al-Mulk who, just a century ago, had played kingmakers, there was less insecurity to the reigning monarch. The Sayyid brothers had crowned and deposed emperors at will, pulling out royal princes living in anonymity in the salatin quarters of Salimgarh and putting them on the throne. The year 1719 had seen four emperors on the Peacock Throne.

45

The Timurid blood that ran in Mirza Qaiser's veins was mixed with the Rajput blood of his mother's family and gave him an imposing air of power and good looks. He was tall, swarthy of complexion, well-built thanks to the military training he undertook, and well-versed in poetry and literature as well as philosophy, mathematics, logic and reason. The princes and princesses of the royal blood were all given an extensive education. Though the extended family was not always included in this, Mirza Qaiser's father, who had himself had the benefit of that education, had personally supervised his son's upbringing.

Mirza Mohammad Aftab hoped that his son may catch the eye of the Company bahadur and get a good post. There were no restrictions on the movements of the salatin now and his son had started attending the morning Jharokha Darshan and even going for the parade on days of the public court.

Everyone knew that it was the Company bahadur that ruled and not the Emperor. When a proclamation was made, it read, *khilqat khuda ki, mulk Badshah ka, hukm Company ka* [the Lord's creation, the emperor's territory and the British East India Company's rule]. Mirza Mohammad Aftab had suffered during his initial years in confinement but now that the Company bahadur was ruling and no one could place a king on the throne, or even succeed their own fathers, things were better. The Company bahadur had to approve even of the names of the *wali ahad*, or heir apparent, and though they recognized merit, they also recognized a rebellious nature and ensured it was tamed. The whole world knew what had happened to Mirza Jahangir, that rebellious, carefree young prince. Favourite of his father, Emperor Akbar Shah II, and mother, Mumtaz Mahal Begum, his appointment as heir apparent was stalled by the angrez sahibs who preferred the sober Abu Zafar Sirajuddin Mohammad Zafar. They had had their way, and Abu Zafar was later crowned as Abu Zafar Sirajuddin Muhammad Bahadur Shah Badshah Ghazi and became the occupant of the Peacock Throne. Mirza Jahangir too had played into their hands, by mocking the angrez Resident bahadur, Sahib-e Kalan Seton sahib, and even taking a pot-shot at him, ending in his being banished to the Allahabad Fort.

Mirza Aftab had noticed his son in a pensive mood. 'How did your shooting practice go yesterday? And did you catch any good *shikar*?'

'My greetings to you Abbajan, may the Almighty Allah keep you safe and healthy. You are always worried about me. The shikar was good. I can now shoot a flying bird with my arrow and a deer with my gun. How I wish there was still an Imperial Army I could join. I really don't understand the point of this daily shikar.'

'My son, I have read in Allami Abul Fazl's account of our illustrious ancestor—Shahenshah-e Hind Akbar Badshah arsh ashiyani—that the emperor would organize regular shikar expeditions; for shikar during peace times keeps the mind and body fit and working in coordination.'

'Tell me some stories about the shikar. I love those old anecdotes, and wish we could have those days back,' said Mirza Qaiser. The nineteen-year-old boy was a prince of royal blood but was sidelined from the royal family because of the fear of dynastic coups. And so, he spent his days living in hope of recognition by the Emperor, fearful of the lifelong anonymity that beset his father before him. His mother had died when he was a child and his father had brought up his only son on tales of valour and the glory days of the Timurids and Rajputs. The Timurid blood in his veins made him restless, inciting him to make a mark, but the wise counsel of his father kept him in check.

Mirza Mohammad Aftab continued in measured tones, 'Ah! If only those days could come back. But the wars of succession and the intrigues of the *wazirs* to play kingmakers, putting puppets on the Peacock Throne. In fact, the end could be foreseen ever since Badshah Alamgir II was thrown off the Jami Masjid in the Kotla of Firoz Shah through the machinations of his wazir, Imad al-Mulk, after which his son Shah Alam crowned himself away from Delhi. Shah Alam Badshah then aligned himself with the Nawab of Bengal and Awadh to fight against the Company bahadur and lost. It was so long ago—I cannot be sure, but I think it was 1764. The next year he had to sign a peace treaty with the angrez and ended up signing away the revenue rights to the richest Mughal province to the angrez sahib, Robert Clive, and the Company. When he did return to Delhi it was as a pensioner of the Maratha leader Scindia. I have heard all these stories from my father, who was enraged at the fact that his uncle and cousin had to become pensioners.'

'Abbajan, are we really pensioners of the Marathas?' asked a shocked Qaiser.

'No, son, we are actually pensioners of the Badshah, but he is a pensioner of the Company bahadur. This happened in 1803 after the Company bahadur defeated the Marathas in Patparganj. Thereafter, the Badshah of the *khandan-e Timuriya* became a pensioner of the same Company bahadur who had come to beg for trade concessions from our ancestor Jahangir Badshah. But why am I depressing you with these stories, let us talk of happier things.'

Shaking his head to shrug off his dark mood he continued, 'Badshah Jahangir has, in his memoirs, described an occasion when Empress Nur Jahan killed four tigers with six shots!'

The surprised son immediately exclaimed, 'Four tigers in six shots! I didn't know that women were such crack shots.'

'Son, the Timurid women have always been very well educated and at par with the men. They could ride, use swords and guns, as well as argue over philosophy with the best of them. Just because they lived in *purdah* doesn't mean they didn't have opportunities or influence. The matriarchs and milk mothers wielded a great deal of influence on the Badshah. The badshahs have always sought their advice.'

'Abbajan, you keep using the word Timurid or *Gurkani*—and that is what you taught me too. So why do the firangis and now even some of the Hindustanis call us Mughals?'

'We are descendants of Sahib-e Qiran Amir Timur. He had married into the family of Genghis Khan and so became his son-in-law or *gurkan* and that's why they write Gurkani after their name.

I remember my respected father telling me that those heathens, the Portuguese, first used the word Mughal for us. All firangis have subsequently used it for they don't understand our culture or even our language though they do study it.'

'Abbajan, the ladies who live in the haramsara now, do they also get education and training like the royal princes?'

'I don't know what is happening now, but when I was young, they did. I am sure the very efficient system established by Akbar Badshah for the haramsara still functions. Your sainted mother used to visit when we were younger and tell me of the very erudite and enlightened women staying there. A female tutor called by the name of Atun Mama would supervise their studies in literature, poetry, philosophy and logic. *Hafizas* or those women who knew the Holy Quran by heart would ensure they learnt about the Quran, *hadith* and sharia.'

'Abbajan, tell me about Ammijan, please.'

'You never tire of hearing about her, do you?' said his father, smiling. 'She was from a very noble Rajput family and our fathers arranged the match. They say that those whom the Gods love, die young—and perhaps it's true. She was the epitome of everything good, be it beauty, piety, charity or learning. You take after her in one more thing.'

'Oh really! What is that?'

'Your curiosity! Your mother had an immense spirit of enquiry, as do you, always wanting to learn more, know more and broaden your mind.'

Father and son shared a good rapport and good-hearted ribbing was a normal routine for them.

'Your maternal great-grandfather was a commander in the army of the Emperor's grandfather and was very trusted by him,' continued Mirza Aftab. 'It is because of his preeminent position in court that I was considered a threat. But now it is only the Company who decides. I have been thinking of shifting from this prison to the city. You will also have a better life there and more freedom.'

'Will the Badshah give us permission?'

'Yes, if the Company bahadur does. I will talk to Sahib-e Kalan, Resident bahadur Fraser sahib. I know he likes me and maybe you can get employment with him.'

'I don't want to work for the firangi, Abbajan,' said Qaiser, 'They are eyeing our country and our kingdom.'

'Who has put these blasphemous thoughts in your mind? For God's sake, son, be careful or like Mirza Jahangir you will be exiled form Shahjahanabad and maybe even imprisoned,' cried out Mirza Aftab in anguish. 'We know that it is they who control everything, and we can only be resigned to our fate.'

'I don't care; anything is better than this life. There is nothing for me to do. All this training and skill and nowhere to use it,' replied the son.

'Would you like to visit your maternal uncle? Maybe a change of scene would do you good.'

'Let me think, Abbajan. Do I have your permission to go to Chandni Chowk?'

'Of course, my son. An outing will do you good.'

'You are always so thoughtful about me. May I be sacrificed over you.'

Qaiser did a quick toilette and set off on his horse towards Chandni Chowk.

The road from the Qila's Lahori Gate led straight to the Chandni Chowk, or Moonlit Square, built by Emperor Shah Jahan's beloved daughter Jahanara Begum.

Though the square was no longer the blushing bride once adorned by a Sufi princess, Chandni Chowk was still beautiful, like a dowager who had endured the vicissitudes of time with her dignity intact. Her loved ones still came to visit her and were welcomed with open arms. The shops were still full of rubies from Burma and pearls from Basra. The paying customer may have changed from the shahzadas, *amir* and *umara* to the British, European and neo-riche Hindustanis but the etiquette of the market remained the same. The salesmen stood outside and advertised their wares. The *attars*, or perfumers, touted the qualities of their *itr* saying its vapour was guaranteed to melt the hardest of hearts and make the beloved swoon in your arms.

The *qahwakhanas* there were full of Qaiser's friends in the evening. Coffee brought by a Sufi named Baba Budan from Yemen to the Deccan had spread to the north. It was said to be a spiritual intoxicant which helped the devout stay awake for their nightly devotions. Of course, the many he-devotees who frequented the Chandni Chowk qahwakhanas were those who worshipped at the altar of pleasure.

China ware, huqqah bases and wine cups were being sold in another shop. The wine cups could tempt even the most pious to take a sip.

As Qaiser's horse trotted briskly, his mind was full of the woman he had rescued from the river and her kohl-rimmed eyes. *Who was she*, he wondered. Not that he would ever meet her again, for the salatin rarely came in contact with the princesses who lived inside the palace. He shook his head and rode on through Urdu Bazar, past the Urdu mandir and onto Jauhri Bazar. There were beautiful shops with awnings and qahwakhanas on either side of the Moonlit Square. These were the haunts of the young blades with pretensions to writing poetry or practising any art form. Sometimes a famous poet would come here, and the raw poets could get to hear some master verses. The custom was that every budding poet had to have an *ustad* who would provide him guidance and correct his verses. Of course, the most famous was Mirza Naushah, but it was difficult to become his protégé.

Qaiser gave his horse to the syce outside the qahwakhana to stable it while he enjoyed some huqqah and coffee with his friends over poetry and sweet nuqtis. As Shah Hatim said:

jahan dekho tahan har aan qahwa
hai bazm-e-aish ka samaan qahwa

Wherever we look, there is qahwa
It is the recipe for pleasure, this qahwa

As usual, a few young bloods were gathered there. The air was thick with the scented smoke of many huqqahs, made heady with the itr and camphor from the lamps decorating the niches and of course the smell of *qahwa*.

As Mirza Qaiser entered, he saw many young men sitting on a carpet with bolsters scattered around them for comfort.

They were dressed in the latest fashion. Chintz jamas with a Kashmiri patka on their waists, bejewelled daggers tucked into them, a matching Kashmiri turban with a sarpech, and pearls and emeralds around their necks. There were many workshops in the Empire, both in the city and countryside, which produced the finest textiles such as *mashru*, silk, chintz, muslin, velvet brocade, *bafta, amru, ghatta* or satin-like velvet for making the dresses of the nobility and elite. Royal workshops within the Qila made the finest of textiles for the royal family. These would be embroidered with *zardozi* and *kamdani*, all using delicate gold and silver wires.

Qaiser stopped to greet Imamuddin Khan, Santosh Lal and Brijnath Zutshi, all students at Delhi College who were discussing the day's lecture by Master Ramchandra and then headed towards his friends.

With the decline or, in reality, the collapse of the Emperor's political power, literary activities had replaced political ones in the city. Delhi College was emerging as an intellectual centre with its departments of English, Arabic, Persian and Sanskrit. Students came from the provinces to study here. Weekly *mushairas* were held, and on those nights, the Ajmeri Gate was kept open late into the night.

Delhi College was just outside Ajmeri Darwaza and had been established by Ghaziuddin Khan Nizam al-Mulk, an eminent noble of Emperor Aurangzeb's reign, some hundred and fifty years ago. In 1825, the British opened a college here for imparting Western education in the imposing double-storey red sandstone building.

The entrance itself was very grand—a lofty central arch flanked by three arches on either side. English had been introduced on the recommendation of Sahib-e Kalan Bahadur Sir Charles Metcalf, may his glory increase, who was the angrez Resident bahadur, of that time though Urdu was the medium of instruction for teaching science subjects. Maulvi Imam Baksh and Maulvi Mamluk Ali of the oriental section were two very famous teachers.

Mohanlal Zutshi, the famous Kashmiri diplomat and author, had been the first Indian student to learn English. His felicity in languages had led to his getting employed by the British as the Persian interpreter of Sir Alexander Burnes when the latter left for Central Asia. He was later appointed as a political agent to the court of Khurasan and Kabul.

His roving eye and numerous romantic liaisons and offspring in different parts of the world had led the Kashmiri Pandit community to disown him. He was living in Shahjahanabad these days with his Muslim wife Haidari Begum. His college, however, was very proud of his successes for the British in Afghanistan.

By 1856, several more institutions had been set up to facilitate learning and encourage further study. At that time, there were three hundred and eighty-five Hindus, four Christians and only eighty-three Muslims who were obtaining modern education at the Delhi College. One of the reasons for low Muslim enrolment was that the royal family and nobility had home tutors and a sense of privilege, and in any case did not need to study for employment. Another was a reaction of the people against modern education, propelled by the feeling that Christian propaganda against Islam and Hinduism would destroy their religion.

As the three students got up to greet Mirza Qaiser with a salam, the latter asked them about their welfare.

'Pandit ji, how are your studies going? I heard you are learning Latin and Greek also?' He asked Brijnath Zutshi, the scion of a prominent Kashmiri pandit family living in Sitaram Bazar and receiving a classical western education.

'Thank you for asking, Mirza sahib. I am trying to work hard. I am learning Greek and Latin at home from a private tutor. I hope to get admission and go to Cambridge University to pursue my higher education.'

'Your dedication and knowledge are admirable. May Allah give you success,' said Mirza Qaiser before moving to join his friends.

Kashmiri Pandits were not only highly educated but also occupied very high posts in most of the governments. They had the advantage of knowing Arabic and Persian apart from Sanskrit and in many cases were well versed in English too. Naturally, not only the Company *sarkar* but also Hindustani rulers employed and rewarded them amply.

In fact, Qaiser's maternal grandfather had a *haveli* in Sitaram Bazar and would stay there to attend the Mughal durbar. Their neighbours were a Kashmiri Kaul family and the young son Bishamber Nath and Qaiser's mother had not only been playmates as children, but she had also become his *munh boli*, or adopted, sister. Even today, Mirza Aftab maintained that relationship. Bishamber Nath had gone to England to study and returned after attaining a degree in medicine from the Manchester Royal Infirmary. Dr Kaul, as he was now known, was a very popular doctor and his friendship with Mirza Aftab had strengthened with time.

On *salona*, Qaiser would go to their house to get a rakhi tied by his daughter, Parmeshwari, and gift her a string of pearls while she would feed him his favourite shakkarpara and halwa sohan.

'Ama *yaar*, we were waiting for you, Qaiser. What took you so long to come?' asked Ibrahim. Kunwar Mohammed Ibrahim was the son of Nawab Azizuddin Khan of Tirhwa. Though the decline of the empire had spelt a steady decline in the fortunes of the Mughal dynasty, the nobles and rulers of principalities were still doing well. Many provincial governors, though ostensibly paying obeisance to the Emperor, were more or less independent and had gathered immense wealth and power. The local *rajas*, *jagirdars* and landlords too were doing well, taxing the peasants on their land and enjoying the good life in the capital. Many had consciously or subconsciously exchanged their loyalties to the new rising power, the Company bahadur.

There had been many changes in Shahjahanabad and its neighbouring provinces. The attacks by the Persian ruler Nadir Shah in 1739 had broken the back of the Mughal empire. It was said that he took away seventy crore rupees of wealth from Hindustan, including the famed Peacock Throne built by Emperor Shah Jahan. Subsequent raids by Ahmad Shah Abdali and local chieftains put the Mughals at the mercy of moneylenders. And gradually a new class of rich traders and moneylenders had replaced the old nobility.

Qaiser had heard all about this from his father, who also said that the only good thing to have emerged from this otherwise lamentable situation was the development of a new language called Rekhta. Its emergence had been hastened by the fact that Persian had lost a lot of its patronage with the fading away of the old nobility. Now, even the Badshah wrote verses in Rekhta, as did Sheikh Ibrahim Zauq, Hakim Momin Khan Momin and Mirza Ghalib. A new poet was rising on the horizon of Rekhta these days, Mirza Nawab, known by his pen name Dagh Dehlvi.

I must ask Abbajan if I can become a protégé of the Badshah Huzur, but for calligraphy rather than Rekhta, thought Qaiser as he presented his salam to the gathered friends and sought permission to sit down.

They say that a dead elephant is still worth a lakh and a quarter, and that could be said for the Shahjahanabad elite as well, who continued to clutch at their old *tehzeeb* and ways.

'How are you, Mirza?' asked Kunwar Zoravar Singh, scion of a Rajput state and related to Mirza Qaiser through the latter's mother. He lived in Delhi and was a disciple of the Emperor in the art of calligraphy, and the two cousins got along very well.

'Ama, tell me about your adventure yesterday,' said Miyan Nabbu, son of a wealthy landlord from Bareilly, who stayed in the capital to spend his father's money and enjoy at the cost of the blood and toil paid in taxes by the peasants. Gulab Jan had visited him at

night and there had been a satisfactory outcome for both. Money
and information had both exchanged hands and of course, never one
to miss an opportunity, Nabbu had enjoyed a night of unbridled
pleasure too. The women working in the Fort were very experienced
in pleasuring their partners.

'What adventure? I lead a very boring life and the only excitement
in it is meeting you all.'

'Come on, don't be shy. Everyone is talking of your chivalrous
rescue of a young princess in yesterday's ladies outing at the Qila,'
said Miyan Nabbu jocularly. Outwardly respectful of royalty, he was
secretly jealous of what he felt were unfair privileges given to them.
He despised his situation: all this money and yet he had to struggle to
find a foothold in society while these princes, sunk up to their necks
in debt, were considered pillars of society.

'Oh, that was nothing. I had forgotten about it. I am sure you
would have done the same if you were in my position. A girl was
drowning, and I helped to save her,' Qaiser tried to brush it off
nonchalantly.

'Arre, what is this talk of rescue? I haven't heard of any of
this. Miyan Nabbu, how do you get all the gossip so fast?' asked
Ibrahim.

'Well, I pay my servants well to keep me informed,' said Miyan
Nabbu with a wink.

Qaiser was a little put off by this conversation, wondering once
again if good manners and etiquette were a sign of ancestry. Miyan
Nabbu's father, though rich enough to have greased the way for his
son into the upper echelons of Delhi society, obviously hadn't been
able to get over his love for gossip.

'I am sorry, but I don't like gossip, nor do I indulge in it,' he said
dismissively.

'Yes, of course. Why would you Qila folks need to gossip? You
have such an efficient network of spies to keep you informed and give
you written reports. We poor mortals must rely on our servants,' said
Miyan Nabbu, piqued.

'Come on, you two,' said Mirza Abu Bakr, a Mughal descendant whose ancestors had long since lost their power and influence in the fort and had shifted out into the city. They had some interests in trade and had done well for themselves and lived in a palatial haveli in Matia Mahal. 'Everyone knows that there are spies, only these days they report to the Company bahadur, not Alampanah. Only the eunuchs and women employees must report on affairs of the haramsara to the Huzur Badshah. I have heard such tales of spies and palace intrigue, but that's for another day. Qaiser, please tell us more.'

While Miyan Nabbu was mollified by this, Qaiser was mortified. Living a protected life in the salatin quarters and brought up by a loving father who fed him tales of bygone days and chivalry, he still clung to the ideals of what he thought of as his heritage.

'As I said, it was nothing. I had forgotten about it. This huqqah smells good, let me try it. Is it a new flavour?' Trying to change the topic he reached out for the beautiful glass huqqah, decorated with golden flowers and with a silver pipe. As was the norm in the qahwakhana, clean *muhnal*, or mouthpieces, were amply provided for use by the patrons, but many of the city's elite carried their mouthpieces. Mirza Qaiser took out a beautiful jade mouthpiece and, attaching it to the huqqah, took a puff.

'I heard there is to be a *tarahi* mushaira in the city?' asked Qaiser. 'Any of you going to try your hand there?'

'Do you mean at the Delhi College?' asked Mirza Abu Bakr.

'Arre Mirza, everyone is getting ready to go to Qutub Sahib[4] for the monsoon months. They are busy packing. I don't think there is going to be any mushaira for a few months,' said Miyan Nabbu. Qutub Sahib had become the monsoon retreat of the later Mughal emperors, and Akbar Shah Sani Badshah had built a small palace called Junglee Mahal, to which his son Bahadur Shah Badshah had added a palatial gateway with beautiful apartments on top.

Mirza Abu Bakr replied, 'The college hosts a weekly mushaira, so I don't think the heat or the packing is going to bother them.'

'Ah yes! I remember now. Something to look forward to then. The heat is becoming unbearable,' said Miyan Nabbu. He was looking forward not to the mushaira, but to the fact that the Ajmeri Darwaza of the walled city would be kept open late into the night. Such wonderful possibilities were coming to mind.

At least that mushaira is something to look forward to, thought Qaiser, seized by an unbearable restlessness. The coffee and the huqqah were not helping and he got up. 'Anyone for a stroll down Chandni Chowk? I think I will take a round in some fresh air and clear my mind.'

He may have nonchalantly dismissed the episode by the river, but suddenly, the girl's face and fluttering eyelashes came unbidden to his mind.

As Mir Taqi Mir said:

shikastah-baali ko chaahe to ham se zaamin le
aseer mausam-e gul mein hamein nah kar saiyaad

If you so wish, I will pledge my broken wings to you
Don't make me a prisoner, in this season of roses, O Hunter.

5

The Dupatta and the Dil

kar sair jazb-e ulfat gul-chiin ne kal chaman mein
toraa tha shaakh-e gul ko nikli ṣadaa-e bulbul

Witness the immersion in love, yesterday when the
flower picker
Broke a flower in the garden, far away the nightingale sighed

—Mir Taqi Mir

Far away in the Qila, Falak woke up from a restless sleep with a verse
of Mir Taqi Mir on her lips. Did Majnu, as Qais was known, really
bleed when Laila's veins were opened for bloodletting to cure her of
her obsessive love for him, as was alluded to in the verse by the poet?
Could there be such a love? What was it that made her suddenly
restless? Was her young prince in trouble? She didn't even know who
he was; how was she to ever find him? Why had no one told her
about love?

She had no idea whom to ask. The royal women she shared her
apartment with were immersed in their lives. The maids, especially
Gulab Jan, indulged in dalliances but these were not affairs of the
heart so she would not know. And Mubarak would be horrified if
she asked any of them.

*

Sikandar Ara Begum, Huzur's great aunt, had of late taken to getting her jewellery broken down. Every day a young boy would come from the jeweller in Jauhri Bazar near Chandni Chowk. She would open a leather bag and give him some sets of stone-studded jewellery from it. His assigned task was to remove the stones from the gold. She would sit there silently and watch him use his thin chisel to carefully prise out the precious stones and put them on a red velvet cloth while setting aside the gold on another piece of fabric. She would then tell her attendant to deposit the precious stones in the treasury and tell the boy to take the gold for his own use. The uncharitable women in the haramsara said she was senile and wasting her jewellery. They said that Sikandar Ara Begum had always been scatter-brained since she was a young girl in the wake of that traumatic time when the Rohillas had invaded the privacy of the haram and ravaged many of the ladies there. They say she had never been the same since that incident. She had also never married and had lived in the palace all her life.

The goldsmiths talked of the fact that even though the Qila had been looted by Nadir Shah, Ahmed Shah Abdali, the Jats and Rohillas, there was still so much left and that these royals would never understand the value of money as they had never had to earn it themselves. And of course, the inevitable whispers of the hidden treasure that everybody talked of but no one knew if it existed or not.

Falak always felt sorry for Sikandar Ara Begum, realizing her loneliness, and tried to spend more time with her.

The royal ladies more or less got along well with each other and provided a support system, of course in a while the jealous attendants and maids would create some rift. But the darogha would always sort it out.

The present darogha was a daughter-in-law of a very famous Sufi saint, whom Huzur considered his spiritual preceptor, and she was a very sensible, patient and very respected person.

Falak Ara went and took her place by the window, gazing pensively at the scene outside.

'Would Zebunnisa Begum have gazed through this same window as she composed her poems? Was her heart also beset by the same unnamed emotions?'

Falak sat in front of the window with a sketch book and a palette full of paint, drawing inspiration from her ancestress. A book of verses, a *diwan,* was lying in front of her. She had borrowed it from the royal library the day before. She had gone to the library in the zenana hoping to find an illustrated manuscript of the *Shahnameh* when her gaze fell on the notations on this book. It had been borrowed by Nawab Malika Sultan uz-Zamani Begum sahiba, who had been her grandmother's mistress. She felt drawn to the connection to her mother.

It was quiet in the chamber as the ladies were engaged in dawn prayers, but in front of her, there was glorious movement and colour as the bathers gathered for their ritual bath in the Jamuna.

Lost in thought, she moved her charcoal pencil on the paper. She had been sitting by the window, lost in thought, for a few weeks now, preparing the *khaka*, or tracing, on a parchment which had been carefully transferred on to the paper.

A preliminary sketch after selecting paper had been made with a piece of charcoal, or a specially prepared pencil called *lekhni*.

The first outline on the surface of the paper, burnished earlier with agate, was made with Indian red, or *garika*, which was mixed with any gum or similar adhesive and could be easily removed if any alterations were required. Over this line of her preliminary sketch in red, she made a black outline, which she improved wherever she thought necessary.

As she was drawing the black lines, Zebunnisa came and stood near her shoulder.

'Why are you drawing over the red in black colour now, Falak Apa?

'Well, the garika was temporary and black is permanent as the pigment is mixed with gum so that any alteration to this has to be made by rubbing it out with white paint. The black outlines also enhance the colour scheme, Zebun.'

'What is it called?' continued the curious Zebun.

'This is called *siyahi*. But another preparation of the siyahi, which was invented by a famous calligraphist of Persia called Mustafa, is called *Mustafa-i roshnai* and is used for writing.

It has the same black pigment as that of siyahi except that it was mixed with the juice of *harra* and amala.'[5]

'How is the black pigment made, Apa?' Zebun was feeling inspired by Falak to take up painting herself.

'Well, the black pigment is the soot deposited when burning mustard oil in an earthen *chiragh*, or lamp. It is also called Indian ink and I have heard from Khadija Bibi that the Chinese painters came to India to learn the art.'

'And your brush is so fine,' said Zebun as Falak's hand moved over the paper, on which she had applied a thin white coat. The black outline was clearly visible.

'It is made from the hair of a squirrel's tail,' replied Falak.

The drawing of the bathing scene on the riverbank was complete. She now needed her palette of delicate hues to capture the movement of the gossamer dupatta draped casually over the shoulders of the young girl she had been watching through the window for two weeks. Just then the girl shook the water out of her hair and looked towards the Qila. She had taken a dip in the river, completed her puja and was now ready to face the world for the day. Every movement was an expression of freedom, of joy, of youth.

'Is she aware that she is so heartbreakingly beautiful?' wondered the girl watching her.

'Falak Apa, what have you drawn today?' asked Zeenatun Nisa, another young cousin who had joined them. 'Show me.'

Falak snapped out of her reverie as her young cousin joined her at the window. All of thirteen years old, Zeenat thought she was old enough to understand the restlessness that seemed to be stalking Falak these days.

'I was working on the dupatta. The creases, the folds and their sudden release when she moves to echo my own longings,' replied Falak.

'Whatever do you mean Falak Apa?' Young Zeenat was perplexed.

'The heart is like a caged bird, constrained to live in my breast. It is full of longings which crease its folds; they house memories and yearnings that are released every time the heart is moved. Oh! How do I explain it! I only know that every time her dupatta moves, I am envious of its freedom. See how it falls and she picks it up with a nonchalant movement of her hand. Sometimes she just lets it trail behind her as if defying the imprisonment of her heart beneath it.'

Falak's hand once again began flying over the paper capturing the twirls of the dupatta, the liberty and captivity it represented, the folds of the dusky skin that could be seen through it and the droplets of water shimmering on her neck and arms. Her doe-eyed face, oval in its perfection, was innocent. She didn't seem beset by the longings of her painter. 'Why is there always a disconnect,' Falak wondered. Her apparently calm face hid the turmoil of her heart. The stillness of the face seemed to be at odds with the seductive movements of the dupatta.

'By the way, Falak Apa, what longings are you hiding in your dupatta?' asked Zeenat, mischievously pulling Falak's dupatta from her forehead.

'Nothing, nothing, at all,' said Falak Ara but the guilt on her beautiful translucent face was very obvious.

> *How hard to read, O Soul,*
> *The riddle of life here and life beyond!*
> *As hard as in the pearl to pierce a hole*
> *Without the needle-point of diamond.*[6]

How could Falak explain the emotions raging in her breast to Zeenat or to anyone else? Growing up without a mother in a corner of the palace, she was used to keeping her counsel and remaining as unobtrusive as she could. Apart from Zeenat and her teachers, the only one who knew her was her old wet nurse, Mubarak.

But no one knew that she was reading the *Diwan-e Makhfi*, a collection of verses said to have been written by Zebunnisa Begum, the daughter of Alamgir Aurangzeb Badshah, Khuld Makan—he whose abode is in eternity. The princess had seen tremendous highs and lows in her life, from being her father's favourite who often appeared in court with a veil on her face, assisting her father in court matters, and being appointed the Badshah Begum, to being imprisoned by the same father for what he thought were plans to overthrow him. She wrote under the name of Makhfi, or the Concealed One, and loose sheaves of her verses were collected many years after her death and compiled in a diwan a few decades ago.

Though no longer a disgraced name, Zebunnisa was still a symbol of rebellion, and her verses were not considered ideal reading material for young princesses. Gone were the days when princesses like Jahanara Begum, Roshanara Begum, Zebunnisa Begum and Zeentat-un Nisa Begum were extremely wealthy and powerful women, who could influence the decision of emperors. The daughters had lost importance. Today the power was wielded only by the Chief Consort and most of the time was spent in conspiring with the British and powerful nobles to ensure the succession of their sons. Nawab Zeenat Mahal sahiba was the daughter of Nawab Ahmed Quli Khan, who was a direct descendent of Ahmed Shah Abdali and considered her son to be the most appropriate to become the next king. The adoring husband indulged her. She kept trying assiduously and relentlessly to promote the case of her son at the English Court. While many were critical of her, only a few understood that a young wife of an aged emperor had to do what she could to stay relevant.

Falak Ara was neither rebellious nor desirous of wielding any kind of power; her sensitive soul was only caught up in thoughts of freedom and perchance, love.

Love!

Why had that word come into her mind? It was far removed from the motherless girl's life. The only love she knew was what she received from Mubarak.

Shaking her head, she went back to her painting. The young girl had finished her ritual bath and puja and was nowhere to be seen.

Ah! The freedom to come and go as you please, thought Falak, not realizing that every girl was bound down by the patriarchal society and freedom was but an illusion.

A few people were still bathing but the Nigambodh Ghat was mostly deserted. The crowds were now swelling under the Musamman Burj, where Bahadur Shah Badshah was sitting after his dawn prayers, and his courtiers and subjects had gathered to pay obeisance to him. He was loved by his Hindu and Muslim subjects equally and all gathered to catch a glimpse of him after their dawn *namaz* or *puja*.

He was sitting in that same window as his ancestors but unlike Sahib-e Qiran Shah Jahan Badshah, who decided matters of life and death, law and order, territories and acquisitions, he was reading his latest ghazal.

> *kiya jo qatl mujhe tum ne khuub kaam kiya*
> *ki main azaab se chhutaa tumhen savaab huwa*

> My murder rests good on you, don't worry,
> You have found grace, I am away from strife.[7]

Sounds of 'waah', 'subhanallah', 'afreen' could be heard as the aged Emperor completed the ghazal.

The sounds of praise and encore were echoing on the sandy banks of the River Jamuna, called *reti*. A few aspiring poets who were his *shagirds*, or disciples, had taken out their pens from the *qalamdan*, hanging in their sash and were copying down the words.

Falak was sitting pensively, holding her face in the palms of her hand. As the Emperor had himself said:

> *Yaa mujhe afsar-e-shahaana banaaya hota*
> *Yaa mira taj gadayaana banaaya hota*

I wish you had made me the master of royals,
Or made my crown the bowl for alms and betrayals[8]

Sahib-e Kalan Resident bahadur Simon Fraser *sahib* was standing on the platform near the *tasbihkhana* beaming at the crowds. It was the writ of the Resident bahadur sahib that ran large since 1803 when Shah Alam II Badshah had signed a treaty with the angrez Company bahadur.

Shaking her head, Falak went back to her drawing. The dupatta and the pulsating bosom were shaping out well, as if jailor and the cage were in perfect tune today.

Just then, Mubarak entered the room and started fussing around. Why hadn't Falak washed her face, had she slept well, why was she looking wan?

'Mubarak, take a break, breathe and let me breathe,' said Falak with a smile. She knew that even the smallest anomaly in her behaviour would be caught by Mubarak. 'I had a good sleep and am just finishing my sketch. Anyway, what's the hurry?'

'It is a glorious day, my princess and I thought a walk in the garden, with the nahr-e bahisht flowing by would put some bloom back in your cheeks,' said Mubarak.

Ashrafun, the attendant of Zohrun Nisa Begum, laughed and said, 'Oye Mubarak, have a thought for the rest of the girls in the palace. Leave some bloom for the other princesses to blossom too!'

The two were friends and started trading jocular insults and Falak went back to her thoughts.

Ashrafun and Mubarak were joined by Saeedan who had just come in from her house in Maliwara.

In a confidential whisper, she told Mubarak, 'You know my son works in the Chandni Chowk qahwakhana. Yesterday, he heard some of the young blades talking about the river incident. The man who saved shahzadi's life is a young price. His name is Mirza Qaiser, and he lives in the Nau Muhalla.'

'You mean he was talking about it?' Asked an agitated Mubarak.

'No, no, he was trying to play it down and refused to talk about it, but the news had travelled, and Miyan Nabbu was teasing him.'

'That Miyan Nabbu is a good-for-nothing young man. His father seems to think he has bought the entire city with his money. Such is life, that the noble have become poor and the poor are rich and ignoble.' Mubarak knew that bazaar gossip was terrible and could spoil her darling's reputation. 'I wonder which of the witches from the mahal is gossiping. I wouldn't put it past that *kalmunhi*, black-mouthed, inauspicious Gulab Jan. I could make out that she has been taking an unusually keen interest. Anyway, among the younger lot of maids, her morals and tongue are as flexible as that piece of new-fangled elastic that the *memsahib* showed Begum sahiba the other day.'

Ashrafun and Saeedan tried to pacify Mubarak that it was just light-hearted banter and nothing that could reflect on the young princess.

Also, Gulab Jan was young and entitled to her share of fun, but no one knew if she was the culprit, so why blame her?

Everyone knew that for the attendants it was *do din ki chandni phir andheri raat* (a few days of fun and then long dark nights). Who would look after them once their youth had faded?

Meanwhile, the young princess, who had been listening with half an ear to their conversation, heard a reference to the river incident and turned her full attention to what was being said. So, her young prince was Mirza Qaiser. *What a beautiful name.* She remembered one of her poetry lessons where her tutor had talked of the famous emperor of Rum, Caesar, who was called Qaiser in Urdu and Farsi.

With a languorous yawn, she packed away her paint brushes and got up from the window. She would now paint in the afternoon after her lessons.

She could see Hariyali in one corner of her room, with her basket in front of her, humming softly.

By now it was midmorning and Mubarak and the other attendants had already arranged the meal for the ladies. The food was cooked in the main kitchen and relayed via a series of khwajasaras and female attendants to all the parts of the palace.

Rose water mixed with musk, rose and saffron attar was sprinkled on the ground from long fluted containers with an aperture to scent the room. Food was after all a spiritual and physical exercise and had to appeal to all the five senses.

Rashid Ara Begum, another cousin of the Badshah, as the eldest lady present, recited *Bismillah* and some prayers to bless the food and waved her hand so the women and children gathered there could begin their meal. Contrary to the meal that Falak had eaten in the Badi Baithak, here it was mostly women. Sometimes the sons of the women would come, but it was rare as most of the princes would get up and go for shikar or some other pursuits. They would visit only in the late afternoon after classes, if they were young or after other lessons that they took. As was the custom once the princes attained puberty they would be separated from their mothers and lived in separate quarters but could come and meet their mothers whenever they wanted with the permission of the mahal darogha. If they were young men, then the darogha would discreetly supervise the visits too. Mirza Davar Shukoh, son of Shahzada Khizr Sultan, had started visiting Gul Bano, the daughter of Mirza Dara Bakht.

There were some lovely apartments made for them near the Shah Burj and Asad Burj.

Young Zebunnisa Begum sat down next to her mother and asked the maid to pass her the qorma. The attendant served her and turned to the mother next, who asked about it. 'It is made with quails, my lady. There was a great catch yesterday. Some of the princes had gone hunting near the reti beyond Salimgarh.'

'Ammijan, can I also go hunting with my brothers?' asked ten-year-old Zebunnisa. She had recently started learning how to hold a rifle from her elder brothers.

'No, you can't. Princesses don't go out hunting with the boys,' said her mother in a matter of fact, dismissive manner.

'But Ammijan, my teacher, Khadija Bibi, was telling me about our ancestress Malika Nur Jahan Begum. She shot four tigers with six shots and Jahangir Badshah rewarded her. We were reading from his memoirs. I want to be like her. I am going to talk to Alampanah, Ammijan,' said the young girl. Her father had been the Badshah's favourite cousin and after his death, the Badshah had brought his widow and daughter into the haram. He pampered the young orphan.

'Be careful, or you may end up like your namesake. Hazrat Alamgir Badshah had imprisoned her in Salimgarh for disobedience,' replied the mother.

'Respected aunt, Shahzadi Zebunnisa wasn't imprisoned for disobedience but because Hazrat Alamgir Badshah thought she was encouraging her brother Mirza Akbar to overthrow him and become the Badshah himself,' said Falak. Like all the royal women, she was also educated by the best female teachers who would come every morning and hold classes on every subject. Some girls had their own designated teachers, while others studied in a group. They were well-versed in history, especially in Timurid history, philosophy, classical literature and poetry, as well as basic mathematics. Those who showed an inclination were also taught how to use bows and arrows and to shoot. Falak Ara, interested in painting from childhood, had taught herself the basics with some help from her teacher.

Though they didn't go out of the mahalsara unless it was for travel, they were very influential and powerful women, given the best education and encouraged to excel in whatever they were interested in.

'These kababs are delicious—just the right taste, soft and flavourful. Please present my salutations to the *rakabdar*,' said Rashid Ara Begum, lavishing praise on the chef to change the topic. It was absolutely taboo to entertain any talk of overthrowing the Badshah. There had been enough bloodshed over it.

Soon the meal was over, and the attendants helped the ladies wash their hands and the betel and cardamom trays made of silver, jade and mother of pearl were brought out. Huqqahs were kept in readiness for the ladies.

The musical sound of the naubat announcing noon could be heard from the *naqqarkhana*. The hours of a day were divided into separate units of time called *pahar*s, and each pahar was announced by the beating of drums.

Soon it was time for the afternoon namaz, known as *zohr*.

Once again, the attendants brought out the ewers and napkins and the ladies performed their ablutions. The prayer rugs were spread out and namaz was offered.

There was a special urgency to her prayers today, as Falak prayed that she may get to meet her soldier-poet one day. In her innocence all she wanted was one meeting, not realizing that to a heart in love, one meeting was nothing.

The teachers had come in and the afternoon was spent studying.

Oh! When will the afternoon end, and when will I get a chance to talk to Mubarak! despaired Falak.

Finally, the classes were over, the teachers had left and Falak was alone. 'Mubarak, where are you, let's go for a walk outside. A little bit of air is just what I need.'

Mubarak, who had been sewing in a corner, folded away everything and came to the entrance of the mahal where Falak was waiting for her.

As soon as the two were outside in the scented garden with the silver fountains gushing water into the marble pools, Falak turned to her. 'Mubarak, what were you talking of in the morning? What is the name of the man who rescued me from the river?'

'Shahzadi, don't pay heed to the gossip of these old hags. They have nothing to do but create trouble. I am just thankful you are safe and the Badshah invited you for ulash. Yesterday I fed twenty *faqirs* near Jama Masjid as a thanksgiving to the Almighty.'

'But Mubarak, don't you think we should also thank the man who actually saved me? Is he a prince or a noble? The fact that he was there by the river on the day of the ladies outing when strange men aren't allowed means he must be someone known.'

'Whoever he is, may God keep him safe.' Mubarak tried to dismiss the conversation.

'Please Mubarak, I put you under an oath to me, tell me his name. Please.' Falak was not to be brushed off.

'He is a salatin. His name is Mirza Qaiser. I knew his mother when she was newly married. She was a Rajput princess and died when the Mirza was a young lad.'

'Where does he live?'

'How does that matter? None of us are going to meet him. And please stop these questions or someone will hear and complain to the darogha or God forbid, the Malika.'

'But I just want to send a thank you note. Surely, I can do that,' begged a distraught Falak.

'No, you can't. You have lived all your life in the mahal and know just as well as I do that the purdah of the ladies in the mahalsara is very important. Now stop it, I beg of you.'

'Mubarak, please,' begged Falak, 'just take a letter from me to him.'

'And get myself dismissed from service, imprisoned or even killed? Absolutely not. And if that pretty head is devising schemes of asking any other attendant to carry out this ill-advised errand, you may forget it. They are indiscreet and you will only earn a bad name! Our Badshah Huzur has just started taking notice of you—don't jeopardize that! You know what happens to rebellious princesses! Now, let's go in. I have a lot of work to do. In less than a month we will go to Qutub Sahib for the procession of flower-sellers. I have to get your clothes ready.'

'Oh yes! I had forgotten about that. That is something to look forward to,' said a disconsolate Falak.

'So much to do there,' continued Mubarak, animatedly thinking about the famed Phool Waalon ki Sair. 'It is a unique and colourful festival. I have not been to any other festival away from Shahjahanabad or Qutub Sahib but my husband, who goes to various places for work, says he has never seen anything that beautiful, even though he has attended the fairs in Haridwar, Bateshwar and Mukhteshwar. And why would he? No other place can compare with the observance of etiquette of the Timurid family. Villagers look forward to it the whole year round and come to the city to attend the festival, and there would be a wonderful, matchless connection between them and the Delhi residents on the occasion,' said Mubarak.

While the royals called the festival Sair-e Gul Faroshan, its more colloquial Urdu translation was Phool Waalon ki Sair.

The bouquets of fresh-scented flowers kept in vases in the niches of the Imtiaz Mahal pool of the nahr-e bahisht were being replaced by camphor lamps as dusk fell. Their heady scent emanating from the lamps as the water fell over it was enough to make anyone feel romantic.

Falak, in the throes of first love, was feeling melancholic. As was her custom, she started fiddling with her locket and quietly traced her way back into the palace.

The pahar was being sounded from the *naubat khana* and the ladies carrying the *raushan chowki* could be seen making their way into the mahal. This was a musical ensemble consisting of the *shehnai, nafiri,* or clarinet, and tabla. They would walk along with the women who came to light the candelabras and chandeliers at dusk every evening.

Badshah Begum had just returned from her haveli in Lal Kuan. The emperor had gifted it to her after their marriage and she spent a great deal of time in its spacious red sandstone and marble interiors. It had been furnished lavishly in the European style with chandeliers, silk curtains and carpets and it even had paintings on the walls. She would meet British officials there, leading to gossip of conspiracies and connivance behind the Badshah Salamat's back, to get her son appointed as the heir apparent. Mirza Fakhru, the eldest surviving son of the Badshah was the present heir apparent.

As her palanquin came into the mahalsara, her attendants rushed around making her comfortable.

The singers were taking their position behind the curtain of the tasbihkhana to entertain the Badshah. The dancers would go into the khwaabgah while the male instrumentalists and singers sat outside in deference to the purdah.

News had percolated into all parts of the mahal and whispers and the name Badshah Begum and angrez bahadur could be heard.

Finally, the day had embraced the evening and from her room Falak could see the bamboo torches in the corners of the palace and the lanterns glowing like fireflies while the palaces were illuminated with exquisite chandeliers, exotic wall lamps and candelabras.

Her heart was also burning brightly as she pecked at her evening meal.

Sakhti-e-ishq jhel le ai dil
Waah re burdbar kya kahna

O heart, bear the vicissitudes of love
I can only praise it for its maturity.

—Wazir Ali Saba Lakhnavi

6

The City of the Beloved

Dilli ke na the kuche auraq-e-musawwar thay
Jo shakl nazar aai taswir nazar aai

The lanes of Delhi were nought but an artist's album
Every face seemed a painting

—Mir Taqi Mir

The sun was bidding adieu for the day, and those who had retired to the cool confines of their houses were coming out. It was rest for the servants who had spent the day pulling fans made of cloth, hanging from hooks in ceilings. The vetiver screens hanging from all the windows had to be kept moist by sprinkling water on them. This is also the season of mangoes. Langda, sindoori, guudra and saroli mangoes were soaked in water to lessen their latent heat and consumed in great quantities, and their effects slept off.

The rooftops of the city would be full of the sounds of doves coming back to their dovecotes, and there would be whoops of excitement if they managed to bring pigeons from someone else's flock. *Ishq-baazi*, as pigeon flying was called, was a serious business in Shahjahanabad. People would give their lives for their pigeons, whom they brought up with as much love as children.

The street from the Qila to the Fatehpuri masjid was brightly lit with flambeaux and torches.

It was time for the men to come out and enjoy. Baths would be taken from water cooled in freshly baked earthen *surahis,* and dressed up in pristine white clothes, pearls around their necks, generous dabs of attar on their wrists and behind their ears, they were ready for their daily jaunt. Anything to escape the oppressive heat.

A few young princes along with Mirza Qaiser were out for an evening stroll. While some of the royal princes were in sedan chairs, Mirza Qaiser preferred to ride.

As Qaiser rode out on his horse from the Dehli Darwaza of the Qila he could see the sherbet sellers lining the sides of the street. The sherbets were garnished with falooda and tukhm, each better than the other. Business was brisk, and no one could keep count of the bowls being handed out to customers. Water carriers known as *saqqa*s stood with their water skins on their shoulders, a coarse, wet cloth over the skins to keep the water cool, offering cold water to passers-by, saying, 'Miyan, should I offer some water? Would you like a sip of life-preserving water?

Qaiser could see the ordinary folks walking or selling their wares, dressed in simple cotton kurtas, a slightly loose-fitting, knee-length, and longer outer garment, with a round neck and side slits paired with loose pajamas or dhoti and a topi on their heads, while the rich and noble wore *angarkha*s with *chikan* embroidery made from the popular cotton materials of the day such as *sharbati*, mulmul, *doriya*, *jamdani*, or *nainsukh*.

Though there were still plenty of palace intrigues, there was no longer a suicidal struggle amongst the princes to ascend the throne. After Badshah Shah Alam's death in 1806, and with the Company bahadur firmly in the saddle, there had been peace for the last fifty years.

While the lamp of the fortunes of the Timurid Empire had begun to flicker, the *shamma-e farozan* burned brightly in mushairas, scented candles seduced visitors to the *balakhanas,* incense sticks intoxicated the devotees in various dargahs. Political activities in the Qila and Shahjahanabad had been replaced by literary activities and became a literary and cultural centre. On one side there was a forced gaiety and a flourishing of courtesans, balakhanas and song and music, and on the other hand there was also an increased interest in mysticism.

Qaiser could catch snatches of interesting conversation on the latest ghazal by Mirza Naushah but he was looking for his friends.

Passing the Urdu Bazar and the Jauhri Bazar, they came to the square shining like fairyland, Chandni Chowk.

The moon was reflected in a pool of water, the lanterns and torches looked like stars twinkling in the water.

Having handed over his horse to a syce, Qaiser joined the other young blades.

'Mirza, you should join the calligraphy classes. Ustad Mir Panjakash was at his sublime best today,' said Hamid, an earnest young man, whose father had sent him to Shahjahanabad to study.

'Panjakash? What kind of name is that for an ustad calligrapher?' asked Miyan Nabbu. Arm wrestling, known as *panja kashi*, was a very popular sport in Delhi and like all young men Nabbu had also dabbled in it. Unlike wrestling or *kushti*, for which the wrestlers were trained in *akharas*, anyone could try panja kashi and it was a common sight in markets and shop fronts.

'That is the beauty of the Ustad's hand,' said Hamid. 'His strokes are as delicate as the butterfly's breath when on paper and as strong as iron during arm wrestling.' Smiling he continued, 'Ustad is very fond of arm wrestling and as he's an ace at that too, so he's been given that name. His name is actually Syed Muhammad Amir Rizvi.'

'May I be sacrificed over him. He has no equal in today's date in the *khat e-nastaliq*. I had some work in the morning, but I did practice,' said Qaiser. 'Mir Panjakash's work is so valuable that one word written by him on a piece of paper sells for a rupee in the bazar. And he is so generous and pious that in the evenings he sits in his haveli in Pahadi Imli and writes one word each on many papers and hands them over to the mendicants who make a line outside it. They then cash them by selling them on the steps of Jama Masjid. May I be sacrificed over his skill and piety. I am but a humble beginner of that art. I have been learning from my Abbajan. I am writing Hazrat Bedil Dehlvi's verse. How beautifully he writes, and his poetry is so apt for calligraphy.

Helplessly practice tracing pain's rending alphabet
For in love's ledger
a line's nothing
but an incision on plain paper.

I pray that my fumbling efforts can do it justice. Subhanallah! What a magician he was. Do you think

They walk as the white camels walk
when kept in check by blows,
While the stunted black ones
go astray.[9]

Do these lines by Ka'b ibn Zuhayr also refer to calligraphy? Emigrants in their battle ranks are described as a troop of majestic white camels that are kept in line by the stick, whereas the scrawny black ones, traditionally said to refer to the Medinese Helpers of the Prophet, 'stray from the road'. Could this allude to students being taught calligraphy—to stay within the lines of the prescribed style and not stray, or am I being overly imaginative?' replied Hamid.

'Didn't Ka'b ibn Zuhayr write in the seventh century? He converted to Islam and wrote this panegyric ode. Calligraphy was in its infancy then. It developed with the transcribing of the Holy Quran mainly in Kufi script and then under Amir Timur, when *nastaliq* script was developed, beautiful literary works were transcribed in it. But what you say does bear scrutiny and I will ask the respected *ustad* about it. Indeed, we are blessed to have the guidance of Mir Panjakash Khush Navez as well as Mohammad Jaan Aga sahib, Ahmed Jaan, Imamuddin sahib and Badruddin sahib. Huzur Jahanapanah is no mean calligrapher himself,' replied Qaiser.

'What are the two of you discussing?' asked Ibrahim as he joined his friends.

'We were discussing our esteemed ustad, Mir Panjakash's classes. I didn't see you in the class either,' said Hamid. 'Also, I haven't seen Zoravar for some time.'

'Ama bhai, I had to go to Qutub Sahib with Abbajan. Our haveli there needed repairs. You know we will be shifting there for the monsoons next month along with the Refuge of the World, Huzur Badshah. Zoravar has gone to Rajasthan for some work, he will be back soon.'

'Oh yes! Something to look forward to. We have taken a house on rent there,' said Miyan Nabbu. 'Mirza Qaiser, I challenge you to win the diving contest this year. I have put in serious practice! I've been going regularly to Sultanji's dargah *baoli* in Aliganj to practice,' he added, referring to the site of Hazrat Nizamuddin Auliya's dargah.

'Miyan, so I haven't been sitting idle either. I have been practising in the Qila baoli and in the dariya-e Jun,' retorted Qaiser, referring latterly to the Jamuna.

'Of course! Don't we know that! And rescuing princesses along the way too,' chuckled Miyan Nabbu.

'I have told you I don't want to talk about that. I was there and I helped. If you were there, you would have done so too. That's all there is to it. I don't even know who it was. There is a gentleman's code to not talk loosely of ladies,' said Qaiser in an angry but firm voice.

'Arre, don't get angry, Nabbu is just teasing you.'

'Indeed Ibrahim, I am teasing him, but if he gets angry, I won't tell him the name of the princess. My maid has a friend in the Qila who knows her maid.' Seeing a fleeting look of enquiry in Qaiser's eyes, Nabbu continued. 'She is Shahzadi Falak Ara Begum.'

'For God's sake Nabbu, please don't bandy her name around. That is not how gentlemen behave.' Qaiser had greedily stored the name in his head but didn't want her talked about or becoming bazar gossip.

The mahalsara was an out-of-bound topic for everyone and though no one's tongue can be stopped, at least he could try.

Just then the melodious strains of the maghrib azan could be heard wafting through the air. 'Should we go to Fatehpuri masjid to offer our prayers?' asked Ibrahim.

'Let's go to the Masjid-e Jahannuma,' said Qaiser, referring to the Jama Masjid. 'We can watch a *dastangoi* performance there. They say a new *dastango* has come from Lucknow and is performing *Dastan-e-Amir Hamza* on the steps of the northern gateway.'

Ibrahim's eyes brightened, 'Yesterday I was there. One *qissakhwan* was reciting *Qissa Hatim Tai*, and I swear there were at least a few hundred people gathered there, spellbound, to listen to that storyteller. His voice was echoing in the dusk, each word as bright as a diamond, cutting through our consciousness. Maybe he will also be there. We can listen to his stories till the night prayers and then leave.'

'It must be Mir Kazim Ali Dastango. He has been given the title of Bulbul-e Hazar Dastan—or Nightingale of a Thousand Tales—and indeed his voice is sweeter than a thousand nightingales, more dramatic and colourful than actual battles—you can actually see Rustam draw his bow—he's cleverer than a thousand sorcerers as he can take you on a journey into a world of fantasy that sorcerers can only dream of. His words have the power of magic, and he can mesmerize his listeners with them. I hope he is there. I have long wanted to hear him,' said Qaiser.

The three friends got their horses and sedan chairs were called and off they went towards the masjid. Others were also making their way to some mosque or the other.

They could smell the kababs roasting over burning charcoals as they neared the steps of the Masjid. Masita's kababs were famous in the city and one of his patrons was Mirza Naushah. The kabab-sellers would be winding up now to say their prayers.

The three friends entered the lofty gateway into the magnificent courtyard with its soaring minarets and majestic domes. It was a Jahannuma, a world-reflecting mosque, though now everyone called it Jama Masjid. The mosque was built after the completion of the Qila on a hillock known as Bhojla Pahadi. As there was no spring on the hillock the *hauz* of the mosque was fed by a Persian wheel from a well behind the *pai'waalon ka muhalla*. The water was always fresh and sweet smelling.

Namaz over, the friends came out.

The kabab-sellers and other vendors put up their shops on the steps again. During the day jugglers and storytellers also showed off their skills on these steps in such a way that even the elderly felt rejuvenated.

But now only the food stalls and dastango were left holding the fort. Many of those who came out of the masjid after praying sat down on the steps to hear the Bulbul-e Hazar Dastan, Mir Kazim Ali perform the *Dastan-e Amir Hamza*.

Dastangoi was an exalted art-form where the dastango, communicating with his audience just by the use of his voice and hands, could transport them into a fairyland where magicians, fairies and demons ruled; where good triumphed over evil but after many twists and turns that kept the audience enthralled.

There was a magical feel to the evenings on the steps of these gateways that only someone who had experienced it could understand.

God be praised, what a mosque, what a city, what inhabitants, what bazars, what spectacles and what magic! Only someone who has seen it can believe it! thought Qaiser and wondered with a pang what it would have been under Badshah Shah Jahan.

The friends went hand in hand towards Matia Mahal, where one of the friends had invited them for the evening meal.

They entered the haveli of Nawabzada Shahrukh Beg, son of Nawab Amir Mirza Khan. The servant greeted them and took them into the well-appointed *diwankhana* or male portion of the haveli.

Pandit Hridaynath Kashmiri had agreed to come and regale the *mehfil* with his sublime sitar play. He was also the ustad of the royal princes Mirza Kale and Mirza Chidiya. It was said that no one could compete with the skill of Mirza Kale in sitar playing.

A white *chandni* had been spread out on the floor which had padding underneath. Exquisite Kashmiri carpets had been spread in various parts of the large room and bolsters and cushions arranged on it. The three friends went and sat down on one of the carpets. Syed Zahir Dehlvi was also sitting on one of the carpets with Nawab Mirza Khan sahib Dagh and Mir Mehdi Husain sahib Majrooh. Syed Zahir Dehlvi was *darogha-e* Mahi Maratib and a disciple of the Badshah Salamat in poetry. Nawab Mirza Khan sahib, who wrote under the *takhallus* Dagh, was the stepson of Mirza Fakhru. He lived in the Qila in Mirza Fakhru's haveli with his mother, while Mir Mehdi Majrooh was a disciple of Mirza Naushah.

The first to play was Mirza Chidiya, so called because his sitar could replicate the sound of birds. People had forgotten his real name. The hall was soon a garden of chirping birds marvelling at the greenery, and the nightingale longing for the rose, stunning the audience into complete silence. Indeed, Mirza Chidiya was a genius with his sitar.

Pandit ji tuned his sitar, and very soon the gathered assembly had been transported into a world of divine love, as he played Raga Madhuvanti—a romantic raga which reflects eternity and colours of love.

The refrain of 'subhanallah' echoed in the room. Mirza Qaiser, who had been greatly affected by the melancholy and sorrow of the sounds of the nightingale coming from Mirza Chidiya's sitar, was now lost in a sea of yearning after Pandit ji's performance.

Aa andalib, milke karen aah-o zaariyan
Tu haaye gul pukaar, main chillaun haaye dil

Come o sweet nightingale, let us lament together
You cry for the rose, while I weep over the state of my heart.

—Rind Lakhnavi

7

When It Poured Love

pareshan ast az bi iltifati subha-yi 'ulfat
zi dil bastan magar jami'at-i baran shavad paida

Inattention spills, intimacy's rosary.
When did binding the heart ever bind the rain?[10]

Unbidden, this verse by Bedil Dehlvi came into Falak's mind, as the dark clouds started gathering in the skies, like the kohl in the eyes of the beloved. The dark, stormy clouds and the promise of heavy rains seemed to echo the heaviness in her heart, the turbulence in her mind. How difficult it was to yearn in silence! She had never felt like this.

The monsoon months were bliss in the city, but this time the bliss wasn't echoed in her heart.

Every year when the rains came down, there would be swings put up in the gardens and the young royals would enjoy singing in the drizzle. The musicians would sing Raga Malhar with the joyful voices of the young princesses joining in. While the older ladies yearned for clear skies and a dry day, the princesses got drenched amidst squeals of delight, soaking in the rainy benediction just as parched lands soaked up water.

Unlike the other princesses, who enjoyed revelling in the rain, the monsoon seemed endless to Falak—a season packed with vague longings, glowing faintly like fireflies at night in her heart.

However, Falak's longings weren't shared by the others as young and old ladies got henna applied on their palms. The bangle-sellers had come with green and orange bangles. The seamstresses were busy stitching green, orange and sandal-coloured dresses for the ladies and girls.

Falak could see young Zeenat and Zebunnisa running around with their cousins in the rain as she stood at the entrance of the mahal.

'Arre Shahzadi, may I be sacrificed over this longing in your eyes, why aren't you out there running around with the others. The water from the first rains is *aab-e rahmat*—and thereby believed to be blessed. It keeps you safe from illnesses. You have been looking pale lately, splashing in the rains with your cousins will do you good.' Mubarak had just come in with a young attendant and a tray laden with fried rice balls coated in sesame seeds as well as fried gram-flour balls. Indicating the andrasas and pakoris on the tray, she genially suggested, 'But before that, eat some of these monsoon specialities.'

As Falak turned to follow Mubarak, she heard the strains of a popular song being sung in the garden by Hariyali as she slipped green glass bangles on slim wrists:

Mera piya gaya hai bides
Mohe chunri kaun ranga de
Baeri sawan aayo re

My beloved has gone abroad
Who will dye my scarf now?
My enemy, the monsoons are here.

Sigh! Was it possible for a season to be an enemy or was her own heart the traitor?

The conversation turned to all the activities of monsoon season in the mahal.

In the Rang Mahal, Malika-e Zamani, Begum Zeenat Mahal was sitting with Nawab Taj Mahal Begum sahiba, Moti Begum, Piyari Begum and Nawab Nur Mahal Begum sahiba. The Huzur had many wives and concubines. All of them were given allowances and wielded some influence in the mahalsara. However, it was Begum Zeenat Mahal who was his Chief Consort and wielded the most amount of power in the haram as well as on the Badshah. Her constant contact with the Company bahadur to ensure that her young son should supersede all his brothers and be declared the heir apparent by them, was the subject of much hushed gossip. The wazir was said to be her conduit to the angrez officers.

The Malika, looking incandescent, was sitting on a brocade couch, leaning against a bolster.

The begums were getting henna applied as was the custom at the first rain. They were covered from head to toe in jewellery. The thin cotton mulmuls, which could go through a ring, had been put away and once again silk flared pyjamas, brocade angiyas and gauze dupattas had been taken out, now that the weather had cooled down. The jamas were embroidered and whereas the male jama would have *karchob* embroidery on it, female jamas were embroidered in the finer style known as *karchikan*. The fineness of embroidery in karchikan characterized the delicacy of the fair sex whereas the karchob had a heavier look.

A beautiful jade huqqah with a gold and silver pipe and a ruby bit, and a gold filigree *khasdan*, was kept on a silver table next to her bed, with a silver spittoon under it. Her pointed, velvet shoes, curving upwards, with long uppers and low walls, called *shirazi*, were kept beside the huqqah.

The plush furnishings, Kashmiri carpets, the gold and silver embroidered cushions and bolsters thrown over the carpets in the mahal were a perfect setting place for the beauty of the Malika.

Their clothes and jewellery reflected the brightly coloured ceiling of the mahal, inlaid with gold, which had resulted in the

Imtiaz Mahal being conferred with the name of Rang Mahal or Coloured Palace.

The maidservants, eunuchs, personal attendants, female guards all stood with folded hands in the courtyards waiting for their orders.

This mahal was magical, with a facade consisting of five beautifully painted arched openings with arched square bays and vaults within. Its beauty was indescribable and the eyebrows of a thousand beloveds could be sacrificed to each arch! The marble of this palace was fairer than the complexion of a thousand beloveds, and the redness of the stones used was more attractive than the ruby-red lips of innumerable beauties.

In the middle was a square with a pool, the beauty of which baffled the mind—made of marble it was built to resemble a flower in full bloom. The Malika's opulent settee, with its gold and silver embroidered cover, was set near it and the beauty of the pool rivalled the bloom on the Malika's cheeks. The tinge on her cheeks and the beauty of each petal of the fountain evoked a similar envy in the hearts of lesser mortals and they wondered which one was more beautiful.

Truly, every jasmine from all the gardens in the world could be sacrificed at the altar of their beauty.

The pool was very shallow, but it had a marble cup shaped like a beautiful flower in the centre from which water bubbled out. It was fed by an underground stream and when the water overflew from it, the flowers and leaves inlaid into the marble seemed to sway.

The eldest two sons and heirs-apparent had died, much to the Malika's secret delight, whispered the uncharitable. Mirza Mohammad Shah Rukh Bahadur, the second son, and Mirza Kaimuraz Sultan Bahadur, the fourth son, had both died some nine years ago in 1847. Mirza Dara Bakht Bahadur, the eldest son and favourite to succeed had been appointed heir-apparent by the British but had died in 1849. There had been an air of grief and sorrow in the fort, but it was rumoured the favourite Malika was happy. She had tried to press her adoring husband to push for her son, but he had shrugged it off as the Malika's son was very young. She made many visits to Sufi saints and mendicants to pray that the British looked favourably on her son. She had started writing again to the sahib bahadurs and pressured His Majesty to talk to them. She was trying to soften the senior officials of the Company by sending them presents. However, nothing seemed to be working. The third son, Mirza Fath ul-Mulk Bahadur, known as Mirza Fakhru, had been chosen by the firangi sahibs and it was rumoured that he had struck a deal with them.

Like the water gurgling and rushing out of the fountain, the Malika's mind was working overtime, and her thoughts were tumultuous as she thought of the rumoured deal. It was said that Mirza Fakhru had promised to vacate the Qila and shift to the Jangli Mahal in Qutub Sahib, giving up all claims to it and giving equality to the British officers. It was said they would not have to stand in his presence. These were things that were unheard of, and the sainted ancestors must be turning in their graves.

Given that there was a fifty-year difference between her and the Emperor she knew that she would outlive him. If she didn't succeed in getting her son on the throne, she would have to leave all this behind and live as a dowager relative of Mirza Fakhru. In a world of intrigues, where men were constantly scheming to reach the top, a woman doing the same was seen with suspicion, however, Nawab Zeenat Mahal was not only beautiful but also determined and intelligent. She did what she had to do and saw no wrong in it. Hadn't emperors schemed to sit on the throne and kingmakers tried to install their puppets on it?

The summer was very hot, and her heated mind was not getting cooled even by the breeze blowing in from the *khas khanas* at the four corners of the Rang Mahal. These small enclosures were lined with swatches of wet, sweet-smelling reeds and during summer months the vetiver screens on them were kept watered so that cool breezes could blow inside and keep the mahal cool, but now with the advent of monsoons, there was no need.

This was the largest of the palaces in the Qila and was used by the Malika and the begums. It was just behind the Diwan-e Aam and there was a beautiful courtyard between it and the Rang Mahal. The nahr-e bahisht flew from the gorgeous marble fountain in the Rang Mahal over chutes cascading into this courtyard and flowing towards the gardens. The chutes had niches in which fragrant flowers were put in vases in the morning and camphor lamps at night.

The royal princes had built their apartments on three sides of it and though it had lost some of its magnificence, it still looked elegant.

The Pai'n Bagh, or Miniature Garden, was on the other side of Rang Mahal, on the bank of the Yamuna, and to praise its beauty was beyond the capacity of a mere mortal. The begums were surrounded by beauty on both sides.

There were two basements below the palace which were used by the attendants and sometimes begums from the other palaces would retreat into it to beat the oppressive heat of the summer afternoons as these quarters were cooler than the mahal on top.

To the ardent audience in the picture gallery, the soothing sound of water helped to highlight the melodious voice of the Malika as she discussed the two upcoming events in the Qila.

Before they shifted to Qutub Sahib to celebrate the Sair, there would also be the salona festival, where the family of the Hindu lady who, as per family lore, had sat with Alamgir Sani Badshah after he was assassinated, would come and tie the thread called *rakhi* on the wrist of the Badshah and other royal princes.

'We have to prepare for the welcome of Ram Kumari's family,' the Malika was giving instructions to her attendants.

One of the ladies who had just entered the haramsara a few months ago asked, 'With respect to you your exalted Highness, I have not heard of the salona festival. Can you tell me about it please?'

An aunt of the Emperor who was also sitting there, narrated the story that had been handed down for generations. It related to the time when Alamgir *sani*, or second, was the reigning monarch but all powers were vested in the hand of his wazir, Imad ul-Mulk Ghazi-ud-Din Khan. The wazir wanted to remove the emperor and place his puppet on the throne. He did not have the audacity to assassinate the emperor in the Qila, so he devised a ploy to lure the emperor out of it. One day, he told the pious emperor about a Sufi faqir who had come to stay in the Jami Masjid of the old citadel of Sultan Firoz Shah Tughlaq. Once the emperor went there, he ensured that his bodyguards stayed outside the Jami Masjid and the emperor went in alone. The emperor was stabbed there by the wazir's men already waiting inside to commit the dastardly crime. The body of the emperor was thrown onto the sandy banks of the Jamuna.

A Hindu lady was passing by on her way to her early morning puja of the Jamuna. The shocked lady saw and recognized the dead body of the emperor. The Mughals had always enjoyed the goodwill of their subjects—Hindus and Muslims alike. She immediately sat down there and waited. Later, the sentries and bodyguards, alarmed by the delay of the emperor in coming out, went in search of him and found the woman with the emperor's dead body. Once Shah Alam II, his son, came back to the Qila as the emperor, she would come on every salona, the popular and age-old Hindustani festival of Rakshabandhan, bearing lots of sweets and would tie a rakhi of pure pearls on the wrist of the emperor. He would gift her clothes and gold coins, as was the custom. This custom continues to date, the aunt concluded.

'That is a captivating story, and I would also like to participate in welcoming their family,' said the begum who had asked the question.

The ceremonial tying of the rakhi was done in the Badi Baithak which would be decorated to welcome the guests. All provisions would be made for the sanctity and welcome of the ladies who came.

'Make arrangements for food trays to be sent to their houses,' the Malika instructed the darogha of the kitchens, 'And tell the darogha of *toshakhana* from which some robes and jewellery can be sourced and kept ready for the return gift. They are very important members of our extended family. We don't have blood ties but are bound by threads of mutual respect and love.'

The Badshah Salamat's mother was Rajput and though she was no longer alive, one of the daughters of the attendants who had come with her at the time of the wedding was also present. She had chosen to stay on and serve the Empress's family after the queen mother's death. Raj bai said, 'It is such a beautiful and ancient festival, and we Rajput women have a long history of tying rakhis on the hands of our brothers. It promises us protection from all evil and that our brothers will give their lives to protect our honour.'

The Malika continued giving orders for clothes to be prepared for the Qutub Sahib visit when sounds of the naubat signalling the pahar came from the naubatkhana. It was time for late afternoon prayers and then preparation for the evening.

The Badshah Salamat usually had his meals in the mahalsara and he would come in after he had offered his prayers in Moti Masjid. There were preparations to be made. When he was younger, sometimes he would send instructions beforehand indicating with which of the begums or concubines he would be spending the night so she could prepare for his entertainment. They would decorate their apartments, get meals and entertainment lined up. Singers and musicians would play music from behind the curtains, while itr would perfume the room.

But now as age had advanced, he just came and spent the time in the Badi Baithak with the Malika and a few other senior ladies before retiring for the night in the khwaabgah.

The musicians would play music, if his respected Majesty so desired, the dancers would perform or the dastangos would tell their stories of Persian classics or he would quietly play *chaupar* with the ladies. Chaupar was an extremely popular game played by royalty and commoners alike. It was played on an embroidered cloth, with two parallel lines of equal length bisecting two others at right angles, forming a little square at the centre and four rectangles each divided into four equal spaces of three rows on four adjoining sides. Two or four players could play at a time and the senior begums would join the Malika and Badshah Huzur. Each player had at his/her command,

four pieces; the shape was the same, but they were made individually
in different colours for the royal players of precious and semi-precious
material. Three dice were used with dots marked from one to six. It
required considerable mental agility to play the game and was good for
the women living an indolent life.

Sometimes the Badshah Salamat would just spend the evening in
prayers and meditation. No one could predict what entertainment he
would like so all had to be in readiness. With no administrative work
to be done or military strategies to be devised for the running and
preservation of the empire, Alampanah patronized the art and music,
which were flourishing under him.

These days Daaran bai was a favourite singer, and she would
often come to the Qila in the evenings to sing. Her memory was said
to be so sharp that she could look at a ghazal and learn it by heart in a
few minutes. She had committed Huzur's ghazals to heart and would
often come and sing them for him.

> *Baat karni mujhe mushkil kabhi aisi to na thi*
> *Jaisi ab hai teri mehfil kabhi aisi to naa thi*

Conversing with you was never so difficult for me
Your assembly is now as if never used to be[11]

—Bahadur Shah Zafar

8

Preparations for the Flower
Seller's Festival

Sada hai is aah-o-chashm-e-tar se falak pe bijli zamin pe baran
Nikal ke dekho tum apne ghar se falak pe bijli zamin pe baran

The sighing glance of the tear-filled eyes has always resulted in
lightening in the sky and rain on the ground
Come out of your houses and see the lightening in the sky
and rain on the ground

—Shah Naseer

The royals had their entertainment from trained musicians and
dancers, but the general populace of the city was quite happy with
their own entertainment. June had ended and with the start of July,
the monsoons had arrived.

At the onset of monsoons, the Jamuna River was in space, and
champions were ready to show off their skills. An annual swimming
competition would be held in the Jamuna River, near Salimgarh
Fort. A small, forested area, called Bela, on the sandy banks of the
river, would be the venue where the swimmers and spectators would
gather. The whole city would pour out to watch it. Vendors would
set up their shops on the sandbanks as everyone would come down
to the river to witness the competitions.

The smell of hot sesame-covered rice balls called andrasa would be served piping hot to the excited crowd. Jamun-sellers would call out, 'Come and try our salted jamuns,' while others would sell juicy mangoes, ripened on the bough. Not to be left behind, the guava sellers would advertise their guavas as tastier than apples from Kashmir.

A spicy savoury preparation made of sliced guavas or boiled potatoes called kachalu was served, while another vendor sold spicy chaat made of gram lentils seasoned with twelve types of spices and lemon.

Each vendor had beautiful jingles to sell their ware and would extol the virtues of their product. 'My bananas are the sweetest, ripened on the bough, grown here itself on the sandy banks of the Dariya-e Jun,' cried out the banana seller.

The star attraction was the famous swimmer Miyan Muhammad Ismail Shahid. First, his disciples would show off their prowess in swimming. Then the master himself entered the water and left the audience spellbound. He could swim underwater for long periods of time, and stay afloat with his legs crossed, and arms folded on his chest. It seemed as if he was a fish, not a man. His body would be moulded to the shape of water. The other swimmers were not far behind; one was floating on his back with his hands and feet stretched out sideways, and another was floating with hands and legs tied up in a bundle. Lo! What is this? One man was jumping in the water in a standing position, just like a fish. He would come up to his thighs and then go back in.

This was a grand spectacle, the Mahabali Badshah would come and sit on the balcony of Musamman Burj; the princes would be seated on a carpeted area prepared for them between the Diwan-e Khas and Hamman. The ladies would be in the Rang Mahal, Moti Mahal and the havelis near Asad Burj.

There was heavy betting going on among the princes on which swimmer could hold his breath for the longest time, or who could jump up the highest, who would swim all the way from here till the tomb of Emperor Humayun. With nothing much to do, the princes whiled away their time in such frivolous pastimes. Gone were the days when the Timurid family ruled, and princes of the blood were trained in warfare and administration. Now that was the privilege of the Company bahadur and the Hindustanis that they chose to serve them.

The last to protest against this had been Huzur Badshah's brother Mirza Jahangir and after him, Huzur's son, Mirza Shahrukh Bahadur, who had chafed at the restrictions and wanted to be free of them. Both had died young and now the angrez were ruling.

Falak was watching from the window of her room as the swimmers could be seen in the distance. She could hear the hawkers cry out in praise of their wares, all of them oblivious to the drizzle as Ustad Ismail showed off his prowess. The cage maybe gilded but it was a cage. Her heart longed to be there in the reti, barefoot, hair streaming behind her, holding her prince's hand as the rain drenched them.

Mubarak had just come from her house and could see the young girl profiled in the morning light by the window. Her face had a hauntingly pensive quality, framed by a sense of longing. 'What is it that troubles you, my child?' she asked tenderly, gathering her in her arms.

'Nothing. Nothing at all. Why would you think that?' asked Falak.

'You think I don't know you? I have brought you up from the time you were an hour old, I've suckled you, nursed you and you are closer to me than my own heart,' said an emotional Mubarak. 'Since the day of the zenana outing you have been wan, pale, peckish. What is it that troubles you my heart?'

'Nothing. Nothing at all. Or at least nothing that you can do anything about.'

'Try me. Maybe I can help you,' pleaded Mubarak. 'It breaks my heart to see you like this.'

Turning around to see that they were alone, Falak said with quiet desperation in her voice, 'Then once, just once, help me meet Mirza Qaiser so that I can thank him for saving my life.'

'You will get us both killed!' said a shocked Mubarak. 'You know you can't meet strange men. The ladies of the zenana are in purdah from all men. You know that.'

'Why does Mirza Davar Shukoh visit Gul Bano then?' retorted Falak.

'My darling, you know that Gul Bano is the Emperor's favourite granddaughter,' said Mubarak, trying to pacify the girl. 'She is the daughter of his beloved son Mirza Dara Bakht. Now that the sainted prince has died, the Emperor has brought his widow and daughter to the mahal, and he pampers the orphan girl. And Mirza Davar is the son of Shahzada Khizr Sultan, another royal prince. He comes to visit her mother.'

'I am also motherless,' said the tearful Falak.

'I know, my sweetheart. However, Shahzadi Gul Bano has her mother for supervision; and Mirza Davar comes to visit the mother. They follow different rules,' replied Mubarak.

'I told you that you can't do anything,' said Falak. 'Now let me be with my thoughts.'

Only yesterday she had heard her teacher recite Mirza Naushah's latest verse:

qafas mein hun gar achchha bhi na jaanen mere shewan ko
mera hona bura kya hai nawa-sanjaan-e-gulshan ko

I'm in a cage; even if they consider my lamentation to be bad,
How can my existence harm the other singers of the garden.

The ustad had explained that the other birds in the garden scorned the bird's lamentation; but now that it had been captured and was no longer in the garden, the other birds had been freed from its lament, so why did they still resent her existence?

There was a feeling of anguish in Mirza Naushah's voice as if he too, felt imprisoned in the city and alienated in strange circumstances.

The teacher had explained that Mirza Ghalib was called Naushah, which means son-in-law, as he was from Agra and had come to Delhi after being married to Umrao Begum, a lady from there. He was fighting a case for his pension to be restored before the Company bahadur and often found himself in debt and generally in impecunious circumstances.

Now, while the splendour of the palace was beginning to lose its lustre, its legacy of courtly poetry—kindled by the allure of Rekhta—was thriving.

The court of the Badshah and the city was home to some of the brightest talent to grace the world of poetry. The poets flourishing were of the calibre of Sheikh Ibrahim Zauq, Mirza Ghalib, Hakim Momin Khan Momin, Mustafa Khan Shefta, Sadruddin Azurda and the Badshah Salamat himself.

Sheikh Ibrahim Zauq had passed away two years ago. He had been the Huzur Badshah's ustad and Mirza Ghalib often felt that his entry into the favours of the Emperor was being impeded by Sheikh Ibrahim Zauq and this was a bone of contention for him.

Whatever be the reason for Mirza Ghalib's sense of alienation, Falak felt herself very far removed from the jovial singing of her cousins, the ladies dyeing their hands with henna or the ones splashing around in the gardens. She wanted to be free so that she could fly and meet her prince. Alas! It didn't seem destined. Perhaps she would die in this cage, her songs unheard, her love unexpressed.

Mubarak was stroking her hair and trying to soothe her frayed nerves. She herself was feeling very unnerved. What if someone had overheard Falak and told the Malika?

'What dress would you like me to get stitched for you for the Sair? There's hardly any time left. Next month we go to Qutub Sahib,' she asked, trying to distract the girl.

Falak's face brightened up. In Qutub Sahib, she and the younger cousins could run free. The rules of purdah were relaxed there as all care was taken to cordon off the areas where the royals went for recreation from the common folks. The princes would also come. Could she meet her prince there?

'Qutub Sahib, I will offer a special floral chadar if you make it happen. You are the *wali*, or friend, of Allah. Please plead my case to Allah. I have always gone to your dargah, offered *fatiha* and accepted you as my Pir, but I have never asked you for anything. Please listen to me.' Eyes closed, with full concentration on her prayers, the young girl was talking to herself and to Khwaja Qutbuddin Bakhtiyar Kaki, the popular Chishti saint of Delhi, known as Qutub Sahib or the Pole star of the time.

'My darling, don't look so woe begone, you will enjoy the Sair and the weeks in Qutub Sahib,' Mubarak tried to console her. You will have more freedom to move about there and can visit the mango orchards, waterfall and the Shamsi Talab.'

Falak closed her eyes and prayed, 'O Qutub Sahib, listen to my plea. Make me meet my prince. I swear I will never ask you for anything else. Just this once answer my prayers.'

After all, he had listened to Mumtaz Mahal Begum.

Malika Mumtaz Mahal, had made a vow to offer a floral chadar at Qutub Sahib's shrine in Mehrauli, if her son, Mirza Jahangir was restored to her. Mirza Jahangir resented the tenacious grip of the British on the Mughal *sultanat* or what was left of it. Irked by their refusal to consider his father, Akbar Shah II's request to appoint him the heir apparent, Mirza Jahangir had not only mocked the British Resident, Sir Archibald Seton by calling him a *lulu* in the open court, but also taking a pot-shot at him from the top of the naqqarkhana. While an annoyed Seton had accepted the flimsy explanation that lulu meant a pearl, the second could not be sanctioned. The prince was exiled to Allahabad.

Miraculously the prince was restored to his mother after a few years. Thus began the annual pilgrimage called Phool Waalon ki Sair, in which not just the royal family but every resident of Shahjahanabad, be they of whichever religion, class or caste participated. It was held on the fifteenth of the month of Bhadon every year.

Akbar Shah II also offered a pankha, a fan made of flowers at the nearby temple of Yogmaya. In the first such procession of flower sellers, the heir apparent Sirajuddin Zafar offered the pankhas with a poem.

Nur-e altaaf o karam ki hai yeh sab iss ke jhalak
Ke woh zahir hai malik aur hai batin mein malak
Yeh bana iss Shah-e Akbar ki badaulat pankha
Aaj rangeen hai raiyyat se laga Shah talak
Zafranzaar hai ek baam se dargah talak
Dekhne aayi hai iss rang se khilqat pankha

All this reveals the radiance of his blessing
Within he is an Angel and without a King
To that great King Akbar do we owe this coloured fan
From prince to pauper, all bedecked to the last man
From the bower to the *dargah*, a wondrous saffron hue
A blessed *pankha* all creation has come here to view

Unknown to Mubarak—and just as well, for she would have started quaking in her shoes—preparations were being made for the Phool Waalon ki Sair in another quarter too. But here the intentions were neither pious nor well-meaning.

News of Falak's accident and her rescue had spread in the city. The servant's network was always the strongest and soon news had spread from one haveli to another and an intense curiosity had been kindled about the young princess.

Tongues were once again wagging, and stories that had almost been forgotten were resurrected and eagerly circulated.

By now many knew who she was, what her mother's name was, who Mirza Qaiser was, and the speculation was about her relationship with the Timurids.

Was she really the Badshah's daughter?

One trader in Punjabi Katra named Hira remembered a story he had heard from his father about a girl named Dil Ruba, whose mother,

Hira bai, had been the darogha of Mirza Salim Shah Bahadur's wife and milk mother to Mirza Firuz Bakht Bahadur. On account of the similarity in their names, his interest in this woman was piqued, and consequently, he found himself absorbing bits of news and gossip that his father would sometimes convey. But of course, for a young boy like Hira, these were just stories.

Hira's father had often met the enigmatic Hira bai in Mirza Salim's haveli in the Qila when he had gone there with the latest bolts of silk from the Deccan. Mirza Salim was very flamboyant and loved to buy dress materials for himself and the ladies of his zenana. As there was very little money in the treasury, the princes were mostly in debt. His mother Nawab Mumtaz Mahal Begum was the Emperor Akbar Shah sani's favourite wife, and so Mirza Salim would often boast that he had the keys to the *real* treasury and that he would soon have access to its riches. Knowing the impecunious state of the Timurid princes the merchants recognized a good story for what it was: just a story to save face.

Mirza Salim had died in his father's lifetime, and all his creditors had to take the loss with stoicism, expressing real sorrow at his death. That night, Hira's parents had a tense but whispered conversation, which Hira had overheard.

'How much did the prince owe you? Can you hope to get it back?' His mother had asked.

'We all know that it is a losing proposition when we deal with the house of Timur,' said his father. 'None of them can pay. They are living on a pension given to them by the Company bahadur. They hardly get much. It is just that at times they give us gifts of precious stones, jewellery and silver that keep us going. Also, we can't refuse to serve them. They may be royal only in name, but their glory is still enough to keep them relevant. We make our money from the prestige of being attached to them when we sell to the English *memsahibs* and nobles. All of them want to be associated with the house of Timur.'

'How on earth will they continue like this?' lamented his mother. 'I hear stories in the bazaar that the Company now wants to exile them to Qutub Sahib and that there are always arrears in the pension.'

'I really have no idea. Unless, of course, they can find that treasure buried by Shah Alam Badshah,' replied the father with some sarcasm.

'What treasure?'

'Oh, just some more royal nonsense,' he responded with exasperation. 'Every few months there are rumours that a map to a hidden treasure is with one of the princes or retainers, and then a scramble begins. The latest is that on her deathbed, Mirza Salim's wife had given a silver locket to her darogha for safekeeping—so that it could eventually be passed on to his son Mirza Firoz. But all this is nonsense—just as hollow as the foundation of the Timurid empire today. Don't pay heed to gossip!'

His wife, however, was not one to give up so easily. She had an instinct for gossip—and enjoyed ferreting it out as much as she relished sharing such tattle with others. 'Who was Hira bai that the Shahzadi trusted her so implicitly? What happened to Hira bai and her husband?'

'Don't talk to me of them! They had more airs and graces than the Mirza and Begum sahiba themselves. Hira bai had been in the service of Nawab Mumtaz Mahal Begum, the mother of Mirza Salim and our Jahanpanah. When Mirza Salim got married, Hira bai was given to the couple to look after them. That's how became Sultan uz-Zamani Begum's darogha. As I said earlier, there were rumours that she was given a locket with the clue to the royal treasures by Mirza Salim's wife before her death, but that must have been nonsense. I had once asked them jokingly if they knew about the treasure—but Hira bai had snubbed me very rudely, saying that these were matters pertaining to the royal house and that I should know better than to poke my nose where it wasn't warranted. Imagine such audacity! How dare she condescend to me! As if she's a royal herself and I, a lowly servant who needs to be shown their place! As if her beloved Mirza Salim and these Timurids are all above reproach when they are the ones who owe *us* money! They must have made many enemies for

I heard they both died mysteriously very soon after. Not that anyone really mourned them. Serves them right, I say. I can never forget my humiliation at their hands when I went to ask for my dues. Anyway, God seemed to be pleased with them for their only daughter went to work as an attendant in the bhinda-khana, after their death. She later became the new Badshah's concubine.'

Though he was sounding tired, the wife prodded further, 'What is the daughter's name?'

'I don't know her name, she was given the title Dil Ruba by the Emperor and she's also dead now. Died in childbirth.'

The wife went on doggedly, 'Do you think that the Mirza or Begum sahiba gave Hira bai some clue as to the whereabouts of this treasure? Perhaps a map for safekeeping?'

'I have no idea. The old badshah also died soon after and there was much excitement with Mirza Firoz running way. And may God forgive us, he is said to be under the influence of that padri named Thompson. These firangis will take away not only our country but our children too if the Badshah isn't careful. But what can we do? We are poor people, destined to follow orders, whether they are from the Mughal king or the firangi.'

'You are right,' agreed his wife. 'Our lives remain the same drudgery. Only money can change it. Think about that map, please.'

'Hmm, there is no way of knowing if there really was a map. Though now when I come to think of it, Hira bai suddenly started wearing a peculiar mango-shaped silver locket around her neck after Mirza Salim's death. At that time, I didn't pay any attention to it. I don't know if Hira bai gave it to Mirza Firoz before he ran away or to her daughter before she died. If this treasure exists, Hira bai would have been told of it. But then again, we will never know. Now I have had enough of this nonsense. I am famished. Please serve me my dinner,' he said with a finality in his voice.

That same night a young girl in their muhalla eloped with a boy from the neighbouring muhalla, and Hira's mother and her friends had something far more substantial to gossip about. 'Such goings on, I tell you,' gossiped the women. 'This is what happens when you don't keep tight control over your children and get carried away by this angrezi notion of free thinking. Our ancestors knew best when they kept girls locked inside houses. The only saving grace was that they were both from the same caste, or else blood would have been shed.'

Hira himself had never forgotten that conversation. Like many other stories of the slights and humiliations suffered by his father at the hands of the wretched Timurids, this too simmered in his heart, patiently waiting for the day when he could avenge his family's humiliation. And now it all bubbled up to the surface again—no doubt sparked by the fresh gossip from the Qila, which also implied quite strongly that Shazadi Falak Ara was the granddaughter of his namesake, Hira bai. Was it true that Hira bai had been given a map of the treasure? Had it been passed on from mother to daughter to granddaughter? Could that silver locket containing a map to the Timurid treasure be with her? He had to find out if Shahzadi Falak Ara wore a locket or not. He did not burden himself with any notion of loyalty to the Emperor—unlike all the other residents of the city who seemed content to bow and scrape to the Qila for all eternity. Hira had survived the hard way. He was aware of just how unforgiving life could be. For him, it was imperative to look after his own interests first—because if he didn't take advantage of the situation to make money, he knew the Company bahadur would. And surely, he had more right to the treasure than the angrez bahadurs? And as for the Timurids, they deserved nothing if they continued to live in denial of their own reduced circumstances, blissfully unaware that the angrez were bent on looting them.

Hira bore a lot of ill will towards the royal family, as he blamed their default in paying their bills, for the failure of his father's business, which had forced them to leave Shahjahanabad and retire to their village. It was typical of the royals to not pay what they rightfully owed to others while sitting on an unclaimed treasure to hoard all for themselves.

While most people discounted the story of a hidden treasure as a myth, Hira was convinced it was a ruse concocted by the cunning royals to hold on to this treasure while not being obliged to honour their debts and to throw dust into the eyes of the Company bahadur so they didn't get their hands on the treasure.

Why else was the royal court unperturbed by how much the Company was already looting them; it must be because they were secure in the knowledge of the hidden treasure being untouched by the Company. If that were true, then the treasure must be vast indeed.

That city abuzz with news of Shahzadi Falak's rescue made it even more difficult for Hira to contain his resentment and greed. Why was she enjoying privileges while he languished in uncertainty. To top it all her grandparents were responsible for facilitating the ruin of Hira's family. These royals were all the same! They took so much for granted, unmindful that others had to suffer on their behalf! They did not deserve the privileges they had. It occurred to Hira that he had waited far too long to avenge his father. He also needed to find out about Mirza Salim Bahadur and his wife, and also about Mirza Firoz. He would find a way to take back what he felt was rightfully owed to him.

The Phool Waalon ka Sair had to be visited. The entire palace shifted there, which meant Shahzadi Falak Ara would also be going there. Now he had to think of a plan to identify her and the locket, and then contrive to take it.

He decided to visit Maliwara, where the gardeners and flower-sellers lived. One of the traders whom he travelled with on journeys for buying cloth lived there and he had heard his friend say that his wife participated in the Sair every year. In fact, she made floral jewellery for the royal ladies during the weeklong fair that took place in Qutub Sahib.

Rahim was sitting outside his modest thatched house, smoking a huqqah when he saw Hira approaching. The sharp contrast between the grandiose havelis of the rich in Maliwara and the thatched mud houses of the poor was glaring. Here, sackcloth curtains protected their inhabitants from rain and sun. Shanties served as shops selling essential items and open drains emitted a foul smell. The residents, stoic in their circumstances, toiled on to provide more and more luxuries for the rich.

'Arre Bhai Hira, did you lose your way? How come you are here?'

'I was passing by and suddenly realized that you live here, and we haven't met for a long time. I hope you don't mind. I just came to talk of the Sair and the opportunities we could both use,' said Hira.

'Arre, my humble house is blessed by your footsteps. Please consider it yours. Come and sit,' he said patting the stool he had brought out for his friend.

They sat in comfortable silence for some time, taking turns to smoke from the huqqah. Most of the residents smoked huqqah and kept an extra muhnal for their friends so that they could share.

'Bhai Rahim are you planning to go to Qutub Sahib for the Sair this year? I was thinking we could make a quick trip to Jaipur and buy some jewellery from there. I'm told that some excellent kundan and studded jewellery has been made there recently and the royal family would be eager to buy them, as would the nobility of Shahjahanabad, who also shifted there. Normally, I bring and sell to the jewellers here, but I was wondering if we could put up a small shop ourselves this time? You work as an assistant to Raja Mal *jauhri* so know the tricks of the trade and can help me. We will divide the proceeds equally, after expenses.'

'That's true, Hira. They are in a good mood and since it's a season of rejoicing everyone's purse strings are loose. Since my jauhri isn't putting up a shop in Qutub Sahib I can take leave and join you. It is a good opportunity to make some extra money, and everything has become so expensive these days. When do you want to go to Jaipur?'

'How does next week sound to you? This week we can go to Qutub Sahib and fix a house for ourselves, to stay in. Will your family also go with you to Qutub Sahib or just you? The house will have to be taken accordingly,' continued Hira.

'I think a house for the two of us is fine,' replied Rahim.

'Your family will continue to stay here?' asked Hira who saw his hopes being dashed.

'My wife goes with the royal entourage and stays with them. That is why I have never gone before.'

'Oh yes! I had forgotten she works in the Qila. So let us go tomorrow or the day after to Qutub Sahib as per your convenience.'

'Tomorrow is fine. Let's go quickly as by now most of the good houses must have already been rented out. The longer we delay it, the more expensive they will become,' replied Rahim.

'Fine, I will fix a cart to take us there and come here tomorrow morning. Be ready after your morning prayers. I will take your leave now.' Satisfied with the outcome of his expedition, Hira left.

> *Sab ko duniya ki hawas khwar liye phirti hai*
> *Kaun phirta hai ye murdar liye phirti hai*

> Everyone is driven and disgraced by greed in this world
> It's this accursed greed that drives us in this world

—Sheikh Ibrahim Zauq

9

Monsoons Bring Tears

Adaa se dekh lo jaata rahe gila dil kaa
Bas ik nigaah pe thahra hai faisla dil kaa

One coquettish glance from you will wipe away all complaints
The fate of my heart rests on one look from you

—Arshad Ali Khan Qalaq

'Abbajan, will we be going to Qutub Sahib this year?' asked Qaiser.

'Yes, of course. That is one of the highlights of the year. I am glad you have reminded me. We need to check out arrangements for living there. Last year we stayed in Bagh-e Nazir. I will ask Khan-e Saman if we can stay there again. It is just behind the waterfall and mango orchard, and it will be so easy to join in all the fun,' replied Mirza Mohammad Aftab.

Bagh-e Nazir, a beautiful, verdant and luxuriant garden near the waterfall of Qutub Sahib, was very well maintained, with blooming flowers and green trees. This garden was built by the khwajasara, Nazir Roz Afzun during the reign of Muhammad Shah Badshah. A wall surrounded the garden and there were many attractive red sandstone buildings built inside the compound. The building in the middle of the garden was the biggest and best of all the buildings there and was used by the royal princes during their stay in Qutub

Sahib, but even the others were attractive and comfortable. Mirza Aftab had stayed in one of the *baradaris* near the gateway that led to the *jharna* and had been very comfortable. It was secluded so they had more privacy, and they were closer to the jharna which was the focus of attention during the Sair.

During Badshah Aurangzeb Alamgir's reign a beautiful jharna along with colonnaded halls and pools, had been built by Nawab Ghiyasuddin Khan Firoz Jang to harness the water of the Hauz-e-Shamsi. The pavilion just below the wall of the waterfall didn't have a roof. It had been covered with flowering creepers and when the water from the waterfall fell it drizzled inside, much to the delight of the people in it.

As the Sair became an annual event both Badshah Akbar Shah II and Huzur Bahadur Shah Badshah had added baradaris to it.

'Yes, that would be wonderful,' said Qaiser. 'I hope we can stay there.'

'Did you go for your wrestling and archery lessons today, Qaiser?'

'Abbajan, I did go but what is the use of it all? The Company bahadur will never allow the Badshah to have his own army. When I was younger, I was part of the *bachera paltan*, but now that I have crossed fourteen I am barred from that too. It seemed there was a purpose to the training in weapons, but I realize now that those skills can only be used for *shikar*.'

Bachera Paltan, or the children's regiment, was made up of young boys of the Qila, created by Huzur Jahanpanah, where they were trained to use guns and weapons. They wore brightly coloured uniforms and accompanied Huzur Badshah on his ceremonial processions. It had been allowed by the Company bahadur only on the condition that once the princes crossed fourteen, they would be banned from it, and that it was only used for ceremonial purposes. The threat that a regiment of trained, older Timurids posed to the British was immense and had to be discouraged.

'My son, I understand your frustration, but I am trying to get you a position with the Company bahadur, and they value these skills. Timurid princes are famed for their prowess in arms and their knowledge of the arts and letters,' said the worried father. He thought for a minute and continued, 'I have been thinking that since you do calligraphy, I will ask Huzur-e Purnur to accept you as his pupil. So far, I have been teaching you, but I am no ustad myself. Would you like that? You will be exposed to great ustads, and Huzur Alampanah will take you under his wing and guide you. I think you know Zahir Dehlvi. He is also one of Huzur Badshah's protégés in poetry.'

The Badshah was an ace calligrapher and his ustad was Mir Kallu. He would often look at the calligraphy and painting *muraqqas* or albums he had inherited from his forbearers and gain inspiration. He considered the calligraphy of Aurangzeb Alamgir Badshah and the unfortunate Shahzada Dara Shukoh to be *tabarruk* or blessings and would try to copy them.

Even though the Badshah had given strict instructions that nobody should be stopped from approaching him because he felt that in this way even the poorest man could be connected to him, Mirza Aftab knew that permission had to be sought through proper channels.

'O Abbajan, may I be sacrificed over you. I don't know how Allah has blessed you with the firmness and love of a father and the nurturing nature and adoration of a mother. You intuitively know what I want and voice it before I can ask for it. That would be wonderful. I have been composing some calligraphic panels and would love to go and show them to Huzur Alampanah for correction and guidance.'

'I will ask for permission to present myself before him today itself and request him with folded hands,' replied the relieved father. 'I will also find the Khan-e Saman, the chamberlain, and talk to him about Qutub Sahib.'

Qaiser left for his archery classes which were held in Salimgarh Fort, built by that Afghan traitor's son while Humayun Badshah jannat ashiyani was in exile. It was built in the middle of the river, and one had to alight on it from the river, but a bridge had been built to it by Shah Jahan Badshah and it was so well integrated that it had become a part of the Qila.

It had been used as a prison for many years. Princess Zebunnisa, daughter of Alamgir Aurangzeb Badshah had been imprisoned here. There was a compound here where young salatins, especially those who could be a threat to the reigning badshah were imprisoned.

Mirza Aftab left his house to go in search of Hakim Ahsanullah Khan, the royal physician and a close confidant of the Emperor. Hakim sahib was not to be found in his regular place, the Khan-e Samani building, where he normally rested with Mahbub Ali Khan. Mahbub Ali Khan Khwajasara was the wazir and very close to the Hakim. He suffered from dropsy and the Hakim sahib helped with treatments.

That's strange, thought Mirza Aftab, *Hakim sahib never goes anywhere at this time. I hope no one is sick.* He asked a passing attendant about the Hakim sahib's whereabouts.

'Hakim sahib has gone to Mirza Fakhru's haveli,' came the reply.

'Is all well?' asked a worried Mirza Aftab.

'May God have mercy, Mirza Fakhru is very sick. He had been unwell, so his physician, Hakim Mohammed Naqi Khan, had given him some medicine to take and prescribed light food and plain soup thinking the start of the monsoons always brings stomach trouble. But he hasn't got any comfort and is now complaining of nausea, vomiting and low-grade fever. As you know, there is cholera in the city and even though Sahib-e Alam is very particular about his diet and exercise, it is suspected he might have got cholera. So today Hakim Ahsanullah Khan has been called as the prince has fainted.'

The attendant walked away to discharge his duty and Mirza Aftab rushed towards the haveli of Mirza Fakhru behind the Diwan-e Aam. Next to it was the haveli of Mirza Babur, in which Mirza Mughal lived now. Mirza Babur, Huzur Purnur's brother, was greatly influenced by the European way of life and had built a European-style haveli for himself. He had even worn European clothes and uniforms.

He found a worried-looking Mirza Abu Bakr, Mirza Fakhru's son, and Nawab Mirza, popularly known as Dagh Dehlvi, his stepson, pacing outside.

'My sons, is everything all right? I have just heard about Mirza Fakhru's illness,' he asked them.

'Sir, we don't know yet. Abbajan Huzur was very unwell, and I went to call Hakim sahib who is with him just now,' said Mirza Abu Bakr

A storm of wailing could be heard from inside. Nawab Mirza went in hastily to comfort his mother. Hakim Ahsanullah came out shaking his head.

'Hakim sahib what is the matter? How is Sahib-e Alam? I heard his enemies aren't well,'[12] asked Mirza Aftab.

'May I be sacrificed over him. I leave it to God, who is all-powerful and can grant health to the sickest of persons on earth. Sahib-e Alam is in a coma. I have given him medicines,' said the Hakim sahib with a mournful shake of his head.

Deeming that the time was not right for his mission, Mirza Aftab, went towards Salimgarh to see the young royals being trained. On the way, he passed by Mirza Mughal, another son of the Emperor who was practising his archery skills on a target.

The Bagh-e Hayat Baksh was fragrant with flowering trees and bushes and laden with ripe fruits as he passed through it to cross the bridge.

This fort housed not only the salatin but also the prisons for royal rebels and those who displeased the Emperor. Now that the salatin quarters weren't guarded and the prisons were empty, it was not as gloomy a place and was used for arms training and practice by the royals.

He met one of his cousins and they walked along exchanging news.

The Yamuna lapping gently at its walls created a sense of security, but this was broken by his cousin's words.

'Aftab, have you been following the fate of Jaan-e Alam Nawab Wajid Ali Shah?' asked Mirza Sikandar.

'Yes, I heard that he had been deprived of his kingdom and exiled to Calcutta by the Company bahadur,' replied Mirza Aftab.

'It is a sad situation, Aftab. Everyone blames the beloved Nawab sahib for being interested only in music and dance, but do they even know how the angrez sahibs curbed his powers?

'Nawab *aali maqam*, he of exalted status, had devoted himself to the organization of the army and he issued orders that after morning prayers all the regiments in Lucknow were to come for the parade at 5 a.m. He himself was in the habit of taking command at the parade dressed in the uniform of a general. He used to drill the troops for four to five hours daily. Furthermore, he issued an order that if he were absent from the parade except through necessities of the state, he was to be fined two-thousand rupees, to be distributed among the residents in the garrison, and an equivalent fine was to be levied if any of the regiments was late to the parade and the soldiers of that cavalry were to remain under arms the whole day. This activity of the Nawab created suspicion in the angrez Resident, who enquired about the cause of his exertions in creating the army and suggested to him that if he required forces for the protection of his provinces, he should employ angrezi troops to be paid out of the revenue of Awadh. The courtiers of his court also advised him not to raise suspicion by his activities, and the discouraged Nawab replied that he would employ himself in other occupations as his interest in an army was not approved of. Hence forward, he took interest only in poetry and dance and music.

'The Resident and the Company bahadur did not agree to any of his reforms and refused to even understand the administrative reforms he described in his book, Dastur-i-Wajidi. Yesterday, I met a friend who had come from Awadh. The Company bahadur has dismissed his army and the soldiers devoted to their beloved Nawab are restless.' Mirza Sikandar lived in the city and being a very social person, met many people in the various gatherings there. 'May Allah save us from ruin. My heart sinks when I hear all the goings on of the Company bahadur. They came as guests, but they have now become owners. I fear for our own Alampanah.'

'Don't worry, Sikandar. I am sure these are just rumours to rattle us. The Company bahadur is giving a good *peshkash* to Huzur Alampanah, and he in turn makes sure that we are all well looked after. I am sure there is no need for us to worry,' replied Aftab calmly.

'You don't understand Aftab. Our ancestors used to talk of the magnificence of this dynasty but now, whichever way you look, you can see that the foundation is exposed and in a state of disrepair. We are fooling ourselves by living in a sense of false glory, the glory of the Timurids departed from this world 150 years ago with the death of Hazrat Aurangzeb Alamgir. And that which you refer to as peshkash isn't a tribute, but a pension given by the Company bahadur to establish their superiority over Huzur Alampanah.

'There are already rumours that Mirza Fakhru has struck a deal with the Company bahadur that he will vacate the Qila and shift to Qutub Sahib when he ascends the throne. You know that the firangis have already stopped the Alampanah from minting coins and accepting nazar. And if the Timurids have to vacate this magnificent Qila built by Sahib-e Qiran Sani Shah Jahan Badshah, what prestige will they have left? I fear for us. Very soon we will be nothing but employees of the firangis.' An agitated Sikandar was letting out pent-up emotions.

'Did you know Mirza Fakhru is very sick?' asked Mirza Aftab, trying to deflect his anger. 'I just saw Hakim Ahsanullah Khan coming out of his haveli. I hope he recovers,'

'What? Let me go and find out about his health. This is terrible news.' Saying so, Mirza Sikandar walked away briskly towards Mirza Fakhru's haveli.

A very mentally disturbed Mirza Aftab walked around the Salimgarh Fort, cast an eye on the archery practice taking place in the early July drizzle, and retraced his steps back to Mirza Fakhru's haveli.

In the two hours since he had been there, things seemed to have taken a turn for the worse and there was quite a crowd gathered there. Wailing and weeping could be heard from inside.

He looked around and found Mirza Sikandar sitting in the
khan-e samani arcade near the Diwan-e Aam with Mehboob Ali
Khan Khwajasara and a few other courtiers.

'I'm afraid the news isn't good. I just met Hakim sahib, and he
says there's no hope. He has gone back to Mirza Fakhru's haveli. I
was about to go back home but then decided to stay on in case, God
forbid, Alampanah requires our support,' said Mirza Sikandar.

As if on cue a fresh storm of wailing and crying could be heard
and Hakim Ahsanullah came out of the haveli saying, 'Verily we
belong to Allah, and verily to Him do we return.'

'What calamity is this Hakim sahib? Is our beloved Sahib-e Alam
no more?' asked Mirza Aftab.

'His soul left his body a few minutes ago. I am now going to
inform Huzur Alampanah,' said Hakim sahib mournfully. 'Sarkar
Mehboob Ali Khan sahib, please come with me. I will need support.'

'Oh! This is terribly tragic,' said the wazir, getting up.

Both Mirza Sikandar and Mirza Aftab joined the wazir and
Hakim Ahsanullah. They went towards the Lal Purdah area, which
was the entrance to the courtyard nearest the Diwan-e Khas, known
as *jilaukhana* or abode of splendour, and kept screened by a red
curtain. From here they sent a message seeking permission for an
audience with the Emperor.

Between the Lal Purdah and the Emperor's private apartments,
there was a small hall where the Emperor sought solitude or held
meetings with special nobles. It was open towards the Diwan-e Khas
with the nahr-e bahisht running through it, leading to the mahalsara
under a finely carved marble screen displaying divine scales of justice.
This symbol served as a reminder for the emperor to be just and
weigh his decisions carefully.

Mirza Ibban, as Bahadur Shah Zafar Badshah was known
before his coronation, was crowned here as Abu Zafar Sirajuddin
Muhammad Bahadur Shah Badshah Ghazi. He replaced the marble
throne used by his father, with an octagonal throne of gold and silver,
named Takht-e Huma, for his coronation. Unfortunately, he used it
only once for ceremonial purposes, as Huzur Alampanah's refusal

to let the angrez sahib bahadur Lord Ellenborough be seated and treated at par and offered a seat in the durbar resulted in the accursed firangis prohibit the Badshah Salamat to sit on the formal throne.

Huzur-e Anvar held durbar here twice a day, seated on a simple shahnasheen.

The Khasi Deorhi, next to it, which led to the Khas Mahal, was where the chobdar relayed the information to the jasolini, who in turn informed the darogha of the mahalsara. The Darogha took royal permission before admitting Hakim sahib into the tasbihkhana.

'Ama, at this time, is all well?' asked the Mahabali Alampanah

'May I be sacrificed over my benefactor, Huzur, the chobdar said it was urgent and he looked very worried and anxious, so I took the liberty of interrupting your sleep.'

The Huzur Alampanah had been sitting on a silver shahnasheen with tiger head arms, reciting the beads on his rosary. There were attendants all around him. They all rushed towards him, as he prepared to get up. One brought his gold brocaded slippers, another brought the chougoshia cap with an emeralds and ruby aigrette on it.

Another went out to tell the chobdar to be ready, as the Huzur-e Anwar was about to illuminate the tasbihkhana with his luminous presence.

'Stand at attention, the Mahabali, Huzur Panah graces us with his presence,' cried out the chobdar. Immediately Mahboob Ali Khan, Hakim sahib and the two Mirzas stood at attention.

A few minutes later the door of the *deorhi* opened and the Badshah Salamat came out in his hawadar or sedan chair, held aloft by four Abyssinian women soldiers. They set it down near the throne chair kept on the plush red carpet of the tasbihkhana. The Emperor got off and took his seat.

The four men bent low from their waists and presented their salutations. The Emperor acknowledged them and looked at them enquiringly.

'If I have Huzur Alampanah's permission, may I speak?' said Hakim sahib.

'Hmm,' said the Emperor.

'May I be sacrificed over my Mahabali Jahanpanah, I wish my tongue had been cut off before I had to utter these words. I am the unluckiest wretch on the face of this earth that I have to relay this tragic news to my beloved monarch,' said Hakim *sahib,* gathering the courage to utter the tragic news.

'*Khuda naa khasta,* has something happened to Sahib-e Alam?' asked the Jahanpanah.

Looking at their bent heads and despondent faces, he realized that it had.

Reciting '*Inna lillahi wa inna ilayhi raji'un,*' he looked towards the wazir and said stoically, 'Make all arrangements for the burial and funeral. He will be buried in Qutub Sahib's dargah. Call me when the *ghusl* has been given and he has been shrouded.'

The Abyssinian soldiers brought the sedan chair, helped the grieving father sit and took him inside.

By now the news that something amiss had taken place had already spread in the haramsara. Everyone knew that Mirza Fakhru was ailing, and they feared the worst. The jasolini who had accompanied the Emperor outside quietly told the darogha who in turn told the ladies.

When the Emperor came inside, bent double on his hawadar, Malika Zeenat Mahal was waiting. As soon as he got down and sat on his chair, she bent in salutation and presented her condolences.

The darogha and a few jasolinis could swear they saw a gleam of triumph or was it relief, in her smoky dark eyes. But then it was very dark inside and the darogha remembered Ustad Zauq's verse:

Laayi hayat aaye qaza le chali chale
Apni khushi na aaye na apni khushi chale

Life brought me, death took me away
I neither came of my free will nor did my wishes have a say

10

Qutub Sahib Beckons

Manam aan rend-e jahaangard-e maseeha nafasi
Ke man een har do jahaan ra nashomaaram be khasi
Agar az eshq-e toam sar beravad goo beravad
Hargez een serr-e nahaan e to nagooyam be kasi

I am a free spirit, world-wandering, of messianic breath
Insignificant are the two worlds for me, no better than straw
In your love, if I lose my head, so be it
To no one shall I reveal your secret, none![13]

—Syed Mohammed Ameen Muntaqi

The sky was black with clouds when the funeral procession left the Qila. The Badshah came to the Diwan-e Khas where the enshrouded body of his son was kept. He recited the fatiha with a quivering voice and tears in his eyes. The courtiers were shocked to see the frail hands raised in prayer. The enshrouded body was put in a palanquin covered with black cloth and the funeral cortege, escorted by bodyguards, attendants and cavalrymen, left for Jama Masjid. Mirza Fakhru's sons, Mirza Muhammad Abu Bakht Bahadur, Mirza Muhammad Farkhunda Jamal Mughal, Mirza Muhammad Sultan Khurshid Alam Bahadur, his stepson Mirza Nawab Dagh, his grandsons and father-in-law Mirza Ilahi Baksh. They princes walked to the gate, then accompanied the cortege in palanquins, weeping copiously, their faces covered with handkerchiefs.

Mirza Fakhru was a very popular prince and many spectators joined in.

Charity was being distributed to the city's poor, so that the soul of the deceased may be blessed and granted entry in heaven.

The funeral prayers were read in Jama Masjid where many grieving residents of the city had gathered.

Only his children and grandchildren along with the bodyguards, attendants and cavalrymen accompanied the procession to Qutub Sahib where he was buried in the compound of Qutub Sahib's dargah.

Once again food and money were distributed there among the indigent.

Arrangements were made for food to be distributed to the poor and prayers for the deceased to be done for forty days.

On the second day after Mirza Fakhru died, preparations for the deceased man's phool ceremony were underway.

Death is a strange thing, thought Falak Ara. While on the one hand, Mirza Fakhru's widows Hatim Zamani Begum and Wazir Khanum were grieving, refusing to eat, and lavish food was being prepared to hold ceremonies for the blessings of the deceased soul. Everyone would gather to read chapters of the Quran and offer prayers for the redemption of the deceased's soul.

The Badshah entered the mahal and gave clothes to Mirza Fakhru's children and their partners so that they could come out of mourning. The widows, however, were given *randsalas* or widow's clothes and were beside themselves with grief.

The Badshah consoled them with tears in his own eyes, 'Please bear it with fortitude. You will not gain anything by crying. Allah does not permit anyone to take their own lives and one can only endure the pain with patience.'

A few weeks later, to the shock of the entire mahalsara, Wazir Khanum was given orders to vacate her haveli behind the Diwan-e Aam by Nawab Zeenat Mahal Begum. Normally widows would be allowed to stay in their havelis to complete their *iddat*—the mandated waiting period of four months and ten days that a woman was required to observe after the death of her husband or even a divorce.

Was it because her beauty made the Malika jealous? No one can stop gossip and tongues from wagging. Now there was speculation that the Malika had a hand in Mirza Fakhru's death for it very conveniently paved the way for Mira Jawan Bakht appointment as heir apparent.

Meanwhile, to cajole the grieving Badshah into a better mood, Malika gave orders to Ustad Miran, in charge of the royal zoo, to bring the famed nightingale, known as Bulbul-e Hazar Dastan to the imperial khwaabgah. Its song was sure to enchant him. Though, the bulbul's golden cage was hung near his canopy, its melodious songs failed to soothe his heart.

The next morning, Sikandar Ara Begum, Huzur's great aunt, Zohrun Nisa Begum and Rashid Ara Begum, his cousins, were sitting huddled in a corner. Moti bai, the Badshah Huzur's wife and mother of the eldest remaining son Mirza Quwaish had come to visit. She was tearfully and also fearfully recounting the events of the past few days after making them promise it would go no further.

'I never thought I'd live to see the day that Alampanah got so swayed by that wife of his that he didn't even wait for Mirza Fakhru's body to get cold before sending letters to the Resident bahadur, asking for his approval to make Jawan Bakht the new wali ahad.'

'What!' Sikandar Ara Begum, who was very fond of Mirza Quwaish, was shocked. 'But the angrez know that there are elder brothers alive with more right to the throne than that impertinent young man. Also, Quwaish has done the Hajj pilgrimage and is a *hafiz* of the Quran.'

'That is why I am so upset Phuppijan. Huzur and Malika prevailed upon them, or should I say, coerced them to sign a paper renouncing their rights in favour of Jawan Bakht. Quwaish tells me that Mirza Mughal, Mirza Abdullah,[14] Mirza Mendu,[15] Mirza

Abu Nasir Bahadur, Mirza Mendhi,[16] Mirza Khizr Sultan, Mirza
Abu Bakr, Mirza Kuchuk,[17] Mirza Shah Abbas Bahadur and Mirza
Muhammad Sher Shah Bahadur were all made to sign that paper and
it was given to the Resident bahadur, Sahib-e Kalan Fraser sahib,'
replied Moti bai.

'And the Resident bahadur agreed?' asked Zohrun Nisa Begum.

'Yes, Apajan. It seems they have agreed on the condition that
the new wali ahad also agrees to all the terms and conditions that
Mirza Fakhru had agreed to. But now Quwaish has told the Resident
bahadur that they were forced to sign the paper or else Alampanah
would stop their allowances. I am so scared Apajan, that is why
I came to consult you, my elders. I am scared not only that they
will stop his allowance but also that there might be attempts on his
life. We all know what happened to Mirza Fakhru,' said Moti bai,
shivering with fear.

Just as well that the residents of the Qila did not know of the
plans being made in faraway Calcutta in the office of the Company
sarkar that after Badshah Bahadur Shah Zafar, the Mughal empire
itself should cease to exist as it was. The next successor would only be
a prince who lived in a haveli in Mehrauli while the Qila with all that
it represented was to be in the hands of the angrez. Lord Canning
had advised the Resident that Mirza Quwaish could be accepted
just as the head of the Timurid family and be called a shahzada.
Only the immediate family would get an allowance or pension from
the Company bahadur and the salatins had to leave and fend for
themselves. Mirza Quwaish would only get fifteen thousand rupees
and not one lakh, as he no longer had to look after the upkeep of
the Qila.

But this was not the case with Nawab Zeenat Mahal sahiba,
who, with her efficient system of spies and allies had come to know
of some of this. Ever hopeful, she knew that life was transient and if
two wali ahads had passed away what was the guarantee that Mirza
Quwaish would live? She persuaded Alampanah to employ the service
of T.C. Fenwick, whose job was to write to the governor-general

pleading for Jawan Bakht to be instated as heir apparent. Though the governor-general had rejected Jawan Bakht's claims, she was pushing the matter.

Meanwhile, Hira and Rahim had reached Qutub Sahib in their bullock cart. The death of Mirza Fakhru had delayed their trip for a few days as Rahim had wanted to participate in the funeral prayers.

The long journey from Shahjahanabad to Qutub Sahib with stops in between was mainly on the gossip of the Qila.

'Ama, Rahim do you know that Mirza Ilahi Baksh is very angry with Huzur Badshah?' asked Hira.

Mirza Ilahi Baksh was a great-grandson of Alamgir II Badshah and father-in-law of the current Badshah. His hopes of becoming the grandfather of the next badshah through Mirza Fakhru had now been dashed.

He had firmly established his relationship with the Qila, after his daughter Hatim Zamani's wedding to Mirza Fakhru. He also had good relations with the British.

'Well, yes, Hira. I have heard from Nasiban that after Wazir Khanum Begum was thrown out of the Qila by the Malika, he took his daughter back to his haveli to complete her iddat. He is said to be a close confidante of the Badshah and the Malika and knows them both well. He is also the chief intermediary between the Badshah and the British. His star had been on the rise but now his anger and frustration are rising too. Of course, he's no babe in the woods either and while colluding with the Malika to ensure that her son Mirza Jawan Bakht becomes the next wali ahad, he was lobbying with the Company bahadur to ensure his grandson becomes the next badshah. He too was said to have his suspicions about the prince's death and swore that he would take revenge when the time was ripe,' whispered Rahim, for fear of the bullock cart driver hearing them.

'Do these Timurids always behave like this?' asked Hira.

'Arre bhai, power is a terrible thing. Brothers can kill brothers, imprison their fathers and even harm their sons. I am very happy to be poor and content with my lot. Not for me the Peacock

Throne. I am happy with just my dry roti and chutney,' said Rahim philosophically.

'Ahaa! Now we are getting somewhere,' thought Hira. Judging it to be the right time to start his temptation, Hira said, 'But don't you wish to buy jewels for your wife, fancy clothes for your children and not have a worry for the next day?'

'Bhai, I don't want to spoil my sleep with these useless dreams. It is my fate to dig a well with my head before I can get a drop of water to drink.'

Thinking that he had sown the first seed, Hira probed Rahim further. 'I heard from an old trader that when Akbar Shah Sani died, he had given the keys of the treasury to the son of Mirza Salim.'

The rocking gait of the bullock cart and the open space and air made the normally reticent Rahim quite loquacious.

He settled back against the cart railing, put a cushion behind him and taking a few puffs of the huqqah, started his tale.

'Though Huzur Badshah Bahadur Shah was the eldest, Badshah Akbar Shah sani loved Mirza Babar, Mirza Salim and Mirza Jahangir amongst his sons as they were born from his favourite wife, Mumtaz Mahal Begum. He, therefore, appointed Mirza Salim as his wali ahad and desired that the Company sarkar also accept and announce the same. However, since Mirza Ibban, as our Huzur-e Purnur was called, was the oldest son, the Company was not ready to accept the Badshah's proposal.

'As he couldn't make any of them his heir apparent, so he had showered them with precious gifts and the responsibilities of looking after the workshops and other services to be rendered in the Qila. All three princes died in the father's lifetime. Mirza Jahangir had been exiled by the angrez to Allahabad for his rebellion against them and though he returned once due to Seton Sahib bahadur's intercession, he was exiled again and died soon after in 1821. Mirza Babur died in March 1836 and Mirza Salim died of a perforated stomach ulcer a few months later. The sainted Badshah had then handed over the responsibilities to Mirza Salim's young son, Mirza Firoz Shah.'

'Did they all die natural deaths?' asked Hira.

'Mirza Jahangir died of alcoholism in Allahabad and his body was brought back to Delhi on Mumtaz Mahal Begum's insistence and buried in Sultanji's dargah,' he said, referring to the dargah of Hazrat Nizamuddin Auliya. 'He was a very headstrong and dissolute young man. The other two also died of ailments due to overindulgence.'

'Oh! But go on, what happened to Mirza Firoz Shah?' asked Hira.

Rahim took a few more puffs of the huqqah, opened his box, took out a paan cone and continued, 'This story was on everyone's lips twenty years ago and many remember it. I had heard it from Nasiban, who heard it from one of the attendants in the Qila, who was there at that time. When Badshah Akbar Shah Sani had been on his deathbed, it was rumoured that he had secretly handed over the keys of the royal treasury to Mirza Firoz Baksh. As I had said, he did not get along with his eldest son and wanted to ensure that one of the grandsons of his favourite consort would succeed him. He gave strict instructions to the boy to use the leverage that the royal treasury gave him to make sure he succeeded as the next emperor. The old Badshah had forgotten or not considered the new dynamics of the angrezi power over succession and their preference for his eldest son.

'The grandson is said to have gone into shock and run away with the keys after the grandfather died. He knew he would never ascend the throne, given the power of the Company bahadur. He is said to have worn the saffron clothes of a faqir and gone into the jungle. There he spent time fretting about his grandfather's advice. As he had expected, with the Company bahadur's seal of approval, his uncle became the badshah. The keys to the royal treasury were missing. After much investigation, one of *marhum* Badshah Akbar Shah Sani's attendants remembered that there had been some handing over of keys to Mirza Firoz, after which he had disappeared. A search party was sent out to look for him. When the nobles found him, he refused to hand over the keys. Then angrez officers were sent, and many promises were made to him, of which the young prince would believe none.

'The prince was promised by the British officer, "If you give us the keys, we promise that all the money and factories that were under your father will remain under you. Apart from that, the Badshah will also reward you well." But the shahzada was adamant and only "no" left his lips.

'After a few days, the shahzada's attendant, who had looked after him as a child and had been with him ever since, came looking for the prince. It was only when an attendant who had literally brought up the prince came to the jungle and appealed to him that the overwrought prince broke down. The attendant reminded the prince of the transient nature of the world and kept repeating, "Miyan, there is no use in living in this disloyal world. One should be unaffected by it and stay aloof from the vagaries of time. This world stands by no one. Huzur, may I sacrifice myself for you, it breaks my heart to see you in these beggar's clothes. These are the days for you to live a luxurious life and enjoy yourself. Had your father been alive, this is what would have transpired. However, we are but puppets in the hands of God."

'The naïve prince, not realizing that there was a conspiracy against him and that his attendant was working for the Company bahadur who wanted the treasury keys back, was taken in by the attendant's words. The attendant said, "Huzur, when you have forsaken the crown, what use are the keys?" and with folded hands, he continued, "Hand back the keys and spend your days in remembrance of Allah to see what fate has in store for you." The young prince was in tears.'

Hira had been listening in rapt silence to this fascinating tale. 'What happened after that? Did he hand over the keys?'

'Oh yes, he did. The poor prince was an innocent man.'

'Was he treated well? I have never heard his name in all the years that I have been living in Shahjahanabad,' said Hira.

'How would you? The prince had to flee for his life after he handed over the keys. His pensions and allowances were stopped.

Now he is said to be living in the central provinces. It was also said that he had developed a keen interest in Christianity. I am glad I don't have a kingdom or treasures and can sleep in peace every night,' concluded Rahim.

By now, they had reached the outskirts of Qutub Sahib. Finding a *sarai,* or inn, they settled down for the night.

The next day they went looking for cheap lodging. To their surprise, they found a reasonably affordable set of rooms near the Shamsi *talab*, a reservoir built in the thirteenth century by Sultan Iltutmish.

It seemed that the news of Mirza Fakhru's death had cast a pall of gloom in Qutub Sahib, and no one was sure if the Sair would be held with the same fanfare or not.

They went to Qutub Sahib's dargah to offer their respects and a chadar and prayed for the success of their mission. Of course, while Rahim was praying for a boost in sales, Hira was praying that he could get his hands on Shahzadi Falak Ara's locket, which was fast becoming an obsession for him.

There wasn't much else to do there at this time of the year and they returned to their sarai and the next day, went back to the city.

Meanwhile, in the Qila, Mirza Mohammed Aftab sought permission and was granted an audience by Huzur Purnur.

'Huzur Mahabali, may your fortune and prosperity always be on the ascendant,' he said after presenting a nazar of a gold coin wrapped in a satin handkerchief along with his salutations.

The hammam had three sections. The first section was a room with delicately embossed marble up to its dado. The eastern side has glass windows and screens through which one could see the river and the refreshing greenery. In the second section, a marble throne towards the north has exquisite mosaic and inlay work. In front of it was a marble square decorated with unique floral designs. A beautiful square pool was set in the middle of this room, and the nahr-e bahisht ran all around it. Hot and cold water flowed into it as per the seasons and the royal wish.

As it was winter, Huzur Purnur went to the *garam khana,* which was the last of the three sections and had hot water. Steam from the fire which heated the water had warmed the room and the beautiful inlay work on the floor, resembling a Persian carpet, shimmered like flowers in full bloom.

Huzur was relaxing there, on a marble *shahnasheen* with his jade huqqah beside him, the gold pipe held by an attendant and the emerald mouthpiece in his hand. The wives of the angrez officers were very taken up with this material and got gowns made from it. Aftab had heard that they were exporting it to their country too.

The nahr-e bahisht, was gurgling gently beside the shahnasheen, the inlay patterns on the floor and walls sparkling from the discreetly lit lamps, the heady smell of camphor and attar filling the air. The nahr-e bahisht had been built by the architects of the palace in such a way that it ran throughout the palaces and fort buildings in marble channels, sometimes underground, sometimes above ground, decorated with the most beautiful fountains and pools.

In summer, the nahr and the fountains kept the room cool, and it was a favourite resting place of the Badshah in the afternoons. He would often hold meetings here.

It is a piece of paradise, not a hammam, was the first thought that came to Aftab's mind as he entered. Since no one could sit in the imperial presence there were no chairs. Aftab came and stood beside the Badshah Salamat and presented his kornish.

'Ama, I am seeing you after a long time Aftab. How are you? I hope all is well,' said the Badshah Salamat.

'With your auspicious hand on our heads, how can anything be amiss, Alampanah.' As he lifted his gaze decorously, he couldn't fail but see that Huzur's beard had more silver and his face, more lines. Whatever the uncharitable might say, clearly Mirza Fakhru's death had hit him hard. *Perhaps, I should have waited longer*, Aftab thought.

Seeing his hesitation, Jahanpanah asked, 'Is there something I can do for you?'

'O shadow of God on earth, we who live in your shelter want for nothing. Your Majesty second-guesses each need.'

Eventually, after prolonged court formalities that demanded nothing could be said without some flowery conversation, Aftab came to the point.

'Huzur-e Wala, refuge of the world, if you would be so kind and gracious as to take my son Qaiser in your shelter, his birth would be successful. The young lad has been learning calligraphy and has learnt the basics, now he wants your blessed hand on his head,' said Aftab.

'Ama, you know I have given orders that anyone can come to me for instruction in calligraphy, poetry, or to become my *murid*. Send him to me tomorrow after *asr* prayers. I will be in the tasbihkhana.'

'Your grace and generosity know no bounds. May God protect you and keep your shadow on us forever. May your star always be on the ascendant and shine in all the firmament.'

So saying, Aftab backed out of the hammam, ensuring that he did not show his back to the Emperor, saluting him all the while.

The next day, Qaiser's classes began. He presented himself before the Emperor, gave a nazar of five gold coins wrapped in a brocade cloth and sat down at the royal feet to begin learning.

> *Shab jo dil do do haath uchhalta tha*
> *Wajd tha ya wo haal tha kya tha*

> My heart leapt with joy last night
> Was it frenzy or ecstasy or what!

—Ghulam Hamdani Mushafi

11

Return to Qutub Sahib

Nami danam chi manzil bood shab jaay ki man boodam;
Baharsu raqs-e bismil bood shab jaay ki man boodam.

I wonder what was the place where I was last night,
All around me were half-slaughtered victims of love,
tossing about in agony.

—Hazrat Amir Khusrau

The Qila was back to normalcy.

Forty days had passed, and it was time to observe the *chaliswan,* or fortieth day, ceremony after death. Attar and rosewater were poured into the earthen grave and a marble tombstone was erected.

A canopy of flowers was erected over the grave, which was covered with a brocade cloth and a chadar. There were orders for purdah and the women came to mourn him. The food, the clothes, and the other items were kept near the grave's headstone.

Later a *qawwali* session was held, and once everyone had eaten and distributed alms, they returned home.

The official mourning was over.

A group of nobles from Shahjahanabad asked for permission to meet Huzur-e Aqdas. They were granted an audience in the tasbihkhana.

After the kornish and formalities, Raja Nahar Singh said, 'Pir o Murshid, if we may have permission to say something?'

After a nod, he continued, 'Alampanah, may we be sacrificed over you. We are lowly specimens of humanity, and it is only your exalted presence which is so forgiving and gracious that we have become emboldened enough to ask if we can make preparations for the Sair. We know that your revered presence and the other exalted denizens of the haveli have also been grieving but now the fortieth day is over. Even the residents have somehow limped back from the cholera plague that had beset them, and a change of air will do them good.'

Huzur Jahanpanah, the beloved of all Shahjahanabad, nodded and said, 'Our happiness is in your happiness. Fix the date of the Sair as the fifteenth of the month of Bhadon. We will also come, for we Timurid emperors can never be separated for long from our subjects. Can a nail ever be separated from the flesh?'

The *nafiri waala* was summoned and was told to immediately announce the dates in the Qila and the city. He set off with his silver nafiri to obey the Badshah Salamat's orders.

The first sound of the nafiri was like a balm to the hearts of all the residents of the Qila.

As soon as Huzur-e Purnur came inside the *mahal* all the princesses and ladies, young and old, started gathering. Huzur-e Wala was on his silver shahnasheen in the Badi Baithak and each lady or girl would come up, make her salutation and sit down on the plush Kashmiri carpets. No one said a word, but their eyes seemed to be pleading with Huzur to take them to Qutub Sahib.

'Ama, we know why you all are here,' he said with a smile. We have fixed the date of the Sair, only a week is left, so all of you start getting ready. We will leave a little earlier so that the residents can come in comfort later. We will also get a few days to enjoy Qutub Sahib and then can open it up for the Shahjahanabad residents. We will leave in three days, early in the morning.

Miyan Mughal, please inform the *filkhana*, *aspkhana*, and the wagon house to get the conveyances for the begums ready. Tell the *filbaan* to get Maula Baksh ready. Miyan Quwaish, please inform Khan-e Saman to get the paraphernalia ready and tell the Qiledar

and Kotwal that we are leaving. I will tell Mehboob Ali wazir and
Hakim sahib.'

With a wave of his hand, the assembly was dismissed, and
everyone moved sedately out of the imperial presence. As soon as
they were out of eyeshot, of course, it was another matter.

Orders were given and preparations began to go to Qutub Sahib
for the Sair as only a week was left for the date fixed by the Badshah
Salamat on which the floral canopies were traditionally offered on the
shrines of Qutub Sahib and Jogmaya Devi. Thousands of boxes and
bags were readied to cater to the imperial guests.

Falak Ara was least interested in the preparations as she couldn't
foresee any change in her situation. She was still heartsick, and these
longings were further heightened by the sight of Mirza Qaiser at the
Jharokha Darshan every day.

Though earlier she would get up just before the fajr or dawn
prayers, of late she had started getting up earlier and on the pretext
of painting, she would sit glued to the window in the mahal that
opened on to the riverside, trying to colour her painting and perhaps
her life.

The dawn was beautiful, and she could hear the call of azan
coming from the mosques, the bells ringing in the temples and
the soft, enticing sounds of Raga Bhairavi being played from the
naqqarkhana, all combining to make her heart restless. Could she
work these sounds into her painting? She wished she had a good
ustad who could teach her these nuances. She had heard of the
renowned Ghulam Ali Khan Naqqash, who had painted so many
spectacular paintings of her grandfather, Badshah Akbar Shah Sani,
and of her father in his youth. There were other ustads, his brother,
Faiz Ali Khan, and nephew, Mazhar Ali Khan, and Mirza Shahrukh
Beg and Muhammad Alam but they were busy painting for angrez
officers and the Company bahadur. In any case, she couldn't learn
from a man and there were no women painters in the city. She
had to negotiate her way forward by studying the *muraqqas* in the
kutubkhana.

She could see beautiful girls and women dressed in delicate
lehengas and *saris* plunging gracefully into the water up to their
waist, and the young girls splashing water on each other.

How she longed to be there. The freedom of coming out of
the river. Bending down from the waist and then flinging the
head up with a great flourish so that the water droplets would go
flying in every direction, much to the squeals of others on whom
they fell.

Falak Ara felt someone coming and immediately bent her head
down to concentrate on her prayer book. Rashid Ara Begum had just
finished her prayers and joined her at the window.

They could see a plump priest, with his *choti*, or ponytail, on the
middle of a shaven head, dressed in a loincloth, sitting cross-legged
on the riverbank. Three small idols of Lord Mahadev, his consort
Parvati, and his bull mount, Nandi, were kept next to him, along
with some shells, conches and items for puja. He was pouring milk
over the idol of Mahadev and scattering flowers around. Devotees
who had just finished their ritual bath in the river were gathering to
pay obeisance to the idols, and the pile of coins next to the priest was
growing. He was putting a sandalwood teeka on their foreheads with
one of the rings on his fingers, and a leaf of tulsi in their mouths.

Young Zebunnisa, who had been woken up by her attendant for
prayers, had also joined them, rubbing her eyes.

'Dadijan,' she addressed Rashid Ara Begum, 'Why are they
praying to an idol? Isn't it forbidden in our religion?'

'My daughter, Allah is one and there are various ways of reaching
him. You should read the Surah Kafirun, which is Surah 109 in
the Quran and ends with "*Lakum deenu-kum wa leeya deen*." This
literally means "for you is your religion and for me is my religion."
Our Alampanah is very enlightened. He knows the truth of the
Universal God and knows that everything springs from one source,
that is why like his forefathers, especially Shahenshah-e Hind Akbar
Badshah arsh ashiyani, he says:

Butkhanon mein jab gaya main khenchkar qashqa Zafar
Bol utha woh but, 'Brahmin yeh nahin to kaun hai?

When Zafar went to the temple with a tilak on my forehead
The idol exclaimed, 'If not a Brahmin then who is he?

'Alampanah treats all his subjects, be they of any religion, as his children and that is why there is such complete communal harmony in the realm. Even as I speak to you, you can hear the temple bells mingling with the sounds of the prayers coming from the mosques.'

The mischievous Zeenatun Nisa had now joined them. While all the other ladies and attendants were engrossed in Rashid Ara Begum's conversation, Zeenat could see that Falak Ara's eyes were constantly darting to the window and gravitating towards an arresting figure dressed in a muslin angarkha, red turban, with a dagger and sword at his waist tied in a silk sash. He was standing under the jharokha where the Badshah was giving darshan.

'Bajijaan, isn't that the same man who saved your life from drowning?' she asked Falak Ara.

'How would I know? I was unconscious and didn't see him,' said a red-faced, extremely embarrassed Falak. 'Also don't disturb me, I am completing my *wazifa*,' she added, referring to the special prayers with Quranic verses that one invokes to find solutions to problems.

'Oho! So were you doing wazifa to find out who your saviour was? Then offer your prayers of gratitude, for there he is! I was standing just next to you on the river and saw him very clearly,' teased Zeenat. She had just turned thirteen and was not only cheeky but had also started understanding romance.

'Don't talk nonsense Zeenat,' scolded Falak Ara. 'There are more important things to worry about. I was praying for Huzur Purnur's long life. There are strange rumours in the wind about the firangi intentions.'

'By the way, Bajijan, your prince comes every afternoon to the tasbihkhana to take calligraphy lessons from our blessed Alampanah.

I think you need to get into the good books of Badshah Begum sahiba Zeenat Mahal so you can go to the khwaabgah and at least hear his voice,' teased Zeenat.

'Shoo, little one. Don't talk nonsense. There is complete purdah between the tasbihkhana and the khwaabgah. Also, who put these foolish ideas into your head?' scolded her mother as Falak stood nearby, red with embarrassment.

By now there was quite a gathering near the window. Rashid Ara Begum had been joined by Sikandar Ara Begum.

'May Allah have mercy on us,' said Sikandar Ara Begum. 'After Mirza Fakhru's sudden death, my heart keeps sinking. There is something amiss in our stars. And then that young begum thinks nothing of plotting and planning with the firangis.' Age gave her the excuse for being outspoken, but the others were more cautious.

'For Allah's sake please guard your tongue, Phuppijan,' said Rashid Ara Begum. 'Walls have ears, and the Begum has spies everywhere. Don't even think such thoughts. You are so religious; you should know that Allah has given everyone a fixed life and death is predestined. No one can take anyone else's life, only Allah has the right to cause death and life. Why blame Begum sahiba for that?'

Rashid Ara Begum knew that the Begum was quite ruthless and while Sikandar Ara Begum would be protected because of her seniority and relationship with the Badshah, the rest were vulnerable.

By then the Jharokha Darshan was over and the people were returning to start their day. In the mahal, the huqqahs were ready for the ladies, as were silver and jade trays with silver-coated cardamoms and betel cones. Falak Ara put her painting and paint brushes away.

The maidservants and attendants were buzzing around getting the clothes ready for the Qutub Sahib stay, seamstresses were busy stitching exquisite garments for the begums and shahzadis. These dresses were elaborately embroidered and embellished with all kinds of gold and silver laces, precious stones and feathers.

Elsewhere, in the male section of the palace, preparations were also in full swing.

Every year, an amount of two-hundred rupees was given from the royal treasury to the flower-sellers for making the pankha and chadars.

Mehrauli and Jangli Mahal were being decorated. Though the mahal was always kept ready, during the monsoons, it was decked up like a new bride's henna. The verdant green all around and the red hills, the drizzle from the skies resembling her tears and the joyous singing and celebrating by the families evoked the atmosphere of a wedding.

The people of Shahjahanabad and Qutub Sahib all looked forward to this sair the year round.

The Badshah was much loved by everyone and as the saying went in Shahjahanabad, if his subjects were the root, he was the tree that had flowered from their love and faith in him.

There was a sense of great joy as the whole city was getting ready to move towards Qutub Sahib. The rich would go in their carriages and phaetons, the courtesans and prostitutes in bullock carts, while the poor would walk.

To the sounds of joyous singing and merriment the residents of the city were also getting ready to leave.

A popular ditty on everyone's lips was:

Qutub ko chala mera Akbar[18] hatela
Naa raste mein jangal naa milta hai thela

My unique Akbar to Qutub is away
He will encounter no cart or forest on the way

12

Swings on Every Tree

Jhoola kinne daalo hai amriyaan
Baag andheri taal kinara
Mor jhinkare
Badal kaare
Barsan laage
Boondein phuniyan
Jhoola kinne daalo hai amriyaan
Bhool Bhulaiyyan
Bholi dole
Shauq-rang saiyyan
Jhoola kinne daalo hai amriyaan

Who has put up the swing on the mango tree?
The orchard is dark, the peacock dances at the edge of the
lake, black clouds splatter raindrops softly,
Who has put up the swing on the mango tree?
All the friends are together,
(Laughing and playing) in the Bhool Bhulaiyyan
(With) Shauq-rang, the beloved.
Who has put up the swing on the mango tree?

—Bahadur Shah Zafar
(writing under takhallus Shauq-Rang)

Strains of Raga Bhairavi being played on the flute, or *ektara,* outside the mahals signalled dawn. Not that the residents needed this daily morning wake-up call today. Some had hardly slept, either from excitement or because of work.

'Have you died in some corner from the excitement, Dulari? I asked you to bring fresh flowers for my braid an hour ago. Are you planting the seeds and waiting for them to grow?' cried out the impatient young princess, Bilqis uz-Zamani.

'Ai shahzadi, please don't utter such inauspicious words. I am here only. I wanted to get the best flowers for my rosebud. But what can I do, this wretch Ashrafun was trying to steal it from me.'

'Oh, go away, you strumpet, may Shaitan urinate on you. Don't you go eyeing my shahzadi's flowers,' came back the angry retort from Durdana, the attendant of Mehr Jahan.

The rivalry between the two maids looking after princesses of approximately the same age was legendary, and they were always blaming and cursing each other, trying to ensure their charge outshone the others.

'If you are spoiling for a fight, let's do this!' said Durdana.

'Fight with you? Even my shoe wouldn't kick you and give you importance,' replied Ashrafun.

'Why didn't you say this before? Let me throw this shoe at your husband's face,' retorted Durdana.

'Arre you are truly a hussy, without a husband. At least I have one. I heard you got your gusset attached to the knee. Good for you, now you won't need to use the drawstrings, there is an easier way up for the illicit seeker of your flower,' snapped an angry Ashrafun.

'Stop this nonsense at once both of you. Can't you see there are young ones present?' Bilqis uz-Zamani's mother, Afroz uz-Zamani Begum remonstrated them. In the next breath, she called out, 'Gulshan, you lazy woman, where are you? Please bring my red brocade box. I think I will wear the red phulkari angiya kurti. And don't tell me it isn't ready.'

'Begum sahib, I would never say this. Everything is ready,' replied Gulshan.

Not wanting to be left behind in this friendly banter, Dulari quipped, 'Arre begum sahib, you have caught her pulse. Her motto is "*suyi tuti kashide se chhuti* [Thank God my needle broke, and I am saved from work]."'

The mahal was in an uproar, with everyone frantically preparing for the weeklong sair.

The young girls were busy getting henna put on their palms, the maids and attendants were packing and getting scolded for giggling and gossiping. Everyone was in a good mood.

Finally, dawn broke, and it was time to leave. The carriages and palanquins were standing in front of the naubatkhana. Purdah arrangements were made with screens on either side for the ladies to reach there. First, the giggling and laughing serving maids and attendants were piled onto the bullock carts.

'A three-legged donkey loaded with nine maunds,' scoffed the driver to himself, praying that the journey was free of mishaps.

But no one cared for anything except merriment.

The last carriage was of Nawab Zeenat Mahal Begum, with her attendants and khwajasaras labouring under the weight of her jewellery boxes. Her carriage was pulled by two pure white horses, caparisoned in gold and silver brocade.

She was escorted by tall, armed Abyssinian women dressed in red turbans and jackets with jewelled aigrettes on spirited horses.

One Abyssinian woman cracked her whip the other would call out, 'Attention, lower your eyes in respect, may Allah protect Hazrat Badshah Begum.'

The preparation for the Emperor's departure commenced with the chobdar relaying instructions to the elephant Maula Baksh.

The Emperor, after consuming his special tonic, finished his morning rituals and gave orders to Mir Tuzuk, in charge of the procession, to commence. Maula Baksh, adorned and bathed, stood ready for duty, escorted by loyal guards and attendants. The procession included soldiers, princes on horseback, and nobles, with Captain Douglas offering salutations upon the Emperor's appearance near the Lahori Darwaza. Nobles mounted their animals outside the naubat khana, joined by camels carrying drummers and trumpet blowers. Mirza Qaiser was also there with his father, in readiness to follow the Badshah Salamat's procession.

Maula Baksh was joined by two elephants at the back, called *bele ka hathi,* from the backs of which charity would be distributed.

Armed and uniformed cavalrymen and infantrymen stood on either side of the road from the Qila gateway to the Dilli Darwaza.

A gun salute was given. The cherished Jahanpanah was coming out, so the shopkeepers of the bazaar had decorated their beloved city with beautiful arches made from flowers, some brocaded, leaves and with tapestries and mirror work.

The streets had been sprinkled with water and the shops and houses decorated like beautiful brides. All the windows and balconies that opened out onto the streets were full of women straining to see the imperial procession from behind screens, curtains or from behind their chadors. They knew this separation was temporary as they would be following him soon to Khwaja Sahib. The Badshah Salamat's eyes reflected his happiness at being among his people and gave them blessings.

Fistfuls of coins were thrown from the bele ka hathi as alms of the Badshah. The sentries at Dilli Darwaza, leading out of the city, gave another gun salute as their Emperor's procession passed by and went on to the road leading to Sultanji.

By the time Huzur Mahabali reached the Kotla, the ladies had reached Mansur ka Maqbara where arrangements had been made for refreshments and rest.

Meanwhile, the imperial cavalcade reached Purana Qila, where the Badshah Salamat got into his hawadar and went into the beautiful red sandstone mosque built by Sher Shah. In gratitude, he rendered *shukrana* namaz there.

The shahzadas were with him. A young prince, whose first outing it was with the men, remarked on the octagonal building near the mosque, where carpets had been laid out and a masnad laid out for the Badshah to rest.

'My son, this is called Sher Mandal. It was built to serve as an observatory and library. Our ancestor, Humayun Badshah jannat ashiyani, slipped from the roof of this building and went to heaven.'

'Dada Huzur, who was Sher Shah? Abbajan says he built the mosque we just prayed in.'

'My child, he was an Afghan adventurer who usurped the Timurid throne, but God was on our side and with the help of the Persian Shah Tahmasp, Humayun Badshah was able to regain it.'

'Dadajan, I heard one guard saying the Persians are very nice and they will be sending help for you also?'

'Where did you hear such nonsense? Mirza Mohammed, please keep a check on your son's activities and company. God forbid the Company bahadur hears all this, they will unnecessarily suspect some conspiracy.'

An embarrassed Mirza Mohammed took his son away, feeling guilty as it was his conversation with some friends that the young boy had overheard and repeated. The ever-growing British influence and power were causing great resentment among some of the Timurid princes and nobility.

In the Qila, several of the princes were talking of a Russian-backed Persian invasion. After the fall of Herat in Afghanistan to the Persian Army in October 1856, the British government declared war against Persia.

Hasan Askari, a Shia mystic who visited the Badshah Salamat often and was very close to him, was supposed to have prophesied that the Persian army would march to Hindustan and reinstall him as emperor.

It was not a new idea as some three years ago, Mirza Haidar Shukoh and Mirza Murad, sons of Mirza Khan Bakhsh and grandsons of Mirza Sulaiman Shukoh, had come from Lucknow where they resided, and in concert with Hasan Askari had arranged and suggested to the Jahanpanah that he should have a letter prepared and despatched to the King of Persia. Sidi Qambar, who was one of Alampanah's special armed retainers, was presented with hundred

rupees through Mahbub Ali Khan for the expense of his journey and
was despatched in the direction of Persia with a letter that had been
prepared in the King's private secretariat. The princes had returned
to Lucknow immediately, and no one knew what the response from
the Persian court was, or if the Badshah Huzur had received any
reply.

After the Anglo-Persian and the Crimean wars, there were a lot
of rumours about Russia.

It was said that they were eyeing Afghanistan and maybe even
Hindustan.

The angrez sarkar had signed a treaty with the king of Afghanistan,
Dost Muhammad in the previous year.

Chafing at the economic and political restrictions and loss of
power to the Company bahadur, some of the shahzadas hoped that
the Russian Badshah would help the Persians to defeat the angrez.

Some light snacks and huqqah were presented. The Badshah
Salamat was a very frugal eater and he pecked at a few nuqtis and
had a sherbet of milk and dry fruits, and a few puffs of the huqqah.

The rest over, Huzur got into the hawadar and left for Humayun
Badshah's *maqbara*.

Once again, carpeting had been arranged and a masnad set up
for the Badshah. He sat down for a little while and after a short rest
and some huqqah, he went into the underground vault with all the
princes in tow. First, he recited the fatiha at the grave of Humayun
Badshah jannat makani. This beautiful maqbara had been made for
him by his wife, Bega Begum.

After that, he stopped at each grave, identified it, recited the
fatiha for the deliverance of the deceased's soul, and told his children
about the persona of the dead man.

'This is the grave of Sultan Daniyal and Sultan Murad. They were
the sons of our great ancestor, Akbar arsh ashiyani. This is Shahzada
Dara Shukoh's grave,' said the Badshah Salamat as he stopped at a
grave. Mirza Qaiser filed it away in his mind. He wanted to have a
conversation with his father on the tragic end of the shahzada.

'These are the graves of our sainted ancestors, Jahandar Shah Badshah, Farrukhsiyar Badshah, Rafi-ud Darajat Badshah and Shah Jahan Sani Badshah, Shahzada Mirza Muhammad Kam Bakhsh and Alamgir Sani Badshah,' continued the Badshah.

'Dadajan,' the young prince, curious once again, asked his grandfather, 'why are no names written on the graves? How does Huzur Badshah know who is buried in each grave?'

The grandfather replied, 'This knowledge is passed on from the Badshah Salamat to wali ahad and shahzadas. If you listen carefully, you can hear the names and remember.'

'Dadajan, why are the names of Farukhsiyar Badshah, Rafi-ud Darajat Badshah, Shah Jahan Sani Badshah, Mohammad Shah Badshah and Ahmed Shah Badshah not written in your seal?' he asked next.

'Son, they were the grandsons of Bahadur Shah I and were put on the throne by the wazirs. We are the descendants of his grandson Alamgir Sani Badshah, who was the son of Jahandar Shah Badshah. There were five other emperors between Jahandar Shah and Alamgir Sani, our ancestor.'

It was now time to leave for Mansur ka Maqbara. The Badshah Salamat got into his hawadar and the cavalcade set off.

The Moti Mahal, Jangli Mahal and Badshah Pasand Mahal were decked up to receive the royal guests. The ladies were ensconced in the beautiful tents with floral designs, with their silver huqqahs and khasdans. The attendants and servants were standing behind them with flywhisks and fans.

The children were running around playing *atkan batkan dahi chatokan*—a version of the game 'catch me if you can'. The young girls were busy trying to get their maids to pluck fruits from the innumerable fruit trees that grew there. The hauz and water channels were full of rainwater, the fountains were gurgling, and the pots and pans were simmering with food and delicious smells were wafting in the air.

Falak Ara was seated under a mulsari tree, lost in thought, with Mubarak clucking around her like a mother hen.

Zeenatun Nisa and Zebunnisa, who had been trying to climb a neighbouring mango tree, were shrieking in delight and fear, when Zeenat screamed, 'Falak Apa!'

With a jolt, Falak shook off her reverie, and her eyes fell on Mirza Qaiser, who had just entered the area with the Badshah Salamat.

Alerted by the shout and Falak's name, Mirza Qaiser too immediately looked towards the tree and his gaze met Falak Ara's. Their gaze would probably have stayed locked forever if Zeenat and Zebun hadn't started giggling and Mubarak hadn't started panicking.

'Shahzadi, there's an ant on your hand,' she screamed nervously. Falak looked down at her hand in reflex and the moment was broken. The Badshah Salamat was getting into the tent prepared for him, and Mirza Qaiser was in attendance.

Mubarak took Falak away to the tent prepared for the young princesses. Falak was in a daze. She had gazed into his eyes and had seen emotions for herself there.

She sat quietly and submitted to henna being applied to her hands.

The henna had already been ground from the bushes growing in the mahal and soaked overnight in filigreed silver vessels. As it was applied on the hands of the ladies, the female attendants sang laudatory songs.

One of the *mirasins* started singing Hazrat Amir Khusrau's qawwali:

Aaj rang hai, Maa, rang hai ri
Moray mehboob kay ghar rang hai ri
Sajan milaavra, sajan milaavra,
Sajan milaavra moray aangan ko
Aaj rung hair i Maa, rang hai ri

There is a glow everywhere, O mother, a bright glow;
There is a glow in my beloved's house.
I found my beloved, I found him!
I found him in my courtyard

Even though the song talked of the Divine Beloved, whom the worshipper was seeking and who was inside his own heart, every word pierced Falak's heart. She had found him and what was more important, she was sure from the intensity of the gaze that he had recognized her! It was balm for her heart.

The girls of marriageable age were the target of all the bridal songs and today Falak felt as if the world was conspiring against her. She tried to dissolve under her mulmul dupatta but to no avail. Her charming confusion just made her look lovelier.

Mubarak was sitting with a group of foster mothers.

The foster mothers were listening to the attendants recounting fanciful tales about their wards. Naseeban had also joined them. She had no idea why, but Hira bhai, her husband's new business partner, had asked her to look out for a mango-shaped pendant on Falak's neck.

Before she could investigate, trays of freshly fried andrasas and luqme had been brought into the tents and no one paid attention to anything except stuffing their face.

The royal party which had left for Qutub Sahib after lunch, reached just as the sound of the maghrib azan could be heard from Qutub Sahib's dargah. Huzur-e Aqdas's immediately transferred to a hawadar and went to the dargah to pay his respects to the saint and say his prayers. The princes had also followed him, while the ladies were ushered into the Jangli Mahal.

The Badshah Begum Zeenat Mahal sahiba was in her special six-horse carriage with special outriders and soldiers accompanying her.

The Jangli Mahal, or Zafar Mahal, as some called it because of the magnificent Hathiya Pol, or elephant gate, that the blessed Badshah had added, was decked up for its royal inmates.

Special carriages had carried the attendants with food trays for dinner while the slave girls, servants and craftsmen from the workshops sat in other carriages. The royal family would be here for a week or maybe more and work had to go on as usual.

The day's travel had tired everyone out and they all fell asleep despite the excitement.

Orders had already been given for purdah for the women from the royal palace till the Shamsi Talab, jharna, amriyan, all the way till Nazir's bagh. Tents had been raised everywhere. Eunuchs and soldiers stood guard and no stranger could enter this area now. It was reserved for the enjoyment of the haram.

Next day, while Hazrat Zill-e Subhani and Malika-e Zamani sat in the *baradari*, the others roamed around. Fires were lit, *kadhai*s were put on them, and savouries and sweets were prepared. Swings were put up on the mango trees and vendors spread out their wares.

The drizzle of the rain, the smell of the savouries, henna, mangoes and flowers were enough to intoxicate anyone's senses.

Falak Ara sat with a group of young girls at the edge of the orchard from where they could get a clear view of the baradari where courtesans were dancing and Tanras Khan was singing.

The Badshah Salamat was surrounded by a group of princes, and a nudge from Zeenat made her aware of something her senses had already felt: the presence of Qaiser.

By now some of the other ladies had also joined and cots had been spread out with beautiful coverlets for them to sit on.

'Waah! What a note, Tanras has taken. Indeed, he has a silken throat,' said Zohrun Nisa Begum.

'Begum sahib, you know Huzur Purnur sends him special yakhni soup every day so that his throat remains supple and strong. It is prepared on the instructions of Hakim sahib,' quipped Ashrafun referring to Hakim Ahsanullah Khan.

'Of course, I know. We Timurids have been great patrons of art, music and literature.'

Falak's absorption was soon noticed by not only Zeenat, the usual suspect, but by Zohrun Nisa Begum, who decided to have a word with the Huzur Zillullah. As a cousin, she was on easy terms with him. She herself had never married, and she was determined that Falak, whom she was very fond of, should settle down with the one she was so obviously enamoured with. He seemed like a nice boy.

The kitchen department had got lunch ready and soon the dastarkhwan was laden with every kind of qorma, kabab, biryani, murabba and qaliya.

Getting the little ones away from the huge sliding rock was a task though. There was too much fun to be had climbing and sliding down it into the water pool. But their attendants managed.

The next two days were reserved for the ladies after which the area would be opened for the public.

Hira had already shifted to Qutub Sahib with Rahim and was waiting for Naseeban's visit to her husband at night. He had to be very careful so that no suspicion was evoked.

He had spent the day trying to awaken a desire in Rahim that he must be with his wife that night. He had even prepared a glass of local wine which was said to have aphrodisiac qualities for the unsuspecting Rahim and had given it to him at lunch and again at dinner. Rahim, now fully aroused, had sent a note to his wife asking her to come to their modest dwelling at night.

That night as the palace slept, exhausted after the day's fun and frolic, Naseeban sneaked out.

'What was the fuss all about?' was all she managed to ask her husband before he had her firmly in his arms. She had never seen him so passionate and was pleasantly surprised and happily gave in.

'Be careful,' she giggled, 'I am no longer that young lass you married.'

'Oh, come on, you are still the girl I love,' he retorted and continued his passionate lovemaking.

'What will your friend think?' she whispered at his heavy breathing and grunting.

'He is grown up and has a wife too, I am sure he knows what we are doing,' winked Rahim. 'Enough talk, woman. Don't distract me.' He opened her drawstrings and lowered her pajamas.

Hira, on the other side of the wall, was listening happily. He decided to invest in some more of that wine. It seemed to be good and would help in leading to the conversation of the locket.

The next three days went in the same fun and frolic.

In the ladies' quarters, preparations were in full swing for a trip to the Qutub Sahib *ki laat*.

'Dadijan, please come with us,' young Zebunnisa tried to cajole Rashid Jahan Begum and Zohrun Nisa Begum. 'We don't know anything about Old Dilli and it would be such fun if you could come with us and tell us your stories.'

'Arre, beti, may I be sacrificed over you. These old bones don't permit these jaunts now,' said Rashid Jahan Begum. 'I will tell you stories when you come back at night. Unless you can persuade Zohrun Nisa to go with you.'

All blandishments at the command of Zebunnisa and Gul Bano, who had decided to join them, were put to use, and Zohrun Nisa Begum agreed.

'While we are getting ready, please tell us a little bit, Dadijan,' pleaded Gul Bano.

'Where should I start, my children? These old eyes have seen the city at its height and are witnessing it now when we are trying to keep up the glory of the Timurid family in the face of opposition from the Company bahadur. Anyway, I will try my best. I have heard from my elders that this is the Dilli-e Kuhna of yore—and now I am narrating it to you.

'It was the same Dilli that had been named Dehlu after the King of Kannauj, Raja Delu, and later became Dhilli or the city of the Rajputs. Though the location kept shifting towards the Dariya-e Jun, the name Dilli endured.

'It was the capital of the Rajputs and then of the Delhi Sultans. Sultan Alauddin Khilji shifted his capital to Nayi Dilli and so did other Sultans. From the time the Rai Pithaura ruled over Qutub Sahib till our sainted ancestor Sahib-e Qiran Sani Shah Jahan Badshah built Shahjahanabad, this city was built and destroyed many times. I have heard that there were five "*pats*", out of which four are still flourishing: Panipat, Sonepat, Marpat and Baghpat. Not much is known about the fifth, which was Indrapat and it is said that Dilli was settled on that "pat". Raja Anangpal Tomar was ruling over this kingdom when the angel of death came to seize his soul, and his maternal grandson, Rai Pithaura Prithviraj Chauhan, who was ruling over Ajmer, became his successor and next king. Fortune smiled on Shihabuddin Mohammad of Ghor, and he defeated Rai Pithaura. Truly, no one is here to stay forever! We must always remember that this world is temporary,' said the wise old lady.

'Yes, of course, Dadijan, but please continue, this is very interesting,' said young Zebunnisa who had just started learning history and philosophy from her teacher.

'Well,' continued Zohrun Nisa Begum, 'Shihabuddin was succeeded by his general Qutbuddin Aibak, whose star shone brightly in the firmament and then faded away. His son, Aram Shah, was a wastrel, and he was removed by Qutbuddin's son-in-law, Shamsuddin Altamash, who came on the throne. He had appointed his daughter, Raziya, as his successor, but the generals put up his brother on the throne.'

'Really? A woman was nominated as his successor?' asked Gul Bano, who had never bothered to pay attention to her studies.

'You know Gul Apajan,' said Zeenatun Nisa, 'all this is described in Tarikh-e Ferishta, which I am reading these days in class.'

'I prefer listening to these stories from Dadijan,' retorted Gul Bano angrily.

'Dadijan, how did she rule? Wasn't she kept in purdah like us?' asked Falak Ara.

'Those days were different, Falak. The Turkish women were very headstrong and brave,' said Rashid Jahan.

Sikandar Ara Begum who had been quietly listening joined in: 'The Timurid princesses have been no less, it's just that no one has been an independent ruler. Malika Nur Jahan, the wife of Jahangir Badshah Ghazi, was a co-sovereign with her husband. She issued *farmans* and coins were stuck in her name. The sainted mother of Akbar Badshah *arsh ashiyani*, Hamida Bano Begum Mariyam Makani was very powerful, as were the mothers of Babur Badshah *firdaus makani* and Humayun Badshah *jannat ashiyani*. Not so long-ago, Shahzadi Jahanara, daughter of Sahib-e Qiran Sani Shah Jahan Badshah, was very influential. They played a very important role in the court and helped the Badshahs make decisions. Why only Timurid princesses, even the consorts of the emperor were encouraged to trade and were powerful. Akbar Badshah's Rajput wife, Mariyam uz-Zamani, used to trade with the firangis and had many ships plying the oceans. The firangis used to bow before her power. And now!' She struck her forehead in agitation, continuing, 'It is since these accursed angrez have come that the Timurid badshahs and malikas have been reduced to playing second fiddle.'

'Ssh Phuppijan, please calm down. The angrez Company bahadur gives a pension to Jahanpanah which he shares with all of us,' said Rashid Jahan.

'Pension! Pension you say! We Timurids were the rulers of Hindustan. The income and revenue are ours. We gave pensions. But an unfortunate decision to let the angrez Company bahadur trade in our lands and then the loss of Shah Alam Badshah Ghazi at the battle of Buxar has made us pensioners in our own empire. I don't want to criticize the dead, but a few wrong decisions and battles of succession led to the wazirs becoming important and putting puppets on the throne. This was the first step in weakening the empire. So much so that Shah Alam Badshah had to flee from the Qila to escape being killed by the wazir. He crowned himself emperor while he was in exile. Those abominable angrez were waiting for such an opportunity and after defeating him and the nawabs of Bengal and Awadh, forced him to sign a treaty giving away the revenue of the richest provinces. I forget the year, but I remember hearing it was in Allahabad. The Emperor of Hindustan was forced to stay in Allahabad instead of coming to rule from his capital in Delhi. Eventually, the Marathas supported him, and he came to Delhi but was always under their influence. Later, Nawab General Lake bahadur defeated the Marathas and the angrez became our masters. They were supposed to give us a peshkash and share of the revenue. They cheated in that too and never gave the money due from the revenue of the provinces and now they have the temerity to call it pension! I will never call it that.'

Seeing that the old lady was becoming very agitated, Falak Ara tried changing the topic and asked Zohrun Nisa Begum, 'Phuppijan, please tell us more about Sultan Raziya Begum. What happened to her?'

'Oh! She was such a great ruler, but men rarely let women rule. She was killed by her brother. Eventually, the entire bloodline of Sultan Altamash was finished by his slave Balban, who also became a Sultan. They all stayed here in Qutub Sahib. His grandson made Kilokari his capital, but he was also killed. Then we had Sultan Alauddin Khilji, tales of whose strictness and excellent administration are famous. He laid the foundation for the fortified city of Siri, to fight the Mongols. His children were replaced by the Tughlaqs who laid the foundation for the cities of Tughlaqabad and Firozabad. There were other rulers, and then our ancestors defeated Sultan Ibrahim Lodi and established the Timurid empire.

'Anyway, that's enough of a history lesson. Go enjoy yourselves. When I was younger, I have often climbed to the top of Qutub Sahib ki laat. Talat, are you going with them?' she asked.

Nawab Talat Shahar Banu Begum was the daughter of Mirza Mughal, Huzur Alampanah's son, and had been recently married to her cousin, Mirza Muhammad Abbas Bahadur, son of Mirza Muhammad Khawer Shukoh Bahadur. Though she lived in the city with her husband, she had come back to the Qila to accompany the family to Qutub Sahib for the Sair.

'Yes, Dadijan. I am going with them. It is one of the highlights of the Sair. I love climbing the laat. I think Mirza Abbas maybe there too.'

By now the girls were ready, and, escorted by the attendants and female soldiers, they left for the laat in their palanquins.

The palanquins were set down in front of the laat and the excited girls started running around enjoying their freedom in the place segregated for the royal ladies. Falak Ara, along with a few others, started climbing up the laat.

They were midway on the second storey when they heard male voices coming from the balcony on the next level. Zebunnisa and Zeenatun Nisa nudged Falak Ara and looked at her meaningfully, for they had seen who was speaking.

Mirza Qaiser, along with Mirza Abu Bakr, the son of Mirza Fakhru was standing on that balcony and was visible from the open door. 'The laat is actually a minaret built as a victory tower,' Mirza Qaiser was saying. He had been reading Tarikh-e Ferishta and had had many discussions with his teachers and father on this.

'Why is it called a laat then?' asked Mirza Abu Bakr.

'That is out of respect to Hazrat Khwaja Qutub Sahib. It is said that this is the laat or staff that connects Qutub Sahib to heaven. That is why this entire area is known as Qutub Sahib.'

Falak Ara had frozen on the steps just below the balcony. She didn't know whether to continue climbing up with her cousins or go down.

'Continue walking, Falak Apa,' said young Zeenat. She had sensed her cousin's discomfiture. 'Once we pass by them, they will automatically go down and out of the laat. I don't think they knew that we would be coming here today.'

By then Talat Shahr Bano Begum had reached the balcony and she saw that her husband, Mirza Muhammad Abbas Bahadur was also there.

She stood just in front of the opening and talked to the men, while the girls squeezed through. The spiral staircase was narrow and dark, with light spilling in only from the ventilation slits and the balconies. One of the attendants had the good sense to bring candles so that the interior was lit and eerie.

Taking advantage of Talat Begum's presence and Zeenat's good advice, covering her head with her dupatta, Falak walked up. The sounds of the anklets and bracelets had already alerted the young men who respectfully stayed on the balcony and as soon as the girls had passed up, made their way out. Talat Begum confirmed that.

'Why is fate playing hide-and-seek with me,' thought Mirza Qaiser to himself. 'I know that was Falak Ara who passed by me. When will the day come when we meet?'

As he had no answer to his own rhetoric, he walked out of the *minar* along with Mirza Abbas and Mirza Abu Bakr and went off to the Nazir ka Bagh where both were putting up in the various elegant baradaris that dotted the place.

The princesses had reached the top and though there had been much giggling on the way up, now they were awestruck as they looked at the lush greenery all around and tried to identify the places they saw.

'Is that the Qila?' asked Zeenat.

'Yes, of course,' said Nawab Talat Shahr Banu Begum. 'There is nothing as grand as the Qila our ancestor Sahib-e Qiran Sani Shah Jahan Badshah has built. It can be seen for miles around. In the olden days, it used to strike terror in the hearts of enemies. When I was younger, I often heard Huzur Alampanah Dadajan talk about the glory days of the Timurids. Now cruel fate has robbed us of power and bestowed it on the Company bahadur.'

Giving herself a mental shake, she continued, 'Anyway today we won't talk of anything melancholy. Let's enjoy ourselves.'

'For heaven's sake, be careful Zeenat and Zebun. The ledge is very low, and we don't want you falling over,' cried Talat Begum. The last and fifth storey of the minar used to have a small cupola but that had been damaged in an earthquake. The Company bahadur, while doing repairs, had got another one built but no one liked it, including Huzur, so Nawab Governor General Bahadur had given orders for it to be removed. There was now a low ledge built around it, but it was not high enough to prevent a fall should any girl go too close.

The happy princesses came down to find that a few of the other ladies had also joined the party and were waiting at the entrance of the laat.

To their surprise, they found that there was light drizzle, though it had been clear on top.

'God is the greatest! Even the clouds are lower than this minaret!' said Talat Begum.

The younger girls were full of questions for their elders.

'How tall is the laat? What is this gateway behind it? Why was it built?'

'Hold on, take a breath and give me time to answer!' said Nawab Zeb Zamani Begum, elder daughter of Mirza Dara Bakht Bahadur. She was in her forties and had received an excellent education.

Meanwhile, Talat took on the task of answering the questions of the young girls. 'This gateway you see is called the Alai Darwaza, it was built by Sultan Alauddin Khilji who wanted to expand Sultan Qutbuddin Aibak's mosque and quadruple its size. He wanted to build four such gateways, but he died before he could finish it.

'The business of the world was left incomplete.

'There is no doubt that had this mosque been completed, it would have had no equal on the face of this earth. It was God's will that only a gateway and some arches should be completed. He was building another minar but that too was left incomplete. Truly, who has been able to predict destiny? It is only Allah who knows what will happen.'

'As for this minar, it is eighty yards high. You have already seen it has five storeys. They say it had seven storeys—that is why it was called a *haft* minar—but now there are only five.'

'Look at the exquisite calligraphy with Quranic verses inscribed on them, on the red sandstone flutings,' continued Talat. 'The words are raised and written by such an accomplished calligrapher that one wants to pay respect to them by touching one's forehead to the stone.'

'How do you know so much, Talat Apa?'

'Mirza Abbas has recently brought home a beautiful book by Saiyed Ahmed Khan called Asar-us Sanadid. He had seen it with some angrez bahadur and bought one for himself. It was written some eight years ago. It gives the history of all the monuments in Delhi. As we were coming to Qutub Sahib, Mirza Abbas gave it to me to read,' she replied.

'Can I borrow it from you Talat Apa?' asked Falak.

'Of course! I think the author is writing another book on the Qutub Sahib, but you can read this one till then,' came the reply.

Now that the younger girls had found someone to answer their questions they kept asking the two older princesses.

They had entered the mosque, which had been built on the ruins of a broken temple. In the centre was an iron laat.

'What is this Talat Apa?' asked a young princess.

'This is the *lohe ki* laat, also called Rai Pithaura's nail. If you have time I can tell you the story that Saiyed Ahmad Khan has written.'

'We are all ears,' came the instant reply from all the girls. Even the elder ladies, who had accompanied the princesses into the courtyard of the mosque were agog.

Talat started her tale: 'Some people say that Sultan Muizuddin Muhammad bin Sam got this pillar installed here as the needle of a sundial, but this seems incorrect. It seems that this needle was already present in Rai Pithaura's temple and Sultan Muizuddin Muhammad bin Sam let it remain as the needle of a sundial, thinking that it would be useful as a tool to measure the hours of the day and would add to the glory of Islam.[19]

'There is another story which I found very interesting. I have seen our Rajput ancestresses do *naga* puja on Naga Panchami. Saiyed Ahmad Khan writes that the soothsayers of Rai Pithaura told him that they wanted to install a nail and as long as that nail held firm, his kingdom would too. Rai Pithaura couldn't understand the reason.

'An old and learned priest told Rai Pithaura, "Maharaj Prithviraj, though I don't want to make this knowledge, available to us sages, public, I will tell you so let us go to a place where we are alone."

'Rajaji immediately took the priest aside, who said, "Listen Maharaj Prithviraj, Raja Basik, the Emperor of Snakes, the master of this whole world, is the God who traverses the whole earth. He is about to come to this area in a few days. If we install this nail firmly on his head, then he will remain permanently in this area and your kingdom will remain forever too."

'Raja Prithviraj understood the importance and gave orders for the nail to be installed. All the priests gathered, ascertained an auspicious time and installed the nail. The raja was suspicious and asked, how he could be sure. So, he ordered the priests to uproot the nail and show him proof. They kept beseeching him not to do it, but he was adamant. He gave orders to the priests to uproot the nail and see if it was indeed wet with Raja Basik's blood. The priests tried to explain the folly of this action to him, but he refused to listen and got it uprooted.

'There was fresh blood on the nail. Raja Prithviraj was very dismayed that he had doubted them and immediately had it reinstalled. This time, however, it was not set properly, as the serpent had moved away, and a little while later he tasted defeat at the hands of the Muslim invaders. Some say that he was killed, while others say that he was sent to Ghor. Thus, Muslim rule came to be established here.'

'What a fascinating story, Talat,' said Nawab Zeb Zamani Begum. 'Even though we Muslims don't believe in the serpent king, it just shows that we must never disbelieve the learned sages and priests.'

The curious Zebun Nisa asked her cousin, 'Apajan, is it true that many temples were broken to make this mosque?'

'Zeb, the nature of monarchy is absolute and thus injustice and justice are both inherent to it. A ruler, ruling as the representative of God on earth, Zill-e Ilahi or shadow of God on earth, as our Badshah Huzur is called, will try to be as just as he can. All rulers, however god-fearing they may be and knowing full well that ultimately only Allah's name will prevail, are also autocratic and want to perpetuate their name. They build grand edifices and name them after themselves. Since they believe that every land in the kingdom now belongs to them, they build whatever they want. This is exactly what Sultan Qutbuddin Aibak did. To establish his imperial rule and stamp his authority and provide a place of worship for his soldiers and nobles he used the pillars of twenty-seven demolished temples of the Jains and Hindus to make a Jami Masjid,' replied Talat.

Nawab Zeb Zamani Begum added, 'Our rulers are just and have many inclusive policies so that the subjects never feel isolated or discriminated upon. After all, so many of our ancestresses were from the Hindu faith. See how many temples exist in our beautiful walled city. Dulari goes to worship in one. She told me about the many Shivalayas in the city. Since so many of the royal officers are of the Jain faith and are rich merchants, I have heard of the extremely beautiful Jain temples in Dharmapura. Badshah Akbar Sani even permitted to build a *shikhar* or steeple on them. But don't get me started on these accursed angrez. They are practising extractive policies and extracting taxes whether people are at risk of famine and what not.'

'Yes,' added Talat, who had been discussing this with her husband, 'It is not that our ancestors did not indulge in their share of exploitation, but they found innovative religious and cultural accommodations, and rarely did they discriminate on the basis of religion.'

This was enough food for thought for the young intelligent princesses as the tired ladies made their way back to the Jangli Mahal, having spent a wonderful morning at the laat.

Umr e daraaz maang kar laaye thay chaar din
Do aarzoo mein kat gaye do intezaar mein

Four days had I asked for my life to be
Two were spent in desires, two in waiting for it to be.

—Seemab Akbarabadi

13

The Supplicants and the Supplications

Uske farog-e husn se, jhamke hai sub main noor
Sham-e haram ho yaan ke diya Somnath ka

The splendour of His Beauty fills everything with light
Be it the candle in Mecca or the lamp in Somnath

—Mir Taqi Mir

The next day, it was time for the pankha to be offered at the temple and the chadar to be offered at the dargah.

All restrictions had been removed once the royal family had enjoyed their picnic. Shahjahanabad's population, Hindu, and Muslim, rich and poor, high and lowly, all had come here. The sweetmeat sellers, bread makers and kabab-sellers had set up shop in the area around the dargah and were doing brisk business. The sweet shops, with big kadhais, or woks, full of ghee heating on the fire, in which sweet and savoury snacks are prepared, were crowded with hungry people. Vendors sold their wares along the roads leading to the market.

The cloth sellers like Hira and Rahim, itr sellers and jewellers were all making money.

Once the royals had left, swings were put up in Andheri Bagh and everyone was enjoying him or herself. Songs of Malhar, the raga associated with rain, were wafting in the air along with the rains and the green hills, making it an unforgettable experience.

There were jugglers, musicians and bear trainers showing off their tricks to make some money. The roués were creating a ruckus on the terrace of their rented houses.

It was a wonderful atmosphere, which was well worth seeing. Thousands of people were diving into the tank in the jharna from the top of the hall and swimming out. There was usually a continuous stream of people diving in. Some bodybuilders jumped in holding as many as five people! Thousands slid down the sliding stone.

The flower sellers were sitting in the jharna buildings and making fans from the flowers, called pankhas. There was a huge tumult here, and the noise was deafening. It was difficult to find space to walk.

Soon it was time for the procession. The pankha came out in a ceremonial procession. In the front were the nafiri players. They were seated on wooden *takhts* which had the naubat khana built on them with thin wooden strips carried on the shoulders of attendants.

Behind them similar takhts had the courtesans dancing on it, with musicians accompanying them. Hira, accompanying them, thought they looked like dolls and were the epitome of culture and etiquette. He could see that he wasn't the only one whose heart was gladdened and mind, rejuvenated. There was so much happiness on all the faces around him.

Hira had visited the balakhanas, or salons of courtesans, in Chawri Bazar but of course, these were derawalis, or the highest-ranked courtesans, and only the very rich and influential had access to them. There were no courtesans like them; they were elite women who performed only for the nobility and elite. Their name, derawalis, or tent dwellers, came from the fact that they were mobile and had no fixed address. They were so talented and cultured that they were easily recognized in a crowd of lakhs. Hira knew that they behaved like teachers with the young noble boys, criticizing their smallest faults and polishing their manners. The rich and noble sent their children to them to learn etiquette and culture. The other two categories of courtesans were *chakla-dhari*, who had a fixed location or balakhanas where they performed mostly for middle-class patrons, including performances at weddings and other celebrations in their residences. The third were called *bazari* because of their affiliation with the bazars, and their pursuits were more physical and commercial.

Then came the nobles and princes on their horses. The procession came to a stop under the Baab-e Zafar jharokha.

Hira craned his neck to see if any princess was visible, but they were hidden behind curtains from which they could see but not be seen by the multitude below.

Soon, Hazrat Jahanpanah joined them at Maula Baksh, and they went to Jogmaya Temple.

The pankha went to the dargah on the next day. Hira knew that this was his only chance, and his plan seemed to be working well. By now, he had Rahim and Naseeban eating out of his hands.

The night before, Naseeban had visited her husband, and Hira had positioned himself in such a way that she had to see him as she left.

'Salam. How are you?' Hira had asked.

'Salam, I am well. I hope you are doing good business,' she had replied. She had never met him before but had been hearing praise from her husband and was grateful for Hira's kindness to Rahim.

'How is everything at the mahal? I was among the thousands who managed to stand in the crowd and got a chance to see the blessed face of the Badshah Salamat as he went to the Jogmaya Mandir with the pankha,' asked Hira.

Though normally taciturn, Naseeban was loquacious today after a wonderful evening with her husband. She had never seen him so relaxed or passionate. Little was she to know of the wine that he was being plied with.

'What a grand spectacle it is,' continued Hira. 'I would love to see the procession go into the dargah. This is my first time, and I never knew there could be anything like this where every faith and sect is together. Is there any way I can come near the Jangli Mahal?'

'Arre bhai it is open for all. There is only purdah for a little while when the ladies go out. Otherwise, everyone can join in. Huzur Purnur is so loved by everyone that everyone wants to see his beautiful face and be blessed.'

'I am sorry for sounding so inquisitive but what can I do? It's just so grand that I am extremely curious about everything. Tell me more about the pankha offering at the dargah. Who goes first? Does Badshah Salamat go with the public or with the ladies? There must be so much excitement in the mahal just now,' replied Hira.

Hira's mind was working overtime. He had to find a way to obtain a glimpse of Falak Ara Begum to ascertain that she indeed wore that locket. If she did, his next course of action would be to find out about her daily routine and then contrive a way to obtain or exchange the locket with a similar one.

He had seen that there was a way in which he could try to hide himself and see the ladies going to the dargah. It would be after the procession had come there. While the procession waited outside, the area would be cordoned off so that the Badshah, princes and the ladies could go inside first. The others would go in after them to offer their tributes.

The day dawned and after much merrymaking in the amriyan, or mango orchard, and jharna the people gathered for the procession to go to the dargah in exactly the same way, with the nafiri walas, courtesans and princes following.

Arrangements were made for purdah and the Huzur-e Aqdas and the ladies left the Jangli Mahal and entered the dargah in palanquins. The ladies stepped out at the *dargah* and took the baskets of flowers, the bottles of scents and brocade chadars to be offered on their heads and followed the Badshah and the princes inside.

No woman could go beyond the marble screen, and they all stopped there while their offerings were taken in by the princes and khwajasaras. Falak was carrying a basket of flowers, a bottle of itr and a brocade chadar. She had spent the whole night in restless wakefulness, praying that she could meet Qaiser and somehow be united with him.

Little was she to know that Qaiser had also spent a similar night of longing and prayers.

Qutub Sahib was known to bring about miracles, could he make one happen for them?

Everyone had their prayers to ask, miracles to seek.

Badshah Begum Zeenat Mahal sahiba was praying with extreme concentration that those accursed angrez would declare her son the next heir apparent, or else all her previous efforts and wheeling-dealing would go in vain.

And was it not a good time to meet the Resident bahadur who was also staying in Metcalfe's Dilkusha? She should send a note to him. Here, in all the boisterousness of the fair, no one would notice these meetings.

The next day she sought a meeting with Hakim Ahsanullah Khan, who was the emperor's attendant physician and close to the British powers.

She had met one angrez bahadur in her haveli in Lal Kuan ostensibly on the pretext that she needed medical care, but it had been to push her son's case forward. Perhaps Ehtreramud Daula Hakim Ahsanullah Khan, who had arranged that meeting and carried her messages several times to the Resident bahadur, could do it again.

The Hakim Sahib's haveli was nearby and a message was sent to him to meet her.

While the Badshah Begum's mind was always busy trying to think of ways to secure her son's future as the next badshah, and thus her own, the rest of the ladies were in the mood for merriment.

Alampanah was also in a good mood. He was sitting in the lovely apartment above Baab-e Zafar, engaged in composing a ghazal when the khwajasara came to ask permission for Zohrun Nisa Begum to come and pay her respects to him. Having grown up together, Huzur Purnur was very fond of her and immediately gave orders for purdah and asked the khwajasara to permit her in.

Zohrun Nisa Begum came in and presented her salam. 'May your reign be perpetuated for eternity, a thousand divine blessings on you, may Allah keep you safe,' she said while proffering a silk handkerchief with a gold coin as nazar to the Badshah.

'May Allah keep you safe, my dear cousin. How are you?' he replied.

The room was furnished in a mix of Persian and European styles with masnads and carpets and floor seating, but paintings hanging on walls. The Timurids had always been great connoisseurs of paintings but those were miniatures painted as illustrations of literary texts/ poems or meant to be held in the hand and viewed. In this room, there was a painting above the fireplace, another European addition and oval frames hanging above eye level on the walls.

A conversation on paintings ensued. Zohrun Nisa Begum had a keen eye for paintings and as a young girl had even tried her hand at making portraits of the ladies in the mahal.

The Badshah, with his fine sense of aesthetics, enjoyed all forms of art.

'This portrait of you over the mantel piece is magnificent. I can feel each jewel on your exalted neck. The colours are brilliant, and the painter seems to have a keen eye for detail, and he has captured the mystical simplicity of your eyes and the picture seems to glow with your *nur*.'

Just as Zohrun Nisa Begum was trying to lead the conversation to the real purpose of her visit, an urdabegni came to seek permission to enter.

Huzur Alampanah looked at his cousin and she had no option but to withdraw. She knew that the urdabegni would not disturb them if it wasn't urgent.

The next day they all left for the Qila. On the return journey, they paid their respects at the dargah of Hazrat Roshan Chiragh Delhi, the successor—or *khalifa*—of Sultanji.

Hira had not succeeded in catching a glimpse of Shahzadi Falak Ara as the palanquins that came from inside the mahal were covered and were put down in the courtyard of the dargah where he couldn't enter. But he wasn't disheartened. He had made money in his shop and become close to Rahim and Naseeban. He would find more ways.

Gah hum se khafa wo hain gahe un se khafa hum
Muddat se isi tarah nibhi jati hai baham

Sometimes I am cross with her, at others she with me
Beautifully have we managed to live with each other

—Shefta Mustafa Khan

14

Rumours and Heartsickness

Toote par hon jis parinde ke Ai Saib
Qafas, bagh, ashiyaan isse ek se hi hain dikhte

To the bird with broken wings, Saib
The cage, the garden and the nest make no difference[20]

—Saib Tabrezi

Diwali was here.

Ramlila, the theatrical reproduction of the Ramayana, had already been going on in the city, with *savaris*, carriages on which men playing the roles of Lord Rama and Lakshman and Lady Sita would be seated, would go out in processions through certain portions of the city, culminating on the tenth day in the Bharat Milap in Chandni Chowk. It was a time of great festivity as Hindus and Muslims of the city joined in and embraced each other as brothers, just as Lord Rama had embraced his brother, Bharat.

Mahabali Alampanah replaced the old copper utensils with new ones in the kitchens of all his Hindu officers and nobles, on Dhanteras, the festival before Diwali, when its auspicious to buy metal. A special Lakshmi Puja at the Red Fort was attended by one and all.

For the three days preceding Diwali, called *pahla* diya, *doosra* diya and *teesra* diya, the streets were full of gram roasters selling puffed rice, sugarcane pieces, candy, clay utensils and toys. Beautifully decorated sweetmeat shops full of every kind of sweet enticed the passersby. The lighting in the markets gave the impression that there was daylight even at night.

The Rang Mahal was lit up with diyas for Jashn-e Chiraghan as Diwali was called.

On the day of third diya, which was the day of Diwali, Huzur Purnur held a special durbar and he was weighed in coins which were distributed amongst the poor. As usual the emperor's sadqa was taken out to avert misfortunes.

The Qila inmates enjoyed firecrackers, lit under the supervision of the Mir Atish, which were burst near the walls of the Red Fort. A special Akash Diya was lit with great pomp, placed atop a pole several yards high, supported by sixteen ropes, and fed on several maunds of cotton-seed oil to light up the durbar.

Diwali signalled the advent of winter and respite from the diseases that summers and monsoons brought.

The grounds were prepared for wrestling matches, where the wrestlers trained by Kale Jamnawaale and Gondu Shah would wrestle each other.

The princes were engaged in kite-flying contests held in Salimgarh. There were several types of kites: *kantara, bagla, angaara, mangdaar, zulfondaar, juniyondar, kunde khuli, sar khuli* and *adrangi pari*. As kites soared high in the sky, each kite-flyer sought to cut another's string while protecting his own. As soon as anyone cut the string of an opponent's kite, loud congratulatory cheering could be heard.

Cock-fighting competitions and pigeon flying competitions were taking place not only in the Qila but also the city.

Back in the mahal everyone fell back into their routines. The princesses went back to their studies and life. And as there were few diversions for them, the young girls found their own.

Gul Bano was wont to sleep under a gold canopy wrapped up in costly velvet and silk shawls. Her mother said, 'My darling goes to bed as soon as the lamp is lit.'

Gul Bano yawned, shrug off her hair from her forehead and said, 'How does it affect you if I sleep and waste my time? You are just jealous of me and scold me unnecessarily.' The mother replied, 'Bano, no never. Why would I be jealous of you? Rest as much as you want. May God give you a peaceful sleep every night. I meant that too much sleep is not good for your health. If you sleep early, then wake up early too. However, you don't wake up till mid-morning. All the maidservants are scared to make a noise in case you wake up and throw a tantrum. What kind of sleep is this? You should involve yourself in some work too. You are now grown up by the Grace of God and will soon be married and go to another house. If you continue to behave like this, you will have a tough time adjusting there.'

One morning Zeenat and Zebun, the two most mischievous princesses, decided to tease Gul Bano Begum, who was quite spoilt and pampered and never really gave them much attention.

Gul Bano would normally wake up late in the winter.

She was still sleeping while the other princesses were doing their lessons.

Zeenat and Zebun put soot and oil on her face to tease her. Feeling something wet on her face she woke up, and seeing everyone laughing, asked for a mirror. Mortified, she peevishly retorted, 'Look here, I don't like this kind of jest. What kind of a joke is this? You have blackened my face, now I don't want you to say a single word to me.' The others burst out laughing: 'Oh what fun! We will burn the burnt, and sprinkle salt on the wounds.'

Just then Mirza Davar Baksh, son of Mirza Khizr Sultan, came into the palace. He had started coming seemingly to visit his aunt but everyone knew that Gul Bano was the real magnet. The practice of purdah or segregation amongst the close members of the royal family wasn't strictly followed inside the Qila, thus Mirza Davar and others could come and go to the palace as they pleased. He also burst out laughing but seeing Gul Bano's anger quickly became solicitous.

Falak Ara, sitting quietly in a corner with the Diwan-e Makhfi, wished that Mirza Qaiser had been the son of one of the royal princes instead a salatin. She must think of some other way; the few glimpses that she caught once in a while were making her longing worse.

Perhaps, she could get a taveez or charm. She had overheard the wife of Mirza Mughal instructing her maid to get her a taveez from the Baba who sat in Chitli Qabr. Her fear was the evil eye of the wicked angrez and the conspiring Malika on her son Mirza Qadiruddin Mohammad Bahadur. They had already made her husband renounce his rights as successor in favour of Mirza Jawan Bakht, and she was scared for her son's life. He hadn't been well lately. She, Falak, would have to use emotional blackmail on Mubarak.

Shaking her head, she went back to reading. Frustrated at not being able to contact her prince, Falak had started feeling more and more like the Makhfi or concealed one. But how long would she have to conceal her longings? She needed some inspiration for her miniatures as well. The bathing scene at the *ghat* painting had been completed and she was trying her hand at illustrating, and what better than the Diwan-e Makhfi?

She was flicking through the book when her eyes fell on a drawing. Was this diwan already illustrated?

The verse next to it in Farsi read:

Within my bosom stirs once more tonight
A voice of song. Love, erewhile slumbering,
Intones his mystery, and the flowers of spring
Relive and bloom. Winter, forbear to smite
My heart's late flowers. Listen! From left and right
Through the green boughs the bulbul's note is heard,
And, wing-clipt and imprisoned, my heart's bird
Flutters against his barriers, wild for flight.[21]

But why for only one verse, and that too unfinished? It wasn't even the same paper as the rest of the diwan and seemed to have been painted later.

Her curiosity thoroughly piqued, she examined it closely. Did the sainted princess, Shahzadi Zebun Nisa, draw as well?

The drawing depicted a lush garden, full of flowers. She recognized it as Choti Duniya or Khurd Jahan, from what she could make out. Of course, the garden wasn't as big now, since Mirza Jahangir had built his mansion there. In fact, she lived in a portion of it. But suddenly Falak saw an anomaly in the drawing. A begum was sitting in one corner—or was she crouching? There was something clutched in the figure's hand. In fact, the figure seemed to be digging the ground. Who was this woman in the drawing and why was she digging? When was this painting added to the book? Was it Shahzadi Zebun Nisa herself or did it have something to do with Malika Sultan uz-Zamani Begum sahiba or her husband Mirza Salim? After all, Malika Sultan uz-Zamani Begum sahiba's name was there in the list of people who had issued the diwan.

She had briefly considered painting over this illustration to practice her calligraphy—the poem above could be beautifully rendered in this way. But something about this painting gave her pause. It seemed to contain a puzzle that begged to be unravelled. Could there be a deeper meaning to this, or was she just letting her imagination get the better of her? Perhaps she could ask Sikandar Jahan Begum about the possible identity of the lady and the meaning of the painting.

Unbidden, another verse by Zebun Nisa Begum came to her mind:

I will not lift my veil,—

> *For, if I did, who knows?*
> *The bulbul might forget the rose,*
> *The Brahman worshipper*
> *Adoring Lakshmi's grace*
> *Might turn, forsaking her,*
> *To see my face;*
> *My beauty might prevail.*
> *Think how within the flower*

Hidden as in a bower
Her fragrant soul must be,
And none can look on it;
So me the world can see
Only within the verses I have writ—
I will not lift the veil.[22]

15

What Does Fate Have in Store?

January 1857

Ulti ho gain sab tadbiren kuchh na dawa ne kaam kiya
Dekha is bimari-e dil ne aakhir kaam tamam kiya

All my stratagems have fallen apart, no cure seems to work
My ailing heart has eventually spelt doom for me

—Mir Taqi Mir

The sun had just decided to start illuminating the earth when the Huzur-e Wala, having finished his prayers, came to sit in the jharokha for his daily interaction with his beloved subjects. The milling crowds below saw the Emperor telling his beads. In between, he would answer someone's call and dispense justice. As the sun rose in the sky he came and took his seat on the throne kept in the tasbihkhana. The nobles and princes gathered to pay their respects and presented their kornish. The Badshah Salamat presented a robe of honour to Mir Qasim Ali Khan, darogha of Shahjahanabad.

Qasim Ali khan presented nazar and gave profuse thanks to the Badshah Salamat's magnificent generosity and blessings. The courtiers in the durbar took their leave as the ushers came and

167

respectfully announced the arrival of the best of paths to reach God, the one blessed with the best manners, Shah Ghulam Nasiruddin, alias Miyan Kale sahib. He was Huzur-e Aqdas's spiritual master in *tasawwuf*, and the Emperor respectfully got up to wish him, taking his seat only when his *pir-o-murshid* had taken his seat. The registers of gnosis and truth were opened.

The Sufi saint blessed the Emperor with some prayers for his well-being.

After this blessed meeting, the papers regarding the department of *bakshi* and the papers of Hidayat Ali Khan's case were presented. The Emperor gave his decision and summoned the Ehtreramud Daula Hakim Ahsanullah Khan, and handed over the case to him.

Slowly and steadily over the years, Huzur Jahanpanah had been handing over the administration of the crown lands to the angrez Resident bahadur, despite protests from his sons and a few faithful nobles. The uncharitable grumbled that if the angrez called him King of Delhi instead of Shahenshah-e Hindustan, he deserved it and he should be careful or else he would become just the owner of the Lal Haveli as the Qila was increasingly being referred to as. However, the Badshah, bowed down by age and intrigues, not being able to trust too many, was satisfied with the outcome of the angrezi policies. If only they would increase the monthly allowance.

The Badshah Salamat's glance fell on a young man, dressed carelessly, who was standing in a corner. The young man, Munnu Khan, was a known ne'er-do-well of the city but his mother had been a very pious lady, who had served the Huzur's mother diligently. She was given a silver coin every month as a pension. Huzur Purnur gestured to the urdabegni to ask him what the matter was. The young man bent low and presented his kornish and upon getting permission, said, 'May Huzur Mahabali have a long life, and may I be sacrificed over you.' On being prodded he said, 'My mother had a hen that laid silver eggs but for the past two months the hen has become barren. I have come to the Huzur-e Anwar's durbar for redressal as we have no other means of subsistence.'

Badshah Salamat had recognized him and understood the cryptic message and smiling in amusement, gave orders for him to go to the Khan-e Saman and find out why his mother wasn't receiving the money. It turned out that the *khoja*, or eunuch, who was in charge of delivering his mother's monthly pension of one silver coin was keeping it himself.

It was then time for his disciples to come and gain blessed knowledge from him. The usher came to call Mirza Qaiser, who had been standing in the waiting area near the tasbihkhana, along with Santosh Lal and Zahir Dehlvi. Santosh Lal was studying Persian in the Delhi College from Imam Baksh Sehbai and wanted to learn how to transcribe his favourite verses in khat-e nastaliq.

Backs bent low, all of them presented their kornish and were rewarded with a smile. They presented the nazar of gold coins that they had brought wrapped up in velvet.

Hazrat Badshah was a student of the late Mir Imam Ali Shah sahib, Zahir Dehlvi's grandfather. From him, he had learnt calligraphy in the Naskh script. Zahir's father, Syed Jalaluddin Haider, was also a famous calligrapher, and after his father's death, he was given the position of ustad to the Badshah in calligraphy. Zahir became the Emperor's student in the art of calligraphy and had been a frequent visitor to the Qila-e-Moalla from the age of eight.

'Ama, what have you brought for me today?' asked Huzur Purnur with a smile.

Qaiser and the others settled down on low stools in front of the Emperor, opened their satchels and took out their *qalamdans* with carefully constructed wooden implements or feathered quills that were dipped in ink. The qalamdan had provision for keeping the ink on one side too.

Their eagerness to learn these unique Arabic/Persian styles such as Kufi, Naskh and Nastaliq for transcribing Quranic verses and Persian poetry was something that the Emperor looked forward too.

'Alampanah, I have tried to transcribe the Surah al-Isra,' said Zahir, referring to the particular verses from the Holy Quran while taking out his work.

'My Lord, lead me in through an entry of truth, and lead me out through an exit of truth,' read the Emperor. 'This is excellent Miyan Zahir. I like the way you have shaped it like a boat. Indeed, we have to traverse this world holding on to truth and exit it with the flag of truth flying high.'

'Jahanpanah, I have written a verse from Hafez for your perusal,' said Santosh Lal.

On a turquoise blue surface, he had written in illuminated Nastaliq characters the following words of the great Persian poet Hafez Shirazi:

> *The realm of love is in higher state than reason*
> *The one who is ready to sacrifice his life, can reach the*
> *threshold.*[23]

—Hafez

'Subhan Allah, Santosh Miyan, this is excellent progress and such beautiful words to start the day with. Indeed, when one loses their self in *ishq-e haqeeqi* or love of the divine, they achieve true happiness and peace,' praised the Sufi Badshah. 'Sacrifice is the essence to those who want to tread the spiritual path. What have you brought Qaiser?'

Mirza Qaiser shyly opened his notebook to show a beautifully transcribed verse from Mevlana Rumi. He had shaded the paper like an oval mirror in pale red and gold and had transcribed the master's words:

> *How do you ever expect*
> *for your heart to become polished like a mirror*
> *without putting up*
> *with the pain*
> *of polish?*[24]

'Alhamdulillah, Miyan Qaiser! Indeed, you have the heart of a student. No one can ever hope to find the path to the divine or reach the stage of *ishq-e haqeeqi* without going through extreme and intense pain. I like the pale red, denoting blood, that you have used. I have spent many a sleepless night praying, meditating, reading and hoping to find that love in my heart.'

The three students had got up when they were praised and offered their salutations, flushed with the generous praise.

'Ama, have you also done the *siyah mashq*? Calligraphy is concealed in the teaching method of the master; its essence is in its frequent repetition, and it exists to serve Islam,' continued the Emperor. 'This saying of Hazrat Ali Abi Talib *raziallahu anhu*, who is traditionally regarded as the first master calligrapher of Islam, lies at the heart of *siyah mashq*, or calligraphic exercise pages.[25] It is very important and even at my age, I practise it daily. It strengthens the hand and teaches us discipline and patience, which are the hallmarks of a good calligrapher. After all, we transcribe the word of God and His chosen creatures and must do full justice to it.'

Just then, the urdabegni came to ask permission for the entry of Mirza Mughal.

The three young men got up respectfully and having made their salutations, withdrew from the royal presence.

It was a glorious day and the three friends decided to walk into the Bagh-e Hayat Baksh and soak in the sun. The sound of the nahr-e bahisht tumbling down from the two exquisite marble pavilions, Sawan and Bhadon, and the gushing silver fountains in the channels relaxed their minds as they sat down to discuss the day's lessons.

Santosh Lal, who had been very diligent said, 'I was reading that Sultan Ali, the famous Persian calligrapher advocates that we should be very patient when writing. He says that each letter of the alphabet warrants careful study: their shape, their ascent and descent, all must be observed very diligently. Carelessness can lead to imperfections.'

'Speaking of ascent and descent, have you noticed that our beloved Alampanah has started looking increasingly worried by the ascent of the British star over Hindustan?' asked Zoravar Singh, who had joined the friends. He had been hearing discussions of a rifle which the company soldiers were opposed to, in his father's mansion. 'The practice of nazar given to the emperor has already been stopped, and now the British sahibs can sit down in the durbar as if, God forbid, on terms of equality. There are rumours flying thick in the markets that a new rifle is being introduced which may corrupt the faiths of the soldiers, be they Muslim or Hindu. Here we are continuing with our normal activities as if there is nothing untoward in the air, but my heart is sick with worry.'

'Arre, where did you hear all this? I am sure everything is well. You worry too much. Which reminds me that I have to go for a mushaira tonight to Raja Ajit Singh's haveli,' said Zahir. 'I am reciting my ghazal there and will go and transcribe it. Are any of you interested, because the Raja Sahib has kindly asked me to bring my guests.'

All the friends were interested and agreed.

All feelings of unease were temporarily forgotten.

Raja Ajit Singh was the uncle of the present Raja of Patiala who had lost his heart to Delhi, where he came as a young man, and stayed on.

As befit the uncle of the Raja of Patiala, he had a rich *jagir* and he would spend lavishly, living like a king. Whenever money would come in from his lands, he would redo everything in his home and change the decoration of his house; chandeliers, carriage, clothes and so on would all be bought anew.

If he attended any gathering where money was being showered on poets and artistes, he would give everything he had away and would say, 'I am a mendicant,' and sleep on a sackcloth!

If his money was over, he would take loans and then his nephew would send money to pay them off.

His eccentric ways were well-known, as well as his generous and informed praise of poets. He was particularly fond of Zahir Dehlvi.

The Raja Sahib was extremely fond of two things: poetry and the flute. Dancers and singers were always present in his court, all year round.

One year, he gifted a female elephant, along with her gold jewellery and silver howdah, and a thousand rupees for her food, to poet Momin Khan sahib, and some elephant jewellery to poet Dagh sahib.

Mirza Qaiser enjoyed the evening of poetry and the Raja's hospitality, but his heart really wasn't in the verses. The longing to meet Falak Ara just once and talk to her was engulfing his being. He felt like a flame burning in it, but there seemed to be no solution to it. How could he contrive such a meeting?

On top of it all the conversation with Zoravar Singh was haunting him. Zoravar would surely know what was going on as his father was pretty close to the sahib bahadurs.

Qahr hai maut hai qaza hai ishq
Sach to yun hai buri bala hai ishq

Love is divine wrath, it is death, it is fate
If truth be told, love is a calamitous fate.

—Momin Khan Momin

Winters also brought with them the month of Jamad-us Sani, in which Huzur Purnur had attained the blessed throne of the Timurids. It was a glorious occasion and called for a week-long celebration. There wasn't time to be morose or melancholy. Everyone joined in.

Preparations were in full swing and the mahal was abuzz with excitement as clothes were stitched. The mahal was also being readied for the guests who would come. It was decked like a bride.

'Dadijan, tell us about the *ratjaga*. I love that ceremony,' said Zeenat nestling down next to her great aunt.

Rashid Jahan took a puff off her huqqah, put a cone of paan in her mouth, checked to see that the spittoon was nearby and started. Talking of customs that showcased the glories of the Timurids gave her great pleasure.

'The night before the jashn was called ratjaga, or staying awake the whole night, and the Malika would soak mung dal to make fried dumplings.'

'Phuppijan, though I have attended many of these jashns in the past few years I have never understood why *baras* signal the start. What is the reason for this tradition?' asked a curious Falak Ara.

'Beti, that's a good question and something I had also asked my sainted mother. She told me that ever since Akbar Badshah married our sainted ancestress, Mariyam uz-Zamani, the Rajput princess of Amber, syncretic traditions have been followed in our families and empire. Akbar Badshah paid a lot of attention to keeping everyone in the empire happy, and we adopted and assimilated many customs from different parts of Hindustan. Local customs were given more importance than any of those that Babur Badshah's people may have brought with them from Central Asia. I don't know when this custom started but in my living memory the soaking of mung dal was considered an auspicious omen at night to start the festivities.'

'Please tell us more about the Jashn-e Tajposhi,' said Falak.

'Oh, I forgot to tell you that all this is done in the Rang Mahal. First, the ladies will enter in a small procession preceded by female guards and attendants carrying torches, candelabras and lamps for illumination, to the singing of female musicians. The Malika will lead and princesses, noblewomen and eunuchs will all follow the Empress as per their rank and status. The Malika will soak seven handfuls of the mung dal in a huge pot, kept in the centre of the Rang Mahal. Mark you, the number seven is very important and auspicious for Muslims, and this is how we adopted and assimilated local customs. The kitchen attendants will then soak the rest of the dal. All the women present there, will offer their salutation and congratulations to the Empress and drum rolls and trumpets will be sounded.

'At midnight, the dal was soft enough to be ground and is brought back to the mahal. Kadhais will be kept on stoves, ready for the *dal* to be fried and as soon as the oil is just the right temperature for frying, and the Malika will begin shaping seven *baras* in her palm and the message will be sent to the Badshah. The entry of the Badshah into the mahal is a joyous occasion and it would be to drum rolls, accompanied by music and dancing. He will arrive on his hawadar and get down to a flurry of salutations from all the ladies present and sit down on the shahnasheen near the fire. Then he will ceremoniously put these seven baras into the oil.

All the ladies assembled there will once again present their salutations and congratulations to the Emperor. The musicians will start playing the drums and *shehnai* to mark the joyous occasion. The Jashn-e-Tajposhi is officially inaugurated.'

Zohrun Nisa Begum, who had been listening added, 'You will see all this in a few days. Remember, Falak beti, we are the people of Hindustan; we are part of this *mitti*, this earth; our ancestors are buried here, and we have to ensure that no one's feelings are ever hurt.'

The night of the ratjaga arrived. All the women, be they queens, princesses or attendants, were dressed in their best.

To Zeenat and Zebun, they looked like fairies flitting around in every colour under the sun.

Everyone had a grand time.

The next day, Zill-e Ilahi held a durbar in the Diwan-e Khas.

The nobles began to arrive. Each one had to dismount at the naqqarkhana as beyond that only the emperor could enter on a mount.

There are various *adabgahs* or stations for the audience to gather and make their salutations before they can reach the throne.

At the gate of the Diwan-e Khas was a red broadcloth curtain, the Lal Purdah. The royal infantrymen, foot soldiers, bodyguards, soldiers and *qullar* stood with red staves in their hands. No stranger could enter here, if they dared, they were removed and punished.

The Diwan-e Khas was beautifully carpeted and curtained, bedecked like a bride waiting for the bridegroom. The 'wedding party' had arrived and a messenger went running to the *deorhi* to inform the Badshah Salamat's attendants that all was in readiness.

The jasolini called out, 'Attention!' The herald and mace-bearer replied, 'God save the king.' When the Alampanah Badshah appeared, the two called out, 'In the name of Allah, the most merciful and beneficent, may the grace and mercy of Allah and his Prophet be on the Emperor. May the Emperor stay safe, and all his friends prosper, his enemies be destroyed and his troubles vanish forever.'

He descended from his hawadar after it was placed beside the Takht-e Taaos, or Peacock Throne. He read two units of the namaz of thanksgiving and then, raising his hands in prayer, he mounted the steps to take his place on the Takht-e Taoos.

The Takht-e Taoos was glittering and waiting for Badshah Salamat. It had three attractive arches on all sides with a wooden baluster running around the throne and a bolster at the back. There were three steps in front of it. It had a vaulted, Bengali-style dome-shaped canopy with golden tassels. On top of it were two peacocks with pearl strings in their beaks.

Of course, everyone knew that the original Takht-e Taoos, called Takht-e Murassa, or Jewelled Throne, commissioned by Shah Jahan Badshah, had been taken away by Nadir Shah and lost to everyone in the raid on his camp when he was killed in Persia. This was just a replacement and not a patch on the original. But it reflected the fate of the badshah who graced the throne; none of them were a patch on the grandeur of Shah Jahan Badshah either.

This hall had been built by the master architects Ustad Ahmed and Ustad Hamid as a piece of paradise, and perhaps that is why the famous Persian couplet was inscribed here:

Agar firdaus bar ru-ye zamin ast
Hamin ast-o hamin ast-o hamin ast

If there is Paradise on earth
It is this, it is this, it is this

With the flowing nahr-e bahisht, the gilded columns, the decorated ceiling and the magnificence of the throne and the glory of its occupant, the hall did seem like paradise to the two young girls hidden behind the wall.

Zeenat and Zebunnisa had taken permission along with all the other ladies from the Malika to peep onto the durbar from the two windows behind the wall. The khwajasaras and jasolinis were cajoled to bring reports, for those who could not find a place.

But the ladies need not have despaired, for a Meena Bazar was arranged for them in front of the Dilli Darwaza. As soon as news came that a special bazaar was arranged for them to celebrate, a few hearts started beating faster. These bazaars were started for women of royalty and nobility by Badshah Humayun and developed by Badshah Akbar and were a regular feature on special occasions. Under Badshah Humayun, these bazaars were arranged on boats on festival days. Only the Badshah himself and princes of the royal blood could attend. Rajput ladies were also invited. Now the regularity of the grand bazars had been reduced though bazars on a small scale were held every few months.

It was a great source of entertainment for the ladies who were otherwise confined, and like the *bagh ka jharokha,* it allowed them to not only dress up but also buy items themselves.

The wives of nobles and prominent city traders would put up beautiful stalls where they sold exotic items such as jewellery, cloth, brocades, sumptuously embroidered silk of the latest fashion, turbans elegantly worked on cloth of gold, fine muslin worn by women of quality, perfumes, unguents, and other articles of high price. And fruits and flowers were sold too.

As soon as the news reached Falak Ara, she started dreaming that her poet-soldier would be there too. She had heard his house was close to the Dilli Darwaza. She sent a frantic summons to Mubarak, for she had to have a new dress made. Saeedan and Naseeban both helped to stitch an angiya of maroon brocade fastened in front with a pearl clasp. A silk peshvaz of light yellow, which was the colour declared for the bazar, and a yellow kamdani dupatta embellished with gota and kinari were readied. Mubarak had managed to get an extra bolt of brocade from Naseeban, and the pajama and angiya were made of the same brocade.

Simple floral jewellery decorated their darling. Every lady was similarly dressed as per their status. Falak extracted a promise form Mubarak that she would help her meet Qaiser if he was there.

When Zoravar heard of the fair, he asked his mother to put up a stall of Rajasthani kundan jewellery so that he and Qaiser could attend. He had been seeing his friend's longing for the princess and his inability to do anything about it. He knew that his morally upright, principled friend would never adopt any stratagem to meet Shahzadi Falak and so it was up to him to arrange some meeting, even if fleeting. Chand Kunwarji, his mother and Qaiser's aunt, who was visiting Shahjahanabad, readily agreed.

The evening of the bazaar dawned, and the ladies left via the Rang Mahal for the bazaar chaperoned by the attendants, nursemaids and maidservants. The mughlanis and the slave girls walked alongside the ladies, holding parasols over their heads and loudly praising their beauty. The annas were warning their ladies of sorcerers, black magic and the evil eye, telling them to cover themselves with a white chador, to stay safe from evil spirits that may be hovering around, while they walked through the vaulted corridors of the palace that lead to the bazar.

Shops selling betel leaves, vegetables, dry fruits and kebabs were already doing brisk business, with the halwai's young sons selling puri, kachori and mithai. Much giggling and bargaining was going on in the shops selling jewellery. Hariyali was sitting on the floor in one corner with her basket of bangles, observing everything with a hawk's eye, crooning to herself.

Gulab Jan was walking with Shahzadi Zebunnisa with a confident swagger, for she knew there were many here whom she could charm and move upwards from Miyan Nabbu's patronage.

'Look at that witch Gulab Jan, Mubarak,' muttered a jealous Saeedan. 'Prancing around in the bazaar. May the curse of the Gods be on all these strumpets, witches, whores—they have lost their sense of decency and are on the lookout for patrons. They just can't sit still! Don't I know that they crawl into every nook and cranny of the city!'

'Ssh, Saeedan. Calm down,' said Mubarak.

Nudging Falak she said, 'Shahzadi bibi, see that is Chand Kunwarji, a relative of Mirza Qaiser and mother of his friend Zoravar Singh. Let us go and see her shop.'

With a shy smile and lowered head, Falak went to the stall and presented her salam. Mubarak introduced them.

'May you always be happy, my precious daughter,' said Chand Kunwarji who had been introduced to the love story and was part of the conspiracy to make Falak and Qaiser meet.

'Let me see what I have for you,' and took out a pair of kundan chand-baliyan. Shaped like the moon they had pearls hanging from the lower part which tinkled as they moved.

'Wear these and see if you like them. I used to love them as a young girl.'

While Falak was trying them on, she heard laughter and gentle ribbing form the stall next to it. Gul Bano and Dawar Baksh were indulging in an innocent flirtation, with the prince teasing her about her habit of lying in bed till late.

Gul Bano, embarrassed and unable to take out her anger on the prince called out to her attendant.

'Zamarrud, get me some andrasa immediately. I am feeling hungry.' Then smiling sweetly at Dawar, she asked him to sit with her on the bench decorated with flowers that was placed there for the ladies to rest.

Zamarrud came running, 'Shahzadi there is no one selling andrasa today. I have brought you some kachoris instead.'

'What have you brought? You can stuff your face with this. The first to eat and the last to do any work!'

'Don't be angry, Gul,' cajoled Dawar. 'The frown will crease your pretty face. Andrasa is only made in monsoons, what can poor Zamarrud do?'

Meanwhile, the other princes had also entered and there was much bargaining going on in every shop, with the princesses watching and begums discreetly joining in the fun.

Falak, heedless of all other activities around her, kept standing at Chand Kunwarji's stall waiting for Qaiser to appear. She had examined each piece of jewellery twice under Chand Kunwar's amused gaze when she felt a frisson of excitement pulse through her body. Surely, he was here.

Sure enough she heard the rich baritone say, 'Tasleem Mumanijan. I hope and pray you are well. How is Mamujan?'

'Bhagwan *ka shukr hai*, beta, we are well. How is Aftab Dulha bhai? Your uncle had met him the other day,' she replied.

'Allah *ka shukr* Mumanijan, we are both well,' replied Qaiser.

Zoravar who had managed to come in by virtue of his relationship to Qaiser, had seen Falak in the corner trying to make herself as invisible as possible while drinking in the sight of Qaiser, and turned in such a way that Qaiser was forced to face her, saying, 'Maa-saa, hope you are doing good business. Qaiser and I are both looking for a sarpech and bazubands. Did you bring any? And what a pretty chand-baliyan. I remember you wearing them when I was a boy!'

Falak dropped the chand-baliyan in her hand in utter confusion. She had not bargained for the forthrightness of Zoravar. She had hoped to just gaze at her prince.

'You have a sharp memory, my son. Yes, I love them and wore them often when I was younger, and now I think they have found their new owner. Shahzadi, these are my gift to you for they frame your face. The moon is meant to adorn the sky.'

'I can't take such expensive balis for free, Thakurain sahiba, please tell me their price. I will gladly pay. That is if you really want to part with something that has such precious memories for you,' replied the blushing Falak.

'No, I insist they are yours. You can't refuse me. I am elder than you and related to you through the marriage of my sister-in-law to Huzur Alampanah's cousin Mirza Aftab.'

Mubarak who had been standing quietly till then, bent low to present her salam and said, 'Shahzadi, take them and present a kornish to Thakurain sahiba. It is being given with a lot of love.'

Shyly, Falak took the embroidered pouch in which the velvet case with the balis was kept in.

Throughout, she had been peeping at Qaiser who had remained silent as soon as he realized her presence.

He was cursing himself for feeling so tongue-tied, but he had not grown up around women and had no idea of how to say anything to her, though his whole body was burning in longing and anguish at separation.

Finally, he managed to say, 'Mumanijan, these must have looked so pretty on you. They are exquisite and will add to the beauty of its already beautiful wearer.'

Zoravar smiled at his friend's awkward compliment, but Falak's heart was about to burst.

Falak saw Zebun and Zeenat running towards the stall and knew that she was about to be mercilessly teased, and catching hold of Mubarak's hand, tugged her away towards a group of young children. Once amid the children, she discreetly turned to see that Qaiser was still standing at the shop. Immediately, she regretted pulling away from there so impulsively. *What do I do about my traitorous heart,* she thought. *It refuses to stay calm so that I can stay longer with my Prince. All those hours of longing and now I couldn't even be with him for more than a few minutes.* What did the teasing of her cousins matter in the face of fulfilling her longing to be around him? But it was done, she could not undo it—and she saw him walking away with his friend and cursed herself, praying for another meeting soon.

Dusk was approaching and it was time to enjoy the moonlit evening, brightened by candelabras and flambeaux. The nahr-e bahisht flowing in the area had diyas scented with camphor floating in them, creating a fairylike atmosphere. The group of young children under the supervision of their nursemaids was having fun in the nahr, splashing each other. A few splashes of water landed on Falak's heated face, though there was no respite from the burning desires that the glimpse of Qaiser had caused. Someone was playing the *dholki*, while someone else was singing. Falak went and joined her great aunts, who had spread out the chaupar board and watched them while keeping an eye out for her poet-soldier.

Fortunately for her, Zeenat and Zebun had not seen Qaiser, and she was spared from their teasing and could spend her time daydreaming and longing.

The next seven days passed off in changing and admiring clothes and jewellery and looking after all the guests. Trays of food called *toras* were distributed to everyone in the Qila and nobles in the city and the clamour of clanging pots and pans added to the general noise in the Qila.

But behind all this was an uncomfortable disquiet in the hearts of quite a few and for various reasons.

In the city, Hira wondered at the extravagances of an empire tottering on its legs and wondered what was being celebrated.

The adage which his father used often, came to his mind: *the husband's false sense of grandeur is belied by the wife's poverty-stricken state*.

Now if only he could find a way to meet Falak Ara, at least his fortunes could change.

Ai sanam wasl ki tadbiron se kya hota hai
Wahi hota hai jo manzur-e-Khuda hota hai

My beloved, it matters not what arrangements we make for our union
Only what God wills can come to pass.

—Mirza Raza Barq

16

The Empress Is Sick

Zaahiran maut hai qaza hai ishq
Par haqiqat mein jaan-fazaan hai ishq

Overtly, love is death and devastation
In reality, love is life-giving.

—Abdul Ghafoor Nassakh

The weather was distinctly chilly for February. Everyone in the palace talked of the cold wave. Small *angethis* with coal fires were kept inside the rooms for warmth in the evenings. During the day, the ladies sat in the gardens, enjoying the hot sun. The princes went out for shikar and enjoyed barbecues in the forests.

The Emperor was sleeping in the Shah Burj these days and seemed to be engrossed in some weighty matters of metre and verse. Daaran bai was coming almost every evening to entertain him and make his heart lighter. She would compose his latest ghazal and sing it on the spot. Her eyes and ears were so keen that she could even suggest minor tweaking in the verses to better suit the raga.

A particular ghazal that the Emperor was composing had kept him occupied for over a fortnight now. Mirza Naushah had also come to help with it.

Though he came for Jharokha Darshan every dawn, Huzur Alampanah had not visited Zeenat Mahal in her mansion in the city, where she often stayed, or in Imtiaz Mahal in the palace.

Badshah Begum Zeenat Mahal had begun wondering if perchance he was unhappy with her. Had he come to know about her meetings with the sahib bahadurs? So much time being spent with Daaran bai, was he tired of her? She was much younger than him and knew her charms were dependent on youth. Which man and that too a ruler had ever been faithful to one woman? With so many sons elder to her son, Jawan Bakht, all she could do was try to manoeuvre her son as his successor. She knew people saw her as a scheming woman but was she the only one who was using strategy to ensure her son's succession? Why was a man's plan called strategy and she was a schemer? Her mind was working overtime.

Huzur Alampanah had just finished Jharokha Darshan and was planning to return to the Shah Burj when Begum Zeenat Mahal's khwajasara came into his presence, and bending low, presented his salutations.

'Ama, Agha Jan is everything, all right? How is the Malika? Please convey my greetings to her,' said the Emperor.

'May I be protected by your Majesty's extreme generosity towards your lowly servants against any trespasses. The fair one, the mistress of hearts, my mistress is not well. She has woken up with a fever. I was just going to Hakim Ahsanullah sahib to get some medicine when I was blessed to see your shining visage. Now, that your Majesty's sanctified gaze has fallen on this lowly man, I know my mission will be successful,' said Agha Jan.

'What? The Malika is unwell? Why wasn't I told earlier?' Saying so, the Emperor ordered the female bearers of his hawadar to head towards Imtiaz Mahal. The qalmaaqni, jasolini and the *urdabegni* were galvanized into action. Huzur Jahanpanah had deigned to grace the haram after an unusually long interval and things had to be just right.

With Agha Jan in attendance, the ushers calling everyone to attention and to stop all activity at once, the royal cavalcade reached Imtiaz Mahal.

The haram was once again ringing with the sound of, 'Attention! Greetings, present your salutations to the Refuge of the World, long live the Emperor, the Refuge of the Universe!'

Begum Zeenat Mahal was lying on her silver canopied bed, wrapped up in expensive Kashmiri shawls, with her attendants around her.

As soon as the Badshah's visit was announced by the usher, she sat up against the bolsters and called out to one of the attendants to quickly dress her hair and settle her dupatta becomingly around her. Once done, she sank back into her pillows. Her gem-studded shoes were kept on the other side of the bed so that the Emperor's seat could be set.

The qalmaaqni and jasolinis had already taken out the Emperor's shahnasheen and set it in front of her bed. They trusted Agha Jan's ability to ensure that Badshah Salamat paid a visit to their mistress.

The Huzur Jahanpanah's sedan chair was put down and he was helped to sit down on the royal seat. He was wearing a *Mughliya chargoshia Taj*, or four-cornered cloth crown with a sarpech, jewels and feathers.

Begum Zeenat Mahal struggled to stand up to present her kornish, but Huzur-e Wala put his hands on her hands and said softly, 'Kornish muaf,' thereby releasing her from an obligation to do the formal salutation. He then chose his words carefully, since it was considered inauspicious to directly allude to someone's ill health. He continued, 'Don't tire yourself out. Ama, I heard that your enemies aren't well, Begum sahiba.'

'Now that your sanctified gaze has fallen on your slave girl, I am sure I will recover in no time at all,' said the Empress in a feeble but very melodious voice.

'Uff, your voice is so feeble, you are really unwell. Why wasn't Hakim Ahsanullah Khan called earlier?' He asked while putting his palm on her forehead.

'I know I am looking my worst and not worthy of your glance,' said Zeenat Mahal Begum in a woebegone voice. 'This slave girl has lost her charms.'

'Wallah! What nonsense is this?' said the Badshah Salamat, going on to quote a newly composed ghazal of his:

shamshir-e-barhana mang ghazab baalon ki mahak phir waisi hi
jude ki gundhawat qahr-e-Khuda baalon ki mahak phir waisi hi

Her hair's parting is a naked sword, the fragrance of her curls divine
Her coiffure enchants, the fragrance of her hair is captured in time

Happy to have his full attention after a long time, the Malika's cheeks were tinged with rose, her eyes sparkling.

She replied:

nashsha-e-ishq le uda hai mujhe
ab maze mein udaa raha kuchh hun

The intoxication of love has given me flight,
In bliss, I let my imagination fly somewhat[26]

'Subhanallah, my beloved Malika replies to me in my own verse!' said a smiling Huzur Badshah Salamat.

samjhe vo apna khaaksar mujhe
khaak-e-raah hun ki khaak-e-paa kuchh hun

Let them think me their humble servant,
I am the dust of the road, of the feet—somewhat,'[27]

quickly replied the now happy Empress.

A jade huqqah belonging to his sainted ancestor, Jahangir Badshah, had been set up for the Badshah and he was content to sit for a while and smoke it.

Agha Jan was standing behind him with the morchal.

By now news of the Malika being unwell and Huzur Badshah Salamat visiting her had spread throughout the palace and the Fort.

There was at least some new excitement in the palace. The ladies changed into new dresses and sought permission to visit. Seeing Huzur-e Anwar present, after presenting nazar, the ladies sat down in the palace as per their status. The palace was full of invocations to the munificence of Allah: Yaa Allah Shafi, Ya Allah Kaafi!'

Two *qalmaqani* asked for permission to enter. They were followed by the *muhri*, who was responsible for carefully sealing the food served to the Badshah Salamat in the kitchen under the darogha's strict supervision. The muhri was carrying a silver tray covered by a brocade tray cloth. The tray was set down in front of the Emperor and the seals on two silver bottles filled with sherbet and khameera syrup were broken. The sherbet was then poured into a celadon cup and offered to the Emperor. It was popularly believed that celadon would crack if it came into contact with poison, and so it was liberally used as a medium in which food or drink was served to the royal family. The khameera syrup—which was prepared daily as per Hakim Ahsanullah Khan's prescription for the Emperor—was also poured into a celadon cup and the Badshah presented it with his own hands to his favourite Empress, saying, 'Hakim Ahsanullah Khan has healing hands. If God wills, you will feel better soon.'

Indeed! The potion was magical, for the Empress was on her feet in a few minutes and fussing around Huzur Jahanpanah.

Pleased to see her swift recovery, Badshah Salamat had left with a promise to come back soon.

Hakim Ahsanullah Khan was being brought into the palace and arrangements for purdah had to be made. The jasolinis and attendants all stood in a chain from the deorhi of the khwaabgah till Imtiaz Mahal while the Hakim sahib was guided inside. A cloth covered his face, as was usual in the palace for men not related to the ladies inside. A purdah screen was set up in front of the Empress' bed and Hakim Sahib came, and bending low, presented his salutations. He sat down and took the cloth off his face. Through a small space in the screen, the Empress extended her hand. Hakim Ahsanullah Khan felt her pulse and diagnosed her and gave instructions for medicine to be prepared immediately so that he could administer the first dose himself.

Saying, 'May I be sacrificed over you, my Malika. You will be fine within an hour,' he examined the beautiful golden cup in which the medicine was brought and smiled with satisfaction when he heard her drinking it behind the screen.

That done, he took his leave.

Thereafter, the Malika was all smiles and pouts and turned her attention to all the ladies who were coming to pay her a visit. It was as if locks on the lips of the ladies had been opened. Soon everyone was chattering, talking, smiling.

The wives of Raja Nahar Singh of Ballabhgarh and Nawab Moti Begum sahiba, widow of Mirza Mohammad Jamshed Bakht, came to enquire about the Malika's health. Huqqahs with individual mouthpieces were presented to them. Giloris of paan were put in front of them.

Conversation was flowing when suddenly it was announced that Mrs Gardner's daughter-in-law was seeking permission to visit her majesty along with some other British ladies.

William Linnæus Gardner had married Nawab Mah Manzil ul-Nisa, the daughter of the Nawab of Cambay, who was later adopted by Emperor Akbar Shah II. They had two sons and a daughter. The eldest was Alan Hyde Gardner; his younger daughter married a Mughal prince named Mirza Anjum Shukoh Bahadur. The younger son, James Valentine Gardner, was married to Malika-i Qamar Sharah Banu Begum, the granddaughter of Mughal Emperor Shah Alam II, daughter of Shahzada Mirza Muhammad Suleiman Shukoh Bahadur and one of the widows of Mirza Salim Shah Bahadur.

After her marriage to Gardner, Malika-i Qamar Sharah Banu Begum, though she continued to dress in the Mughal style, had learnt English manners and was quite at ease with the British. She

had come to Delhi from Khasganj to visit her daughter by Mirza
Salim Bahadur, Zeenatun Nisa Begum sahiba. This time she had
decided to visit the Lal Qila and brought angrez ladies with her.

Memories of a visit by Mrs Fanny Parkes, another angrez lady,
to meet Emperor Shah Alam Sani's mother, were fresh. Sergeant
Fleming's wife often visited the Nawab Malika, but the rest of the
family was rarely present in these meetings, which would often
take place in Lal Kuan in the Zeenat Mahal. Everyone was eagerly
awaiting the visitors.

Salutations over, the three ladies presented the customary nazar
to the Empress and settled down on the plush settees leaning against
velvet bolsters and cushions as huqqahs with crystal bases and silver
pechwan and crystal muhmals.

While Malika-i Qamar Sharah Banu Begum was enquiring
about the health of the Empress, the two angrez ladies were
devouring the scene with their eyes. They had heard a lot about
the royal zenana, and how the women here were almost slaves
who needed to keep the old Badshah happy! However, to their
surprise, the women seemed quite happy. Their clothes seemed
quite ornate, though uncomfortable. The Empress herself was
wearing a pair of yellow brocade wide-legged pajamas and a gold
embroidered angiya, with a silk jama on top of it. Her turquoise
dupatta reflected the blue edging on the pajamas. It was heavily
embellished with gota, kinari of gold and silver. Pearls were sewn
on to the embroidered roses giving it a shimmering effect. It
looked beautiful and exotic but how comfortable was it?

One of the ladies decided to have a go at the huqqah, and taking
the pechwan into her well-manicured hands, took a puff. It seemed
very like the pipe that the men smoked, and she decided to get one
for herself. It was fun to see the water bubbling in the crystal base.

Little did she know that while she was busy judging the women
around her, the courtesy was being returned. A group of young girls,
Falak Ara among them, was sitting in one corner talking quietly
amongst themselves. Some of them had never seen an angrez lady

so closely and her frock seemed distinctly uncomfortable to them: it
had so much of gather, was too long and was so tight on the waist,
and where were the pajamas?

The sight of the lady's manicured hands catching the pechwan
led to much merriment amongst the younger girls. Why were her
nails so long? They had been taught to cut their nails every month
as per *shariah*.

'Doesn't food get caught in her nails?' asked Zeenat.

'Shh . . . she will hear you. We have to respect our guests,' said
Falak softly but firmly. 'They eat with spoons.'

The ever naughty and quick-witted Zeenat made an immediate
comeback. 'Do they clean their bottoms and do *aab-e dast*, with
spoons too?' referring to the cleaning after relieving themselves.

All the girls burst out in laughter and everyone's eyes turned
towards them.

'Sshh,' hissed Falak.

Naseeban, who had also come, saw Falak sitting there laughing
and remembered that Hira had asked her to check if she wore any
unusual locket that he had heard she inherited from her mother. Yes,
indeed she did. Oh! What a lovely girl she was. Even in that group of
young girls, she looked luminous.

By now the singers had come in and the *mirasans* followed. The
room was full of congratulatory songs on the occasion of the Empress
having regained her health.

Then came the requests from the gathered ladies. They were
requests for *khayal*, *thumri* and *tappa*.[28]

These mirasans had been trained by ustads. They had learnt
thumri from Sada Rang, Phool Rang and Khush Rang; their
master in the art of khayal and qawwali was Tanras Khan. Tanras
Khan was a favourite of the Badshah, who had given him this title
because of the harmonies he could sing with fluid ease. His real
name was Meer Qutub Baksh. He was a scion of the legendary
qawwal bachhe trained by Hazrat Amir Khusrau in the art of
qawwali singing.

This was before Tanras Khan was exiled from the fort by the Badshah for committing the cardinal sin of falling in love with Pyari bai and meeting her secretly. What a scandal that was!

Soon exclamations of praise were floating in the palace: a chorus of '*afreen*', 'subhanallah' and 'waah'. The ladies were sending their requests along with money to be showered on the singers.

Nawab Alia Sultan Begum sahiba, wife of Mirza Nili, the son of Shah Alam Sani Badshah, had come over from her apartment near the Asad Burj. A maid was carrying a box and seated next to her. At a gesture from her, she opened the wooden box to reveal a compartment full of gold coins. Naseeban was awestruck. She had much to tell her husband and now close friend Hira, tonight.

Meanwhile, a group of ladies who had come from the city, sitting next to the princesses, were holding forth on the effects of spirits.

'May I be ransomed over the Malika, but I heard from Roshni, the Malika's personal attendant, that just yesterday she went out in the Mehtab Bagh, after her bath in the evening. She was wearing a white dupatta, her hair was wet and open, and she had freshly strung *mogra* and *chameli gajras* in her curly tresses and on her wrists. She had hoped to find Huzur Jahanpanah but instead, I think she caught the fancy of a *jinn mamu*. All of us know that the spirits especially the jinn mamus like beautiful ladies. I always tell my daughters and daughters-in-law not to go out in the evenings with open hair,' said Meher Afroz Begum. Her husband was a courtier and Nawab from Farrukhnagar.

'Well, she will be sending Roshni to get some charms and amulets from Hazrat Deen Ali Shah Qalandar, the famous and respected saint, who lives in Farrashkhana,' said Birjis Zamani Begum, a Timurid princess living in Matia Mahal.

'The Malika is a great believer in black magic, I have heard. Hazrat Deen sahib isn't the only one she patronizes, there is this *amil* that she patronizes whenever it seems she needs some black magic done against one of her enemies or some incantation performed to increase

Hazrat Bahadur Shah's love for her and keep him seduced with her charms. Naseeban arranges it for Roshni,' whispered Khurshid Laqa.

'Shh, for heaven's sake keep quiet,' said Meher Afroz Begum in alarm. Her eyes darted around to see that no one had heard.

Though they had been whispering, Falak Ara, sitting nearby had overheard them. She was also looking for some charm that could help her attain the love of her heart. Those daily glimpses during Jharokha Darshan were not enough. The Meena Bazar meeting had awakened all kinds of strange desires which she had no understanding of, or control over.

Lost in thought, she left along with all the others after a while.

The uncharitable of course were now gossiping that this was just the Empress' excuse to get Huzur Purnur into the palace and make him aware of her love for him. He had been absent for many a night, busy writing ghazals and listening to Daaran bai.

How else did she recover so fast?

Un ke dekhe se jo aa jaati hai munh par raunaq
Voh samajhte hain ki beemar kaa haal achchha hai

On seeing her when one's face is then infused with such a glow
She starts to think the one who ails for her is better now[29]

—Mirza Ghalib

17

Black Magic and Much Else

jin jin ko tha ye ishq ka aazar mar gaye
aksar hamare saath ke bimar mar gaye

Those who were tormented by love, passed away
Frequently, my fellow sufferers in love, passed away

—Mir Taqi Mir

'Mubarak, do you know Naseeban well?' asked Falak Ara the next morning.

'Yes, I do, my princess but why are you asking?'

'Please ask her to visit that qalandar, Hazrat Deen Ali Shah, and get me a taveez,' replied the heartsick princess.

'May I be ransomed over you my darling,' said the agitated and worried Mubarak, 'These are dangerous paths you want to tread. These old eyes have seen the world. These charms and amulets bring nothing except trouble.'

'Please, please Mubarak, I beg you. If you love me, do this for me,' begged Falak.

'Why don't you show me what you have painted?' Mubarak tried to distract her.

'Oh yes! I have been copying this painting I found in the diwan of Zebunnisa shahzadi. Tell me, how is it?'

'Arre, this is the Khurd Jahan. How beautiful it looked when there were no buildings here. But, what can anyone do? As the

193

families increased, provisions had to be made for the royal offspring. And this lady? Who is she? What is she doing?' asked Mubarak.

'That's what I was hoping you could tell me.'

'I think you should ask Sikandar Ara Begum sahiba,' said Mubarak. 'She has been living here forever and would be the best person to answer your questions. She has seen that garden before Mirza Jahangir's haveli was built.'

'That's a good idea. I will do that. Now come back to Naseeban, please tell her I want to meet her tomorrow.' There was such finality in Falak's tone that Mubarak thought it better not to argue. She could always say she had forgotten.

Meanwhile, Naseeban had gone home with much to tell her husband.

'May my tongue be wrenched out of its socket if I exaggerate, but miyan, that box had more *ashrafis* than I have ever seen in my life.'

'Slowly, slowly! Where did you see all these gold coins?' asked Rahim.

'Arre, I am getting old. Yesterday, the Malika had fallen sick and the Emperor came to visit her. She immediately became better and then there was a *jashn-e sehatyabi*,' she replied.

'How could she become better so soon? Is the Badshah a magician?' asked an incredulous Rahim.

'Well, the uncharitable say that this was just a ploy to get the Badshah to visit her. He hasn't been coming to the palace for some weeks now. They say he is busy with Daaran bai. She sings his compositions,' said Mubarak.

'Daaran bai, that famous courtesan?'

'Yes, the same. She not only dances very well but also is a very accomplished singer. You know that these Timurids are *rasiks* of good music and dance and always patronise them. These courtesans are so well trained in classical kathak and Hindustani music that the ustads pale in comparison. She is Huzur-e Anwar's favourite at the moment because she sets his ghazals to music. And of course, I am sure one thing must be leading on to another.'

'Astaghfirullah!' said the pious Rahim. In his mind, courtesans meant no good, as he had heard of many a rich noble falling prey to their charms and squandering their fortunes over them. 'I have never understood why these rich people can't be satisfied with what they have. They get married at such great cost to rich, beautiful and powerful women, yet keep hankering after the courtesans in the bazaar. Zeenat Mahal Begum's beauty is famous, and God knows she spares no effort to stay charming and keep him charmed.'

'Arre, miyan we are different. How would we understand the ways of the rich? I am so glad we aren't rich, and you are satisfied with me,' said Naseeban, snuggling up to him. Daaran bai, ashrafis were all temporarily forgotten as they noisily and passionately made love.

Much later, Rahim went back to their earlier conversation. 'So, who had this box of ashrafis?'

'Mirza Nili's wife brought this box with her to throw over the mirasans. Of course, they are excellent singers, but do they deserve so much money?' asked Naseeban more rhetorically than anything else. She knew that her royal employers were eccentric and bad at keeping account of their money.

'I don't know whether they deserve the money or not, but I do know that so many of these Mughal princes are heavily in debt to the moneylenders in the city. Of course, Mirza Nili is no more, but his sons are also in debt. She should give it to them.' Rahim was shocked at what he regarded as wasteful expenditure.

'Yes, I know. The blind will always differentiate and favour his own. They are not born from her, so she prefers to squander on her pleasures. But what can we do? We are their slaves and do their bidding. If someone smiles at us and says a good word, we feel blessed. But like you, I wonder about their lives. They seem so disconnected from reality. I wonder if they know the struggle that our Huzur Alampanah has to undergo to make ends meet with the money he gets from this wretched Company bahadur. Never did I think I would live to see the day when an angrez would demand a chair to sit in the presence of our Mahabali Badshah! I am so glad he has refused them that, even though that meant he can no longer use the Takht-e Huma.'

It was as if the dam of grievances that Naseeban had had burst, flooding her eyes and mind. 'These blasted firangis who don't even know how to wash their bottoms and wipe them with paper are now dictating terms to us! Just yesterday, I heard that our raja and amirs are expected to take their elephant mounts to a corner so that an Englishman, who could be coming in his carriage to the market, is not inconvenienced. I wish I had died before hearing all this.'

'Don't be so distraught, Naseeban. This is an old order. Also, if the Badshah has agreed to it, what can we do? In some way, the Badshah's sainted ancestors are to blame for handing over all this power to the Company bahadur. Now he continues it. Just a few days ago, Munshi Sher Ali Khan had come to our jewellery shop and was talking to the Lala. The contract of the Chandni Chowk Bagh, which had been laid by Jahanara Begum, has been taken away from him and the revenues and upkeep of it has been given over by Jahanpanah to the Resident bahadur for the English administration. He was saying the revenue of so many royal provinces has also been given to them. I overheard my owner saying that this was harmful to the interests and future of the Timurid monarchy.'

'Arre, miyan, only the rich and powerful can understand what they do. It is beyond my understanding. And as if that is not enough, Sikandar Ara Begum sahiba has started throwing away her jewellery. Every day she calls the jeweller's young son, Badri, and makes him extract the gems from gold jewellery—and while the gems are kept in the tosha-khana, the gold is for that Badri to take. Imagine that!'

'Every day?' asked Rahim. 'But where did she get all this jewellery from?'

'God alone knows where she got so much jewellery from. She never married, so it can't be from her trousseau,' replied Naseeban. 'Perhaps she got it from her grandmother, who was Shah Alam

Badshah's wife. It is not for us to speculate. We can only watch silently and carry on with our tasks.'

Shaking her head, she said, 'Which reminds me, if you meet Hira please ask him to come over. I have some news for him, regarding the questions he had asked.'

'Hira wasn't here the day before. He had gone to Punjab after the Sair because his mother was very sick. Let me find out if he has returned. Ughh what is this smell of burning hair? This amil is becoming a nuisance. Every day, there's some nasty smell coming from his house,' said Rahim wrinkling and putting his *gamcha*, his shoulder cloth over his nose.

'Miyan, this is that amil practising black magic. I am sure Malika must have sent her personal maid Roshni to him. She gets a lot of magic done and charms made for her to overcome her enemies and keep Huzur-e Wala interested in her,' replied Naseeban.

This magic and charms had been occupying Falak Ara's mind and she tried to distract herself by painting.

She was sitting in the Khurd Jahan garden performing some magic of her own with her paints. The diwan with its illustration lay open in front of her.

The sketch was ready, and it was time for *rang amezi* or adding colour to the drawing. The first to be added would be the secondary colours, then combinations of red and finally the gold. Gold was where extreme skill was needed and Falak was still unsure of her abilities, but since she was making an illustration for a poem of Zebunnisa Begum, she would give it her best.

Just then Mubarak came out, fussing as usual that her precious was sitting in the sun and her face would get tanned or, God forbid, freckled.

After many days of extreme cold, it was a glorious day and Zohrun Nisa Begum came out to enjoy the warmth. Seeing the young girl painting with a pensive look on her face, she remembered that she hadn't gotten around to talking to the Badshah about Qaiser.

Resolving to do that she came near Falak.

'Arre, you have sketched this garden. It is looking so different. I am glad you haven't added this ugly haveli. I don't know what Huzur-e Wala our sainted uncle Akbar Shah Sani, was thinking when he allowed Mirza Jahangir to build this! The poor sainted Shah Jahan Badshah must be twisting and turning in his grave at the spoiling of his careful symmetry. But then I have seen my cousin Jahangir twist him around his little finger.'

'Phuppijan, I am copying a design made by someone when this haveli hadn't been made,' replied Falak.

'What is that? Show me,' said Zohrun Nisa Begum.

Falak took out the diwan, opened it to the illustration and gave it to Zohrun Nisa Begum.

'This is fascinating. Only one sketch, and that too unfinished, in this diwan. Our ancestors used to get full books beautifully illustrated. Maybe this isn't part of the book,' she said examining it closely. 'Oh yes! If you see, the paper is different.'

'I had noticed that but thought that maybe the painter and calligrapher were not working in tandem,' said Falak.

'And who is this woman? She looks like a begum but why would a begum be digging?' Zohrun Nisa Begum was perplexed. 'Perhaps Sikandar Ara Phuppijan might recognize her.'

With the paint being applied, the contours of the lady were more visible, as were her clothes. She was very clearly a begum, and a bag could be seen next to her. Her face seemed to express extreme anxiety.

'Maybe, the original painter was illustrating the anxiety felt by mortals in this transient world and she was reminding herself of the afterlife by digging a symbolic grave,' said Zohrun Nisa Begum. 'I have heard that preparing your grave in your lifetime makes you more righteous as the threat of punishment on the Day of Resurrection is ever present.'

'And what is that bag? It all seems very morbid to me,' said young Zebun.

'Maybe she is burying her sins, and that bag is symbolic. I don't know what the original artist intended but they used to paint allegorical and philosophical scenes portraying life and death. I have some paintings in the kutubkhana,' said Falak Ara, intending to show it to Sikandar Ara Dadijan.

Zohrun Nisa had been noticing the young girl looking wan for some time and asked her, 'Child, your face looks very pale. Are you well? Is something troubling you?'

'Arre phuppijan, don't you know our Apa is in love,' said the irrepressible Zeenat.

'Sshh Zeenat, what nonsense is this? Please don't speak rubbish,' an embarrassed Falak didn't know whether to die or pray that the earth swallowed her up.

'Hmm,' said Zohrun Nisa Begum. Catching Falak's face in her palms she asked her, 'Don't mind these naughty girls, Falak. Look into my eyes and tell me the truth. I will help.'

The young girl blushed and lowered her eyes.

'Aah, I see,' said the old begum, well-versed in the ways of the heart. Before Falak could be teased or embarrassed further, the mid-morning meal was served, and the girls and their aunt left for it.

Falak saw Naseeban coming and called out to Mubarak and pleaded, 'Mubarak please ask Naseeban to get me a charm.'

Mubarak pacified her charge by promising to do so later in the evening. 'Shahzadi, I can't do this here, I will go to her house at night.'

Aah tul-e amal hai roz-fuzun
garche ek muddaa nahin hota

Aah! My desires multiply daily, yet
The one thing I want, I don't get.

—Momin Khan Momin

Mubarak knew that now she had no more excuses left, and since she trusted Naseeban, she decided to pay her a visit at dawn. The streets of Shahjahanabad were almost deserted.

No one who didn't have to wake up to make a living woke up before eight or nine o'clock on cold winter mornings; everyone remained lazily cuddled up under his or her blanket. Even though the braziers burnt brightly in their houses, the shivering did not stop.

She could only hear some movement and snippets of conversation in the *dhobi basti* in Chatta Shahji, in front of Kucha Mir Ashiq, near Chawri Bazar, as the washermen and women got ready to go to the ghat to wash clothes.

The bells around the bullocks' necks were chiming and some of the men were singing ditties as they went about loading the bullock carts with soiled clothes. The squalor of their surroundings and the impoverished dwellings made a sharp contrast with the brightly coloured and rich fabrics that they were going to wash for their noble patrons.

A dirty drain ran through their basti giving it a foul smell. A few shops on one side provided their daily needs, while on the other side were some water tanks for washing dirty clothes and ovens for boiling dirty soiled clothes as a backup to the ghat.

In one mud house around a muddy courtyard, Kallan dhobi and his wife Laado were talking to Wazira while untying their bullock from the pole he was tied to.

'Eidu and Mangal haven't got up as yet,' said Laado, rubbing sleep out of her eyes.

'Eidu was having trouble with his bullock yesterday. I told him these young bulls are like a new wife, have to be treated firmly from day one and broken immediately, or else they trouble one forever,' said Kallan.

Laado, who had borne the brunt of this schooling early on in their married life, rubbed her back reflexively and continued loading the now untied bullock with clothes for washing. She knew that, unlike the dirty clothes they cleaned and made sparkle, her fate was destined to be dark and grimy.

Mubarak passed by them to reach Maliwara. Naseeban was at home, talking to one of her friends, Dulari. The conversation was

about a young girl named Tasliman, who had recently joined the
balakhana of the famous courtesan Zamurad bai. Trained by Zamurad
bai herself in singing and dancing, she had shown a lot of promise. But
just two evenings ago, some young blades had come and forcibly taken
her away to their mansion in Matia Mahal. They had been identified as
a Timurid prince and his friends. She was being held in captivity and
Zamurad bai was seeking her honourable release. Dulari's husband,
Chote Lal dhobi, washed the clothes in the balakhana and so was privy
to information and was loyal to his employer.

'I tell you Naseeban, these young men have still not learnt that
their power is going, has gone. It is the angrez who rule the roost
today. Instead of trying to get back their glory they are steeped in
luxury and debauchery. My husband tells me of the conversations
on the balakhana between the angrez patrons and the princes and
nobles. The angrez act as if they own us all!'

Mindful of her job in the Qila, Naseeban was trying to stem the
flow of Dulari's anger and indiscretions. But Dulari was too full of
anger to stop.

'The angrez of course are spending their own money, but the
princes and the nobles borrow money to spend on the girls in the
balakhana,' grumbled Dulari adding, 'Of course the angrez can afford
to, considering that they have looted us so much and appropriated all
our land and money. They have turned the balakhana into a kotha
where instead of learning and appreciating etiquette and culture, the
emphasis is now on physical relationships.'

'Shh Dulari, what are you saying? We are poor people and should
only be concerned about making our living. I am an employee of the
Qila and loyal to them. Huzur Purnur is very wise and knows what
he is doing. Also, I think Zamurad bai should appeal to the Huzur.
He is very fair and will give her justice.'

By now Mubarak had joined them and added her endorsement
to Naseeban's. 'Dulari, I am sure that our beloved Alampanah will
give justice to Zamurad bai. He has always given so much respect to
these singers and dancers and appreciates their art and skill.'

The sounds of azan from mosques and temple bells could be heard. Dulari left saying, 'It's time for us to go to the ghat to wash the clothes. My husband must be waiting for me. We have to work after all, no one is going to give us pensions!'

'Arre Bi Mubarak, how are you? How come you have come here so early in the morning?'

'It's been so many days since I came and had a cosy chat with you, Naseeban. I am always in a hurry and so are you. Today, I thought I would come over. So, tell me how you have been?'

Naseeban launched into a description of herself. It was rare that she found an audience for that. The boot was always on the other leg as she was either listening to her royal employers or her husband.

Mubarak sat patiently, waiting for an opportunity to start a conversation on charms, when she smelt hair burning. 'Arre, what on earth is that?' she asked.

'Don't ask me about it! We are fed up. It is that amil doing black magic. Ever since that day when the Malika fell sick, her maid visits him daily and takes all kinds of charms and amulets from him.'

'Do they really work?' asked Mubarak. Here was the window she had been waiting for.

'God knows if they work or not. But Durdana and Roshni come regularly and a lot of money exchanges hand,' said Naseeban, adding, 'This amil is becoming very popular in the Qila. The other day, Pyari Begum also asked me to get a charm for her.'

What does Pyari Begum need charms for?' asked Mubarak.

'I don't know, she didn't tell me but maybe that is why Huzur-e Wala didn't come to the mahal for so many days, and the Malika had to fall sick. Only the rich know what they think, it is beyond my comprehension.'

'Accha can you get me a talisman to ward off the evil eye for my darling? Of late I feel she is becoming very listless and looking wan. God knows there are enough people who are envious of her looks and temperament. It is my deepest desire to see her married and settled before I die. I don't want her to languish in the Qila all her life.'

Mubarak was so sincere and emotional in her words that Naseeban agreed and added, 'Mubarak, why don't you talk to Zohrun Nisa Begum. She is very fond of Shahzadi Falak Ara. Maybe she can talk to Mahabali Jahanpanah and fix a marriage for her. That young prince, Mirza Qaiser, is very nice. She would be happy with him.'

Hearing Naseeban's advice, Mubarak perked up. 'Yes, that's a good idea. Why didn't I think of it earlier? Let me do it today itself. Meanwhile, can you get an amulet for my shahzadi?'

'Yes, I will get one for her well-being and happy life. But not from this charlatan who does black magic. I will get it from Hazrat Deen Ali Shah qalandar. Rest assured Mubarak, we will manage to get her settled soon. She has always been very kind to me and I remember her mother fondly,' said Naseeban reassuringly.

Satisfied that she had done her darling's bidding and still been discreet, Mubarak left for the Qila.

She could hear the chanewalas and halwa puri vendors in the streets. She knew soon the residents would be out to eat hot halwa, parathas and fluffed-up chickpeas. Hot nahari and khameeri roti stalls would do brisk business as the workers ate their morning meal before going off for manual labour.

Later in the day, the pampered residents of Shahjahanabad would gather enough courage to step outside, and even at that hour, their teeth would chatter. It was unusually cold this year. Everyone on the streets resembled a shivering bundle of wool. God forbid it rained, thought Mubarak as she walked towards the Qila. For then, the nights and days would become bitingly cold and even the fires didn't give enough warmth. Sometimes the water would freeze at night because of the frost and the poor had a tough time going about their morning business.

Meanwhile, the young prince in question was spending time practising his calligraphy and trying hard not to think of Falak's bewitching eyes or how she would look in those chand baliyan.

Shaking his head, he decided to go to Chandni Chowk, maybe the air would do him good and he could meet some of his friends.

The bazaars and alleys were full of pedlars and hawkers by now. Cries of, 'These carrots are sweeter than candy. They are from Shah-e Mardan in Aliganj,'[30] could be heard. The sweetshops were decorated with trays of varieties of halwa; some offered carrot halwa and others a variety of gajak and crisp rewri. Huge sacks of apples, grapes, pomegranates, pistachios, almonds, walnuts, pine nuts, cashew nuts and other dry fruits that came from far-off places, were being sold in the markets.

His friends were indeed all sitting in the qahwakhana and Tasliman was the topic of conversation here also.

'Who is Tasliman?' asked Qaiser as he sat down on the *masnad* and tucked his feet under, reaching out for the pechwan of the huqqah.

Miyan Nabbu, the gossip, had already found out everything. 'She's a new flower blossoming in Zamurad bai's balakhana. However, her fragrance has been looted before it could be enjoyed by the visitors to the garden. Mirza Tahawwar Shah and Nawabzada Shamsuddin Khan kidnapped her from under the eyes of the wily lady who had hoped to cash in on her. It seems that one of the firangi officers was also interested in her. She has the voice of a nightingale and the face of a fairy. Some money had also exchanged hands between Zamurad bai and the angrez. Now Zamurad bai doesn't know what to do.'

Kunwar Mohammed Ibrahim chipped in, 'Mirza Tahawwar Shah and Nawabzada Shamsuddin Khan are notoriously badly behaved. There have been complaints about them earlier too. I suppose Huzur Purnur will have to intervene.'

'Hmmm. Difficult situation,' said Zoravar Singh. 'There has been trouble brewing between Mirza Tahawwar Shah and the angrez officers. He lost to them in chess and had to sell some of his lands to pay off the debt money. This must be his way of flexing his muscles. It has come at a bad time as there is tension brewing in the cantonments due to the new cartridge. This is not the time to be getting on the wrong side of the angrez. They will flex their muscles against the Mirza as they know that he or his father no longer wields any real power. We all know what happened to Mirza Jahangir.'

A worried Mirza Abu Bakr said, 'I agree with you Bhai Zoravar. We must accept the way the wind is blowing and protect our future interests. I will have a word with Mirza Quwaish Bahadur. After Mirza Fakhru's death, Huzur Purnur started relying on his younger son, even though he petitioned the Company bahadur to recognize Mirza Jawan Bakht as the heir apparent.'

'I heard Mirza Quwaish and Mirza Mughal and some of the other brothers have informed the Company bahadur that they were forced to renounce their rights and the Company sarkar is reconsidering. Of course, the Nawab Zeenat Mahal sahiba is lobbying hard to ensure Mirza Jawan Bakht is installed as the heir apparent. Let's see what happens,' said Zoravar Singh.

Mirza Qaiser, who had come to find relaxation, was now even more worried. In these circumstances how could he hope to find some employment and talk to his father about marriage?

Mirza Qaiser need not have worried, for unknown to him, Zohrun Nisa Begum had decided to take matters into her own hands. Whether it was the qalandar's charm or Falak Ara's yearning face bent over her painting that had worked its magic on Zohrun Nisa Begum, a few days later she sent a message to the Badshah Salamat that she would like to meet him that evening in the Mehtab Bagh, through her khwajasara.

Huzur-e Wala sent back his agreement and the cousin was satisfied and started preparing for the evening. She had to wear a white dress since the theme in the Mehtab Bagh was white.

The ladies would often go to the Mehtab Bagh in the evening and purdah arrangements would be made.

The architects had designed a moonlit garden with white flowering bushes, trees and plants. It was for enjoyment in the heavenly evenings and nights when the scent from the flowers overpowered the senses, the camphor lamps and candles from the Sawan and Bhado'n pavilions made one languorous and dreamy.

The Badshah walked here with his begums, the princes and princesses perhaps dreamt of crowns and palaces.

In this garden was a dargah of Qadam Sharif, believed to contain an imprint of the footprint of the Prophet, and the ladies often went to the dargah for *ziarat*.

Zohrun Nisa Bagum's palanquin bearers had been called and in the evening, she set off towards the Mehtab Bagh, passing by the beautiful Sawan Bhado'n pavilions, with its gushing fountains and chutes replicating the sound of monsoons. The camphor lamps added to the intoxication of the fragrance of flowers in the Hayat Baksh Bagh.

Alampanah was sitting on his marble shahnasheen with a marble huqqah kept near him. In keeping with the white theme, sparkling white *chandnis* and white brocade bolsters and cushions were spread on the masnads. The palanquin was set down and Zohrun Nisa Begum got out in a flurry of lace and white silks. As was customary, she presented her salam and nazar to the Mahabali Jahanpanah and then allowed the attendants and Khwajasaras to seat her. A silver huqqah and khasdan were set before her.

'Ama, how are you? It has been ages since we had a chance to talk,' said Huzur-e Aqdas.

They were of the same age and had been great friends in childhood, but her marriage had taken her away and when she had returned after her widowhood, he had become busy with his regnal duties.

'God is kind, Huzur Jahanpanah. I am reasonably healthy and am fortunate to have got shelter in the mahal. God didn't deem it fit to bless me with children of my own, but I am now surrounded by so many children. I spend my time with them. They keep me young and happy.'

'Arre Zohrun never think of yourself as heirless. We are all there for you. My children are yours,' said the Badshah.

'You are very kind and gracious, Alampanah. Indeed, I am very comfortable and well looked after,' said Zohrun Nisa Begum.

Some more small talk ensued, and Zohrun Nisa Begum then decided to come to the point.

'Zill-e Ilahi, your daughter, Falak Ara, is turning out to be a very beautiful girl. What have you thought about her future?' she asked.

'Ama, we have been very busy with settling our affairs with the Company bahadur and our disciples but yes, she has been on our mind. Do you have any suggestions?'

'Yes, Huzur. There is this young salatin who I think will be suitable for her. His name is Mirza Qaiser, son of Mirza Aftab.'

'Wallah! What a wonderful suggestion. That boy comes to us for calligraphy lessons, and we are also very impressed by him and his sincerity. He is a very disciplined and upright young man. It is rare to find such principled young people today. We will summon his father tomorrow,' said the Badshah.

'Thank you Badshah Salamat, may your reign be perpetuated, and Allah grant you a long and healthy life. I had hoped for your agreement and approval for this young, motherless girl. She is always looking after me and taking care of all the old ladies in the mahal. A true example for her younger cousins. This makes me very happy.

'And speaking of wayward young men, Naseeban was telling me about Mirza Tahawwar and some singer. May I be ransomed over you and forgiven if I speak out of turn, but I have seen the world and both you and I grew up in different times. Today such behaviour will cause an uproar and our Timurid blood can no longer excuse excesses. I am no one in front of you, but I have been worried. When my late husband was alive, he knew some of the goras and I have heard that they think themselves far superior to us. Though what they have to be superior about I don't know!' She ended sarcastically.

'Ama, we know Zohrun. I have asked Quwaish, who brought this to our notice, to order Tahawwur to return the girl to the balakhana. Zamurad bai has always been loyal to us, and she is an excellent performer. We will tell Quwaish to arrange a performance by the girl for us in his haveli by way of mollifying her. This should also send a message to the angrez officer,' said the wise Badshah.

'Gul Bano is also growing up and maybe you can betroth her to Davar Shukoh and they can be married after Ramzan, which is just two months away. I like the young man and he seems very suitable for Gul Bano,' said Zohrun Nisa Begum.

'Ama, yes. Gul Bano is very close to our hearts, but we didn't realize she had grown up enough to get betrothed. Tomorrow we will grace the Baithak and call all the ladies. We think we need to see our children, nieces and grandchildren.'

Satisfied that she had done her part, Zohrun Nisa Begum departed after some more small talk.

Khaali ai chaaragaro honge bahut marham-dan
Par mere zakhm nahin aise ki bhar jaenge

Healers all your concoctions may be at an end
But my wounds show no signs of being on the mend.

—Sheikh Ibrahim Zauq

18

The Proposal

Hai wasl hijr aalam-e tamkin-o-zabt mein
Mashuq-e shokh o aashiq-e diwana chahiye

In the world of dignity and restraint, union and separation
are the same
Needed is a mischievous beloved and a mad lover.

—Mirza Ghalib

The day dawned bright and clear.

As always, the royal musicians were playing the Raga Bhairavi to signal the advent of dawn.

Huzur Bahadur Shah woke up in his khwaabgah with the *kalima* on his lips and sat up against his bedstead. Fresh flowers had been set on all sides and the fragrance was beguiling

The jasolini called out to everyone to be alert: 'Attention!' The attendants replied: 'As Allah and his messenger are my witnesses, we are alert.' Everyone bent down from the waist and saluted the Emperor, who blessed them. A footstool covered with green velvet was put for the Emperor to step down. While preparations were made by the female attendants for his ablutions, jasolini set a Persian prayer rug on the sandalwood settee for Huzur to come in and say his prayers after his ablutions. By then, the face of the fair goddess of morning was peeping in from the windows.

Prayers completed, it was time to read and hear verses from the Quran. The jasolini respectfully announced that the *hafizji* had come to recite the Quran. The sound of Quranic verses recited melodiously by the hafizji and joined in by Huzur echoed, blessing the mahal.

The hakim came and after checking the royal pulse, congratulated everyone on the Badshah's health and left. A cooling drink was brought from the royal dispensary covered in a green velvet bag, which had been sealed to prevent tampering. The seal was broken in front of Huzur-e Wala and served to him.

By the time the Badshah Salamat came in his sedan, the royal bath had been prepared in the Hammam-e Athar. To the strains of the *raushan chowki,* ensemble of musicians, attendants in charge respectively laid out towels, silver dishes containing gram flour, *ubtan* and *khali*, cups, combs, a pumice stone and silver jugs containing water. The wardrobe attendants and jewellery in charge set out the clothes and jewellery sent from the toshakhana for that day.

The royal bath completed, Huzur Purnur went to the Musamman Burj for the Jharokha Darshan. Jahanpanah Badshah sat for some time and then sent a message to the Malika that he would be coming to the Baithak for the morning meal and wanted to meet all the ladies. The excitement in the mahal was palpable. The ladies were flitting around like fresh blossoms, chirping like nightingales, for it was many days since the Badshah Salamat had graced the mahal for the morning meal.

The Malika-e Dauran and the other begums were visions of beauty. Falak Ara was sitting in one corner dressed in a soft peach pajama and turquoise jama and dupatta. Gul Bano had been woken up early to meet her grandfather and looked like a vision in white silk and organza, with pearls and diamonds on her neck and ears; but the effect was somewhat spoilt by her sulking face.

Both the girls were invited for ulash and were the centre of attention. Gul Bano's mood had been restored by that honour, and she was speaking to her grandfather, the Badshah, telling him how much she missed her father. Falak as usual sat quietly, trying to make herself as unobtrusive as possible.

The meal over, the Mahabali Jahanpanah left for the tasbihkhana to hold durbar.

It was now time to hear petitions. Sahib-e Alam Mirza Quwaish Bahadur, who had been in the Baithak, had accompanied his father while Mirza Aftab had received a summons the night before and was present in the deorhi.

The first order of business, of course, was to reduce the tension between the goras and Mirza Tahawwur but without losing face.

'Ama, Mirza Quwaish, we were thinking that it has been many days since we have attended a mehfil. We have heard that there is a new girl in Zamurad bai's balakhana who is excellent in *khayal gayki*. Please convey our respects to her and arrange a mehfil in your haveli,' said the Badshah.

Turning towards Mahbub Ali Khan, the wazir he added, 'Make sure that all the arrangements are made. Invite the Resident bahadur and a few of the senior officials of the company. Sahib-e Alam can invite his friends too.'

Satisfied that he had ensured that the girl was returned to the balakhana as he knew Mirza Tahawwur would not contravene his direct wishes, he turned to the urdabegni and gave permission for Mirza Aftab to come into the durbar.

Mirza Aftab had been wondering at the summons and hoping that his beloved son, a piece of his heart, had not stepped out of line or displeased Huzur-e Anwar.

Kornish done, nazar offered, Mirza Aftab stood silently in front of the Badshah waiting for him to speak.

'How are you Aftab? It has been a long time since we met,' said the Badshah Huzur with affection.

Mirza Aftab, heaving a huge sigh of relief that his son had not done anything wrong, said, 'Zill-e Ilahi, one can only be well when your shadow is on us. After God, you are our benefactor, and we are very well looked after.'

'That is good to hear,' replied the Badshah Salamat. 'It is our duty to ensure that every person in our empire is comfortable.'

'Ji, Huzur-e Anwar, Qaiser and I are indeed blessed to have your hand on our heads. We could ask for nothing more. May God keep you safe and healthy and may your reign be forever,' replied Mirza Aftab.

'Ama, yes. That is what we wanted to talk to you about. Qaiser is a very wonderful young man, and we thought it was time he settled down. We have arranged his marriage with our daughter Falak Ara, to be solemnized on the eighteenth Ramzan of this year,' pronounced Huzur-e Aqdas. Turning towards Mahbub Ali Khan he said, 'Ama, inform the darogha and tehwildar of the zenana to make arrangements.'

'Huzur Purnur, how is it that you divine what is in our hearts! You have always taken the decisions that are in our favour. May your reign be perpetuated, and you continue to rule our hearts,' replied the delighted father. He knew that getting his son married to the Emperor's daughter would also enhance Qaiser's future career. 'I will start preparations,' he added before bending low and taking his leave. That day was tenth of Rajab, and there were two months left.

The efficient network of spies that existed in the mahal ensured that the news reached the zenana with a few minutes. The first to know, of course, was Zohrun Nisa Begum for she had stationed her khwajasara in anticipation. Soon, it reached Mubarak.

Mubarak was in a swoon. This was indeed her heart's desire come true. Even though the charm was yet to come, it had worked. Was she alive or in heaven?

Ye be-takalluf phira rahi hai kashish dil-e-ashiqan ki us ko
Wagarna aisi nazakaton pe khiram-e-naz ek qadam na hota

Warm in her lover's attraction, she roams without a care
Else her dainty feet, a single step wouldn't dare

—Momin Khan Momin

Falak Ara, bent upon her easel, found herself tightly embraced by Zeenat and Zebun. 'Apa, Apa, pack away your paints. Start getting ready, you are leaving us in two months.'

'Leaving! Why am I leaving you?' said a startled Falak, wondering if she had made a mistake that deserved banishment.

'Arre Apa, don't be so naive. Your prince is coming to take you. Huzur-e Anwar has just fixed your *nikah* with Mirza Qaiser on the eighteenth Ramzan,' said Zebun.

The ever-naughty Zeenat teased, 'Now you don't need to peep out of the window to see him every day. He will be there for you all the time.'

'What do you mean, Zeenat? Apa has to get through these two months too! If she doesn't peep through the windows, how will she survive?' Zebun joined in.

The blushing, ecstatic Falak didn't know whether to laugh or cry. This was her deepest desire come true.

The other young girls who were fond of her gathered around her, laughing and teasing.

Mubarak had also reached her charge and was embracing her tightly. She then led the young princess inside so that she could pay her respects to the older ladies. The first person she went to was Sikandar Ara Begum, who gave her blessings and a pair of gold and diamond bracelets. Next was Zohrun Nisa Begum, who caught her in a warm embrace and said, 'We will miss your gentle presence in the mahal, but I am so glad that you are getting married to someone of your choice. Bless you child, may you always be happy.'

'We can never thank you enough, begum sahiba,' said Mubarak with a low salam. 'You have proved to be Falak's fairy godmother. May Allah bless you with a long and happy life. I am your slave for life. Yours to command whenever you wish.'

Mirza Qaiser was getting ready to go to Salimgarh for weapon practice with his friends when Mirza Aftab reached home.

Seeing his father's broad smile he asked smilingly, 'May I be ransomed over you, my dearest Abbajan. You seem happy today. May Allah keep this smile on your face always.'

'My son, may I be ransomed over your happiness. I have much to be happy about. And why didn't you tell me?' he teased his son.

'Tell you what Abbajan? I tell you everything,' said the puzzled son.

'Really? You tell me everything?'

'Of course, Abbajan. Who else do I have? You are my world,' replied Qaiser.

'Achha! I may be your world, but today Huzur Jahanpanah has fixed your place in the grand *falak* above,' he said, indicating the sky.

'Falak?' asked an embarrassed Qaiser.

'Yes, Falak! And now I don't have time to stand around and gossip with you. Your nikah has been fixed by Jahanpanah for the eighteenth Ramzan. We have just two months to prepare,' teased Mirza Aftab.

'Nikah with whom?' Qaiser's heart was beating fast hoping against hope that the reference to *falak* was to his princess. For if the Huzur had fixed his nikah with somebody else there was no getting out of it.

'Arre, *meri jaan*, may God always look after you, don't act so innocent. The Huzur Badshah has fixed your nikah with his daughter, Falak Ara. Now I have to arrange for *haq-e meher* and the wedding ceremony.'

A blushing Qaiser could only bend and present his salam to the father to hide his confusion. This was what he had hoped and dreamt of but wasn't sure if he was worthy enough to be considered a suitable match for the princess.

Mirza Aftab continued, 'I will talk to the Resident sahib bahadur to see if you can get some employment in the central office. We will need to get a house on rent for you. You will need to set up your own household. Uff, I miss your mother, she would have shared my work. Now I have to do everything. I must inform your maternal uncles too.'

'Abbajan, I love you and can never repay what you have done for me. You have been both mother and father to me. If I may be so bold as to request you to talk to Mufti Sadruddin Khan Sahib Azurda, if he can accommodate me in his office. I would rather work under him than an angrez sahib. And Sadr-us Sudur Azurda sahib has a lot of influence and is also a friend of our beloved Jahanpanah.'

'As you say my son. I will ask him tomorrow. Meanwhile, till you start working, don't slack in your classes and make sure you go for your weapons training to Salimgarh too daily.'

'Ji Abbajan. Your wish is my command. As God is my witness, neither you nor Huzur Alampanah will ever find me wanting,' said the young man with great sincerity.

Mirza Aftab called out to his groom to take out his carriage and left for the city to meet the Sadr-us Sudur.

Finally alone, Qaiser sat down to savour his happiness. His torment was at an end. Soon, he would be united with the girl whose eyes had enchanted him and tied him to her.

He hoped he would prove worthy of the trust put in him by the Huzur Purnur. He was nothing but an ordinary salatin. Granted his father was a cousin of the Badshah and his mother from a royal Rajput family, but what had he done? Nothing!

Shaking his head, he thought of all the things he wanted to do but his hands were tied. All his arms training was nil, to be used only for shikar because the Timurid empire no longer maintained their own army. And what fun was there in killing innocent birds and deer? Big game was another matter, at least they offered a challenge and honed one's reflexes, but a poor pheasant?

Anyway, now was not the time to think of all this. If only Abbajan could get him some work in the Mufti's office where he could be of some use to his people.

Meanwhile, Gulab Jan, who knew the interest that Miyan Nabbu had taken in the affair, found some excuse to leave the Qila and went straight to his house in Maliwara.

Miyan Nabbu's house, as befitted his economic status, was newly renovated. One entered through a large wooden doorway into a small garden which led to the *diwankhana,* or salon for men, and then a big courtyard with a marble fountain and flowing water. There were flowering trees and bushes and singing birds hanging in cages.

Of course, Gulab Jan used the *chor* darwaza, which was an inbuilt postern in the gateway for lesser mortals. She sent her salam and was immediately called into a sleepy Miyan Nabbu's bedroom.

'Am I dreaming or in heaven? A visit from a houri so early in the morning? But why should I complain,' said Nabbu pulling her into his arms.

Like many of the serving maids in the Qila and in the city, Gulab Jan was very acrobatic and well-trained to satiate sexual desires. Miyan Nabbu's lust took a few hours of sweaty and passionate love-play and love-making to satisfy, but he was finally spent.

Nibbling her fingers he asked her, 'Upon my word Gulabo, there is no one like you. You never disappoint or say no and meet every blow of mine with a vigorous thrust of your own. And your body! It's not only lissom, it's apparently boneless. I can take you from every angle and more.'

'Arre miyan, you are making me blush. Your slave girl is happy that you are pleased. I am nothing but a vessel into which you can discharge your seed and become more vigorous and stronger,' said a very happy Gulab Jan, for she knew there would be a generous monetary reward for her. Trained from childhood to please men, she, like many others, knew no other skill but the art of making love and keeping patrons happy. They were trained in the principles listed in the *Kamasutra* and the *Ananga Ranga*. While the Kama Sutra was very old, Gulab had heard from one of the more learned serving women in the haram that *Ananga Ranga* was written by Kalyana Malla, some three centuries ago and had been translated into Hindustani and Persian as *Lazzat al-Nisa*. She had also told Gulab that one of the great Hindustani traditions was exuberant, passionate and guilt-free sex, as sensual pleasure was an ecstatic expression of life and death. Gulab didn't understand the philosophy behind *kama* and *ishq* but being very agile, she grasped all the positions that offered pleasure. They were also taught to mix aphrodisiacs and creams, but Nabbu didn't need those. All Gulab Jan needed were potions and ointments to ensure she didn't get pregnant. The wise serving woman had taught her those too.

He was already stroking her and Gulab decided to give him the exciting news before another marathon.

'Miyan, this slave girl has some news for you. Huzur Purnur has fixed Mirza Qaiser's nikah with Shahzadi Falak Ara, to be finalized after two months in Ramzan.'

Nabbu who had been lolling indolently till now, stroking her breasts, sat up. 'That's some news!' he said. 'When did this happen?'

'I came here as soon as I heard. And you know I hear everything immediately,' she said with a naughty wink.

'O you naughty one, come on, don't tease me further,' and saying so, he caught her tightly in his embrace.

Gulab Jan left after another few hours, completely satiated, for very few of her lovers could satisfy her as the young and lusty Miyan Nabbu could, and with a purse full of gold coins.

News had also reached Naseeban, and she wanted to hurry home to the new best friend of her family, Hira. Hira had returned the night before and she had to tell him about the locket, the wedding and the charm.

But with the mahal in a tizzy of excitement over the coming nuptials and Mubarak holding on to her for support, she could only get back by late evening.

'My fate seems to be smiling tonight,' said Rahim, punning on his wife's name. Since the Mehrauli stay, there was an extra warmth and bonding between the two. Their physical relationship had also improved, and Rahim seemed to have become quite demanding.

'Arre, miyan, there is some happy news I wanted to share with you and Hira bhai,' she said before he could get carried away for she had caught the lusty gleam in his eye.

'What is it? The angrez have gone away? Is that why you are late and smiling so much?' laughed Rahim.

'Don't make such jokes,' said Naseeban sharply. 'Remember I work at the Qila.'

'I am sorry,' he said asking, 'Tell me more.'

'Today, Alampanah Badshah announced the betrothal of Shahzadi Falak Ara and Mirza Qaiser. That is why I got delayed. Mubarak is of course maddened with happiness and trying to make all arrangements in one day, as usual,' replied Naseeban. 'Let's have dinner and go over to Hira bhai's house or send him a message to come over.'

'And what about me? Don't I count? I have been waiting for my jewel to be joined with me all evening. Now I have to wait not only for dinner but also Hira's visit? Let Hira go to hell. I am hungry but not for dinner,' he said pulling her into his arms. He had had a difficult day and was looking to release his pent-up emotions.

I am lucky, thought Naseeban *that my husband desires me and not some wench from the market.* Naseeban happily acquiesced and soon there was silence as Rahim and Naseeban joined together in a happy union of bodies. Theirs was the gentler lovemaking of two persons comfortably married and holding the other in affection.

Kya rang jahan mein ho rahe hain
Do hanste hain chaar ro rahe hain

O what spectrum of colours this world displays
While two laugh, there are always four who weep.

—Momin Khan Momin

19

The Day Approaches

Piyaa baaj pyaala piyaa jaaye na
Piyaa baaj yak til jiyaa jaaye na

Without my lover I cannot drink from the cup
Without my lover, I cannot live a moment more

—Qutub Quli Khan

News has a way of spreading and becoming gossip in moments.

Very soon not only the Qila but the whole walled city was abuzz with tidings of the upcoming nuptials. The winter had been difficult, and this was something to look forward to. The royal weddings were lavish affairs and there was entertainment and food for everyone.

The last grand wedding was of Mirza Jawan Bakht four years ago, and even though this would not be on the spectacular scale of the royal couple's favourite son, it would still be lavish. Mirza Jawan Bakht's wedding had been on a scale of magnificence that had not been seen in a century.

The next day, Mirza Aftab reached the haveli of Sadr-us Sudur Mufti Sadruddin Khan Azurda near Matia Mahal. He went past Chitli Qabr, the *mazar sharif* of the famous fourteenth-century saint, Syed Roshan Sahib Shaheed. As coloured mosaic tiles were used on the mazar, it became famous as *chitli,* or multi-coloured.

The Haveli Azizabadi also stood here. It was the mansion of the Nawab of Azizabad which had been in the possession of Nawab Mufil Beg Khan but was now part of the crown lands. There was an old, ruined mosque inside this mansion which has been repaired at great cost by Sadruddin Khan Bahadur sahib. He also got a new well dug here. The Sadr-us Sudur was not only a very learned man who wrote poetry and prose under the name Azurda, and the chief qazi of Shahjahanabad, but was also a very philanthropic and deeply religious man. With his own resources, he had organized the renovation of the Dar-ul-Baqa madrasa, situated near the Jama Masjid's southern gateway. Perhaps no one even in the past was so generous with his time and money. Not only were broken-down rooms refurbished, but teachers were also employed and now students had once again returned. Their board and lodging were paid for from the royal coffers. The primary principles of both religion and logic were being taught.

The Mufti sahib's haveli used to be the mansion of Lal Hazar Beg which was bought by Mufti Sahib and rebuilt from scratch, transformed into an architectural marvel filled with gardens, canals and fountains—all of which Mirza Aftab admired after he disembarked from his carriage and went inside.

The Mufti sahib was waiting for him in his diwan khana, and as soon as Mirza Aftab saw him, he was struck by the thought that no pen had the strength to even begin to capture his magnificence in words, no tongue could adequately attempt to spout his praises. His virtues and qualities were just so many. There is no other person in the firmament of the world today who was such an excellent scholar. He could solve insoluble problems in the twinkling of an eye and learned people would be awestruck at how he could do it all so easily.

In fact, Mufti sahib was so intelligent that he could understand everything instinctively; nothing needed repeating, however difficult the subject, and he didn't need subtext or nuance in the conversation or text. Acutely aware of all this, Mirza Aftab was confident that Mufti sahib would have already guessed the reason for his visit.

'My humble abode is honoured by your eminence's visit,' said Mufti sahib as he rose from the pile of carpets, cushions and bolsters on which he had been sitting. He had been reading the *Dehli Urdu Akhbar*, an Urdu newspaper that had been in circulation in Delhi since 1837— along with *Sirajul Akhbar*, the court gazette, named after Badshah Salamat, whose name was Abu Sirajuddin Zafar.

Maulvi Mohammed Baqar, the editor of *Dehli Urdu Akhbar*, was a friend of Mufti sahib and a very learned man. His forefathers had come to India from Hamdan in Iran during the reign of Nadir Shah and settled in Shahjahanabad. His father, Maulana Mohammad Akbar, was a well-known *mujtahid* of Delhi and had a madrasa in his own house. It was very popular, especially among the Shia sect and this is where Maulvi Baqar studied. Initially, Maulvi Baqar had joined Company bahadur's service and was appointed *tehsildar* but subsequently left it to become a teacher. And since 1837, he had been running the newspaper, which was very popular in Shahjahanabad.[31]

Huqqahs and trays of paan and cardamoms were kept in readiness.

'I am indeed privileged to have been able to get some time with you, Janab Mufti sahib. I know how busy you are.'

Protocol and decorum necessitated some leisurely chit-chat while taking deep puffs from the huqqah before the business at hand could be broached. This continued for some time, till Mufti sahib led the conversation, saying, 'I believe *mubarakbad* is in order, Mirza sahib. May Allah keep your son and the shahzadi sahiba in His protection and happy forever.'

'Please keep them in your prayers, Mufti sahib. They are young and you know the way things are in the city,' replied Mirza Aftab.

'Yes, of course, there is no need for you to tell me,' responded Mufti sahib. Knowing that asking for a favour will not be easy for the Mirza, he continued, 'In fact, I was about to come and visit you. I need a young assistant in the office and my thoughts had gone to your sahibzada. I know how well you have educated and trained him. He is also a protégé of Huzur Alampanah and will be an asset to my office. If he is agreeable, please ask him to come and meet me tomorrow.'

Immense relief engulfed Mirza Aftab. 'May Allah elevate your station and give you all the good in this world and after, Mufti sahib,' he said. 'You have relieved my heart. He is a good lad, very sincere and eager to learn. Insha'Allah, you will not be disappointed.'

His eyes then happened to fall on the *Dehli Urdu Akhbar*. He asked, 'Mufti sahib, I was reading about Maulvi Muhammad Baqar's concern about the economic situation in Hindustan. I know I can talk to you openly. He is very concerned at thousands—no, lakhs—of rupees being sent from here by the angrez officers to *wilayat*. What will happen to us Hindustanis, we have no power now, and soon we will have no money either.'

Mufti sahib thought for a while then said, 'Mirza sahib, that is why our children need to get a good education, cultivate a scientific temperament and move with the times. It saddens me to see our youngsters only worried about cockfights and kite-flying while all high offices of the land are occupied by the sahib bahadurs. Anyway, we will discuss this some other time. Please ask Qaiser Miyan to meet me tomorrow.'

Mirza Aftab got up, thanking his host, and left for the Qila to give the news to his son.

The Sadr-us Sudur's phaeton with two white mares tied to it was waiting to take him to court near the Kashmiri Darwaza. He was one of the very few Hindustanis who owned a phaeton and it was quite a grand sight when he drove in it to his office.

On the blessed occasion of the thirteenth Rajab, Hazrat Ali's date of birth, Mirza Qaiser started his new job.

Every festival was celebrated with great enthusiasm and gusto by the residents of the Qila and the city. On that auspicious morning, Huzur-e Wala got up early and went to the dargah. He recited prayers of thanksgiving and consecrated the various fruits, sweets and dry fruits that had been kept ready in gold and silver crockery. Partaking of a small portion, as custom required, he then left. These would subsequently be distributed in beautifully covered trays to all the Qila residents.

When it came to the mahal where Falak Ara was sitting, the elder ladies were the first to taste the special fare before calling out to the younger girls.

'Falak, this will be your last Rajab with us. I pray to Hazrat Ali to keep you safe. My daughter, remember at any time if you have any problem, recite Nad-e Ali,' said Rashid Ara Begum.

Little Bilqis, who had just graduated from the nursery to the company of the ladies asked, 'Dadijan, my anna is teaching it to me, please tell me its meaning.'

> *'Naad-e Aliyyan mazhar al-ajaib*
> *Tajidahu awnan laka fin nawaib*
> *Kullu hammin wa ghammin sayanjali*
> *Bi wilayatika, Ya Ali! Ya Ali! Ya Ali!*
> *Call Ali! Call Ali!*

Call aloud to Ali
Who is the manifestation of wonders
He will help dispel hardships and calamity.
All grief and anxiety will disappear
By Your power and Authority!
O Ali! O Ali! O Ali,'

said Rashid Jahan Begum.

'I have seen beautiful calligraphic pieces of this in the kutubkhana,' said Falak. By now she knew that her poet-soldier was more interested in calligraphy and hoped he would make one for her to safeguard her from all evil.

As usual, it was Naseeban who brought all the news and announced that today, Mirza Qaiser had started working with the Sadr-us Sudur and the shahzadi would be kept in as luxurious a life as in the Qila.

'Shahzadi sahiba, I think you should also do a nazar of Bibi Fatima as thanksgiving,' said Ashrafun.

'Ai, have you gone mad?' exclaimed an indignant Mubarak. 'Young girls don't give thanksgiving for future husbands or their jobs. That is the work of the older. You seem to have forgotten all boundaries of modesty and propriety that govern the behaviour of young girls. I hope I have taught my shahzadi better.'

Rashid Jahan Begum tried to douse Mubarak's anger by calling Bilqis and saying, 'Come here, beti, I will tell you about the nazar of Bibi Fatima. This is food consecrated in the names of the holy Prophets and his household, known as *ahl-e bait*.'

'Dadijan tell us about the *sahnak*. I love that ceremony,' said Zeenat, nestling down next to her great aunt.

'Arre beti, there is so much work to do, and you want me to spend the day telling stories?' said Rashid Jahan Begum.

'Falak Apa will be going away, and she must learn how to do all this in her home too, shouldn't she?' said the quick-witted Zeenat.

'Well, sahnak is a nazar of Hazrat Bibi Fatima, the Prophet's— Peace Be Upon Him—daughter and Hazrat Ali's wife. She is the best of women and the chief of all the women in heaven. Her chastity and purity have been celebrated by all, and no man can taste the sahnak. Amongst the women also only the chaste are able to taste it.'

'But how do you know who is chaste and who is not?' asked a woman present.

Rashid Jahan Begum explained, 'Well, rice bowls and a plate of slaked lime are placed on a clean, white dastarkhwan along with bangles, henna and missi in packets, itr bottles tied with red thread and wrapped in red paper. There are printed, red dupattas, along with a hundred rupees for illumination, and seven types of cooked vegetables. The food is consecrated by the ladies, who put mehndi on their fingers, wear the red dupatta, and sit down to eat the sahnak. However, everyone has to test their piety first and eat the slaked lime. The mouths of the pious ones do not get cut by the slaked lime. Only after that can they eat the rice and curd dish.'

The girls were hanging on to each word and asked in bewilderment, 'But how does the lime know which mouth to burn and has it ever happened?'

Ashrafun, who had been listening, said, 'Begum sahiba, if I get immunity for my life, may I be permitted to speak? I am a lowly woman, but I have seen an occasion when a mouth did get burnt.'

'Yes, Ashrafun, you have my permission.'

Naseeban and Mubarak wondered if Ashrafun had lost her mind and was about to describe the time when, twelve years ago, Nawab Jahan Akhtar Begum sahiba, daughter of Sultan bai, had run away from the haram. No one knew where she was and with whom or how she had run away, but they did remember that her mouth had been cut by lime that year and she had tried to hide it, by immediately stuffing herself with dahi. Of course, no one was fooled, but she was a royal princess, so the attendants kept quiet.

'Begum sahiba, you would remember Pyari bai, the singer? She was the Huzur-e Wala's favourite and spent a lot of time in the haram with us. Just before she ran away with Tanras Khan, I remember her mouth was cut. That lowlife serpent was hiding such craven desires in her heart and of course, the Almighty knows what is in our hearts,' said Ashrafun.

'Oh, is that why Tanras Khan no longer comes to the mahal?' asked Zohrun Nisa Begum.

'Yes, begum sahiba. That *nigodi*, cursed wretch, bored a hole in the very plate she ate from. Not even for a minute did she remember the many favours of our blessed Badshah Salamat.'

'Where is he now?' asked Zeenat.

'Shahzadi, don't worry your head about such ingrates. That wretched man wandered from doorstep to doorstep, but who would employ someone who has bitten the hand that feeds him? However, our Huzur-e Aqdas's generosity has no parallel. Though he has prohibited Tanras Khan from entering the Qila, he still sends him a salary every month,' replied Naseeban, who was in touch with many singers in the city.

The nazar for the thirteenth Rajab done, it was time for Holi, which fell just four days later. Basant Panchami had signalled the onset of the festivities and people were carrying squirt guns with colours and smearing *gulaal* on each other's faces. Mustard flowers were offered in temples and sprays of gulaal flew in the air.

Flowers from the tesu plant were immersed in earthen water pots. It is believed that Lord Krishna played Holi with Radha using colours made from the red tesu flower, which blooms during the spring season.

Folk songs and ditties were on everyone's lips. One of the most popular was Hazrat Amir Khusrau's:

kheluungii holi, Khaaja ghar aaye,
dhan dhan bhaag hamare sajni,
Khaaja aaye aangan mere

I shall play Holi as Khwaja has come home,
blessed is my fortune, o friend,
as Khwaja has come to my courtyard.

Preparations for Eid-e Gulabi, as Holi was also called, were in full swing. Colour ruled the roost, and perhaps this is what made Falak Ara's pale face even more noticeable to Zohrun Nisa and Rashid Jahan Begum. They could guess the reason for this. After all, they knew that Mubarak guarded her charge jealously, and so must have refused to let the lovelorn girl get any news or glimpse of Mirza Qaiser.

Taking pity on their niece, the two ladies were inclined to be benevolent. And Holi seemed to provide a good opportunity for them to help Falak meet Qaiser.

That day as Hariyali came to sell her bangles, Rashid Jahan Begum summoned Mubarak and Hariyali to their part of the apartment where they would be undisturbed. Rashid Jahan and Zohrun Nisa had already debated whether Mubarak should be into their secret plans. Ultimately, they conceded that this including Mubarak was unavoidable because the alternative could prove disastrous: protective as she was of Falak Ara, Mubarak would have been the first to notice that the girl was missing, and if so, she was bound to raise hell.

'May I be sacrificed over you, my ladies,' said Hariyali to the royal ladies. 'Which colour bangles should I take out for you? Green will look so nice with your dupatta.'

'Arre, we haven't called you for bangles,' intoned Zohrun Nisa Begum. 'We want your help—taken under an oath of secrecy.'

'Of course, my ladies, my life is at your service,' replied Hariyali.

Mubarak was perplexed at this exchange. But although her eyes were full of questions, she remained quiet.

'Then listen carefully,' said Rashid Jahan Begum. 'We are trying to think of some way to help Falak meet Qaiser. She has been looking so pale and morose despite the festive atmosphere. It's not good for someone so young. And she's such a good girl too. How can our hearts bear to see her this way? We feel that meeting her future husband—the man she is so keen to marry—will no doubt lift her spirits. And we want to help her. Now, I know you are a very resourceful woman and will come up with some great suggestions.'

'How about you come here tomorrow with an assistant?' suggested Zohrun Nisa Begum, looking closely at Hariyali. 'You can ensure she has a long *ghoonghat* on her face. In the mid-morning, when the fair is being held on the reti, everyone will be busy. At that time, you could perhaps exchange the clothes of your assistant with Falak Ara and take her to meet Qaiser.'

But Mubarak could hold back no longer. 'My begums,' she uttered, clearly disapproving of this plan but careful to maintain decorum. 'May I be sacrificed over you, and forgive this lowly woman's impertinence, but I speak out of great concern for my darling. How can you think of substituting Falak with Hariyali's assistant? What if someone was to find out? There would be hell to pay—and that too so close to their wedding. And to leave the palace itself holds so many unknown horrors! Please, for God's sake, do not put such ideas into Falak's head. This is a very dangerous plan.'

Hariyali had been in deep thought while Mubarak was speaking. She knew that Mubarak's fears were justified, but she too wanted to help Falak and wondered if there was indeed a way to rise to this challenge while avoiding any dire consequences. With tact, she said, 'May God bless my thoughtful and loving begums for thinking of the young lovers. However, something occurs to me. Even if I manage to take Falak out, where will we find Mirza Qaiser? We will need to get him involved in our plans as well.'

'Yes, and he is unlikely to agree or will probably not be in the Qila premises for he has started working in the Sadr-us Sudur office,' said a relieved Mubarak.

'Don't worry about that,' said Zohrun Nisa Begum, dashing Mubarak's hopes. 'It is Holi, after all—a holiday—and so he is very likely to be in the Qila.'

'My ladies,' continued Hariyali, as an idea started to take root in her mind, 'I think the best way would be for you to call Mirza Qaiser to visit you. He is going to be married to your beloved niece and you have every right to interview him. I can go and convey your summons to him. Then we can arrange for Falak to be present there.'

In fact, Hariyali had over the years helped many a lover meet safely, in the course of her work of selling bangles for betrothed couples. And betrothed couples weren't the only ones grateful to Hariyali—she had also been adept at helping lovers meet away from watchful eyes as well as enabling well-wishers of the mulk and Badshah to communicate in secret. She was good at keeping secrets and famed for standing up for her convictions.

'That is an excellent suggestion,' said Rashid Jahan who, confronted by Mubarak's emotional interjections, had started wondering if she was being too reckless about Falak's reputation. But Hariyali's ingenuity had banished these fears.

'Where will we meet him?' asked Zohrun Nisa Begum.

'You can send a summons to him, asking him to meet you in the Khurd Jahan garden,' replied Hariyali. 'I will escort him here and then bring Falak there too. It will seem natural and even if anyone comes to know, there is nothing to offend. I do believe that we can find a way to solve this puzzle without getting into trouble. But, of course, we must take necessary precautions to avoid any possible adversity.' Then she turned to Mubarak, and said, 'Keep your precious girl ready but don't tell her of the treat in store for her—not a single word—or else her excitement and nervousness will betray her to everyone, especially the ever so observant and sharp Zeenat.'

'Hariyali, you are a genius,' said a happy Zohrun Nisa Begum, offering the faithful bangle-seller a gold coin from her *batua* as a reward. 'Tomorrow, mid-morning, when the young ones will be busy watching the Holi mimicry on the reti.'

'Ji begum sahiba, as you wish.' Hariyali took the coin and left, followed by an agitated Mubarak.

As soon as they were out in the garden, Mubarak was unable to contain her mounting distress. 'Please Hariyali, be careful. You know how much is at stake here. Don't do anything that can jeopardize my darling's future.'

'Don't worry, sister,' soothed Hariyali, 'I am well aware of the dangers and that is why I have suggested the safest possible way. All will be well, and your darling girl will be safe. Now, I must hurry. I have to be off to meet Mirza Qaiser and tell him to be ready. And I will inform Agha Jan just before the Mirza comes so that there is no time for gossip.' With that, she swayed her way out of the mahal, her basket balanced on her head.

Her first stop was at Mirza Aftab's house.

'I was meaning to send you a message to come,' said Mirza Aftab, 'but as usual you know what is in our hearts before we do.'

'You are very kind to this slave girl, Mirza Sahib,' said Hariyali. 'I am very happy to be of service. I remember selling bangles to Begum Sahiba for Mirza Qaiser's *chhati* ceremony when he was just six days old, and it is my privilege to bring bangles for Begum Sahiba's son's bride. She must be smiling from the heavens above. Is Mirza Qaiser at home? I just wanted to take out his *sadqa* and bless him.'

'Yes,' responded the happy father. 'Today and tomorrow are holidays for him on account of Holi. I will call him.' A clap of his hands brought forward the servants. And Mirza Aftab instructed them, 'Tell Qaiser that Hariyali wants a few minutes of his time and take her to him.'

Very soon, Mirza Qaiser came into the room. 'Abbajan, I am yours to command. The attendant said you had some orders for me?' said Qaiser.

'Not me, son, but Hariyali wants to bless you. I will take your leave as I have some work to do.' So saying, Mirza Aftab left the room, allowing the two of them to converse in private.

'Yes, Hariyali, how can I serve you?' said Qaiser with a smile.

'Arre Mirza sahibzade, it is I who will always serve you and not the other way round. I bear a message from Rashid Jahan Begum and Zohrun Nisa Begum, soon to be your aunts. They want to meet you and satisfy themselves that you are indeed worthy of their niece.'

Qaiser's smile deepened. 'How can I ever be worthy of such an exalted princess of the Timurid line? I can only strive and aim to keep her happy to the best of my unworthy abilities. But yes their wish is my command. When should I go?'

'I will come at 10.30 tomorrow morning. You be ready,' said Hariyali. 'And, Mirza Sahibzade, may I be sacrificed over you, don't mention this to anyone except your father of course.'

With this, she presented her salam and left his house and the Qila.

Mirza Qaiser was on tenterhooks not knowing how to while away the hours till tomorrow. His nervousness about meeting the aunts-in-law was peppered by the thrill of possibly getting a glance of his beloved—for he knew they lived in the same part of the mahal. The thought gave him pleasure.

While the two aunts and Hariyali were satisfied with their work and serenely looking forward to the next day, Mubarak felt as if she was walking on hot coals.

Naseeban, sensing her confusion and anxiety, suspected something was amiss and asked her about it as they both left the Qila for their home.

'Oh, it's nothing Naseeban,' replied Maubarak. 'I am just nervous in the hope that everything goes off well as the date of my darling's nikah comes closer.'

'Don't be nervous, Mubarak,' said Naseeban squeezing her hand. 'We are all there to support you.'

'Just pray that everything goes off well and there is no trouble.'

'Why should there be trouble, Mubarak?' said Naseeban, genuinely confused by Mubarak's remark. She put an arm over Mubarak's shoulder and said reassuringly, 'The Huzur Alampanah himself has fixed the wedding. There will be nothing to worry about.'

Seeing that something was still gnawing at her friend from within, a sympathetic Naseeban probed further gently, hoping to alleviate Mubarak's concern.

Mubarak was eager to confide in someone to help relieve the mounting fears that threatened to overwhelm her—the distressing visions of the many ways in which so much could go wrong and disrupt the happiness she had come to know with Falak. However, she was also aware that total secrecy of the plans for tomorrow was of utmost importance. And so she must do nothing to arouse Naseeban's suspicions. 'What can I tell you, sister,' she finally said, 'just that I am anxious about any untoward incident hampering the wedding, especially now that the happy day is fast approaching.'

But as the two women talked, Mubarak realized how utterly alone she was in this—after all, the two begums might have meant well, but they would never understand the urgency of Mubarak's concerns and there was no way to challenge their authority either, and she couldn't even confide in Falak for fear of saying too much. Tears began to prick her eyes as she realized how deeply she missed Dil Ruba!

And so it was that her yearning for a confidante got the better of Mubarak's misgivings. In that quicksilver moment, Naseeban was being so sympathetic—her words so reassuring, her embrace so warm—that before she could stop herself, Mubarak spilled the entire scheme to her friend. If Mubarak had any lingering qualms about this impulsive act, they were swept aside by the compassion in Naseeban's eyes as she sought to console the older woman.

'Arre, sister,' said Naseeban, 'that isn't anything to worry about. The aunts are senior enough to call whomever they want and if the shahzadi happens to be nearby, who can fault her? It is not as if she had made these secret plans!'

By the time the two women bid each other farewell, Mubarak was feeling lighter in spirit as she walked to her quarters. Surely, she thought, confiding in Naseeban was worth the risk. Naseeban also loved Falak dearly and would do nothing to jeopardize the situation for Falak. Nothing will go wrong . . .

*

Around mid-morning the next day all the ladies in the mahals were enjoying the sights and sounds of the mela held beneath the Qila walls on the reti. A huge crowd had gathered, spreading from the Qila up to Raj Ghat. The courtesans were dancing to the euphoric sounds of tambourines, cymbals and trumpets. Groups of travelling musicians and artists had converged upon the scene to display their tricks and talents.

Suddenly Zeenat and Zebunisa burst into peals of laughter, attracting the older ladies to the window. The mimics were imitating the Emperor, prince and princesses. All along the riverfront of the Qila, from the Badshah to the Malika, to the shahazadas and shahzadis everyone was watching and laughing. 'Don't take offense; it is Holi!' said one, and Huzur Mahabali Badshah sent down a fistful of gold and silver coins to reward the mimic and signal his pleasure.

Amid that confusion and excitement, Hariyali quietly led Mirza through a wicket gate into the empty garden. The two aunts had been waiting and immediately advanced, unnoticed, when they saw Mirza Qaiser. Hariyali had already greased the palm of the khwajasara guarding that part of the palace. Qaiser stood quietly with his head bent down, heart in turmoil, till he heard the two ladies approaching him. Bending low he presented his salam to them and said, 'This slave is at your service and yours to command, begum sahiba.'

Hariyali quickly went inside and sought out Mubarak. Falak was preoccupied at her window perch, searching the crowds below for a glimpse of her prince, when she felt Hariyali tug her elbow. Quietly, she came away from the window with a question in her eyes. 'Shahzadi,' said Hariyali, 'may I be sacrificed over your beauty, your aunt Zohrun Nisa Begum wants you to help her.' And with that, she led the princess towards the garden.

Mubarak made sure to accompany them, muttering prayers for their plan's success and invoking Bibi Fatima and Hazrat Ali to keep her charge safe. When they reached the garden, they saw the two elderly ladies sitting on a bench with a young man in front of them.

Falak was transfixed. The sexual tension that built up within her inexperienced limbs was enough to tell her who he was, and her charming confusion and startled 'O' immediately brought the eyes of the three on her.

'Come here child, next to me,' commanded Zohrun Nisa Begum. Stumbling in adorable confusion, head bent low, heart almost leaping out of her throat, Falak did as she was commanded.

'Children, you have a few minutes to yourself,' said Rashid Jahan Begum.

'Mubarak and we will ensure no one sees you or disturbs you.' She rose to go to a bench closer to the entrance of the palace, to better guard the privacy of the betrothed couple for no one would dare cross her path without permission. Likewise, Mubarak and Hariyali positioned themselves near the garden gate.

Alone with the prince of her desires, Falak's heart and mind were in a swirl. She looked up into his passionate gaze and with a blush lowered her eyes again.

Out of sheer nervousness, the upright prince could think of no words of passion to match the fervour in his eyes. Quietly, he said, 'My princess, may I be sacrificed over you. My lowly self will always endeavour to protect you and give you every happiness in the world.'

Falak could not summon a suitable response. Shyly raising her eyes, she smiled into his, her heart in them. She lifted her palms, and he caught them tightly, without realizing his strength. Her involuntary cry of shock returned him to his senses, and he immediately let go of her hands, stuttering an apology. Falak smiled gently and said, 'I wasn't hurt. It's just that I can't believe that I am speaking to you. I have dreamt of this so often.'

'As have I,' he replied.

There was so much more to say to each other, but both were oddly reticent—each was struggling to find ways to frame their sentences with the right degree of sensitivity, clarity, wit and charm. Why was it so difficult?

The normally reserved Qaiser suddenly realized that he could say anything in the world to the woman who sat before him. And yet he remained tongue-tied.

He gazed deep into Falak's eyes, and this unexpectedly steadied him instead of fuelling his nervousness—and this is how he knew he had found a soulmate. Never loquacious, he sought refuge in the words of Mirza Naushah, which he knew would describe his state of mind more eloquently than anything he could come up with himself. He spoke earnestly, the passion evident in his voice: 'Now I know what Mirza sahib meant when he said':

> *mohabbat mein nahin hai farq jiine aur marne kaa*
> *usii ko dekh kar jiite hain jis kafir pe dam nikle*

There is no difference between life and death, in love
The beloved for whom I die, also causes me to live

'Hai Allah,' said Falak, 'Don't ever talk to me of death. You are my life and may I never have to live without you.'

The plaintive note in her voice compelled him to reach out to her. He stroked her hair gently with one hand and cupped her chin with the other. Her skin awakened to his touch. The pleasure of this moment of proximity made their surroundings melt away.

'Fear not, my dear Falak,' he said, his eyes fixed on hers. 'You are my life, and I was just speaking rhetorically. You bring out the poet and philosopher in me. But I will be more careful in my choice of words. May we always be together in life and the hereafter.'

A smile crept into her eyes.

'See,' he continued, trying to tease her into a good mood, 'I have learnt to obey your commands so fast. I won't use words that displease you.'

Her smile deepened, and he was pleased. Her woebegone face was not the memory of her he wanted to take with him.

'My prince,' said Falak, 'since you now obey my commands, come again to visit me soon.'

She had noticed the aunts approaching them from the corner of her eyes. Qaiser had become aware of this too and dropped his hands immediately. But it pained him to put more distance between himself and Falak, and so impulsively he reached out again to clasp her hands tightly, saying, 'I will try my best, my shahzadi, but you know I have to be careful and not let even the slightest smirch come to your fair name.'

Falak squeezed his hands longingly in turn. She was about to say she didn't care for her fair name, and all that mattered was seeing him; instead, she said, 'Now I will live to see you and if you want me to live you will have to come.'

Before he could respond, the aunts made their presence known and signalled Hariyali to take Qaiser away. The entertainment on the reti was over and the attention of the residents of the mahal could not be diverted much longer.

Hariyali quickly took him outside, thanking the khwajasara at the gate.

Mubarak rushed Falak inside, sending grateful thanks to Allah that her precious hadn't been seen conversing with her prince. While Mubarak spread out her prayer mat to offer namaz of gratitude, Falak sank into her bed in a state of ecstasy. Her young body was aflame with desire, and she had no idea what to do to lessen it. She lay quietly trying to calm herself.

It didn't help that Zeenat and Zebun saw her lying down and came fussing around her, asking her if she was well and if she had seen the mimics. Falak answered them in a daze, like an automaton.

Meanwhile, the subject of her desire was walking on air as he reached his house. The meeting had been too short and left him dissatisfied and full of longings, but there was not much he could do about it. He had given an ashrafi to Hariyali, hoping silently that she would help them meet again. Hariyali left well satisfied with her day's work for she had some urgent business to attend to and said she would come again soon.

She could see bands of entertainers going around Shahjahanabad, entertaining the aristocrats and the rich in their havelis. There was much good-natured leg-pulling with entreaties to not take offence because it was Holi! Children were entertaining elders with their antics. People were squirting colour on each other.

Soon, Hariyali joined this sea of colour. She not only carried a basket on her head, but she also wore colourful bangles herself and was going from mansion to mansion, house to house, to sell her bangles, squirt colour, give her *mubarakbadi*. This was the day when all class distinctions were relaxed in honour of the festivities.

'Pour colour on them—colour them!' were the words on everyone's lips.

Hariyali spent a little extra time in the haveli of Thakur Madhav Singh. Thakur sahib's wife and daughter Radha were regular customers and of late she had used this excuse to meet Thakur sahib too for some work.

'Is this the time to come on a festival, Hariyali? Our guests will be arriving any minute and Banno, and I still haven't worn new bangles.'

'Arre, Thakurain sahiba don't set me off. I have been on my feet from dawn. I had to go to Lala ji's mansion, Diwan ji's haveli, to the houses of the jewellers in Dariba and now I have come here.'

'Oh, all right. Sit down. Arre Balram, bring some sweets and *bhang* sherbet for Hariyali. Hariyali, we will try the bangles while you rest your feet.'

'Thakurain sahiba, these gold and silver bangles will look very beautiful on Radha *bitia's* wrists. She is blooming these days,' said Hariyali proffering some bangles to her daughter.

'Hariyali, you go to every house. If there is some suitable match for my Radha, please tell me.'

'Ji, Thakurain sahiba I will keep an eye out. But where is Thakur sahib? He knows all the best families. Our Radha bitia should get married to a prince.'

'I don't know what her father is up to these days. He spends all his time with Imam sahib and Mir sahib, playing Shatranj and talking. He refuses to tell me anything,' replied an exasperated Thakurain.

Sated and rested and a little intoxicated by the bhang, Hariyali said with uncharacteristic indiscretion, 'Don't worry Thakurain sahiba, all will be well. Soon all our troubles will be over.'

'Over? How? Whatever do you mean?' asked Radha who had been silent so far.

'Arre, bitia, what can I tell you except that our days of slavery are going to be over. Our Huzur Badshah will once again become powerful,' said Hariyali, the tiredness in her limbs combining with the intoxication of the drink to make her words slur a bit. 'The accursed angrez can start counting their days,' she continued, all but unintelligible, before passing out.

'Poor Hariyali,' said the Thakurain sahiba to her daughter. 'She works so hard. Instead of living off the earnings of her son, she and that sick husband of hers are dependent on what she makes selling bangles. The Company sarkar caught and executed her son as they thought he was spying on them and colluding with some other disgruntled nobles against them. Let her sleep off the effects of the bhang; Balram must have made it extra strong for her. She can go home later.'

Meanwhile, the musicians and the courtesans eventually reached the Qila, where the Emperor, Huzur Alampanah, and his noblemen sat on one side of the jharoka and the women on the other. Groups of revellers came to the jharoka to take their rewards.

The royal courtesans played Holi by squirting each other with their squirt guns, singing coquettishly in the presence of the Badshah, the *Hori* written by him:

> *Kyun mope maari rang ki pichkaari*
> *dekh Kunwarji du'ngi gaari*

> Why have you squirted me with colour?
> O Kunwarji I will swear at you.

> *bhaaj saku'n main kaise mosso bhaajo nahin jaat*
> *thaa'ndi ab dekhu'n main baako kaun jo sun mukh aat*

> I can't run, I am unable to run
> I am now standing here and want to see who can drench me.

> *Bahut dinan mein haath lage ho kaise jaane deoon*
> *Aaj main phagwa ta sau Kanha faita pakad kar leoon.*

> After many days I have caught you, how can I let you go
> I will catch you by your *cummerbund* and play Holi with you.

> *shokh rang aisi dheet langar sau khelay kaun ab hori*
> *mukh meedai aur haath marore karke woh barjori*

Who can play Holi with such a mischievous Kanha

My face you have coloured and my wrist you have twisted in your playfulness.

At night, there was a grand celebration in the Qila, with singing and dancing throughout the night. Famous courtesans from throughout the country had come here. The most popular song was Bahadur Shah Zafar's *Hori*. Qawwals were singing Hazrat Amir Khusrau's:

Aaj rang hai Maa rung hai ri
Moray mehboob kay ghar rang hai ri

There is a glow everywhere, O mother, a bright glow;
There is a glow in my beloved's house.

These verses, written by Hazrat Amir Khusrau, referred to the glow that emanates from God who is pleased with the saint and is reflected in his beloved's face, for Hazrat Nizamuddin Auliya is Mehboob-e Ilahi or Beloved of the Divine. These verses were composed by the poet after his first meeting with the saint at a very young age, and simply called 'Rang', capture his rapturous emotions on finding a *pir,* or spiritual mentor. Composed in the thirteenth century, they were very popular on Holi and reflected the spirituality of the occasion.

The Qila wasn't the only house they were being sung in, the entire shahr-e panah rang out with the sounds of revelry at night. Mehfils were held in every area of the walled city with the aristocrats, traders and shopkeepers all enjoying themselves there.

The dhobis of Kucha Mir Ashiq basti had a rollicking time in the day, with rounds of *bhang* being ground and mixed in the sherbet. They sang and danced, all drenched in colour. Tomorrow, they would be busy trying to clean the city's clothes soiled with all the vegetable dyes squirted on them, but today was theirs.

Holi was celebrated by a few families with flowers, the night before and the gardeners of Maliwara had been busy collecting colourful flowers for the occasion. Naseeban had supplied many baskets of roses to the haveli of Lala Roshan Lal, in whose huge courtyard the young girls would assemble to swing, to the sounds of music and songs.

While the Qila and Shahjahanabad were ringing with sounds of festivities and squirting of colour, a part of Hindustan was reverberating to a different sound.

Zoravar Singh sent a message to Mirza Qaiser and asked him to come to his haveli. When Mirza Qaiser finished his day's work, he guided his horse towards Phatak Hasbash Khan, where Zoravar Singh's family owned a huge haveli.

Today Mirza Qaiser had no time to admire the handsome naqqarkhana which housed the guards, drummers, trumpeters, and other household musicians of this Rajput family, past the beautifully designed garden with its silver fountains and pools. He entered the large forecourt surrounded by a row of rooms under an arcade and passed on to the diwan khana, elaborately furnished with silk and brocade curtains and cushions, fine carpets and chandeliers.

Zoravar Singh, oblivious to his surroundings, was pacing up and down, a frown on his face.

'Ama, is all well Bhai Zoravar?' asked Mirza Qaiser, dispensing with the normal formalities of greetings when he saw his worried friend.

'Oh, I am so glad you have come. I didn't know who else to trust or turn to,' he replied. 'But I am being amiss. You must be coming here after your day's work, and I should offer you some refreshments. Please be seated brother,' said Zoravar indicating a thick pile of silken carpets with cushions and bolsters scattered around. He clapped his hands and summoned his servant, Ram Khilavan. 'Bring some refreshments for Mirza Qaiser, and Ram Khilavan ensure that only you come to this area. I have some important work with Mirza Qaiser and don't want to be disturbed.'

Mirza Qaiser waited, for he knew that his cousin needed time to sit down and discuss whatever it was that was worrying him so much.

As soon as Ram Khilavan came bearing silver trays laid with nuqtis, luqmas and sherbets, Zoravar asked the retainer to put the trays down and close the door behind him and to ensure no one came within hearing distance.

'What is the matter Bhai Zoravar? I can see it's very serious.'

'Yes, Bhai Qaiser, I just heard all this from my munshi, who is a friend of Mirza Moinuddin Khan, the thanadar of Paharganj. Munshi ji had gone to his village in Marwar for Holi and on his return, went to the thana,' he said, referring to the police station there, 'as he had some work. There he heard Mirza Moinuddin Khan discussing the passing of chapatis throughout Awadh and areas near Delhi. He was sitting there in the thana when the village watchman of Indraprat came and reported that the watchman of Sarai Farooq Khan had brought him a chapati, which he showed him, and then instructed him to cook five similar chapatis and send them to the five nearest villages of the neighbourhood with orders that each village *chowkidar* was to make five similar ones with for distribution. Each chapati was to be made of barley and wheat flour about the size of the palm of a man's hand and was to weigh two *tolas*.'

'Are you sure that man is not mistaken?' asked a shocked Mirza Qaiser. Working in the court he knew that the Hindustanis had many grievances against the angrezi sarkar, but this seemed weird.

'Yes, brother. Thanadar Moinuddin Khan had heard a similar report from his brother, Mirza Muhammad Hussain Khan, who is the thanadar of Badarpur, just sixteen miles from Delhi, according to my munshi and Ram Khilavan, whom I set about to find out if the statement of the watchman is true, and if these chapatis are being distributed in the villages. Sometimes a piece of goat flesh is also added to the chapati. There is something dangerous afoot and since you are with Mufti sahib, I thought I must warn you,' replied Zoravar Singh. 'An event which will undoubtedly create an atmosphere of great alarm in the minds of people is about to happen throughout Hindustan.'

'This is very alarming,' said Mirza Qaiser.

'Yes, Bhai Qaiser. Only a few days ago I had heard that the 19th Regiment of Foot at Barrackpore had refused to use cartridges and the 34th Regiment, also in Barrackpore, had behaved similarly, and that seven companies of that regiment had been dismissed. They fear that the cartridges have been greased with the fat of pig and cow and these are unacceptable to both Muslims, for whom the pig is considered impure, as well as the Hindus, who revere the cow. I am too junior to say anything, but I keep my ears open. Bhai, this is the beginning of a time of trouble. Information on the behaviour of the different regiments was circulated widely in the press in an Urdu newspaper published at Ambala. Perhaps you should tell Mufti sahib. He will know how to deal with this,' suggested Zoravar Singh.

'I am sure he knows. The angrez sarkar has spies everywhere and Mufti sahib too has his informers. If it was in the newspapers, then I am sure he must be aware. But yes, I am glad you have kept this confidential. We don't want a thousand tongues wagging and suddenly chapatis being distributed in all corners of Shahjahanabad,' said Mirza Qaiser.

Having unburdened himself, and seeing that it wasn't as alarming as he had thought, Zoravar Singh asked Mirza Qaiser, 'So what is the programme this evening? All your friends are talking about your absence. Should we go to the qahwakhana?'

'Yes, let us. We can go to Jama Masjid for prayers and will also get to know if there's further news,' said Mirza Qaiser. 'But first, let me go home. Abbajan will be waiting for me. I will change and meet you there.'

munh par us aftaab ke hai yeh niqaab kya
pardah raha hai kaun sa ham se ḥijaab kya

What is this veil on the face of that sun?
What purdah has remained, for us, why the veiling?

—Mir Taqi Mir

20

Baghavat in the Air

Hasti ke mat fareb men aajaiyo Asad
'alam tamam halqah-e daam-e khiyal hai

Don't be beguiled by the deceit of life, Asad
The universe is nothing but a web of consciousness.

—Mirza Ghalib

That evening, Naseeban finished her work early. She and Rahim were to visit Hira. There was something about the wine that he gave them that was conducive to long, passionate lovemaking. She must remember to ask him where he got it from. Of course, it wouldn't be wise to offer it to Rahim often, for she was a poor working woman and there were all those delicious aches and pains which she wanted to savour in bed, not while running errands.

Walking through Katra Ashrafi and Ballimaran, they crossed Chandni Chowk which was sparkling like a pearl in the moonlight and went into the Fatehpuri Bazar and past Katra Neel. A road to their right led into Punjabi Katra, a residential area thus named because this was where traders from Punjab would alight when they came to Shahjahanabad. It was here that Hira lived.

They passed by an attractive and appealing mosque whose beauty seemed beyond Naseeban's ability to describe. It had been

243

built by Nawab Aurangabadi Begum, wife of Alamgir Aurangzeb Badshah, completely of red sandstone, with a tank in the rather large courtyard that was fed by water from the Faiz nahr that ran through Shahjahanabad. However, now it had been encroached on the sides and people were using water from the tank for water supply to their own homes. The nahr that supplied water earlier was choked in many places and the water supply was intermittent.

Hira was waiting for his guests. He lived alone, as his wife had been living in the village to look after his parents and now, after his mother's death, was needed to tend the land and cattle. He had the clay huqqahs ready, the coals were glowing in the chillum, and the wine was kept in a coarse glass bottle and ready to be poured into tinned *katoras*.

'I am so sorry about your mother,' said Rahim after embracing him. 'Parents are Allah's blessings and it's always a tragedy when they leave us. May Allah give you the fortitude to bear the loss.'

'Thank you. Yes, I pray that Almighty gives her the highest place in heaven. Tell me how have you both been? Hope all is well.' He was impatient for news and gossip that might lead him to the hidden treasure; and having already spent a few weeks mourning his mother in the village, he was now eager to return to the task at hand.

'Well, there has been much excitement in the Qila, but Naseeban will tell you,' said Rahim. He had settled down comfortably with a huqqah and a katora of wine. Though wine was forbidden in Islam, like many of the royals and nobility, he too drank wine though only on special occasions.

Naseeban had refused wine but accepted a katora of sherbet and was relaxed enough to be garrulous. 'Bhai sahib, you won't believe me but since you left there has not been a single quiet day. First, the Nawab Malika sahiba fell sick and the Hakim sahib had to be called. Then there was all that fuss about a taveez that the amil had given the Malika sahiba to win back Huzur Badshah's attention. So many others are asking me for a taveez too. Oh yes! Alampanah has announced the betrothal of Shahzadi Falak Ara to Mirza Qaiser, so now she won't be needing any taveez. My head is spinning; there is just so much going on. Now I have to help Mubarak with the wedding preparations too. And I forgot to ask, how did you guess that Shahzadi Falak Ara wears a silver locket? I saw her fiddling with it when she was told of her impending nikah. Otherwise, it is hidden in her clothes.'

'Slow down, slow down, *bhabhi*,' said Hira who had got more information than he had hoped for. Now the question was how to turn it to his advantage. 'Who is this person who gives a taveez, seems like a useful person to know. The way things are these days, I never know when I might need a taveez myself.'

'Arre Hira bhai, where is the time to slow down? I have so much work to do. If you want a taveez, go to Hazrat Deen Ali Shah qalandar at Farrashkhana; he is a learned man. That amil is a scoundrel, a charlatan who does black magic. I rue the day I got involved with him, but what could I do? Roshni persuaded me against my wishes to introduce her to him. He lives behind our house and every day I can smell hair being burnt. Stay away from him. That's the advice I gave Mubarak too,' said an agitated Naseeban. Knowing that only men would drink wine, Hira had spiked the sherbet with a drug that had made Naseeban loquacious, but her tiredness was now making her sleepy. However, she was alert enough to realize that Hira hadn't answered her question. 'And bhai, you still haven't told me how you knew about the locket?'

Hira was unable to think of a plausible answer that would satisfy Naseeban's curiosity. Trusting the spiked sherbet to do its work, he hoped that a change of subject would distract the woman. And so, dodging her question, he asked instead, 'Why did the shahzadi need a taveez?' Under different circumstances, Hira would have questioned her slowly and deviously, but now he had to rush since he wasn't sure when he would get a chance to meet Naseeban again.

'Oh, why do young girls need a taveez,' she replied with a smile. 'But now that the Badshah Salamat has fixed her nikah with her young man I don't suppose she will need one. Of course, Mubarak is another matter. She's going around clucking like a brood hen whose chicks are about to be snatched away from her. She is worried about the evil eye and has already asked me to get a nazar *battoo* for her precious one. And nowadays, she is petrified as the two aunts are making plans to let the Shahzadi meet her Mirza. They are senior begums and there is not much Mubarak can do to overturn their schemes, so she is in a perpetual state of panic.'

'I am sure she has reason to be worried,' said Rahim, who had been listening. 'The shahzadi is said to be very beautiful. Now that she's to be married, she is even more vulnerable. Do help Mubarak, and I hope that the elderly aunts know what they are doing. Who is helping them? You must ensure secrecy and safety. Mubarak has always helped you and she's been a good friend.'

'That dratted Hariyali is always ready to help in any risky scheme. She is helping the begum sahibas,' mumbled Naseeban.

A plan was forming in Hira's mind as he absorbed this conversation. After all this while, he could finally discern an opportunity to get the locket. He was always good at concocting stories, and so jumped into the fray, 'Rahim bhai is right, bhabhi. If they are meeting secretly, it is even more imperative that she has prayers and charms to help her stay safe and ensure that their meetings remain undetected. You must help your friend. And, of course, I can help too if you want. In fact, I now recall that I do know a hafizji in Maler Kotla who gives taveez for such situations. The Nawab sahib's family there swears by him. One of my relatives is employed in the palace and she told me. I had just gone to meet him when my mother was sick. But he told me that her end had come, and I should give her a loving farewell and that is all I could do.'

'Bhai,' said Naseeban, doggedly returning to the matter of the unanswered question, 'you still haven't told me how you knew about the locket.'

'You seem fixated on this, Naseeban!' said Rahim with a good-natured laugh. 'Hira bhai has returned after an ordeal, and we must not be overwhelm him with questions.'

'No, please!' said Hira, worried now. 'Forgive my bad manners. My mind was . . . drifting. I did not intend any rudeness by not answering earlier.'

Hira realized that any further silence on his part would only arouse Naseeban's suspicions, and that would be detrimental to his plans. It was imperative that he say something—anything—to prevent the situation from unravelling further. 'You know Bhabhi,' he said, turning to Naseeban, 'my father used to supply silk and brocade to royal princes. He had told me that there was a Timurid custom that the emperor's daughters born of courtesans wore a mango-shaped locket, while those from legally wedded wives wore a rectangular taveez.' Hira's mind was working overtime and he added glibly, 'This was to differentiate them in matters of inheritance.'

'Really?' murmured Naseeban incredulously. 'I must say, I have never heard of this custom, and I have been working in the Qila, serving the ladies, all my life. Nobody else wears such lockets and there are many children born of concubines in the haram. Yes, many wear a taveez when young. I suppose there is always something new to learn. Anyway, thank you, bhai. I will talk to Mubarak and let you know.' Then, turning to Rahim, she said, 'I am very sleepy now, Rahim, I think it's time we went home.'

Hira's mind was racing. He had made slow progress in getting hold of the locket, but he was pleased that he may have finally found a way. All he had to do was to stoke the fears and superstitions of these two old women who loved the shahzadi. Now that he knew the mahal was not impenetrable, he decided to find out more about Hariyali and co-opt her into his schemes. If she was helping the begums take such a risk, she was probably not averse to helping others too—for a price too, perhaps. All he had to do was devise a way. Perhaps he could suggest that a new taveez be inserted in that locket. If Naseeban couldn't help, he would try Hariyali who evidently seemed very resourceful.

While it was early to bed and early to rise for the working Naseeban in her mud hovel, the indolent rich had just started their evenings in their mansions.

Mirza Qaiser and Zoravar Singh had both reached their favourite qahwakhana, where Kunwar Ibrahim and Mirza Abu Bakr were already seated with their huqqahs in front of them.

Steaming hot qahwa was placed in front of them in sparkling glass *istikans* encased in filigreed silver. The conversation turned to Mirza Qaiser's coming nuptials and his friends were teasing him when suddenly, Santosh Lal came rushing in and sat down blindly on a cushion.

'Ama Santosh, is all well? You look very perturbed,' asked Mirza Abu Bakr.

'Mirza sahib, you will also be very perturbed when you hear this. I just heard this from one of the Bengali students at the Delhi College and thought I would tell you.'

'Has doomsday been foretold Santosh?' asked Kunwar Ibrahim speciously, for what could be of such import?

'Arre Kunwar sahib, when you hear this you will realize. I myself don't have much knowledge about it, but my friend, Anirban Bandyopadhyay, was telling me that a soldier had been executed in Bengal for refusing to use the Enfield cartridge. He was a high caste Brahmin and he said that his caste was being defiled as the cartridge was greased with the fat of cows,' said Santosh in a rush.

Mirza Qaiser, who had been listening intently, asked, 'When was this?'

'A few days ago, Mirza sahib,' said Santosh.

Mirza Qaiser and Zoravar Singh exchanged glances. Soon after, both the friends left.

Meanwhile, Miyan Nabbu, always curious to know about everything around, whether it concerned him or not, had gone to meet two friends who had come from Lucknow.

They were meeting in Gali Chabuk Sawar. This was the place where the horse trainers and horse-breakers used to stay in the Shahjahani era. Now a few mansions had come up of families who had done well in the horse-trading business. Every month, a mehfil of storytelling would be held in the house of Ustad Mohammad

Baig, himself an eloquent and acclaimed storyteller. The winner was the one who told the tallest tales. It naturally attracted every loudmouth who considered himself a storyteller or wit. This mehfil of *fiqra kashi*—renowned for enthused exchanges of witticisms and repartee—attracted some riffraff too, as all were allowed regardless of status or rank. Though Ustad Mohammad Baig was an ace wrestler too and was famous enough to keep all in check, the elite of the city stayed away.

A few years ago, Baig had been invited to the court of Nawab Shah Jahan Begum of Bhopal court by her regent and mother, Sikandar Jahan Begum, but his flowery eloquence shrivelled, and he returned. Which flower can bloom if cut off from the dust of its garden? That too when the garden is as luscious and verdant as that of Shahjahanabad. The bulbuls and flowers of this garden were not only talented but also very faithful. Since then, his mehfils had started attracting travellers and raconteurs from far and wide.

Miyan Nabbu's senses were assailed by a wide variety of sounds and smells as he entered. He knew that the class he aspired to be a part of didn't frequent this place but his appreciation of the vulgar and loud pulled him here. He wondered to himself what these stiff-necked noblemen were so proud of. All they had was their lineage, for wealth and power had left them decades ago, yet they lived in an imaginary world of luxury and pleasure. Even though power had been lost, their sense of entitlement remained.

The mehfil hadn't started and people were gathering and arranging themselves around a small carpet with an embroidered masnad decorated with colourful gold and silver bolsters and cushions. Miyan Nabbu took his seat right in front, and taking out his silver muhnal, started puffing from the huqqah kept near him. Ustad Mohammed Baig sahib, dressed in a white chikan angarkha, fashionably worn to expose his left breast, over a white mulmul kurta and white khada pajama, also called *churidar*, came and sat on the masnad. Many storytellers, wits and sharp-tongued men who had been waiting for him, sat up. Normal etiquette was not followed here and no one got up to wish their host, they just nodded in the direction of whoever recognized or acknowledged them. This was indeed a mehfil where freedom of expression had broken free from the shackles of courtly confinement. The only restriction was that the words be clever, phrases witty and expression pithy.

The ustad signalled the evening open with the words, 'Miyan, there are no limitations to imagination here. Let everyone have fun. The only rule, it should be witty and humorous.'

The evening started, with insults and witticisms being exchanged humorously. Each glib remark was met by an even wittier repartee, and it was praised loudly and generously, encouraging others to join in the conversation.

One wit was ready to pluck the stars from the sky, another boasted he could bring the devil from its underground abode. The evening was going par its course when one stranger, dark-skinned, swarthy and pot-bellied, still wearing the soiled clothes of a traveller, pushed his way into the centre of the room.

Unable to place him, the ustad asked him his name.

'What business do you have with my name,' replied the stranger, 'I am told this is a mehfil of *zabaan-darazi* and verbal sparring. Let my tongue speak for me. If there is someone who can match it, let them come forward.'

Ustad replied, 'You have just entered, you will find your '*aqib* too.' But he had meant to say '*raqib*' or competitor.

The stranger smiled and said saucily, 'Are you hungry? You just ate the 'r' of raqib. It seems that food is expensive here, that is why the residents of this city eat words.'

Ustad smiled and said, 'Yes, indeed you are right. Donkeys and asses from other cities come and consume the food, making it expensive.'

The stranger persisted, 'It seems this is not a city but a stable yard of strange animals.'

'Yes, Miyan and you seem to have broken from your chains and escaped here. We will soon yoke you to a cart and put you to work.'

'Don't worry. I won't take your bridle away. A donkey's bridle would never fit a horse's neck,' replied the stranger.

'You seem more like a frog from a monsoon pond, who croaks only during the rains and doesn't even remember his own name afterwards,' said the Ustad.

'I am that bird whose name is so beautiful that it is not to be revealed in a murder of crows!' said the stranger triumphantly.

But he had underestimated the ustad who immediately sallied, 'Yes of course Miyan, murder is the right word to use for how you treat this beautiful language of our exalted city.'

The stranger said defiantly, 'My name is Sharafat—though the "nobility" it implies seems a little out of place in this ignoble assembly.'

Not one to let go of an opportunity and after all, an ustad of witticisms, the Ustad replied. 'Alas! The person bearing the name came to our mehfil but forgot to bring the attributes of the name with him. Which reminds me, I was present at your naming ceremony. In fact, I was the one who gave you this name. You were born for this name.'

'Thank you for complimenting me on my name. You do have some substance it seems, and don't just talk in the air,' replied Sharafat.

The curiosity of the gathered assembly was thoroughly piqued, and they wanted to hear the story.

'Well, if you insist,' said the Ustad. 'When I was young, I wanted to be a world traveller. One day I packed up my bags and set off in the jungle. I must have walked a day when I came upon a clearing in the jungle and heard a baby crying from within a hut. I went near the door, thinking the child may have been abandoned. I heard loud voices coming out of the hut. The parents of the baby were arguing over what to name the baby. Seeing my shadow at the door, the father came out. He was as thin as a pine nut, with a head like a walnut, small raisin-like eyes and a pista for a nose, and his wizened cheeks seemed to have been scratched by a vixen's claws. I thought to myself, what kind of baby has he begotten that he is in this state? Just then, the mother called out in a shrill voice and said, "If there is any man there, call him in. Let him be an arbitrator." I asked him what the matter was. The man was so full of his woes that the dam of his patience burst, and he said, "Sahib my wife is a calamity for which there is no cure. In fact, her name is also Aafat—calamity. She has the genes of a witch. See what she has done to me."

'Just then the lady of the house shouted, "You offspring of a puny pine nut, if only you were man enough to satisfy me, you wouldn't call me a witch. Anyway, this is neither here nor there. Tell that man why we are fighting, perhaps he may have a solution." I asked Miyan Chilgoza what the matter was. He replied, "Sahib we have been blessed with a son."'

'I immediately said, "But that is wonderful. Why aren't you celebrating instead of fighting?" He replied, "Sahib, I am saying that as it is a son, he should be named after me. If it was a daughter then it was another matter and my wife could name her after herself." Just then the shrill voice screamed from inside, "He is my son. Mine. Only mine. I am going to name him. Who are you to tell me what to name my child? Go to hell you shrivelled *chilgoza* of a man!" I tried to calm the waters by saying, "Why don't you let her name the baby? I am sure you will have more children and you can name them as per your wish." Hearing this the thin man stood up with pride and said, "No one will name this baby except me." Fearing an impasse I asked him, "All right tell me your name, maybe I can help find a solution." He was very reluctant but then finally said shamefacedly, "My name is Shar—evil. My parents kept losing their children in childbirth and one faqir told them that they should give me such an evil name that even death would maintain a distance from me. So, they named me Shar. The same case was with my parents' neighbours. On the recommendation of the faqir they named their daughter Aafat, and when we grew up, we were married off to each other. What an inauspicious conjunction of names. Since then, there has not been a moment of peace in my life. We fight constantly. Now that this baby has come, and there should be some happiness, we are still fighting." I smiled at them and said, "Miyan Shar there is no need to fight. Both of you can have your way. Why don't you name your baby Sharafat, which is a combination of both your names: Shar and Aafat?" When the mother heard this name, she was thrilled that their child could get such a noble name and peace prevailed. So, you see Miyan, this is how I gave you your name.'[32]

The stranger knew that he had been outwitted and, amidst the laughter of the gathering and the sounds of 'waah waah' for the ustad, he left.

In the confusion, Miyan Nabbu noticed another stranger who was staring at him. The stranger gestured to him to come outside. Still amused by the outrageous story of the ustad, he stepped out into the cool air. In any case, the gathering had become very stuffy, and his Lucknow friends had not yet arrived.

The stranger was standing in a corner of the street; from his comportment, he looked like a Company soldier.

Miyan Nabbu walked up to him and asked, 'Who are you? Why have you called me outside?'

'Walk with me, sahib. I will tell you.'

Since Nabbu was armed and a good shot he agreed, his hand on the pistol tied to his waistband.

When they reached the entrance of Kucha Dina Beg, which was deserted, the stranger sat down under a tree. He said, 'Sahib, I have come from Bengal. In fact, I have run away from there. I came to Shahjahanabad and was looking for someplace to eat when I saw many people going into this house. Since there was no restriction on entry, I went in thinking I would get some food here. But it seems only tall tales are exchanged here. I don't have much time as the Company spies must be on the lookout for me. You seemed the only man present there who could have resources, so I called you out to tell you my story.'

'What story? You seem like a scamster to me,' said a suspicious Nabbu.

'No sahib, I am telling you the truth. If you know somebody then you tell them that there is trouble brewing in the Company

Army. They are asking us to use a cartridge that is greased with the fat of pig and cow. The firangis are hellbent on corrupting our religion. Both Hindus and Muslims have refused. From my regiment in Barrackpore, Mangal Pandey refused. I was with him when he refused. He had a loaded musket and was screaming, "Kill the firangis." When he was caught he tried to kill himself but survived. They hanged him a week after and all those with him were also hanged. No one noticed me and I took advantage and ran away. But now someone will notice I am missing and will hunt for me.'

'This is a tall tale you are telling me. Taller than anything I heard inside. How do I know what you are saying is true? You seem a scoundrel to me. Where are you from and what is your name?' asked Nabbu.

'Sahib, I am from Kanpur, but I came here because I know this is the last place they will look for me. The *sipahis* are very angry and so are the Company officers. I fear there is trouble in the air, and I have news that I must share with someone. My name is inconsequential. I don't know if I will live to see tomorrow but at least I can be content that I have passed on my message.' This man was still speaking when another emerged from the shadows and violently pulled him away. Both vanished into the darkness.

Miyan Nabbu had no idea what to do with this information or whom to pass it on to. He went home in a troubled state of mind, leaving the decision for the morrow.

> *Un ko haal-e-dil-e-pur-soz suna kar utthe*
> *Aur do-chaar ke ghar aag laga kar utthe*

I got up after narrating the state of my burning heart
A few more homes were burnt before I left.

—Zahir Dehlvi

21

The Heat Surges

Kahne detii nahin kuchh munh se mohabbat meri
Lab pe rah jaatii hai aa aa ke shikaayat meri

Love doesn't let me voice my emotions
My grievances remain unvoiced, caught between my lips

—Dagh Dehlvi

The early morning breeze from the Jamuna was caressing Falak Ara's cheek as it blew in from the stone *jaalis* into the mahal. The maalans had put baskets of flowers near the beds of all the ladies which was giving out a beautiful fragrance. The young musician was playing Raga Bhairavi on his ektara to signal that dawn was about to break.

The sound of the azan calling the faithful to prayer and the temple bells were mingling with the raga and it was time to get up for prayers.

Water was ready in ewers for the ablution, the attendants and servant girls were standing in readiness to pour water and then wipe the royal hands and faces with napkins and soft towels.

Prayers over, the older ladies sat down to read the Quran *sharif* and the younger ones to follow their interests.

Mubarak had just entered the mahal and was fussing around Falak Ara when Naseeban entered. She called Mubarak aside.

255

'Mubarak, yesterday I met a friend of my husband called Hira, who is from Maler Kotla. Very nice man. I was telling him about the amil near my house and taveez when he said that there's an old faqir sahib in his village who gives taveez to safeguard against the evil eye. I know you were looking for one. Should I ask him to get one made for Shahzadi Falak? May I be sacrificed over her; she has been blooming since her engagement was announced.'

' O Naseeban, is that even a thing to ask? Please get a taveez for my baby. I can't believe just a month is left for the wedding. I am already in a state of panic. May Allah make everything easy for us, Insha'Allah.'

'Very well, I will tell him today itself. And don't be so anxious, we are all here to help. The begum sahibas are also helping with the trousseau. It will all be done on a grand scale, as befits the shahzadi's status.'

Naseeban left to attend to her duties while Mubarak kept on clucking around like a brooding hen over her eggs.

After freshening up and saying her prayers, Falak Ara took up her station near the window. She had to finish the painting of the young girl bathing in the Jamuna. Of course, a glimpse of Mirza Qaiser as he came to attend the Jharokha Darshan was the added incentive. And didn't the naughty Zeenat know that!

Wo aaye ghar mein hamare Khuda ki qudrat hai
Kabhi hum un ko kabhi apne ghar ko dekhte hain

S/He has come to my house, its God's grace
At times, I look at my house and others at her face.

She quoted Mirza Naushah and asked impishly, 'Apajan, what is he wearing today?'

A blushing and embarrassed Falak, whose eyes had been darting around the ghat looking for her love, returned to her painting and said, 'I don't know what you are saying Zeenat. I am finishing my painting of that bathing girl. See her dupatta is now complete but I haven't got that exact movement.'

Sikandar Ara Begum, who had been reciting the Quran nearby, heard and called out, 'Show me what you are painting Falak. I had also learnt a little bit of painting from Sahifa Bano's disciple.'

'Who was Sahifa Bano?' asked Falak.

'She was one of Jahangir Badshah's slave girls and the pupil of Aqa Riza, the famous Persian painter. I don't know much about her, but she signed her paintings as "daughter of Mir Taqi". She had taught one of her attendants and I learnt by observing the attendant paint. Those were the days I was young and the durbar and mahal were far more prosperous than now. Anyway, show me your painting.' A frown creased her forehead as if trying to remember something unpleasant, but immediately she shrugged her shoulders and shook her head.

Then she sat for a long time looking at her painting and gave her suggestions: 'The reason the dupatta isn't falling is that the swell of her breast should be reduced. When drawing the female figure you have to keep in mind that her breasts are small, her waist tiny, hips generous and the lower body tapers to produce a triangular shape. The ankles are slim and shapely. You can use gold to burnish the ends of the dupatta, which will give it that gossamer effect I think you are looking for,' said Falak's great-grand aunt. She had been very close to Mirza Salim and his wife and carried a kindness in her heart for Falak, whose grandmother had served them. The old lady glanced at the locket on Falak's neck and tried to remember where she had seen it. She knew it was a link to her past—some deep-rooted instinct told her this. But try as she could, her mind became blank whenever she attempted to follow the thread of her memory to wherever it wanted to lead her. This girl was definitely a link to her past, and maybe one day she *would* remember.

'Dadijan can I come and take your advice once in a while? I am just learning, and I have no one to guide me,' asked Falak.

'Of course, beti. You can come anytime. In the mornings I am normally free. It is only when I am getting my jewellery repaired that I get busy.'

The bathers had now gone home, the Jharokha Darshan was over and preparations for the mid-day meal were in full swing in the mahal. Falak retired to her corner to read the Diwan-e Makhfi.

Hariyali came swinging and singing to find Falak frowning into the distance, her thoughts clearly elsewhere. 'Shahzadi sahiba,' she exclaimed, lavishing the girl with compliments, 'why are you fretting?'

'You know the answer, Hariyali. That day the meeting was so short, and I couldn't really express my thoughts. Can you arrange another meeting?' asked Falak hopefully.

Hariyali knew that arranging another meeting would be near impossible, if not immensely risky, but she did not want to dishearten Falak. Instead, another idea occurred to her.

'I will see what I can do, my dearest shahzadi but till then why don't you write to him? I can promise that I will deliver the letters in his hands and bring you his reply. Perhaps if you know about each other's movements, a chance to meet again might present itself more easily.'

'That is a wonderful suggestion, Hariyali,' said Falak, cheering up. 'I will immediately write to him. But please don't tell Mubarak or my aunts. Mubarak is in enough of a flap already.'

'My dear, you write a letter and leave the rest to me. I will come on my return and collect your missive.' Saying this, Hariyali left singing Hazrat Amir Khusrau's immortal verse for his pir o murshid, Hazrat Nizamuddin Auliya:

Ghar naari ganwari chaahe jo kahe,
Main Nijam se naina laga aayi re.

Let the women say whatever they want,
I have stolen a glance from Nizam's eyes.

Meanwhile, Naseeban sent Rahim to Hira's house with the message that the saint in Maler Kotla should give the taveez to ward off the effects of the evil eye from Falak and keep her safe. Grabbing the opportunity, Hira replied, 'Rahim bhai, I had sent a message to the pir faqir as soon as we had our conversation. In fact, the *dak* runner brought the message last night. Pir sahib has said that the best results will come if the taveez is inserted into the locket which he could see her wearing mentally. So, if Naseeban could get that via Mubarak, I will get the taveez made and brought well in time for the shahzadi's wedding.'

The message was duly conveyed to Naseeban and via her to Mubarak.

'Please tell Hira bhai that he can get the taveez from the pir sahib, and I will insert it myself into the locket that shahzadi wears. Or he can make another locket, and I will pay the price for the silver. I don't think it is possible to take this one off. I had promised my sainted mistress on her death bed that I would ensure her daughter wore it all her life,' replied Mubarak.

Meanwhile, the sun in Falak's firmament was shining. Her letter had reached Qaiser and a reply had come with the dawn. The inexperienced Falak had no idea how love letters were written and started by prosaically describing her painting, and the problems she had been having over rendering the dupatta's fall. But this outpouring of words on the page steadied her and brought new confidence. And with that, she found the courage to give vent to her feelings: *my heart is beating wildly, and I don't know whether this is because of the fear that you may think me too shameless for writing to you in this way—instead of decorously waiting for the day I can come lawfully to your house as your bride. Even as I write these words it is as if a thousand butterflies have taken residence in my heart. I don't know if, in my inexperience, I am breaching etiquette or being too bold for I never had a mother to teach me the niceties of such customs. All I know is that I am caught in the enchantment of love, a realm that until now remained a distant dream. I know that I can trust you to understand and forgive my trespasses.*

When Hariyali came to give Qaiser the letter and told him who it was from, he took it shyly and went to his room to read. If Falak felt that there were a thousand butterflies in her heart, he felt as if a thousand bulbuls had clustered deep within him, singing of love and passion. As was his wont whenever he became emotional, the first thing that came to his mind was poetry.

Is this what Mevlana Rumi meant when he said, 'Be drunk in love since love is everything that exists. Without the occupation and trading of love, there isn't any door to the Beloved.'

Poetry also came easily to him since Qaiser had been learning and practising verses for his calligraphic panels. And so, after a somewhat stilted beginning in which he wrote about his work in the Sadr-us Sudur's office where he helped the Sadr by reading the case files that came up before him and making notes for the Sadr so that he could dispose of the cases easily. He realized it was boring stuff, but it took him time to loosen up and then there was no stopping him as he poured out his heart to her:

How can this be a trespass? Our love is divinely ordained and the minute I looked into your eyes that fateful day I knew that I had found my soulmate. Your gaze touched the deepest corners of my soul, awakening within me emotions I never thought possible. This must be the ishq-e majazi that my ustads taught me about. Our emotions are pure, and our lives are entwined by destiny. Be sure, I will protect you with my life. In fact, you are my life, and I will always cherish you.

He didn't stop to reread it as he sealed the envelope and kept it in readiness for Hariyali who had promised to pick up his message in the morning. He looked out of his window to see the sun shining.

The sun wasn't the only thing that had decided to brighten the world that day. The pride of the Timurid family, Alishan Gurkani Hazrat Zill-e Subhani, may he reign in perpetuity, had illuminated the throne in the Diwan-e Khas with his presence.

The *arkakeen-e saltanat*, these pillars of the state, after presenting their kornish and salutations, came and stood in their customary places with great humility and reverence.

Syed Qasim Alim, son of Mir Qalander Ali Khan, was given a robe of honour and five pearls for his exemplary service. Syed Qasim Ali Khan presented nazar and gave profuse thanks to the Emperor's magnificent generosity and blessings.

The Emperor waved his hands and said *takhliya*, bidding the others to leave, and the courtiers in the durbar duly obeyed. Only the urdabegni and officers for protocol remained. The Huzur-e Anwar was to meet his spiritual mentor, that guide of straying travellers on the path of Allah, Shah Ghulam Nasiruddin, popularly known as Miyan Kale sahib. This was an intensely personal moment for the Huzur when the registers of gnosis and truth were opened. After this blessed meeting, Ehtreramud Daula Hakim Ahsanullah Khan was called. The papers regarding the department of the bakshi, or paymaster-general, were handed over to him. It was now time for the Badshah to have his meal, pray and retire for the afternoon before he reappeared to meet his calligraphy students.

The next morning, having dispatched his reply with Hariyali, Mirza Qaiser was getting ready to go to the Mufti court in Kashmiri Darwaza. He wondered if he should go to Mufti sahib's house first and convey the information about the chapatis or let it be. *Abbajan will know what I should do,* he thought and went to search for him.

Mirza Aftab was sitting with his account books because he had to put together the money for the dower, which the bridegroom had to the bride at the time of nikah. Amongst the Muslims, it was the bridegroom or his family who made all the expenditures. Of course, now the royal family had adapted to Indian customs and also gave a trousseau but the Islamic tradition of meher continued. The dower had been fixed at five hundred ashrafis. The stipend given by the Badshah was generous but then so was their lifestyle. It was covered by the dower which his wife had brought. After her death, he had inherited those villages and orchards in Rajasthan that had been hers and he got a fair bit of income from there. God willing, their son would be married in a style befitting someone who was going to be the Badshah's son-in-law.

'Abbajan, my salam. If you have a few minutes, can I ask you for your advice?'

'Of course, my son. I am always free for you. I was just making arrangements to get the meher money. Your wedding is now only a month away and all arrangements have to be made. Today, I am going to see a house in Lal Kuan area. My friend Sikandar has talked to someone there. There is a haveli with a small diwan khana and garden. MashaAllah now that you are in service and going to become a householder, you will be getting visitors, official and personal.'

'Abbajan, yesterday Zoravar had called me to his house. He told me about a story that his munshi told him. Apparently, chapatis are being passed in the villages throughout Awadh and areas near Delhi. And whoever gets them is instructed to cook five similar chapatis and send them to the five nearest villages of the neighbourhood with orders that each village chowkidar was to make five similar ones for distribution. Each chapati was to be made of barley and wheat flour about the size of the palm of a man's hand and was to weigh two tolas. Abbajan, I don't know if this information is credible and whether I should inform the revered Mufti sahib about it or not?'

Mirza Aftab lifted his head in surprise and said, 'Chapatis? What message can chapatis convey? I think the munshi ji must have consumed too many intoxicants—perhaps he'd eaten bhang fritters and even drunk milk flavoured with it on Holi—and imagined all this. Mufti sahib is already so busy, let us not disturb him with the fantasies of an intoxicated mind. But do keep your eyes open. If you hear something similar from anyone else, then you should go to Mufti sahib.'

Relieved that the chapatis were nothing serious, Qaiser took his leave mounted his horse rode towards the Kashmiri Darwaza, where the court was located.

The cases brought to the court were mundane and had to do with robbery, non-payment of dues and matters of land revenue. They were easily sorted out. He spent some time writing to Falak as he knew Hariyali had promised to bring her next letter at dawn and collect any messages that he might have for Falak.

When Hariyali came with the shahzadi's letter of that day, Qaiser's reply was ready. He read about her day and her painting. He was overcome by a similar pang when he learned of her feelings at their separation, but he was still thankful that she could at least communicate with him. In return, he mentioned how blessed they were to have Hariyali as their angel in this matter. He reassured Falak that there were just a few weeks of separation left and then went on to share his anxiety about the chapatis, and that thankfully his father had dismissed his fears. He felt lighter. They had fallen into an easy intimacy via these letters which were being exchanged daily.

Miyan Nabbu woke up when the noon azan was being called out from the mosques. He stretched languorously and called for his servants to bring the water for the toilette and ablutions. After freshening up he rushed to the masjid near his house to pray. He was to meet his munshi after that. His father had sent him with some money and accounts for him to check from their lands.

The afternoon was spent in account books at which he was very good. But now Nabbu needed a break. He went towards Chandni Chowk, hoping to find some of his friends. His friends were busy, but he saw Brijnath Zutshi, speaking earnestly with Santosh Lal and another Kashmiri student at Delhi College.

As everyone seemed busy, Nabbu returned to his house and sent a message to Kunwar Ibrahim asking him if they could meet in the evening. By now, he had forgotten the stranger he met the previous night.

Brijnath Zutshi and his friend Mani Ram Kaul were discussing the upcoming meeting of the Anjuman-e Latini, an informal gathering of the Kashmiri pandits, where they discussed the latest strides in scholarship in the Latin world and perfected the art of dancing the quadrille and waltz. The Kashmiri Pandit society comprised great scholars with a sound education in Greek, Latin, English, French, Sanskrit, Farsi, Arabic and Urdu, and were very learned in statecraft, being appointed to high posts in the Company sarkar and invited to balls and parties thrown by them.

That evening, in a haveli in Sitaram Bazar, where they gathered under the auspices of the Anjuman-e Latini, the conversation turned to the swelling rumours of discontent amongst the sepoys of the East India Company, but since none of them was connected to the army, and rumours were not substantiated by facts, it was soon given up. Theirs was a rational society where intellectual pursuits were followed, not a place for bazar gossip.

There were more important matters to discuss, such as the lines by William Wordsworth:

I had melancholy thoughts . . .
a strangeness in my mind,
A feeling that I was not for that hour,
Nor for that place.

These were people whose ancestors had left their motherland of Kashmir to seek their fortunes in the courts of the Mughals. Now that the Mughals themselves had lost their political power they were looking in other directions; in provincial courts and the British Company. Though Delhi College was one very good reason for them to stay in Delhi, its other charms were diminishing. It seemed as if the gaiety of the city which they had taken for granted was forced, and now these rumours added to the general air of melancholy. The city maybe experiencing a cultural renaissance, but it was a city that was past its best years.

The heat was also becoming unbearable. Should they repair to Srinagar for the summer months, or perhaps go to Shimla as the angrez did?

Exams were approaching and they had to do well to secure a position in the Company or as in the case of Brijnath, to apply for admission to Cambridge University. Studying in cooler and climes with alluring scenery might be more productive.

Many such questions were vexing their minds.

Kunwar Mohammed Ibrahim and Hamid Ali Khan had received Nabbu's message and with their day's work done, decided to meet him in the qahwakhana. It was as good a place as any to spend the evening. However, as the qahwakhana was deserted the three friends decided to grace the mehfils of Mushtari bai with their presence. Her prowess in khayal gayki was spreading far and wide and they had not visited it as yet.

As they were leaving, Imamuddin Khan entered the qahwakhana. 'Ama, where are you off to? I was hoping to meet one of you here and spend some time. I have been studying and need to refresh my brain.'

'Miyan, we have just the cure for you. Come with us,' said Hamid.

'Where?' Imamuddin asked.

'To listen to the singing of Mushtari bai, guaranteed to dust off all the cobwebs in your mind and rejuvenate your senses,' replied Nabbu.

'But isn't she a tawaif?' asked Imamuddin, who, hailing from a very religious family was shocked at the idea.

'Yes, she is,' said Ibrahim. 'But tawaifs are skilled in singing and preserving etiquette. Our ancestors have always patronized them. It is a pleasant way of passing an evening.'

'Ama Miyan Imamuddin, how do people of your town pass the evenings? I am sure they can't only be listening to religious sermons or their wives' harangues?' asked the irrepressible Nabbu. He continued, 'And you need only listen to their song. You don't have to look at them or touch them if you fear it will corrupt your soul.' He himself, of course, had other ideas.

Seeing Imamuddin's reluctance, Hamid chipped in with Mir Taqi Mir's famous verse:

Tujh ko masjid hai mujh ko mai-khana
Waiza apni apni qismat hai

For you the mosque; For me the tavern
O preacher, a different destiny each of us yearn.

'Isn't this a sin?' asked the earnest Imamuddin.

'What is a sin and what is a virtue?' asked Ibrahim. 'These are women who are highly trained in classical music and dancing. They are repositories of a high culture that has been on the decline since the angrez took over our country. And they bring solace to the heart with their pure vocals. Their music never fails to elevate my heart. Isn't that a virtuous act? After all, that is what music is supposed to do; connect you to your maker. It is a matter of perception. Of course, if you misuse it then that is a sin,' said Ibrahim.

'That is exactly what a sama mehfil does too,' said a relieved and immature Imamuddin and fell in step with his friends, determined to keep his eyes closed and only listen to the vocals.

The four friends climbed the steps of Mushtari bai's balakhana. These salons were always on the upper floor, which is what gave them that name. The ground floor was usually given on rent to shopkeepers, which earned the courtesans a good rent. Running a sophisticated set-up, training the girls and paying the various ustad and musicians who came to train or accompany them was an expensive business. The tawaifs did have generous clients and generally a single rich one but they relied on their resources to maintain their high standard of living and independence. They were amongst the highest-earning members of the city.

The friends entered a room lit up with chandeliers in which scented candles burnt, incense sticks and the smell of itr and fresh flowers created a heady atmosphere. The floor was covered by a white chandni and Persian carpets were thrown over them in different corners with beautifully embroidered bolsters and cushions, huqqahs kept near them. Flagons of wines were kept with crystal glasses on low stools for those who wanted to partake of it. A few patrons were already seated, taking sips of the wine and puffs from the crystal huqqahs.

Mushtari was sitting in the middle of the room towards the back wall. She was dressed in a mauve peshvaz and khada pajama, with a bright orange organza dupatta carelessly draped over her head. Her broad forehead was decorated with a maang-teeka and a diamond and emerald jhoomar on the right side of her head, as per the courtesan custom; begamat wore a jhoomar on the left side of their head. The young Imamuddin, who soon forgot his vow to keep his eyes closed, had never seen such a vision, her dark hair with the twinkling teeka and jhoomar looked like a glittering stretch of the milky way. He did wonder why her jhoomar was on the right and not the left, like the women in his family wore it.

An older lady, dressed in a more subdued manner, sat on the carpet next to her. A huge silver *paandan* was kept in front of her and it was she who would control the proceedings in the balakhana. The musicians who sat beside her on a separate carpet would wait for her command to start playing or stop. The compositions to be played would be chosen by her.

Mushtari got up with languorous grace to present her salutations to each new entrant, her anklets tinkling and jewellery twinkling. The four friends took up their stations on a carpet, leaning against the bolsters. One of the maid servants, also finely dressed and bejewelled, brought a silver tray with paan on it and presented it to the four friends. She was poised in front of the wine flagon and presented it to those who wanted to partake of it. She would also ensure the smouldering coals in the huqqah were replenished from time to time. All this was done as unobtrusively as possible.

A few angrez officers were also present.

One of them, named Templeton, said in broken Urdu, 'I am in fairyland waiting for the enchantress to entwine my heart to hers.' He was one of those who was more knowledgeable about the Indian traditions. Unlike his friend who had come with him, he did not think of Mushtari as a prostitute, but as a performer. This was her Covent Garden stage.

Mushtari smiled and said, 'Sarkar, you are plucking stars from the sky and elevating this lowly person to the sky. I don't deserve such praise.'

Another assembled Indian noble said, 'It seems that his eminence likes to roam the skies. That is why his head is always in the sky.'

The older lady who was experienced in keeping peace and diffusing tensions said with practised ease, 'Sarkar, I am glad that our humble efforts have been able to give you a peep into the heavens. Isn't that what we all yearn for? A few moments of escape.'

She gestured towards Mushtari and said, 'Beti, which new ghazal do you have for us today?'

Mushtari collected her thoughts together and arranged herself in such a way that she could face the assembled men. She started with khayal and *tappas* and once the mehfil was filled with her magical, smoky voice, started singing Mir Taqi Mir's famous ghazal:

Ultii ho gain sab tadbiren kuchh na dawa ne kaam kiya
Dekha is bimari-e-dil ne aakhir kaam tamam kiya

All my stratagems have fallen apart, no cure seems to work
My ailing heart has eventually spelt doom for me.

Her throaty sensuous voice, the twinkling of her huge diamond nose-pin as she moved her face and the graceful movements of her hands as she emphasized some words soon transported the gathering into another world.

Nawab Sahib Jaan Mohammed Ali Khan said, 'Waah, waah! This is what I needed. My destiny has been upside down from the day I was born,' he said punning on the word '*ulti*' which means upside down. 'But I feel that while earlier I had been hanging upside down in ecstasy like Harut Marut, today my fate has been up righted.'

'Waah, *khoob*. The song transported us into fairyland and Nawab sahib, your analogy has added to it.'

The angrez friend who was with Templeton asked him what Nawab sahib had said. Templeton explained the Quranic story of the two angels who prided themselves on their ability to never sin. They were sent by Allah to earth to test the premise that they could withstand carnal desires, even if they were no longer angels. They were tempted by a woman. And so consumed were they by carnal desires that the fallen angels were condemned to serve their penance by hanging upside down in a well until the Day of Judgment.

Imamuddin was very struck by this analogy too and was talking about it to Ibrahim and Hamid. Nabbu, who seldom troubled himself with deep thoughts, was looking around. He saw a curtain lift and fall at the back of the hall. To his surprise, the person who had peeped out was the same man who had pulled away the sepoy he had met last night in Kucha Dina Beg. He wanted to explore further but the evening was over, and everyone was getting ready to leave.

He left, thinking he would return to investigate.

He was still humming one of the verses of Mir's ghazal that Mushtari bai had sung when he reached home.

Nahaq hum majburon par ye tohmat hai mukhtari ki
Chahte hain so aap karen hain hum ko abas badnam kiya

She accuses helpless us, of being in control,
She does as she pleases and defames us needlessly.

22

The Hunt Begins

Yaan ummid-e-qatl hi ne khoon kiya
Rah gayi hasrat dil-e-jallad mein

It was my desire to be slain that got me killed
Leaving the hangman's wish unfulfilled.

—Mustafa Khan Shefta

Hariyali came in singing a thumri in Raga Bhairavi that expressed the pain of longing:

Bajuband khul khul jaaye
Sawariya kaisa jadu daara re

My armlet keeps opening,
O beloved what magic have you cast on me.

At this time everyone was preoccupied with dawn prayers, she found Falak on her prayer rug and, bending down, dropped Qaiser's missive in her voluminous dupatta before making herself scarce. Falak finished her prayers and went to a corner to read the letter and keep a reply ready.

She savoured his words, 'meeting you even if for a few minutes, was like the water of Zamzam being poured on a parched soul. You are my heartbeat, nay my soul.' Seeing this passionate side of him was balm for her parched soul too.

She read with interest about the chapatis. By now she had come to understand his passionate loyalty towards the Badshah Salamat and Takht-e Timuriya. She had also started appreciating his concerns over the intentions of the angrez.

By the time the Jharokha Darshan was over and the respected Shadow of God on Earth left for shikar of wild ducks and fowls, she had composed her reply. She replied that her life seemed meaningless without him, and she was living in anticipation of being with him soon. She asked him not to fret but to keep his ears open for any further news. Sheltered as she was from the hustle and bustle of the world with only her aunts and cousins and attendants for company, Qaiser's letters opened another world for her, and she was getting acquainted with things he held dear. And with that, she felt even more aligned with him.

The month of Shaban was drawing to a close and within a few days, the new moon would herald the start of the blessed month of Ramzan.

Huzur Alampanah would be spending his time in prayers and devotions and so there were more petitions to be taken care of. The widow of royal employee, Jagjeevi Das, who had died recently, was sent a *do-shala* as a mark of condolence. The summer months also brought an epidemic of diseases with them, and no area was free of disease. Every resident of the city would be troubled and confounded by these illnesses and there was no guarantee left of life.

A house which was full of happiness today maybe a house of mourning tomorrow. The Huzur Badshah condoled every death with prayers for the soul of the deceased and a do-shala for royal employees and money for funeral expenses if they were salatin—of royal descent.

There was a sense of excitement that Ramzan always brought with it. This was the most blessed month of the Islamic calendar to be spent in prayers and introspection. Everyone would get up much earlier for *iftar*, the pre-dawn meal, and it would be a melodious recitation of the Holy Quran that would wake everyone up instead of Raga Bhairavi. Cannons would announce the start of the fast in the Qila and the city. The city would sparkle like a bright jewel throughout the night with the hustle and bustle of the men visiting friends for iftar, or the evening meal, when the fast was broken. The residents would partake in the eateries. At dawn, after prayers, a lazy slowness descended on the fasting populace who would wake up just before noon prayers.

The friends had decided to meet in the qahwakhana before Ramzan.

Mirza Qaiser rode back to his house, freshened up and left for Chandni Chowk. Miyan Nabbu, Kunwar Ibrahim, Mirza Abu Bakr, Zoravar Singh and Santosh Lal had already reached. Brijnath Zutshi was sitting with some Kashmiri and Khatri friends in another corner discussing the diwan of Hafez.

Greetings and pleasantries over, the friends caught up with each other's news. The conversation drifted to ghazals.

Badshah Huzur's latest ghazal was very haunting:

Nahin ishq mein is ka to ranj hamein ki qarar o shakeb zara na raha
Gham-e-ishq to apna rafiq raha koi aur bala se raha na

In love, I have no regrets that I have lost my tranquillity and peace of mind
Sorrow in love has always been my friend, whether anything else remains or not, who cares?

Miyan Nabbu, whose poetic sensibilities were not honed, stayed disconnected from this conversation. He was thinking of the improbable story that the man from Bengal had told him. He decided to take his friends into confidence.

'I am feeling suffocated here, can we go out for a walk? Perhaps in the Begum ka Bagh outside the Qila,' he asked.

The friends, surprised that Nabbu was feeling at odds since he was always amiable and what seemed to them as insensitive, agreed and walked out.

The Begum ka Bagh, planned by Shahzadi Jahanara when the Qila was built, was just on the other side of the Chandni Chowk, behind the Begum ki Sarai, also built by her. Also called Chandni Chowk Bagh, it had beautiful flowering and fruit-bearing trees and bushes, pavilions and baradaris to sit and enjoy in. Even though of late its upkeep wasn't as good as it should have been, it was a beautiful garden and yielded a good income to the royal treasury. Huzur would come here too, to enjoy the flowers in the spring and winter.

Having seated themselves in the baradari, the conversation returned to ghazals when Nabbu who had been fidgeting said, 'I don't know why but I am feeling very restless.'

Having caught his friends' attention, and on their enquiry, he described the event of his meeting with the man in Kucha Dina Beg.

'I had dismissed it as the rantings of a crazy man, but I saw him in Mushtari bai's balakhana yesterday and I have heard strange rumours from my servants. Apparently, some chapati is being distributed. I don't have much knowledge about such things so thought I would discuss it with you. What do you advise? Should I ignore it, or do we tell someone?'

Zoravar Singh and Qaiser exchanged glances. This was the second time they had heard it.

'This is worrying Nabbu Miyan,' said Zoravar. 'I know there is some trouble over the cartridges. However, I think these are just rumours that are being spread to cause trouble. I am sure that the Company sarkar will sort it out.'

'I agree,' said Mirza Abu Bakr, 'but we must all be on our guard.'

Santosh Lal, who had been listening silently added, 'This is not all. A few days ago, there were rumours in the College that someone had pasted posters on the walls of Jama Masjid, saying that the armies of Russia and Iran were coming to attack these firangis who had established their control over Hindustan and secure the kingdom for Huzur Purnur. We went to check with Master Ramchandra and Zakaullah, who took it seriously, but there was nothing there. They dismissed it as rumours. I don't think I heard of anything more ridiculous.'

Kunwar Ibrahim joined in the conversation. 'My servant had also brought this news to me. According to him, there was a great crowd gathered in the Jama Masjid. I ask you if crowds don't gather at Jama Masjid before Ramzan, where else will they gather?'

Mirza Abu Bakr, who had been hearing them all silently added now, 'That is true. But there is discontent amongst the nobility and common people against the Company sarkar. The rich and noble are resentful because their privileges have been taken away and the poor are concerned because the Company sarkar does not care for them the way the Mahabali Alampanah did. Everyone also resents the way our beloved Alampanah has been stripped of his powers. There are rumours that the royal family will have to vacate the Qila and shift to Mehrauli. The angrez will live in the Qila built by Badshah Shah Jahan. It is enough to make any man's blood boil. But I am still not sure if there will be a *baghavat* against them. The angrez are too powerful and their army has the best weapons.'

Qaiser, who had been a silent and worried spectator so far, said, 'Yes Bhai Abu Bakr, I agree with you. By disbanding the Royal Army, the Company sarkar has ensured that they control the land of our ancestors.'

'Not just the land, Mirza Qaiser, the revenue of it too,' said Ibrahim. 'We pay so many taxes on our lands and it all goes abroad— far away to wilayat. Our peasants are in a bad state and the lands are becoming infertile. The Company forces the peasants to grow what they want to use. The lands were always taxed heavily by the badshahs but they loved this land and invested in it, decorated our country. We were our own masters and our own slaves. If we were good, it was for ourselves, and if we were bad, it was we who suffered.

'Where did the ghee go?

Into the khichri.

Where did the khichri go?

Into the stomachs of our loved ones!'

Now everything goes to the firangi lands.'

'Yes, Ibrahim Miyan, our days were like Eid and nights like *Shab-e-Barat*. But forget it, what will we gain from repeating something that's there for everyone to see?' said Mirza Qaiser disconsolately.

Seeing that his cousin was distressed, Zoravar changed the subject, saying, 'Your days are once again going to become Eid and the nights will be grand, bhai. There are less than three weeks for your nikah. Have you finished preparations? How can we help?'

The conversation turned to Qaiser's upcoming nuptials and all the friends started teasing Qaiser. The topic of chapatis, cartridges and invading armies was forgotten.

He came home and, as had become habitual for him these days, Qaiser poured his heart out in his letters and kept them ready for Hariyali to pick up and deliver.

Likewise, Falak would be waiting. Since this epistolary exchange had begun, she had got into the habit of spreading her prayer mat a little distance from the others for greater privacy. The excuse she offered, when she got inquiring looks, was that she didn't want her *qirat*, or loud recitation of the Quran, to disturb anyone.

Hariyali came in singing in Raga Pilu:

Tum Radhe bano Shyam,
Sab dekhenge Brij Baam
Moro kaha tum eko nahin maanat
Aaj pade re mose kaam
Sab sakhiyan mili naach nachave
Yeh hai brij dhan Shyam

> Shyam, disguise yourself as Radha
> No one will recognize you
> You don't listen to me
> Today you need something from me.
> All my friends make you dance
> This is the custom of Brij.

This extremely popular thumri had Radha pleading with Shyam, or Lord Krishna, to come dressed as Radha herself so that they could meet without anyone recognizing him.

It echoed Falak's sentiments, but it was only another three weeks for their nikah and till then she was grateful for these letters.

The fact that the chapati story was being repeated was of grave concern to her and she advised Qaiser to talk to Mufti sahib about it. Since no one knew of her letter exchange there was no one within the palace with whom she could share her worries. She wondered, however, if she could discuss this with Hariyali.

The next day, Hariyali came singing Hazrat Amir Khusrau's immortal verse in Raga Bhairavi:

> *Zihaal-e-miskeen makun taghaful,*
> *Duraye naina banaye batiyan*
> *Ke taab-e hijran nadaram ay jaan,*
> *Na leho kahe lagaye chatiyan*

> Do not ignore my misery
> by turning away your eyes and weaving tales,
> My love, I can't bear this separation
> Why don't you clasp me to your bosom.

How apt her songs were, thought Falak. When Hariyali dropped the letter, she asked her if they could talk. Hariyali indicated that she would return after she had completed her rounds in the mahal.

By the time she reappeared, Falak was sitting with her paints.

'Hariyali, I have no one to speak to about this as no one knows I am exchanging letters and God forbid anyone comes to know. You are my only confidant. You also go everywhere in the city. Have you heard of chapatis being distributed? Of some discontent in the air?' Falak voiced her concerns.

A startled Hariyali replied, 'Shahzadi I haven't heard of any of these incidents. Perhaps they are distributing sadqa? After all, the month of Ramzam is on our heads and it is also the month for generous charity.'

So saying, she left. But her mind was in turmoil, and she knew she had to consult Thakur sahib. While Mirza Qaiser and his friends were unaware of the truth behind the distribution of the chapatis, Hariyali knew about them and the plans afoot. In fact, she was supposed to meet one of those 'discontented' soldiers tomorrow.

Meanwhile, preparations for the month of Ramzan were in full swing. Dromedary riders had been sent off in all directions to spot the Ramzan moon. Their testimony would be corroborated by the local qazi or landholder of that area, especially if clouds marred a clear sighting.

The news that everyone had been waiting for was here!

The Badshah consulted the ulema and ordered the cannons to be fired to signal the month of Ramzan. Eleven cannons were arranged to blast ceremoniously when the moon was auspiciously sighted, and the same eleven would be similarly deployed to herald the end of Ramzan, either on the twenty-ninth or thirtieth day of Ramzan, once again as per the sighting of the moon.

This was the night that Hariyali did brisk business and did not get the time to meet Thakur sahib. Every lady wanted to wear new bangles for this month of fasting and reaffirmation of one's faith and devotion.

In the palace, the begums, the ladies of the haram, the royal children and singers and dancers felicitated the Emperor. And in the ensuing days of festivity, the Qila and the city were brightly illuminated and the beating of the naubat announced the time of the day. The Badshah distributed earthen cups and cottage cheese to everyone.

The preparations for the pre-dawn meal of the first *roza*, or fast, were in full swing in every house, whether it was the mahal or a mud dwelling. As soon as the gongs rang out to announce the start of *sehri*, in the Qila and the Jama Masjid, the dastarkhwan were laid out with food.

The sehri would be very elaborate or simple depending on the circumstances of the person fasting. The Badshah ate the sehri on the third gong, took some puffs of his huqqah and went for the morning prayers. A cannon announced the end of sehri. The Badshah rinsed his mouth and drank *aab-e hayat* as Ganga *jal* was called, and which was the only water that the khandan-e Timuriya drank. Now, there would be no more eating or drinking till iftar.

Everyone made the vows of roza and would spend the next hour reciting the Holy Quran, which had descended on earth in this blessed month.

During late afternoon, the tandoors were lit in the courtyard. It was time to start cooking the food for the breaking of the fast.

There was much playful banter amongst the ladies. When someone's rotis were cooked well, she was delighted. If someone's roti was burnt or fell inside the tandoor, or was undercooked, the others laughed in good humour.

Rotis weren't the only thing being laughed about. If a *rozakhor*—someone who had missed keeping the fast—passed by, they were mocked with rhyming taunts that playfully cast them as culprits in the eyes of Allah. Since menstruating women are not supposed to fast, they would stay away and pretend to fast, to avoid attention and embarrassment.

The ladies from all the mahals were gathered in the courtyard.

Zeenat was teasing Falak: 'Apajan, will you miss us next Ramzan, or will our Dulha bhai make up for our presence in your life?'

A blushing and embarrassed Falak bent low over the greens that she had been chopping. It was hot, and they would eat a light meal.

Various sherbets were prepared and kept in ice to cool; the heat was sapping everyone's energy.

The houses in the city also saw a similar flurry of excitement. There would be arrangements for iftar in the houses of the noblemen, in the various mosques and of course, Jama Masjid, so that no one was bereft of Allah's blessings. Trays of food were sent from the Qila to Jama Masjid, Fatehpuri Masjid, Akbarabadi Masjid, Aurangabadi Masjid and Sirhindi Masjid. The last four had been constructed by the wives of Shah Jahan Badshah and were specially provided for.

Involving themselves in the preparations meant that time flew past.

The begums and shahzadis went around buying flowers and garlands from the maalans who had set up shop in one corner of the courtyard. There was playful bargaining as they overcharged the ladies at four times the normal price.

The time to end the fast was close and everyone was drained of energy and waiting eagerly. Complaints of parched throats and hunger could be heard from the younger ones, while the older ladies consoled them and told them stories from the Quran and hadith to while away the time.

Every minute seems like an eternity.

Finally, the sun set and the Badshah gave the order for the cannon to be fired. The *harkara*s waved their flags, and as soon as the shot was fired, the azan was given. An unbelievable atmosphere of happiness descended on the city.

The fast was broken with a sip of *aab-e zamzam*, or dates from Mecca. Sherbet was sipped delicately. The lavish meal that had been prepared would be eaten only after everyone had finished with the evening or maghrib prayers.

When the time came for the night prayers, the azan for isha could be heard everywhere.

The Diwan-e Khas was turned into a mosque and prayer rugs were spread out. The attendant informed the Emperor that the congregation was ready. The Badshah appeared and read his prayers with the congregation and heard a chapter and a half of the Quran in the *taraweeh*. He returned to his apartments, partook of the huqqah, and rested.

The whole month would pass by like this, every year.

The city was quiet, as though in deference to the *rozedar*, or those who duly fasted—even sweet shops would be discreet in selling their wares to others. Hariyali, with her swaying hips and seductive gait, passed by the puri, halwa shops in Chitli Bazar and came towards Chawri Bazar, singing:

Khusrau raen suhag ki, so jagi pii ke sang
Tan mora, man pihu kaa, so dono ek hi rang

Khusrau! It was our wedding night and I woke up with my beloved
The body is mine, but the heart belongs to my lover; both dyed in the same colour.

She made her way to the balakhana of Mushtari bai.

Mushtari bai had gone to sleep after the sehri and dawn prayers but there was someone else who was awake and waiting for Hariyali.

Bhooray Khan, resident of Awadh, whom Nabbu Khan had seen with the Bengal soldier, was one of the disbanded soldiers of the Awadh Army. After the annexation of Awadh and the exile of the beloved nawab, the Company sarkar had thought it essential to disband the army and its auxiliary forces, maintained by Nawab Wajid Ali Shah. This had caused much resentment. The Company sarkar had raised three new battalions and given the option to the sepoys to join. The Turk cavalry and those who were serving with their horses were repeatedly asked to give their assent, but only two hundred joined. The rest refused. Bhooray Khan was one of those who had joined as he had a large family to feed. But Lord Hardinge decided to remove one hundred and fifty of these sepoys, retaining only fifty in the Company's service. The men had appealed to Lord

Hardinge saying they were neither lazy nor ever shirked from their responsibilities. After appeals and commissions of enquiry, the men were told that since the Company could not afford the upkeep of their mares, the sepoys would have to pay rupees one hundred and fifty for that. Most could not afford that and were asked to leave. Bhooray Khan had not been able to get another job after that. How could he? Eighty-seven thousand servants who were employed by the Nawab of Awadh had been rendered jobless and were on the verge of penury. Bhooray Khan had retired to his village, which was near the Delhi border, and had received the chapati. One of his friends in the village, who had been the Nawab's employee, had sent him to Delhi with a letter to Mushtari bai, and he had been here since March. He had heard of the revolt of Mangal Pandey from the sepoy whom he had been following and had forcibly brought with him to the balakhana. He had since sent him away but was a worried man. Along with two of his friends, Bindeshwar Pandey and Maulvi Qurban Ali, he had been making plans to overthrow the angrez. Pandey and Maulvi sahib had both been part of the disbanded Nawabi Army and resented the overthrow of their beloved Nawab Wajid Ali Shah. Bhooray Khan had come to Delhi on the pretext of selling brocades and satins from Banaras, and since the wealthy and well-dressed courtesans were regular customers of such wares, there would be no eyebrows raised if he stayed at Mushtari bai's balakhana.

They had fixed 31 May 1857 as the day to start the baghavat throughout the Company sarkar's Bengal Army. They were trying to contact three senior Indian officers in each regiment who would coordinate with them. The sepoys themselves were ignorant of the plans.

Hariyali entered from the back stairs as was her wont. Though they were not destined to marry, the tawaifs thought of themselves as suhagans and were her regular customers.

Bhooray Khan was waiting for her in the storeroom behind the kitchen.

'What news do you bring Hariyali? Could you find any connection in the magazine?'

The magazine near Kashmiri Darwaza, which housed the arsenal, was a key factor if the baghavat was to succeed.

'Bhooray bhai, salam. Let me put down my basket and rest my tired feet. I have been on the move since dawn.' 'Yes of course, I have been remiss. Salam, Hariyali. It's just that I have been so worried that I am not able to think,' he said with a sigh.

'Don't fret so much bhai. If God wills it, everything will be in our favour. I have located a young jeweller in Khanum ka Bazar whose uncle is a guard in the magazine. I will go to his house today. I know his mother and will go to sell bangles to her. But we can't meet him here. He will never agree to come here.'

Bhooray Khan thought for a while and replied, 'I don't know what we would do without you and other female sympathizers like Mushtari. Can we meet in Zeenat ul-Masajid on Friday after the jumma prayers? I am not known here so it will be easy for me to slip out. But then how will we recognize each other?'

'Give me a few moments to think,' said Hariyali. Her quick mind and the fact that she was a familiar in almost every house in the walled city showed her the solution. 'I know that Thakur Madhav Singh is meeting a few other people who want to get rid of the firangis. Let me talk to him and we can use his house for the meeting.'

Hariyali went off with her basket on her head, sighing and saying Momin Khan Momin's verse to herself:

Tuu kahan jaayegi kuchh apna thikana kar le
Hum to kal khwab-e-adam mein shab-e-hijran honge

Where will you go, find someplace to shelter for yourself
We will be taken away by death, a night of separation awaits you.

23

The Plot Thickens

Hum tujh se kis hawas ki falak justuju karen
Dil hi nahin raha hai ki kuchh aarzu karen

O heaven, which desire should I seek from you?
I no longer have a heart whose desires I can pursue.

—Mir Dard

It was an unusually late hour for Hariyali to be about, but since it was the month of Ramzan—and the streets were filled with those who had set out to enjoy themselves after a day spent indoors, fasting—no one paid her any notice. Her basket on her head, her skirt swirling and bangles tinkling, she made her way to Thakur sahib's haveli.

The city was decked up like a bride. All the shops were brightly lit, and the boys employed by the shopkeepers were busy advertising their wares. They were spinning a silken web with their words, tempting passersby to make a purchase. The kulfi-sellers and barf ka gola, or ice candy shops were in great demand, because of the heat. Shops selling various types of sherbets were crowded with those who had stayed without water the whole day and were now satiating their thirst.

'Arre Hariyali, how come you are here at this hour?' asked Lakkhan the guard at the gate.

'Bhai, what can I do? Everyone is fasting in the month of Ramzan, so I try and rest and set out at night like the rest of the city. I think I have found a very good *rishta* for Radha bitia, but first I need to ask Thakur sahib if he is agreeable. Then I will talk to Thakurain sahiba. Can you please tell him that I have a *message* for him?' She deliberately emphasized the word for 'message'—*paigham*.

Lakkhan soon returned with the message that Thakur sahib was waiting for her in the diwankhana.

Thanking Lakkhan, Hariyali went in.

Thakur sahib, regal in his sherwani, with his mace stick in hand, was sitting on a chair, swirling his moustache. A tall, well-built man, he posed an imposing figure. Since the word 'paigham' was part of a secret code, he had agreed to meet her.

'Well, Hariyali, how come you are here at night?' he asked.

'Sarkar, may I be sacrificed over you, but this beggar woman has eaten the salt from your table, and it is my duty to serve you. In fact, Huzur, not just salt, but the chapati on my humble stove is cooked because of you. This chapati is a message to our country—it tells of good things to come.' Since these were the words decided by the *inqilabis* who were striving to overthrow the firangis, Thakur sahib nodded. It was true that he, Mir sahib and Imam sahib were meeting Hariyali regularly for a few months as a source for getting and relaying information, but nonetheless, the protocol of secrecy was maintained by use of a password. The password was also changed regularly as a precaution. The three were notable men in the city and could not afford to let the Company bahadur or its spies become suspicious of them and their activities.

'Sarkar, I come with a message from Bhooray Khan. He wants to meet Yusuf Ali, a young jeweller from Khanum ka Bazaar and recruit him to the cause. Yusuf Ali's uncle is a guard in the magazine. Can he meet them here or in Imam sahib's house?' she said in an urgent whisper.

'Hariyali, it is not safe to meet anyone here. I have been told Gami Khan has been seen lurking around the house. He is an angrezi spy.'

'Sarkar, since I have come here with the excuse that I have found a match for Radha bitia, why shouldn't you call a jeweller to prepare her trousseau? You can send a message for him to come with some designs. I will bring Bhooray Khan with me. He can get some bolts of brocade and satin for her dresses. Since he can't go into the zenana, I will take the cloth inside to show it to Thakurain sahiba and you can talk to him in the meanwhile.' The quick-witted Hariyali had found a solution.

'Hmm, that sounds very sensible. I can invite him on the day Mir sahib and Imam sahib come for our regular game of chess every Friday evening. But will he agree?' asked Thakur sahib.

'Sarkar, that we can only find out after we speak to him, but I have heard him talk fervently against the angrezi sarkar. His father was embroiled and executed unfairly by them on the pretext of selling them copper as gold. He has been agitating since then.'

'Well, that's fine then Hariyali. I will send Lakkhan to his house to invite him with samples on Friday evening. Meanwhile, give me some names of possible rishtas. Radha's mother is going to question me on that. In fact, I am surprised she hasn't come here herself to find out. By now, she must have heard from the servants that you are here for that purpose.'

'Oh yes. Sarkar, there are two boys. Their family is also very good. Apart from the fact that I am very fond of Bitia, we need this cover. Thakur Sher Singh's son is very suitable. The family is well-to-do, with *jagirs* near Ghazinagar. Thakur sahib is the diwan of Alwar state and the son will succeed him. The second is the young Thakur Zoravar Singh. I think you know his family very well. One of the finest young men in the city.'

'May all your troubles disappear Hariyali. Zoravar is an excellent suggestion. Why didn't I think of him myself? I will talk to his father. Let's meet on Friday evening and keep an eye out for Gami Khan. No one should know why we are meeting.'

'Yes, of course, Sarkar. My lips are sealed. Sarkar, it is my duty to tell you that the word chapati is being bandied about in the city.

It seems Thanedar Moinuddin Khan and his brother heard reports of chapatis being distributed in the villages. These reports have come to the ears of Mirza Qaiser and Thakur Zoravar Singh. I heard this from Shahzadi Falak. I am only repeating it to you because I trust your discretion. I hope our plans are not pre-empted.'

Having thus unburdened herself of the secret and knowing it was now in capable hands, she picked up her basket of bangles and walked out, humming softly to herself. She had one more stop to make before retiring for the night.

During the month of Ramzan, the balakhanas were normally empty as the courtesans too observed Ramzan. Only devotional songs, in praise of Allah or his Prophet, were sung, whether by them or in the courtyards of dargahs.

Hariyali entered the compound, calling out loudly, 'Are there any takers for my glass bangles here? They are the colours of the rainbow and once you wear them on your fair wrists, they will remind you of God's glory.'

Mushtari bai was sitting with her musicians, setting a verse of Mevlana Jalaluddin Rumi, the famous mystic, with her musicians. She was humming *Ei nuskha-e nama Ilahi*:

> *You are:*
> *a copy of God's scripture*
> *You are:*
> *mirror of that Regal beauty*
> *Whatever is in the world is not beyond you*
> *Seek it inside you*
> *Whatever you seek you are that*[33]

As soon as she heard Hariyali's voice, Mushtari sent the musicians away.

'What have you brought for me, Hariyali?'

'Bai sahiba, may I be ransomed over your beauty and your voice. I don't understand what you were singing but it seemed divine,' said Hariyali setting down her basket.

'Hariyali, this is a poem in Farsi by the famous Sufi saint, Mevlana Rumi. It tells us to seek God within us,' she replied. 'Indeed, Ramzan is the month of reflection and I spend my free time understanding the mystical beauty of Mevlana Rumi and Sheikh Hafez.'

'And not Mirza Naushah's ghazals?' Hariyali asked mischievously. 'Nawab jaan sings so many of his ghazals in her balakhana and swears by their mystical quality.'

Mushtari smiled and replied:

Ye masail-e-tasawwuf ye tera bayan Ghalib
tujhe hum wali samajhte jo na baada-Khwar hota

Oh, these problems of mysticism and your words Ghalib
We would have taken you as a saint, had you not been a wine drinker.

'Arre, bai sahiba, what do I know of this *falsafa*. I am a simple woman and hardly have time to indulge in such philosophy. My time goes into earning my daily chapati for my family.'

At the mention of the word chapati, Mushtari bai replied, 'This is not an ordinary chapati Hariyali, *yeh chapati mulk ke naam paigham hai*—this bread is a message for the country . . . Tell me, what is your news?'

'Bai sahiba, can you call Bhooray bhai here or should I go to the storeroom to meet him,' she asked in a whisper. 'I have some news for him.'

'I will call him here.' Saying so, she called out to her personal maid, 'Akhtari, please ask Bhooray to come here. I want his opinion on a piece of property that Hariyali tells me is coming up for sale in Awadh.'

Bhooray Khan came in and after presenting his salam to Mushtari bai sat down. He then greeted Hariyali.

'Bhooray Khan, Hariyali has brought news of a property up for sale in Awadh. I am interested and since you are from Awadh you can find out what it is worth and negotiate the price for me.'

'Jee, Bhooray bhai. It is being sold by Thakur Madhav Singh. It belongs to a jeweller's family that lives in Khanum ka Bazar. Since I go to his house to sell bangles to his mother, they asked me to find a customer. I know bai sahiba has been on the lookout for a good property, so I came here immediately,' said Hariyali.

'Of course, bai sahiba. I can never repay your favours to me and if I can help you in any way, it is my honour and privilege. Tell me when and where, Hariyali,' said Bhooray.

'On this Friday in the evening. And Bhooray bhai, Thakur sahib's daughter is getting married soon, so it can be useful to you too. Please take some of your best bolts of silk and brocade for their selection. I will come and pick you up from here after *maghrib* prayers.'

Hariyali went home, satisfied with her day's work and looking forward to her nightly meal with her husband and the comfort of sleep.

But someone was awake in Punjabi Katra.

Hira had received the message that Falak Ara would not remove her locket, come what may, and there were barely two weeks left before her wedding. He was trying to rack his brains as to how he could get his hands on the locket. When he could not see any way forward, he slept on the thought that he had heard that Mirza Qaiser was setting up a house with his bride in the city, and a house had already been earmarked. It wasn't so far from his own house, and maybe out of the protocol of the Qila, Hira would find it easier to reach Falak. He could always use some form of blackmail once she was more accessible. After all, he had understood from something Naseeban said that Shahzadi Falak was meeting Mirza Qaiser on the sly.

Thakur Madhav Singh sent a message the next day to Yusuf Ali to come with some jewellery to his house on Friday evening. He met Mir sahib in the house of Imam sahib. Since the three were old friends and played chess often, these meetings were nothing to take note of.

After pleasantries were disposed of and sherbet and savouries had been served, the servants were told to leave the friends alone with their game.

'Mir sahib, we have found a connection to the magazine. I have called Yusuf Ali, the jeweller to my house on Friday evening when we have our regular game of chess. I have asked him to bring some jewellery for approval for Radha's wedding,' said Thakur sahib.

'That's wonderful news Thakur sahib. May God reward you with a good match for our bitia. And may she get married in a world that is free of this angrezi tyranny,' replied Mir sahib.

The two friends had been victims of the angrezi sarkar and had had their lands taken away on silly pretexts and were seething against them. That is what had led to them getting together with a few of the Bengal Army Indian officers and sepoys in their plan to overthrow the angrez.

'*Ameen*, their eyes are fixed on the throne of Hindustan and they want to capture it and take over our country and change our way of lives,' said Imam sahib. Imam sahib, like his two friends, considered the angrez to be trespassers and that feeling had been intensified after the annexation of Awadh by them. Imam sahib was an admirer of Maulvi Ahmadullah Khan, who had come to Awadh from his native Madras last year in November and had found an ardent audience. His mystic gatherings had become famous and alarmed by his cries for jihad against the angrez, the Company sarkar had jailed him in Faizabad.

Thereafter their competitive spirit kicked in and a serious game of chess ensued.

Thakurain sahiba, who had been told about the rishtas suggested by Hariyali, asked her husband if he had done anything about it. She was in favour of Zoravar Singh, who, from all accounts, was a very bright and upright young man.

'Why don't you talk to Mirza Aftab sahib? He is your friend, and Zoravar is related to him through his late wife,' she suggested.

'That is a great idea. I will send a message asking when I can meet him,' replied Thakur sahib.

As it was Ramzan, Thakur sahib met Mirza Aftab the next day in the evening. Mirza sahib had invited him to break his fast with him in the Qila.

Thakur sahib arrived a few minutes before the maghrib azan.

'Salam Mirza sahib, I hope you are doing well,' he said as he entered. The greetings over, Mirza sahib sat down on the sparkling white chandni that was spread out on the floor of the house, with carpets and bolsters decorating it. Qaiser was also there and had stood up on seeing his father's friend and wished him respectfully.

As soon as the thread of darkness appeared on the sky, the cannon was fired to signal the end of the roza. A manservant appeared immediately with a silver tray bearing dates and a glass of water.

Reciting, 'O Allah! I fasted for You and I believe in You and I put my trust in You and I break my fast with Your sustenance,' Mirza sahib and Qaiser broke their fast. Thakur sahib also followed suit and put the dates in his mouth.

The servants came out and spread the dastarkhwan and laid out various sherbets and savouries. The men drank a glass of sherbet each and nibbled at some nuqtis when the sweet sounds of the azan could be heard ringing from the mosques in the Qila and city.

Excusing themselves, Mirza sahib and Qaiser went to the Chobi masjid in the Qila to pray. Since their house was very close to it, it took them a few minutes to reach. In the meantime, the dastarkhwan had been laden with food, and Thakur sahib was being plied with various cooling sherbets.

The huqqahs and silver filigree paan trays were brought. While one attendant remained to refresh the huqqah the others discreetly withdrew. Qaiser also asked for permission to withdraw but Thakur sahib asked him to stay.

'Son, I want you to stay as you can give me valuable advice,' said Thakur sahib.

'It is my honour if my humble self can be of any assistance to you, Chachajan,' replied Qaiser with a salam and sat down.

'Mirza sahib,' said the Thakur, addressing Mirza Aftab, 'as you know, my daughter is now grown up. We have been looking for a suitable match for her. Someone suggested Zoravar Singh's name. Since he's related to you and a good friend of Qaiser Miyan, I came to ask for your assistance in this matter.'

'Ama, that's a wonderful idea! Zoravar is a very upright and steadfast young man with a bright future and will make Radha bitia a good match. I will talk to Thakur Sangram Singh and suggest it,' replied the Mirza.

'What do you say Qaiser miyan?' Thakur sahib turned to Qaiser.

'Chachajan, Abba and you are the wise ones and your idea is certainly guided by divine grace. I can only concur and say that it would be a perfect match.'

The chit-chat between friends continued for a short while before Thakur sahib took his leave. He knew that Mirza and his son would soon go for the night prayers and the long tarawih or supererogatory prayers, which followed it, on the nights of Ramzan.

It was also a Thursday night when special prayers were said for the departed and as Thakur sahib was carried aloft his sedan chair through the lanes of Shahr-e Panah to his house, he could see the brightly lit mosques and dargahs.

He stopped his bearers in the lane just outside his house. He had to fulfil his weekly Thursday custom of giving an offering and lighting a diya at the Saiyid Badshah's *ala*. These small niches, dedicated to Saiyed Badshah, an imaginary Sufi saint considered to be the patron saint of the walled city, were decorated with floral garlands every Thursday evening. The residents of that area would light diyas, incense sticks and make offerings and pray that Saiyed Badshah would protect them from evil and evil spirits. Today, Thakur sahib had two prayers to make. That his daughter gets happily settled, and his land be freed from foreign presence and restored to the rightful ruler, Alampanah Bahadur Shah.

That done, he went home and relayed the evening's events to the Thakurain, who had been waiting.

Thakurain sahiba had visited Ladliji ka mandir in Katra Neel to pray for her daughter's happiness. It was the only temple apart from the one in Barsana near Mathura dedicated to Radhaji, and they said she heard the pleas of women, especially those in love, and mothers.

Radha, eavesdropping from the next room, was quite thrilled too. She had once caught a glimpse of Zoravar Singh with Qaiser bhaijan at a Dussehra mela, where she had accompanied her parents.

Her dreams were sweet that night.

Raha khwab mein un se shab bhar visal
Mere bakht jage main soya kiya

I met my beloved in my dreams the whole night
My luck was awake, while I slept.

—Ameer Minai

24

Friday Night

The Sixth Ramzan

shamshir hai sinan hai kise dun kise na dun
ek jaan-e-na-tawan hai kise dun kise na dun

I have a sword and an arrow, to whom should I give it
or not give
I have but one frail life, to whom should I give it or not give

—Ameer Minai

The first day of May was also the first Friday of Ramzan, 1273 Hijri. It was sweltering hot, and the heat exacerbated the thirst of a *rozedar,* but the entire Muslim male population of the areas around the Jama Masjid of Shahjahanabad was present for the *khutba* and congregational prayers.

Mirza Mughal, Mirza Khizr and Mirza Abu Bakr represented their imperial father and grandfather. The majestic mosque was echoing with the sounds of the azan and everyone stood in rows to pray behind the imam.

Awnings had been put up to protect the faithful from the hot sun beating down on everyone, but despite that, the congregation was wet with perspiration. Not that it mattered, for religious fervour was at its peak during the month of Ramzan.

After the prayers, everyone embraced one another and went back to their homes to rest.

Yusuf Ali was also amongst those who had prayed in the Jama Masjid with his uncle, Rahim Baksh. He was engaged to his uncle's daughter, and their wedding date was two months away.

Instead of resting like others once he was home, he immediately got out his bag from an old safe in his room, and, ensuring that the room was locked, decided to lay out the jewellery neatly for the evening's inspection by Thakur Madhav Singh. It was his first independent order and he wanted to ensure it went off smoothly. His home in Chitli Qabr was a modest two-room thatched affair. Sparsely furnished, he hoped to do it up before his wedding, and the profits from this order would go a long way in helping with that.

Satisfied that he had everything in order, he lay down to rest.

The evening saw two carriages coming to Thakur Madhav Singh's house, but it attracted no notice, for every Friday evening, a game of chess was played here. Gami Khan, a clerk employed in the Company office, who also served as their spy had been keeping an eye on unusual activities in the walled city and carrying reports to his angrez masters. But this did not invoke his curiosity. Like everyone in the area, he had also heard of the wedding plans for his daughter, so the arrival of a young jeweller with boxes of jewellery did not cause much excitement. Yusuf Ali had come with an armed guard for protection supplied to him by Hariyali. She had brought Bhooray Khan, looking impressive in his sherwani and turban, carrying a pair of pistols.

Silent concentration greeted him. Imam sahib, huqqah bit in hand, was watching his two friends engaged in mental combat, and Yusuf Ali stood there quietly till Mir sahib's joyous cry of checkmate echoed in the room.

The three friends noticed Yusuf standing and called him near them.

He bent his head and presented his salams before taking his seat on the wooden takht, covered with a white coverlet. The servants brought sherbet and some savouries, a fresh mouthpiece for the huqqah, refreshed the chillum and were told to withdraw.

Yusuf asked for permission to open his jewellery boxes, and once that was done, Imam sahib intervened.

'Miyan sahibzade, of course, Thakur sahib needs jewellery for his daughter's trousseau, and he will buy it from you. However, that was just an excuse to call you here. We have heard that your uncle is the guard at the magazine. We have also heard you are very courageous. From what Hariyali has told us we glean that you are very faithful to your religion and hate the foreigners,' said Mir sahib.

Thakur sahib added, 'Miyan, your mulk needs you, your Badshah needs you. If we want to live with our heads held high, we need to get rid of the firangis before they enslave us.'

Yusuf, taken aback, said nervously, 'I pledge to protect my land with my life and belongings, however, I am a lowly man and don't know how I can help.'

Meanwhile, Imam sahib had taken out the Holy Quran which he carried with him and said, 'I keep this Quran Sharif in front of you. Keep your hand on it and make a vow that you will maintain secrecy and never repeat what has transpired here. And that you vow to help our cause.'

'Of course, huzur. You need not fear that. I have eaten the salt of this land and the Badshah Huzur's innumerable kindnesses to us will ensure that I will never be unfaithful to him.' Saying that he put his hand on the holy book and swore to maintain confidentiality about this meeting and added, 'I am scared of taking a vow to help you, for this is too big and sacred a vow. Please excuse me from this. However, I pledge to help your cause if it is religious or spiritual, with my life and belongings.'

Mir sahib reacted to his earnest reply saying, 'Yusuf Ali, we will not ask you to do something that you can't do. Just vow to fulfil your duty to the Badshah and your mulk. That is enough for us.'

Yusuf Ali, with his hand on the holy Quran, pledged his allegiance of the cause of the Badshah and the land to the best of his ability.

That done, the three friends then outlined their plan.

Thakur sahib said, 'We just want you to somehow gain access to the magazine offices and obtain the duplicate keys kept in the cupboard in the main office. We have come to know that the British are conspiring to destroy the faith of the Hindustani soldiers and have greased the cartridges with the fat of pig and cow. When the soldiers have to bite the cartridges to load them in the rifles, their faith will be compromised. If this information is correct, then there will be some papers relating to it in the magazine, bring those too. We need proof of it so that we can take revenge in the name of God.'

Yusuf had promised to help, but he was young and scared. He said fearfully, 'How will I do that huzur? The firangi are very strict and cruel. Just recently I heard they had executed a few Hindustanis for what they called "treason". Huzur, how can helping our own Badshah be called *ghaddari* or treason?'

'Exactly why we want to overthrow these usurpers, and having access to the magazine and its arsenal is of utmost importance for that,' replied Thakur sahib.

Bhooray Khan, who till now had been a silent spectator, now contributed to the conversation. 'Huzur, as Hariyali has told you, I am Bhooray Khan and am coordinating with Bindeshwar Pandey and others in this effort. If I have your permission, may I speak?'

'Of course, go ahead, Bhooray Khan,' said Thakur sahib.

'Yusuf Ali, your uncle works in the magazine as a guard. You are engaged to his daughter. Could you ask him to get you a job there? That would place you in an ideal position to access the documents and keys.'

'Sahib, you are all of course much wiser than I am, but how will that help?' asked Yusuf.

'We have got news that eighty-five Hindustani soldiers of the 3rd Bengal Light Cavalry at Meerut have refused to use the new cartridges and are about to be court-martialled. Their lives are at stake. They are part of our cause and we want to prove that their refusal was correct. That is all you need to know for your own safety,' replied Bhooray Khan.

Yusuf replied, 'Sarkar, I don't visit my uncle's house these days. It is going to be difficult for me to get a job at the magazine.'

Imam sahib smiled and said, 'I know that you are engaged to your uncle's daughter and that is why you don't go to his house. However, you don't need to go to his house. You just become more friendly with him and start going with him to the magazine. Then you can try to get your hands on that paper.'

Yusuf said, 'Even if I do manage to go to the magazine, it will be impossible to lay my hands on the papers and keys there. The sahibs there don't leave important papers lying around.'

Imam sahib reassured him, 'Don't accept defeat before you start. You start going there, God will give you divine help and we will also guide you.'

Yusuf agreed and left. He was now trying to think of ways and means to fulfil his promise.

After he had left, Bhooray Khan asked the three men present there, 'Huzur do you think we can trust him? He seems very young and nervous.'

'We don't have a choice, Bhooray,' said Mir sahib, adding, 'Maybe you and Hariyali can follow it up with him. He will need your help and motivation.'

'We need to get into that magazine on or before thirty-first, so that the arms and ammunitions are in our control when we strike,' said Thakur sahib. 'So we need him ensconced there.'

Mir sahib, an avid reader of *Dehli Urdu Akhbar* and *Tilism-e Lucknow*, was aware of happenings all around his world. The unrest in their world due to the new policy of the Company sarkar of snatching away kingdoms from Hindustani rulers because they didn't have children was causing an uproar. Everyone knew that in Hindustan, adoption, or *goad lena,* was an age-old practice. And then of course, the banishment of beloved Akhtar Piya Nawab Wajid Ali Shah was a constant wound, causing pain to everyone all the time.

He was worried that events in Meerut were gathering speed and that things might erupt before they were ready. The thirty-first was the date they had decided upon, and they had a month in which to get their act together. Thakur sahib confirmed his fears.

'Mir sahib, Hariyali brought news that the word chapati and news of its distribution is being bandied about in the city,' said a worried Thakur sahib to his friends. 'Thanedar Moinuddin Khan and his brother were told about it. Quite a few people are talking of it, it seems.'

'That is my constant fear Thakur sahib,' said Mir sahib. 'But what can we do except pray?'

'We have done our part,' said Imam sahib, 'now let us leave the rest to God. He will assist us because we are on the right path.'

The cantonment of Meerut, situated at a distance of thirty-six miles from Delhi, was one of the biggest military stations in North India. Besides European troops of Horse Artillery and Foot Artillery and a Light Field Battery, there were three Hindustani corps stationed there: these were the 3rd Light Cavalry and the 11th and 20th Native Infantry. The disaffection caused by reports about the greased cartridges and the mixing of bone-dust had even found its way to the ranks of the sepoys in Meerut. Mahtab Khan, a clerk in the Meerut cantonment who sent regular news to Imam sahib, had informed him that Colonel Smyth, commanding the 3rd Cavalry, had thought it was necessary to call the sepoys to parade and explain to them that the cartridge could be used without being touched by the mouth. The parade had been ordered for 24 April, and eighty-nine men had turned up, out of which only four accepted the cartridges; the rest refused on the grounds that their religion forbade them, and they would become outcasts in their community if they agreed. The commander-in-chief had ordered them to be court-martialled, and the men were sentenced to ten years of rigorous imprisonment.

Barely a week was left for Falak's nikah and Mubarak was a bundle of nerves. Though Malika Zeenat Mahal herself was taking an interest and had ordered her seamstresses to get the trousseau made, Mubarak was still unsatisfied.

On top of everything else, Naseeban, who had promised to help, was complicating her life with continuous references to Shahzadi Falak's locket. Of late, Sikandar Ara Begum had started taking an interest in it too.

Then there were the petty jealousies to handle.

Gul Bano, though a year younger than Falak, was jealous that her marriage to Mirza Davar Shukoh had not been announced too. His visits to the mahal had been discontinued by her mother, who felt that he was showing too much familiarity with Gul and frowned on these intimacies.

Ramzan meant that the days were not as productive since everyone wanted to pamper their fasts by resting in the hot summer afternoons. It made it easier to spend the day without food and water. Nights were spent reading the Holy Quran and other prayers.

Falak Ara herself was in a daze. Her dreams were coming true, but would her fate support her? Was so much happiness written in her fortune?

She tried to stay calm as her measurements were taken and she was teased or pampered by those around her. But a murmur of anxiety could not be kept away. It had been a while since she had heard from Qaiser—their letters had also stopped once Ramzan started, and since then all she could do was reread the old letters whenever she was alone.

Hira, growing ever more desperate and now nearing the end of his tether, decided to risk it all and asked Naseeban to take him into the mahal to sell jewellery to the ladies.

'Oh, you can't go in there,' she said, a bit surprised at the absurdity of his request. 'Only young prepubescent boys can go in, like that jauhri's son, who comes to polish Sikandar Ara Begum's jewellery. No strange man is allowed.'

'No one?' asked Hira.

'Well, sometimes, a few men do come in, such as the physician, but they are summoned. And in any case, their faces are covered. They are blindfolded. Do you want to go in blindfolded? I can ask Mubarak,' she replied.

'No, no, bhabhi, I am not that desperate to sell my work,' trying his best to maintain his composure. 'I like to see the customer appreciating my jewellery. And I just remembered about that taveez. Did you get a chance to ask Mubarak about it?'

'Let me ask Mubarak again tomorrow.'

'Yes, please do,' said Hira. 'Now that the shahzadi's wedding is approaching, she needs that taveez very urgently. I don't know why, but I have developed a fondness for this young shahzadi whom I've never seen. I would like to help her, but the Imam sahib said that he has to place the taveez in something she's always worn. Since he can't come himself, he has appointed me as his agent in the matter and taught me the prayer I should chant while inserting the taveez.'

'I will ask Mubarak,' promised Naseeban before leaving for work.

True to her promise, Naseeban sought out Mubarak and conveyed the message. A harried Mubarak, clutching at straws to stay sane, rashly promised to see what she could do the next day. Maybe the taveez was what was needed to make everything go off like a charm. She decided to call Naseeban's friend to the mahal after the *maaiyoo'n* ceremony. The taveez would be taken off only for a few seconds so that the new paper with the invocations written on it could be inserted. She would take permission from the darogha to get him inside, explaining the situation.

The maaiy'on ceremony was fixed on the fourteenth of Ramzan for Falak Ara, and on the sixteenth for Qaiser. Maaiy'on was a marriage ritual which took place a few days before the wedding day, after which the bride and bridegroom would give up all their outdoor activities, wear yellow clothes and stay at home till the nikah.

All the attendees also wore yellow clothes and there was singing and dancing. The *rangrez* or dyer had to be given the clothes for dying. Shahzadi Falak's dress had to be readied. The mehndi ceremony would take place a day before the wedding so that the colour of the henna was fresh and bright.

Mirza Aftab had elicited the help of Qaiser's aunts to get the wedding preparation done. Zoravar's mother, Chand Kanwarji, and his own sister Mahtab Ara Begum were constantly in and out of their house. As per custom, Chand Kanwar had her face covered in a ghoonghat when she came face to face with men.

Aftab had taken the haveli in Lal Kuan on rent and was personally supervising its furnishings. His son would never feel the lack of a mother if he could help it.

'Apajan, have you checked the progress of the bridal dress?' Aftab asked his sister. As per custom, the dress and jewellery that the bride wore at the time of nikah would given by the bridegroom's family. 'I will be giving my daughter-in-law the jewellery that belonged to her mother-in-law. I have kept it carefully for this day. If only she was alive to see this day!' He exclaimed with wet eyes.

'Bhai sahib, she's watching us from above, and it will be everything she would wish for and more,' said Chand Kanwarji.

'Aftab,' said Mahtab Ara, 'don't worry. I have the seamstresses sitting in my house even as I speak. I have also got the plain, uncut dress ready for the actual nikah, and then the heavy peshvaz and pyjama that she will change into later.'

'Oh!' said Chand Kanwar, 'You also don't use a scissor on the bridal dress? How similar our customs are! They say that scissors should be kept away from the bride's clothes so that there is no fighting between the bride and bridegroom.'

The points having been suitably discussed, the conversation went on to the *walima*, or reception. Mahtab Ara Begum would be the hostess for the zenana, and she wanted to ensure no one was left out.

The list of invitees to the walima that the bridegroom's family gave, was being made. Since it was the month of Ramzan, the walima would be held at the time of iftar.

'Have you sent an invitation to the shahzadis?' asked Mahtab Ara. The royal family will have to be invited,' she added referring to the daughters of the Emperor.

All invitations, beautifully calligraphed, would be sent along with trays of sweets to the various houses.

'Of course, of course,' he replied.

'Bhai sahib have you put down Dr Bishamber Nath Kaul's name on the list?' asked Chand Kanwar.

'Yes, yes, I have,' he replied. 'I have written all the names down, along with Qaiser's friends. This will also be a good occasion to introduce you to a few suitable girls for Zoravar beta. In fact, I think that Thakur Madhav Singh's daughter, Radha, would be ideal for him. I will talk to Bhai Sangram Singh about it. Thakur sahib had come here for iftar a few days ago. He is very keen to find a good groom for his beloved daughter.'

'Bhai sahib, that's a great idea. I like the family and I have met Radha; she will indeed be a suitable match for Zoravar. I will talk to Thakur sahib. You also broach the subject with him,' replied Chand Kanwar.

Thankful that things were going as planned, Aftab heaved a sigh of relief as he got ready to go to the mosque for prayers.

Shamaa ki maanind ham is bazm mein
chashm-nam aaye the daaman-tar chale

Like a candle to this gathering
I came with wet eyes, and left with a damp hem.

—Khwaja Mir Dard

25

The Fourteenth Ramzan

Sohbat-e-agyaar-o-yaar dekhiye kab tak rahe
Mujhse yeh daar-o-madaar dekhiye kab tak rahe
Ghair se dil tera yaar saaf hai aaina waar
Meri taraf se ghubaar dekhiye kab tak rahe

Let's see till when the company of the stranger lasts
Let's see till when this having and not having lasts
From the stranger, O beloved, your heart is crystal clear
Till when shall I throw dust on it, dear?

—Zahir Dehlvi

Fourteenth of Ramzan donned bright and clear. It was hot, but the heat of the summer sun could not match the heat that was emanating from Falak's heart. Today she would sit in her maiyyoo'n function, which meant that after this she would not step out of her small room and all her needs would be met there by various servants till her nikah was solemnized and she would leave for her husband's house.

The *mirasins* were singing Hazrat Amir Khusrau's evergreen song where the girl is asking her father:

Hare hare bans kata more angna
Neeka madha chiwao re
Parbat baans manga more babul
Kaanu mandha chiwao re
Sagri najumi jyott babul
Sabko bhej bulao re
Jaiso laadli bitiya re baabul
Waisa hi taaj racha re
Hare hare baans manga more angna

O Father get green bamboos cut and make pretty mandap made for me
Get the bamboos from the hills O Father to make a mandap for my wedding
All the astrologers and fortune tellers, please invite them all O Father
As beloved and pampered as your daughter is, wed her in that fitting manner.

While Mubarak was cracking her palms on her darling's face to drive away the evil eye, Hariyali was distributing bangles; today she had been commissioned to bring several baskets of bangles by the darogha of the mahal.

She had brought a few assistants, hoping she could slip out in between, as Thakur sahib had called her. With 31 May approaching, they were all getting restive. Wondering if these pretty heads knew what was happening, she slipped on red bangles onto Nawab Talat Shahar Banu Begum's wrists. She herself hadn't known a moment of peace since her son had been killed. Whatever curses she gave the accursed firangis were less; wouldn't she have been welcoming her own bahu now?

There were a few dancing girls, and *mehndi waalis*, waiting to apply henna; Naseeban and a few other attendants were making floral jewellery.

Everyone had gathered in the Qila for the maiyyoo'n. Falak Ara, dressed in pale yellow, was getting ubtan put on her hands and feet, her head bowed, eyes lowered, hair flowing around her, when there was an announcement that the Malika was coming.

Immediately everyone settled themselves, and the servants stood in attention as the Malika's *palki* arrived.

She got down in a flurry of yellow gauze, organza and mulmul, with gold and yellow sapphire jewellery illuminating and framing her. Her maids fussed around her, made sure everything was just so before their Malika could take her seat.

As was the custom, while the rest of the ladies came up to present their salam to the Malika, she herself went up to Sikandar Ara Begum and Rashid Jahan, the aunts and elder cousins of the Badshah.

She gestured to the darogha of the tosha khana, who had accompanied her, to hand over a box of jewellery and some clothes from the royal collection to Falak Ara.

The blushing girl stood up and presented her kornish and handed over her gifts to Mubarak for safekeeping.

Allah re nazuki ki jawab-e-salam mein
Haath us ka uth ke rah gaya mehndi ke bojh se

Allah! So delicate is she that when she raised her hand to reply to the salam
Her hand was bent by the weight of the henna.

—Riyaz Khairabadi

The Malika left after hearing a few more songs and amply rewarding the singers, dancers and other attendants.

In another corner of the city, Yusuf Ali who had been visiting his uncle in the magazine, had found work.

He had been coming to meet his uncle since the day they had met in the masjid.

The heat was intense, and since he was fasting and could not relieve the thirst with water, he would chant the names of Allah and find strength within himself to do the work that he had set out to do. He knew that fighting for his Emperor and for his mulk was also his religious duty, for one had to pay *mitti ka qarz*, the debt owed to the land. It so happened that a few days after Yusuf Ali had been visiting his uncle at the magazine, some repair work was needed in one of the rooms of the magazine which the sahib used as his office. A wall had to be rebuilt as it was shaking, and the magazine needed to be very strong as it housed the British arsenal.

The magazine was short of some men, and Rahim Baksh, being a trusted employee, was asked if he could help. 'Huzur, my nephew who is also engaged to my daughter, is looking for some work, before his marriage to my daughter. If you permit, he is a strong pair of hands and can help.'

'Yes, of course, send him.'

Yusuf Ali started work and demolished the wall in a day along with the others.

On the fourteenth Ramzan, Yusuf Ali went to the office with the other employees and started picking up the rubble from the wall that had been demolished before another wall was to be put in its place. He had mentally made note of all the cupboards and desks, and wherever it was possible to store the duplicate keys and papers. When the rest of the employees went for lunch, he stayed back, citing that he was fasting and so would not be eating. Having already fixed in his mind where the papers that Imam sahib needed could be, he removed them during the lunch break on the fourteenth Ramzan and hid them in his pyjamas. They weren't frisked every day but in case he was that day, the papers were safe. He still had to figure out how to obtain and secrete the keys to the magazine out. The keys to the magazine and arsenal were also crucial to the success of their mission to overthrow the angrez. Only the angrez had such kinds of arms and armour in Hindustan.

That same evening, he decided to take the documents to Bhooray Khan in the balakhana.

When he reached the balakhana, Mushtari bai told him that Bhooray had been summoned by Thakur sahib in connection with the Awadh land deal.

Dejected, he came to his room and hid them in his bedding. He had no idea what was written on it. His work was not done for he still had to find the keys.

In Thakur sahib's haveli, a worried Thakur sahib, Mir sahib and Bhooray Singh were holding a conference.

It had been brought to their notice that a rebellion was being started in Meerut, and they were afraid it would upset their carefully laid-out plans.

A horse rider dispatched by Mahtab Khan, who was their contact in Meerut, had reached Imam sahib, who had sent the information to Thakur sahib.

Troops of the 3rd Bengal Light Cavalry were being court-martialled by the angrez Bahadur, and if found guilty they would be given punishment.

In fact, the sentencing was today. What if they rebelled on being given severe punishment? The sahibs would definitely come down hard on them for they would not brook defiance of orders. For them, religious and caste concerns did not hold much importance.

The men weren't ready, they still hadn't secured access to the magazines and the inhabitants of Qila were happily singing and dancing their way to what could very well be their doom.

Bhooray Khan knew the power that the angrez wielded, he had seen first-hand his beloved Nawab Akhtar *piya* get disfranchized by them.

'I wonder what he is doing today in far-off Calcutta, longing for his beloved Awadh,' he muttered to himself.

Unknown to them, the sepoys had indeed been handed strict punishment and jailed.

Hariyali, having finished her duty in the Qila, was on her way to the city, singing a thumri in Raga Khamaj, the night Raga as she walked with her sensual swaying gait, with her basket of bangles on her head, hiding the turmoil in her heart:

Chhavi dikhla ja banke Sanwariya
Dhyan lago mohe tera

My beloved show me a glimpse of your face
I am lost in thoughts of you

She reached home and set her basket down and enquired after her ailing husband. Today had been a good day of earning for her, and she could afford to buy some halwa poori from Ghantewala *halwai* for him. She soon had the fire burning and put some rice to boil while she massaged his feet. Their two-room mud house had one room where they slept and another where she cooked and stored their meagre belongings. A tiny privy was attached to it. They bathed in the kitchen itself, from the water she would fetch from the nearby well.

'Hariyali, how was your day?' asked her husband.

'Did you eat your lunch? I had kept it next to the bed so that you wouldn't have to move.' He had been running a temperature for a few days and she was worried as summers brought its own share of pestilence and disease.

'I did.' He smiled. 'You are always worried about me. Did you eat? You must be tired too.'

'Never too tired to look after you,' she smiled at him, thinking that had her son been alive, she would have had a daughter-in-law to take care of her husband. Now she was left alone to look after him and ensure that those blasted trespassers were thrown out, and their beloved Badshah Salamat restored to his rightful place. However much the angrez tried to win them over, in her heart she knew that no Hindustani accepted them, and they were trespassers on their land. This feeling had been intensified after the annexation of Awadh.

The rice was cooked, and she fed him that along with dal and halwa poori that she had brought.

'You rest for a bit while I go to the Hakimji and get some medicine for you. This fever is not leaving you.'

Wondering whether she should also visit Thakur sahib's house she went to the Hakim sahib's house.

She was bone tired and weary, and since she had nothing of any importance to tell him except the stories of merriment in the Qila, she returned home.

She had also seen Gami Khan lurking at the end of her lane.

Aatte ka chiragh bahar rakho to kauva le jaaye,
andar rakho to chooha khaa jaaye

If you keep a lamp made of flour, outside, the crow will snatch it,
If left inside, the rats will eat it,
(An old Delhi idiom)

26

The Day of Reckoning

The Sixteenth Ramzan/11 May

ai dil tamam nafa hai sauda-e-ishq mein
ek jaan ka ziyan hai so aisa ziyan nahin

O heart, there's only gain in the frenzy of love
It entails loss of a life, but that's not such a loss.

—Mufti Sadruddin Azurda

The gong for the sehri struck.

Many people were already awake, for they were reciting the Quran sharif, or praying. It was unusually hot for 11 May and those leading lives of leisure felt it was advisable to stay awake at night and sleep the roza through. Only those who had to work for a living slept a while at night to retain some energy for their work.

Huzur Purnur finished his fajr prayers and came to sit in the jharokha for the daily darshan to his subjects.

In the shahr-e panah, Bhooray Khan, throwing caution to the winds went running to Thakur sahib's haveli. He had received information from Baldeo Singh, the darogha in charge of the Jumna Bridge, that there had been a fight between the Europeans and Hindustani soldiers in Meerut, and that the latter were marching

310

straight upon Delhi, burning all the bungalows, and killing all the Europeans and Christians along their route. The mutineers were said to be very close to Delhi.

The Collector had at once ordered Baldeo Singh to rush to his post and ensure that all city gates leading to the Jamuna bridge were closed. Having given this news, Bhooray Khan ran towards the courthouse to find out that the collector had driven off in his buggy in the direction of the Commissioner's house. Bhooray Khan had taken Mushtari Baji's *tabalchi*, percussionist, with him to show him the way. The tabalchi, by virtue of his position in the kotha of one of the city's prominent courtesans, knew many people.

One of the sentries at Fraser's residence was Bhooray Khan's friend. From Darshan Lal and Rashid Khan, they had learnt that Fraser had been woken up and informed of all that was happening.

The day before, the sepoys in Meerut, goaded by the women, had rebelled and set their officers and colleagues free. They had murdered and killed the Europeans and burnt their bungalows and set off for Delhi.

One of the officers had managed to send a letter to Mr Simon Fraser, the commissioner and the Resident bahadur of Delhi. However, when the rider reached with the letter, Fraser was asleep in his chair after a heavy dinner and some delicious port. Fraser had rebuked Rashid Khan, who had gone to inform his master about the arrival of the rider. Eventually, he had taken the letter from the servant's hands mechanically, put it into his pocket and fallen asleep again.

Even though the rider kept repeating that the matter was urgent, and that great confusion had erupted at Meerut, that he had in fact been urged to gallop at speed with this letter, no servant had the courage to wake up the sahib bahadur.

Meanwhile, Mushtari bai sent a message to Hariyali that she should rush to the Qila and find out what was happening there.

Hariyali reached the mahal to find chaos. The nursemaids and milk mothers were guarding their charges, some of the senior begums were having hysterics and everyone was generally running around like headless chickens.

Gul Bano was still sleeping, while her mother was wailing that they would be murdered in their beds if she didn't get up.

'Stop exaggerating Ammijan. Nothing can happen to me in Dada Jan's Qila. I am safe here.'

'Arre beti, you don't know, all those huge soldiers—*sawars* and *purbias* and *tilingas*—have entered the Fort with their dirty boots and huge rifles. They are now in the Diwan-e Khas. May Allah have mercy on us.'

She sat down on her haunches and started wailing loudly. The attendants were trying to calm her when Hariyali passed by. Gul Bano was still yawning languorously and demanding that she be woken up only when Raga Bhairavi was sung.

These royals have no sense of impending doom, thought Hariyali as she rushed towards Khurd Jahan.

As she passed by the Choti Baithak, she saw another mother trying to wake her daughter up. Ghamzah Begum, daughter of Mirza Abu Bakr, was still sleeping. Her mother was wailing, 'A *ghadar* has started in Meerut and the forces which have rebelled against the British have arrived under the Qila, and the Qiledar is speaking to them from the jharokha.' Her attendant was trying to wake her up.

Ghamzah Begum was accustomed to riding inside the Qila every morning but for some reason, against her usual practice, today she had still not woken up. She would get up before the first light and finish her riding before the first light of dawn. Chandni picked up a rose from the basket and softly stroked Ghamzah Begum's cheek with it. She just rubbed her face with a soft cloth and continued sleeping. Chandni put the rose under her nose and Ghamzah Begum finally got up. She looked at Chandni and said playfully, 'O you wretch, you are trying to tease me! Just wait, I will punish you.'

Hariyali shrugged her shoulders at this insouciance and continued. Mubarak and Naseeban would know what had happened and none of the begums there were prone to hysterics.

Though not quite hysterical, a very emotional Sikandar Ara Begum was weeping in a corner remembering tales of Ghulam Qadir's devastation of the haramsara.

'What if they come here! We know what happened when Ghulam Qadir's soldiers entered the haram,' she cried. 'Is that why Allah has given me such a long age, so I can witness this? Why aren't I dead!'

Rashid Jahan Begum, Falak Ara and the attendants were all massaging her feet and her shoulders to calm her down.

'What has happened Mubarak?' Hariyali asked her friend.

Mubarak had reached the Qila at dawn after her sehri to get an early start on the wedding preparation and had witnessed most of the events. She had come and described them to Sikandar Ara Begum, and now regretted it. The lady was inconsolable.

Hariyali dragged Mubarak away from the old princess and asked her to relate the day's happenings.

'*Arre kya bataun* Hariyali, *qismat phoot gayi hamari* [what can I say, our fate has turned, and bad days are here]. Arre why did this sawars have to come just today! My shahzadi's nikah is the day after; how am I going to do anything when there is so much confusion?' 'Don't panic Mubarak we will all help you, but tell me what happened? Who are these sawars?' cajoled Hariyali.

'I don't know, these *karam jale sawars* [they of bad deeds], have rebelled against their angrez officers and come to the Qila.'

By then Falak Ara, who had managed to make Sikandar Ara Begum sleep, came to Mubarak for some work. When she heard Hariyali's questions she said, 'Sit down Hariyali. I saw everything from the window, let me tell you.

'Some twenty cavalrymen from Meerut came to *zer-e jharokha*, just under the balcony, and started shouting for mercy. "*Dohai*, Badshah Huzur, dohai," they called out. You know how soft-hearted our Huzur Purnur is. He asked them what had happened. "Our faith is being corrupted, Huzur," they told him.

'Our esteemed Badshah replied that he is but a faqir and has no powers and would recommend their case to the angrez officers.

But they insisted that the Badshah lead them against the angrez fauj. Meanwhile, Huzur had summoned Captain Douglas, the Qiledar. I couldn't see him from here, but I could hear him trying to pacify the sepoys.'

I heard Huzur-e Anwar tell the captain, 'What is all this trouble that has erupted? How has a religious fight reared its head? This is a case of faith and principles. Religious persecution and bigotry are very bad things. Many kingdoms have been destroyed by it, and innumerable people have been killed by it. It's essential that this be sorted out immediately.

God forbid that the sedition and riots spread all over the country and innumerable people are killed and there is a loss in revenue. The prevailing peace and prosperity will suffer. As far as possible, we should work with a cool mind and use a gentle approach. These people are illiterate. One should cajole them and insist that they desist from this. I am surprised that you didn't know of this problem already.'

The Qiledar said he would sort it out and left. Huzur withdrew to the khasgah as he was very upset.'

Mubarak, who had calmed down a bit, said, 'But that is not what I am worried about. The sawars have stormed their way into the Qila. I heard that they have entered the Qila.'

Hariyali had heard enough and knew that Thakur sahib's worst fears had come true. The ghadar had started twenty days earlier. She had to rush to his house. Picking up her basket, she made her way out of the Qila to see that there were sawars everywhere. They seemed to have taken over the Qila.

As she exited the Qila, she saw scenes of mayhem. The residents were running away to safety and the shopkeepers were closing their shops.

The city of Shahjahanabad was buzzing with the news of the arrival of the sepoys and sawars from Meerut. The *badmashes,* 800 ordinary criminals whom the sepoys had freed from prison in Meerut, had accompanied the sepoys and were looting and plundering the bazaar and killing people. With more prisoners being set free in Delhi, local scoundrels had joined in the looting.

Meanwhile, Zoravar Singh had reached Mirza Qaiser's house. Qaiser and Mirza Aftab were pacing restlessly in their home. They had already heard details of what had happened under the jharokha.

Seeing Zoravar, Mirza Aftab asked, 'Do you have any news? What is happening in the city?'

'Salam Phuppajan. Yes, my clerk brought news for me from the thana. It seems that yesterday in Meerut when the officers were preparing to go to the church for evening service, they heard sounds of muskets followed by columns of smoke and realized that the sepoys of the 3rd cavalry had rebelled against them. The rebels then opened the jails where their comrades were imprisoned and released not only those eighty-four officers but also all the badmash who were incarcerated. They then attacked and killed their European officers and burnt their houses. Soon after sunset, the rebel sepoys took the road to Delhi.'

'Didn't the officers anticipate this? They are usually so wise,' said Mirza Aftab.

'Phuppajan, they are wise, but they are also puffed up in a sense of their own importance. They never thought that these "natives", as they refer to the Hindustani sepoys, would rebel against them. They had failed to take pre-emptive action and were caught absolutely unawares. As it was dark, they couldn't take any action either. Now these sawars have stormed into the city and Qila. I saw a few of them chasing Mr Simon Fraser and Capt. Douglas into the Lahori Darwaza.'

Just then, a retainer walked in. He was shivering in fear.

'Afzal Baig, is everything all right? *Khuda khair kare* [may God have mercy]. What has happened?'

'Sarkar, I wish my eyes were gouged out, my tongue had been cut off before I saw and had to describe such brutality.'

'What happened, Afzal Baig?' By now Mirza Aftab was extremely nervous.

'Sarkar, the Resident bahadur, the Qiledar bahadur and the Padri sahib, along with his daughter and her friend, Clifford missy sahib, have all been murdered by the sawars who came from Meerut. The two missy sahibs were so young and pretty. So innocent. They were murdered mercilessly. What had they ever done to wrong these sawars? The sawars were aided by some badmashes. These sawars didn't once remember that they had been eating the salt of the angrez, drawing salaries from them!'

Mirza Aftab sat down in shock. Matters had gone out of hand. He had thought he'd go to Hakim Ahsanullah sahib and seek his help in bringing back peace.

'Abbajan, I know that the sepoys, and indeed all Hindustanis were getting restless and restive at the oppressive policies of these firangis, but this is outrageous! I heard that some of the sawars had given the reason for their faith getting corrupted by the cartridges, and they wanted to save it. But to kill? Which mazhab permits this barbaric behaviour?' lamented Qaiser.

'Ji, Huzur,' replied Afzal Baig. 'Hakim Ahsanullah and Sharf ud-Daulah, the royal *wakeel*, had reached the palace as soon as Captain Douglas was wounded and sent a message to Alampanah asking for some men and a palki so that the ladies may be carried away to the haram, where Nawab Zeenat Mahal Begum sahiba would protect them. Hakim sahib even asked for two guns at the request of Bada sahib. A messenger had gone to Huzur Alampanah who was with begum sahiba in the Khas Mahal. Huzur immediately dispatched a palki and gave orders for two guns to be sent from the artillery. Hakim sahib left for the Diwan-e Khas to make more arrangements. But the badmash killed the Bada sahib on the stairs of the commandant's quarters and after that, several men with drawn swords went upstairs and after a while news came that everybody had been killed. They slaughtered the Qiledar sahib and all the innocent men and women!'

The father and son duo sank down in a state of shock. After a while, Qaiser said, 'Abbajan, if I have your permission, may I go and see if Mufti sahib needs any help?'

'Son, of course you must go and find out if Mufti sahib is fine but let me first ask Hakim Ahsanullah Khan if he needs any help. In fact, why don't both of you come with me?'

The three of them made their way towards the Khan-e Saman office near the Diwan-e Khas. They could see sawars on their horses in the area beyond the naqqarkhana. This area could only be accessed on foot by anyone else except the emperor and princes of royal blood, but the sawars were heedless of royal protocol.

Thinking that these people are absolutely disrespectful, Mirza sahib continued on his way.

They found the Hakim sahib and Mahbub Ali Khan, the wazir, sitting with their heads in their hands. They all started praying for peace and reciting 'Oh unique originator of goodness' as they devoutly thumbed their rosaries.

Just then, there was a loud explosion, and it was as if the earth had been rent asunder and the day of reckoning had come.

All they could do was call out to Allah for forgiveness.

When the sky is rent asunder
And hearkens to (the Command of) its Lord—and it must needs
(do so)
And when the Earth is flattened out
And casts forth what is within it and becomes (clean) empty

—Quran 84:1-4

27

The Streets of Blood

maut ka ek din muayyan hai
neend kyun raat bhar nahin aati

When a day of death is pre-ordained
Why does sleep escape me all night?

—Mirza Ghalib

Contrary to the swaying, carefree gait with which she usually negotiated the labyrinthine bazaar, today Hariyali had hurriedly forced her way through the teeming streets to reach Thakur sahib's house. Shops were being closed, and groups of badmash who had now been let out of Delhi jails by the sepoys were roaming around, trying to loot whatever they could. She could hear some sepoys screaming in front of a haveli that the inmates should give up the firangis they were hiding inside, but she had no time to find out. Her mind was inflamed by the suddenness of the events and what effect it could have on their plans.

Mir sahib and Imam sahib were already there. It was close to nine in the morning.

The sentry at the door saw her agitated state and just let her in without questioning saying, 'Thakur sahib is in the diwankhana and Thakurain in her room. You know the way, just go in.' Then he shook his head and said, 'The world has gone mad.'

Hariyali walked up the path that led to the diwankhana, through the garden. The fountain was flowing gently, and Hariyali wondered whether it was washing away her sorrows or shedding her tears. The much-anticipated revolt had started but it had started prematurely, and she was apprehensive of its results.

In the room, Thakur sahib was sitting with Mir sahib and Imam sahib, who had also rushed there when they got the news. She asked for permission to enter and sat in a corner.

The three were discussing news that Mir sahib had brought, that the British were being murdered, mansions were being burnt, and there was chaos everywhere as loot and plunder were afoot.

She had just sat down to get her breath back when there was a huge explosion, and the foundations of the city seemed to be shaking; it seemed as if the earth had split open and everything had been buried inside.

'Astaghfirullah, may Allah forgive my sins,' said Imam sahib as he jumped up, startled. 'Allah *reham*, mercy. What calamity is this?'

The three men and Hariyali had no clue and were looking scared and worried. 'What have we got ourselves into, I wonder,' said Mir sahib.

Just then, Bhooray Khan, who had gone into the city to investigate, came rushing in.

'They have blown up the magazine, sahib,' he told the shocked assembly.

They found out later from Rahim Baksh, that the Joint Magistrate, Sir Theophilus Metcalfe, had escaped Delhi on a horse, by taking off the clothes that set him apart as a British, dressed in only his shirt and underdrawers. He later took a native dress from one of the police sergeants.

Metcalfe had left instructions for Lieutenant George Willoughby, the officer in charge, to secure the main munitions magazine, and under no circumstance let it fall in the hands of the sepoys. When Willoughby realized that the sepoys had brought ladders to scale the walls after having failed to batter the gates down, he gave orders for the munitions to be blown up.

Yusuf Ali had gone to work as usual, hoping to get his hand on the keys. He had just got down to work when he heard the commotion and heard the sepoys, sawars and badmash trying to scale the wall.

Rahim Baksh, who had stood away from the gate so that the sepoys could climb in, was saved. He saw bits and pieces of cannon balls pelting down from the sky like a hailstorm. That day thousands were killed and injured. Yusuf Ali was a part of those who were released from attendance in this world. The sky was filled with smoke for hours and screams of the injured could be heard all around.

The explosion had shaken the ladies, and while the younger ones were crying, the older ones sat on their prayer mats and prayed. Just then, Gulab Jan came. Everyone pounced on her for news. She had just seen a very pretty European miss, who had been captured by the sepoys from the city, brought to the palace. The khwajasaras persuaded the sepoys to take her to Nawab Zeenat Mahal, who agreed to shelter her if the Badshah agreed.

'Ama, of course. Not a single life should be lost,' he said.

However, some of the badmash, rascals who had escaped from the jails, goaded the sepoys into taking her back into their custody.

The Badshah relented when they promised to treat her well. They promised that all fifty-six men, women and children captured from the magazine, where they were hiding, and various other places, were being kept safely in the old kitchen.

As news of the death of the popular Dr Chiman Lal and Padri sahib spread through the city, all the undesirable elements of the city—rascals, thieves, pickpockets, shoplifters, pilferers, impounders, swindlers and embezzlers, who were always on the lookout for such opportunities—came out of their houses and joined the rebels in large numbers. Now, for every sawar, there were at least fifty of these undesirable elements running alongside them.

While the sawars tyrannized, these rascals indulged in loot and theft and left a trail of destruction behind.

Hira had gone to Dariba for some work: a family had asked for some jewellery to be repaired. With the princess' wedding day approaching, his hopes of getting the locket from Falak Ara were fading. He may as well make money from his profession.

He heard a great deal of noise emanating from the area where Begum Samru's kothi had been located, and which was now the Delhi Bank.

Some sepoys, sawars and the badmash had attacked it. The angrez bank officers were defending it. A few women and children had also taken shelter here. The angrez refused to give up the money in the bank and armed themselves to fight the rebels and scoundrels. Hira could hear shots coming from two sides and knew that both sides were engaging in a gunfight.

A great tumult prevailed for some time but eventually, the rebels scaled the garden wall and set the roof of the kothi on fire. Hira and the other spectators watched aghast as the huge beams on the ceiling of the mansion caught fire and began to fall. The flames rose high and the billows of smoke from the kothi darkened the sky. Soon, the front of the mansion was destroyed and all the brave men defending it were burnt to cinders. This was the sign for the rebels to enter the bank and loot it. The inner rooms, which housed the treasury and vaults, were safe from the flames. The men entered the bank from the back and broke all the locks on the chests and carried away as much as they could carry away.

One of the men standing near Hira said, 'These shameless looters, the sepoys had rebelled in Meerut and come to Delhi with their platoons. They had also been joined by the local weavers, shoemakers, washermen, water carriers, grocers, butchers and paper sellers from Kaghazi Mohalla and sundry other rascals from the city. Bodybuilders, musclemen, cudgellers, petty thieves, pickpockets and many others were also present. There are no men from decent families there. All those who live good and honest lives are locked inside their houses, totally unaware of what is happening in their city.'

Hira was debating whether to join the looters and when he saw them coming out with bags of coins, he decided to make some money for himself.

He pushed his way in, kicked a few people and managed to reach the treasury room. He saw two bags in someone's hand and punched that person, snatched the bags, and ran out.

The Mughal treasure may be a myth, but this was real. He would take this and try for that later.

He ran straight home and hid the bags to count later. There was money to be made just now as he headed out to the bazaar to join the purbias and tilingas.

Meanwhile, shaking off the dust that had engulfed the surroundings after the explosion, Qaiser and Zoravar made their way outside. They wanted to find out what had happened and the reason for this explosion.

They didn't have to go far. They met Mirza Abu Bakr and Ibrahim near Jauhri Bazar and made their way to the qahwakhana. They found it had been closed, and Abu Bakr invited them to his house nearby. It was extremely hot, especially for the rozedars, and they wanted to find a shady place to sit. The azan for asr prayers could be heard. Evening wasn't far off.

They found Brijnath Zutshi standing in front of the Tripolia in a daze. He had just come from the Delhi College.

Seeing his state, they asked him to join them.

Brijnath Zutshi was on his way to Delhi College when he heard of the happenings of the morning. He was pushing his way through the milling crowds when he saw Dr Chiman Lal standing in front of his dispensary surrounded by angry sawar and sepoys.

The sawars had just killed the Padri Imamuddin sahib, who lived in Daryaganj, and had now come to the dispensary.

Dr Chiman Lal was a kayastha by birth, but a while ago he, Padri Imamuddin and Master Ram Chandra had converted to Christianity. The sawars entered the hospital as angels of death for Dr Chiman Lal. They started questioning him.

'Which religion do you follow?'

'That of Jesus Christ,' Dr Chiman Lal had responded.

The sawar who had already killed Padri Imamuddin dispatched the doctor to join the priest with his next bullet. They then vandalized the hospital and destroyed it completely.

Brijnath had immediately rushed to Delhi College to find out how the principal and Master Ramchandra had fared. He saw the library in flames, books and pages thrown about. Mr Taylor, the principal, and Master Ramchandra had somehow managed to escape.

He was on his way back home when he met his friends and came to join them to get some moral support.

It was time for breaking the fast when Bhooray Khan found his way to Thakur sahib's haveli. Hariyali had long since left, but the three friends were discussing the blowing up of the magazine, looting of the bank and the murders. With his informal network of spies, Bhooray Khan had more news to tell them.

'How on earth did the sepoys and sawars go so wrong, Bhooray?' asked Mir sahib.

'Mir sahib, may I be forgiven by Allah, for the truth is, none of us expected it to happen so fast or that the badmash of the city would join them. I just heard that the jailor, Lala Thakur Das, who had been maintaining discipline, and not letting the criminals escape from the Delhi jail has also been overcome. After hearing that the angrez had been overthrown, the criminals were complaining that they were being deprived of their share in the plunder. He stood them off for as long as he could, but eventually, fearing for his life he went home. Now they have also escaped, like the criminals from Meerut, and are scouring the city, showing their villainous colours.'

'I just heard that Mr Taylor, the principal sahib, had escaped from the college but was discovered in his hiding place and beaten to death,' said Imam sahib.

In the palace, Hakim Ahsanullah Khan had gone to meet Huzur Badshah. By the time Alampanah had given the orders to close the gates of the Qila, it had been too late. The sepoys had already entered and would not allow the gates to be closed. They had sent a message to the Badshah Salamat through his khwajasara, 'We have come to fight for our deen, our faith and pay our respects to Huzur Alampanah. Please ask him to meet us.'

The khwajasara had taken the messages to Huzur who had come out. They had presented their salam and said that they wanted him to lead them against the Company bahadur.

Alampanah had replied, 'I have neither troops, magazine or treasury. I am not in a condition to join anyone. I am just a mendicant, whiling away my time in prayers and making the best of what fate has dealt me.'

'*Hamare sar par aap apna haath rakh dijiye* [bless us with your support, and we will manage everything]. We will provide everything.'

Hearing this, Huzur Jahanpanah had gone inside the khwaabgah.

The sawars had gone off to the Mehtab Bagh and camped there, but the sepoys remained in the Diwan-e Khas.

By the evening, 300 sawars and three regiments from cantonments and two from Meerut had taken up quarters in the Qila. One regiment was camping in Salimgarh and the rest in the Diwan-e Khas, stables and naqqarkhana.

In the evening, Hakim Ahsanullah Khan presented himself before the Alampanah. Nawab Zeenat Mahal Begum sahiba was also present.

Hakim sahib said, 'It is necessary to write an account of these occurrences to the Lieutenant Governor at Agra, for there is no government here.'

Badshah Salamat replied that the Malika would write a royal missive and send a camel sawar to Agra. Nawab Zeenat Mahal Begum sahiba summoned her munshi and got the clerk to write the letter. Then she signed it and handed it over to be carried by a camel sawar to Agra. However, the khwajasara to whom the munshi handed over the letter alerted the two chief khwajasaras of the mahal, Basant Ali and Nasir. These two informed the sawars and this led to the suspicion that Hakim sahib and the Malika were in league with the angrez. They knew that Nawab Zeenat Mahal Begum wanted her son to succeed to the throne and that this revolt could overturn her plans—which is why she might feel compelled to aid the angrez.

To counter this influence that the Hakim sahib and the Malika had on Badshah Salamat, they decided to empower the shahzadas who did not get along with the former.

In this, they elicited the help of the wazir, Mahbub Ali Khan Khwajasara.

Though the *shuqqah* was intercepted, the angrez bahadur had got the news.

Two young signalmen William Bendish and IW Pilkington, posted in *Telegraph* office on Lothian Road, near St James Church in Old Delhi, had managed to send a brief warning of the disaster to 'Umballa' late in the afternoon, before fleeing themselves. The signallers were able to report only that Europeans 'had been killed' before they signed off with the cryptic sentence, 'We are off.'

> *Ba-yak gardish-e-charkh-e-nilofari*
> *Na nadir baja manad wa ne nadiri*

The revolving sky of destiny is a fraudster and cheat
It creates many excuses for the oppression of men

—Zahir Dehlvi

28

The Shahenshah of Hindustan

The Seventeenth Ramzan

Aafat shab-e-tanhai ki tal jaye to achchha
ghabra ke jo dam aaj nikal jaye to achchha

The faster the calamity of this night of loneliness gets over
the better
If I die today from the confusion it is better.

—Rind Lakhnavi

The city was up early once again for sehri. As Hariyali passed by
Kucha Mir Ashiq, she heard the dhobis discussing the events of the
day before, when one of the elder men got up and said, '*Bahut ho gayi
gupshap* [put an end to the gossip], we have to go off to work. What
difference does it make to us? We are going to benefit neither from
the angrez nor the Badshah. *Khoon ho yaa gulal hamari qismat mein to
usse dhona hi likha hai* [whether it's blood or the colours of festivity,
we are condemned to wash it only].'

Hariyali, however, wanted to wash the grief of her son's death by
ensuring the firangis were removed and Badshah Salamat was once
again made the sovereign.

She reached the palace to see that no one had slept at night due to anxiety, and were now dozing or praying. Mubarak had stayed on in the Qila that night and was waiting for Hariyali or Naseeban to come with news.

Sikandar Ara Begum and Rashid Jahan Begum looked at Falak Ara, sitting in her corner, and started conferring with each other.

'I think it is very important that the nikah take place as planned tomorrow. The Company bahadur will soon sort out this mess, and how long can Falak sit in maiyyoo'n?' said Rashid Jahan Begum. The senior lady agreed, and a message was sent to the Badshah asking for his permission to carry on as per programme, via the khwajasara.

The Badshah had much more weighty matters on his mind, as did the Malika, but they sent a message via the khwajasara that they were in agreement. Another khwajasara was dispatched to Mirza Aftab's house to inform him.

Mirza Aftab and his sister Mahtab Ara Begum had been discussing the same when the khwajasara came. Today was Qaiser's mehndi, but that function could be held in the evening and very simply. Only a few of Qaiser's friends and Chand Kunwarji were invited.

Qaiser was getting ready when he was informed that his nuptials were going ahead as planned since Falak had already sat in maiyyoo'n.

'Ji Abbajan, as you decide,' he replied.

'Are you ready? Come with me to the Diwan-e Khas. I have heard at night many more regiments have come and some of the sepoys have now made the Diwan-e Khas their living quarters. I didn't expect that I would see such sacrilege in my life, but what can we do? What can anyone do now,' Mirza Aftab said rhetorically. 'What Allah has written in our fate will come to be.'

The two reached the Diwan-e Khas to see it filled with sepoys and sawars. They were demanding an audience with the Badshah Salamat. Mirza Mughal, Mirza Abu-Bakr and Mirza Khizr Sultan were also there.

The shahzadas were thrilled at this turn of events. They had a chance to overthrow the oppressive Company rule and resurrect back the glory of the khandan-e Timuriya. They knew that they had a great fighting chance, with the six regiments trained by the British themselves that had come to offer their services to the Badshah. The biggest arsenal of the angrez had been damaged and though they hadn't been able to procure the weapons, the angrez couldn't use them against them either. They were sure more men would join them, and their lack of experience didn't bother them. The blood of Babur and Akbar Badshah ran in their veins. They were born to conquer.

Subedar Gulab Shah ordered his men to get the Takht-e Huma, which had been in storage since the Badshah's *tajposhi*, from the basement. It was dusted and kept in readiness for Huzur Mahabali to appear.

Mahbub Ali Khan sent Agha Jan khwajasara with a message. Mirza Aftab and Mahbub Ali Khan were trying to bring some semblance of order in the Diwan-e Khas when the *naqib* called out, ' Attention! Greetings, present your salutations to the Refuge of the World, long live the Emperor, the Refuge of the Universe!'

The sawars, sepoys and the courtiers who had gathered there stood up in attention. The Hindustani soldiers of Subedar rank presented tribute and described themselves as faithful soldiers awaiting his orders. Muinuddin Khan, who had been the thanedar of Paharganj, was appointed as kotwal of the city and instructed to maintain law and order there and to bring the plundering and looting under control.

Hakim Ahsanullah Khan, Zahir Dehlvi and many others had also reached by this time.

Huzur Alampanah was seated on the Takht-e Huma and pronounced as Shahenshah of Hindustan, nazars were given by all present and they all pledged to fight under his banner against the Company bahadur.

Emperor Bahadur Shah Zafar called on Hindus and Musalmans to fight loyally for the cause of freeing Hindustan from foreign rule.

For this, he made the Hindus swear by Ram and the Ganges while each Musalman had to pledge this by placing a copy of the Quran placed on their head.

As per the confabulations of Gulab Shah and Mahbub Ali Khan, Mirza Mughal was announced as the new commander-in-chief of the Hindustani forces, of the infantry, cavalry and other branches of the army. He was ordered to inspect the city and make such arrangements that the powerful could not exploit the poor, and the kotwal was ordered to declare in the city that if someone had weapons or material from the magazine in his house, he must submit it to the Badshah otherwise he would be treated as a criminal and punished accordingly.

The other royal princes, such as Mirza Kuchak Sultan, Mirza Khizr Sultan, Mirza Mendu and Mirza Bakhtawar Shah, were made colonels of the various infantry regiments, and Mirza Abu Bakr was made a colonel of the 3rd Light Cavalry.

The shahzadas were given two guns each and ordered to take charge of their regiments at the Kashmir, Lahore and Delhi Gates so that they might help bring about order in the city.

Mirza Mughal was ordered to control the disturbances made by the fighting soldiers in the city. The Badshah Salamat retired to his Khas Mahal, but Hakim sahib took permission to meet him and respectfully warned him, 'Huzur, no dependence can be placed on these sawars and sepoys. They have already looted and plundered the city and as more come, there will be utter mayhem in the city.'

While Mirza Aftab, Qaiser and the rest went home, the shahzadas stayed with the soldiers and Hakim sahib went to confer with the leading men of the city. In consultation with Mahbub Ali Khan, Aminuddin Khan, Mirza Ziyauddin Khan it was decided that an executive council was to be formed, to maintain order in the city and provide food for the soldiers. Though the council broke up without any definite decision, they arranged for supplies of food for the soldiers to prevent their plundering.

Qazi Mohammad Faizullah and Abdul Hakim were appointed as city kotwal and Naib Qazi for the administration of justice.

Letters were dispatched to the Rajas of Jaipur, Patiala, Jhajjar, Ballabgarh, Bahadurgarh to march at once upon Delhi with all their forces to join the Badshah's army, and to repel any attack on the city by the English.

This news was conveyed by Bhooray Khan to Thakur sahib and Mir sahib. Bhooray also conveyed the shocking news that the sainted Alampanah was made to parade through the city on his elephant by the soldiers, to bring some peace to the city and order the grain shops to open and allay the fears of the citizens and order the people to resume their ordinary occupations.

'That I have to witness such a day when the Badshah-e Hind has to come out on the streets to control law and order,' lamented Mir sahib.

'What are the newly appointed officers doing that the Badshah Salamat had to go forth himself?' asked Thakur sahib.

'Sarkar,' said Bhooray, 'One of the soldiers told me that the Badshah Salamat heard of plundering of the houses in Churiwalan and ordered one regiment to be placed at strategic points for he said, 'We do not like that our subjects should be plundered.' When he heard that looting continued unabated, he sent Mirza Mughal with a company of infantry to stop the looters. Mirza Mughal visited all the police stations and gave orders that anyone caught looting would be punished with the loss of their nose and ears. And since shopkeepers weren't opening shops and refused to supply essential rations to the soldiers, there was also panic that those who did not open their shops would be confined and imprisoned.'

'Why then did Huzur Purnur go out?' asked Mir sahib.

'Sarkar,' answered Bhooray, 'when the Badshah Salamat got more complaints of food not being available to the soldiers, he mounted Maula Baksh and with Jawan Bakht seated behind him, went out in a display of imperial might and to show the residents that now he was in control. He went through Chandni Chowk with two regiments of Telinga infantry. The soldiers were shouting "Bahadur Shah ki Jai ho".'

And so, at least for the moment, the chaos had been stemmed, the shops had opened and the city's residents were able to stock up on supplies.

Meanwhile, Hariyali also came with the same news that the Badshah Salamat had ordered the shahzadas to send every mutineer out of the city, locating regiments in separate places, and leaving only one regiment in the Palace for the defence of the city, and another on the sands in front of the Palace, between the Fort and the river. Another regiment was ordered to hold the Ajmeri Gate of the city, a fourth the Delhi Gate and a fifth the Kashmiri Gate. These orders had been partially carried out.

Thakur sahib, Mir sahib and Imam sahib were in tears. Their carefully thought-out plans were being derailed by these undisciplined soldiers.

There was news of the massacre of Europeans who could not flee the city and that was not what should have happened. The fight for rights should not include oppression. It seemed as if the Hindustani rebels were only hellbent on destroying old systems without putting anything new in place, and the formation of the executive council brought some solace to their hearts. Maybe, the shahzadas could control the sawars and sepoys and guide them in this war.

They decided to form committees in each mohalla and ensure that law and order prevailed.

In the Qila, Zebun and Zeenat were teasing Falak, as Mubarak and Naseeban, accompanied by the mirasins on the dhol, were applying freshly ground henna on Falak's hands and feet.

'Apajan, *dulhe miyan ke bhi mehndi lag rahi hogi* [the groom must be getting mehndi put on his hands]. Let's see whose colour is brighter, for surely that person loves the other more.'

Qaiser was indeed getting mehndi put on his hands. His friends were teasing him. Chand Kunwar and Mahtab Ara were singing songs while Mirza Aftab looked on with affection, missing the presence of his wife.

Qaiser, who, in the morning, had thought that getting married under such circumstances was unadvisable, was at peace now. Huzur Alampanah was once again given his rightful place on the Takht-e Huma and the Sahib-e alams, royal princes, were in charge of the soldiers. Insha'Allah victory would be theirs. Coins had been struck in the Badshah Salamat's name. In fact, Mirza Naushah had written a verse on that:

Bar zari aftab o nuqra-i-mah
Sikka zad dar jahan Bahadur Shah

On the gold of the sun and on the silver of the moon
Bahadur Shah has struck his coin[34]

Earlier in the day, the Emperor had appointed Mufti Sadruddin Khan Azurda as judge of the civil and criminal courts.

He fully intended to take permission from the Badshah Salamat, his father, Mufti sahib and of course, his wife, and join them.

The thought of Falak as his wife made him blush and think of Mirza Naushah's verse:

Is sadgi pe kaun na mar jaye ai Khuda,
ladte hain aur hath mein talwar bhi nahin

Who would not be slain by such simplicity;
She slays and nary a sword in her hand.

29

Together

tum mere pas hote ho goya
jab koi dusra nahin hota

In such a way are you with me
That no space for anyone else can ever be.

—Momin Khan Momin

The maalans, female gardeners, under Naseeban's expert guidance, had decorated the mahal in which Falak lived. The air was heavy with the fragrance of *champa*, *juhi* and jasmine. The mirasins were singing bridal songs written by Hazrat Amir Khusrau. Of course, he had written them in the spiritual context of the union of the soul with Allah, but they were popular in weddings, sung to the accompaniment of a *dholak*.

Goondho ri maalan phoolon ka sehra
Goondho ri maalan phoolon ka sehra
Aaj badhava, Sajan ghar baaje
Goondho ri maalan phoolon ka sehra

O maalan, make a floral chaplet
O maalan, make a floral chaplet

My beloved will come home wearing it
O maalan, make a floral chaplet.

Nijamuddin Auliya ke bal bal jaaun
Mukhade par motiyan sehra biraje
Mukhade par motiyan sehra biraje
Aaj badhava, Sajan ghar baaje
Phoolon ka sehara goondho ri maalan . . .

May I be sacrificed over Nizamuddin Auliya
Face decorated with the chaplet he has come
Face decorated with the chaplet he has come
My beloved will come home wearing it
O maalan, make a floral chaplet . . .

Under her veil, Falak was thinking not of the union of bodies, but of the union of souls. Living in seclusion in the zenana she had no descriptions to go by but had read extensively of the Sufi idea of *visaal*, when the Soul (lover) went to meet the Maker (beloved) and they were united forever. She hoped that her union with Qaiser would be forever, and their love would endure in this world and the next.

The circumstances of their wedding were strange, but that could not be helped. Who would have thought that the Hindustani soldiers would suddenly rise up against the Company bahadur?

The nikah was to be held around 10 a.m., and all preparations had to be done quickly, was the thought driving Mubarak as she bustled around, supervising the servants, checking with the darogha that garlands for the groom's family were ready, stopping to blow some prayers on her precious charge to protect her against the evil eye. Since everyone would be fasting, no special food was being prepared.

Zeenat and Zebun, Bilqis and Mehr, along with all the younger girls were squealing in excitement, getting their toilettes done by their annas.

'Why isn't Falak Apa getting ready?' asked Bilqis.

'She will get ready when her clothes and jewellery are sent by the *dulha*'s family,' Mubarak replied.

Nawab Talat Shahar Banu Begum, Nawab Zeb Zamani Begum and Amani Khanum had come in the morning itself as they had a fondness for Falak. They were sitting with Sikandar Ara Begum and Rashid Ara Begum, discussing the events of the past two days.

Now that Mirza Mughal was the commander-in-chief, his wife, Amani Khanum, had plenty of news to give.

'Phuppijan,' she said addressing Rashid Ara Begum, who had just congratulated her on her husband becoming commander-in-chief, 'Mirza Mughal has got things under control but even he is finding it difficult. You know that Hakim Ahsanullah Khan and Zeenat Mahal Begum sahiba are in constant touch with the angrez bahadur. They even sent a letter to the Bada sahib in Agra but the shuqqah was intercepted. The Malika still hopes that Jawan Bakht will be declared heir. She doesn't realize that there is no Bada sahib now. It is Mirza Mughal in charge, and he will be the heir once we win this war.'

Sikandar Ara Begum shook her head, 'I have seen plenty of young women wrapping their older husbands around their fingers but this one has crossed all limits.'

Just then the khwajasara came to announce the arrival of Mahtab Ara Begum, Chand Kunwar and Rani Meera Devi, Qaiser's maternal aunts.

They were accompanied by servant girls who were carrying the *suhag pura* and *suhag ka joda*, bridal decoration, jewellery and clothes for Falak. Since the expenses of the wedding were to be borne by the groom and his family, everything needed for a bride was in these trays. Mirza Aftab had left nothing out. All the jewellery belonging to his late wife had been sent for Falak. The dress was very simple in comparison, since, as per Hindustani customs, scissors should not touch the nikah dress. It was torn by mouth and hand and stitched by hand. It was a sack-like kurta and pyjama with a heavily embellished dupatta.

While the groom's family was being welcomed with songs and garlands, Sikandar Ara Begum, as the oldest present, had garlanded

Mahtab Ara, and Rashid Jahan Begum had garlanded Chand Kunwar, while Zohrun Nisa Begum garlanded Rani Meera Devi.

Though everyone else was fasting, they politely offered sherbet and sweets to Chand Kunwar and Rani Meera Devi, but they refused saying that during Ramzan, even though they didn't fast, they respected a rozedar by not eating in public.

By now, the bride was ready, looking like a vision in red and green, wearing the nath she had longed to wear not so long ago.

The khwajasara announced that the Qazi sahib had come to read the nikah.

As was the custom for any male entering the mahalsara, the Qazi sahib was blindfolded and led to the room where the bride was sitting by the khwajasara.

After reading the terms of the meher and the covenant between the bride and groom, the Qazi sahib asked, 'Falak Ara Begum, *binte* Abu Zafar Sirajuddin Bahadur Shah Badshah Ghazi, do I have your permission to solemnize your nikah with Qaiser ibn Mohammad Aftab, with the mehr fixed at five hundred gold coins?'

The blushing, nervous bride could say nothing. The Qazi sahib repeated his question. When he repeated it for the third and final time, Sikandar Ara Begum nudged her and said, 'Beti, say *qubool hai.*'

Falak said in a soft voice, '*Qubool hai.*'

The room was filled with tears and joyful voices and blessings for the couple.

Since the purdah between the bride and groom was maintained till after the nikah, Qaiser was in his house along with his father and friends. He was dressed in a muslin kurta, embellished with gold embroidery, with a *nima* over it, a type of tunic made of the fine material *mashru* which was woven from silk warp and cotton weft yarns, in accordance with the shariah. Over that he had a brocade sash in which his diamond and ruby studded dagger with a gold and gemstone decorated sheath was attached. Qaiser, who preferred to dress simply, had been cajoled by his father and Zoravar into getting dressed up as an ode to the bride. He had shyly agreed. His narrow trousers were made of silk.

A turban of silk was wrapped around his head, with an emerald and diamond sarpech decorating it. On that was tied a pearl *sehra,* or chaplet, that once been worn by his father. A floral sehra was tied on top of it.

A seven-stringed pearl necklace that had been gifted by his maternal uncle Raja Jaswant Singh, who had come for the wedding.

Ordinarily, he would have gone to the Diwan-e Khas and the nikah would have been solemnized there with the blessings of the Badshah Salamat. But nothing was ordinary today and the Diwan-e Khas was full of sepoys.

The Qazi sahib then went out of the mahal and towards Mirza Aftab's house, where the groom's Qazi was waiting. The nikah was finalized and congratulatory voices filled the room.

Mirza Aftab lifted both the sehra carefully and kissed his son's forehead.

Sweets were distributed in carefully packed silver boxes to all the attendees. The feast would only be at iftar.

The *doli* was sent to bring the bride and was accompanied by Raja Jaswant Singh till the deorhi with male and female attendants.

The doli was carried inside by the female attendants and taken to Khurd Jahan, where the young girls were teasing the bride. Mubarak was crying copiously, and Mahtab Ara Begum was trying to reassure her. Rani Meera Devi came up with the idea, 'Mubarak, why don't you come with the dulhan and stay with her in Qaiser's house as you did here?'

This mollified her and she also started bidding goodbye to everyone.

The doli reached and the mirasins started singing the *bidai,* farewell, another popular composition of Hazrat Amir Khusrau:

Kahe ko biyaahi bides
Arre lakhiya baabul mohe
Kahe ko byaahe bides

Why have you married me off to someone in an alien land
O, my wealthy father
Why did you part me from yourself?

Hum to babul tore bele ki kaliya
Arre ghar ghar maange hain jaaye
Arre lakhiya baabul mohe
Kahe ko byaahe bides

Dear father, I am a blossom in your orchard
Every household asks for us.
O, my wealthy father
Why did you part me from yourself?

Bhayiyon ko diye babul mahlay do-mahlay,
Hum ko diya pardes, ray, lakhi babul
Hum to hain babul tere khoontay ki gaiyyan,
Jid haankay hank jaayen, ray, lakhi babul . . .

You gave a palace or two to my brother
And to me o my wealthy father you gave exile . . .
We are just your tethered cows
To be driven by whoever bids for us
O, my wealthy father
Why did you part me from yourself?

This song always evoked emotions in the heart of every woman who listened to it, for they all realized they were dispensable objects, to be given away, snatched at times, and married off at the father's will.

Of course, Falak was getting married to someone of her own choice, but it could just as easily have been otherwise. It had often been otherwise when girls were used as pawn in power struggles, victories and defeats, married off against their will to further their guardian's ambitions or compensate for his defeats.

A message came from the Malika-e Dauran that she and the Badshah Huzur were waiting in the Khas Mahal to bless and bid Falak Ara goodbye.

The *kahharans* picked up the doli, the aunts showered coins as almsgiving and to protect the bride from the evil eye, Khadija Bibi, her teacher, who had also come, was reciting Surah Rahman, and Falak Ara left the room where she had lived for sixteen years to go off to a new house.

She was sobbing, when Talat Begum hugged her and said, 'You will come back to visit us Falak. Don't cry and don't miss us. Your new family will cherish you.'

Accompanied by Mahtab Ara Begum, Chand Kunwarji and Rani Meera Devi in their respective palkis, she reached Khas Mahal.

Badshah Salamat and Nawab Zeenat Mahal begum were waiting. The doli was set down. Huzur tied a gold embroidered *imamzamin* on her right forearm and breathed Ayat al-Kursi on her; Zeenat Mahal blessed her and gave her a bag of coins as a gift. The Qazi sahib, who was waiting in the public area gave the azan as the doli emerged out of the mahal taking its precious inmate to her new house. May Allah be her protector and keep her safe and happy.

The doli left the mahal amidst a shower of coins and reached Mirza Aftab's house.

Mubarak was walking beside the doli, carrying and guarding the jewellery box, for she had heard of the looting done by the soldiers in the city. The jewellery and clothes had been gifted to her precious darling by the inmates of the mahalsara and the Badshah Salamat, and she would die guarding it. Other attendants walked beside the palki with clothes and fruit trays.

In her doli, Falak Ara came out into the public portion of the Qila for the first time in her life. She had heard it described by Mubarak and other attendants but had never gone beyond the Baithaks. Even when they went out of the Qila for Mehrauli or other excursions, they were carried out in dolis via the Meena Bazar route, which had cloth screens put up on either side for purdah and went directly to Dilli Darwaza. But nothing was normal today.

With her head bent, covered with a heavy dupatta and eyes downcast, she could see nothing, but the artist in her could feel each step. The peace of the Qila, which would have normally only echoed with sounds of work, was now disturbed by the Hindustani soldiers, walking about, talking, laughing in breach of protocol.

Chand Kunwarji was also thinking of the breach of protocol; no one except the Emperor and princes of royal blood could enter the naqqarkhana on their horse or elephant. Yet these sawars were galloping on their horses and had sent decorum flying to the wind. She knew that no one spoke in front of the Emperor unless given permission, but she had heard that they were not only speaking but also addressing him irreverently.

Falak Ara's heart was thumping with nervousness and a sensation that she might faint. Inexperienced Falak was in the throes of a passion which she could not understand.

The palkis were set down in Mirza Aftab's haveli. All the male relatives had come to greet them while the ladies were sitting in the baithak. Since purdah rules were more relaxed here than in the Qila, a few ladies were also seated there in a curtained area.

Qaiser was sitting inside, surrounded by his friends. Miyan Nabbu, who had gone home for Ramzan had returned the day before after hearing about the rebellion of the soldiers. Like his father, he was faithful to the angrez but he would not miss out such a chance for action. As soon as he heard of Qaiser's wedding, he found the perfect excuse to enter the Qila.

While Mahtab Ara Begum, Rani Meera Devi and Chand Kunwar walked into the baithak, the bride was brought inside in her doli and the palki was set down in the curtained area.

Amidst a shower of alms money and recitation of Quranic verses, the bride, helped by Mubarak, was taken out of her doli and made to sit on a low masnad with gold-worked cushions and bolsters all around her.

Head-bent, the bride sat down. The mirasins continued singing and money was given to them.

'May I be sacrificed over your beauty, my daughter,' said Mahtab Ara Begum lifting the veil so that all the ladies could catch a glimpse.

As per the custom, everyone gave gifts and the *munh dikhai*, or ceremonial unveiling of the bride's face, was conducted.

Mirza Aftab was called. The ladies did purdah while Mahtab Ara Begum sat near the bride.

'Only God is without blemish,' he said, 'may I be sacrificed over your innocence and moon-like beauty.'

Hearing these comments and feeling her presence, Qaiser was burning inside and trying to appear calm on the outside.

Nabbu nudged him and said, 'Dear groom, is your heart somersaulting?'

Zoravar and Ibrahim hushed him and sat on either side of him to keep him in control.

It was time for asr prayers and the preparation for the iftar was in full swing. Mirza Aftab had called his friends and relatives to celebrate his son's wedding.

The ladies helped Mubarak to take Falak to the bridal chamber decorated for the newly wedded couple.

Considering the situation, Mirza Aftab had decided that the two should live with him till things calmed down.

The room was lit by a red and green chandelier, which gave it a mysterious glow. The four-poster bedstead was covered by a gold embroidered canopy, with flowers hanging in garland strings from the top.

Since both the bride and groom were fasting, they would meet in the evening after breaking the fast. Intimacies were not allowed during the period of fasting.

As soon as Mubarak was alone with her charge, she made her lie down to get some rest.

Outside, some of the men were discussing the day's events, away from the hearing range of Qaiser and Mirza Aftab.

Mirza Abu Bakr was updating Ibrahim and Zoravar, who had been with Qaiser from the morning, of the happenings in the city.

'I don't know when this will stop! It has to, or else we are doomed. These purbias, as the sepoys were called for most of them belong to Eastern Awadh and Bihar, will ensure the destruction of our mission.'

'What happened Mirza?' asked Zoravar.

'These accursed men had been surrounding the kothi of Raja Sahib Kishangarh. He had given shelter to some thirty odd European men, women and children. They had been hounding the Raja, but as they were in the *tahkhana* and it is an old, heavily fortified kothi, their bullets went waste. Today morning, they lured the thirsty and hungry angrez outside on pretext of giving them water and shot them all.

Badshah Huzur sent Mirza Quwaish to prevent them from taking lives but they had murder on their minds. And they aren't done yet. Even as we speak, there are more being hunted in the old houses. I just hope the angrez manage to escape to Punjab for safety.'

Just then the gong from the naqqarkhana announcing that it was time for iftar sounded, and everyone went inside.

The men were seated on a dastarkhwan in the main hall while the ladies were seated behind the curtain.

The mood was sombre for the sound of guns could be heard in the background.

Mufti Azurda, Thakur Madhav Singh, Dr Bishamber Kaul, Thakur Sangram Singh, Mirza Abu Bakr, Zoravar Singh, Miyan Nabbu, Kunwar Ibrahim, Mirza Sikandar, Zahir Dehlvi and Nawab Mirza Dagh were all gathered at the iftar.

The conversation purposely stayed away from the ghadar raging outside and focused on the wedding and the young couple's future.

Falak Ara was in her room with Mubarak. Her iftar had been brought here. She was too nervous to eat anything, but Mubarak cajoled her.

Finally, it was time for her to change and for the *rasm*, ceremony, of *arsi musaf*, which would be followed by dinner. Keeping the weather in mind the dress for this ceremony had been especially made of muslins, *tanzeb* and chintz for her by the finest seamstresses, personally supervised by Mahtab Ara Begum.

The pajamas were light green, made of cotton called *bulbul chashm*; a geometrical pattern similar to the nightingale's eye. Her jama was of delicate red tanzeb and as the name implied, it really did embellish her slim body. Underneath it was a golden angiya made in the Rajput style to honour Qaiser's mother, with a back and front neckline.

Kundan, diamond, pearl and gold jewellery completed her ensemble.

But wait, the final touch was still to be added.

This was the gossamer like net dupatta, heavily stitched with zardozi work embellished with pure gold and silver lachka, gota and kinari.

Mahtab Ara had asked for permission to enter along with Chand Kunwarji.

They stood looking at the vision in front of them and with 'Surely, only Allah is free of blemish. You are looking like the sun and moon have come out in the night sky together, Dulhan bibi. May I be sacrificed over your beauty.'

Chand Kunwarji, after praising Falak and showering sadqa over her, turned towards Mubarak, 'All the ladies are ready for the munh dikhai and rasms. Let us take the dulhan out.'

Hariyali and Naseeban had also come to help Mubarak and together with the two senior ladies, they put Falak on her feet and into her *kaf-e paa* sandals, and slowly walked her to the zenana area.

Every pore of Qaiser's body was aware that Falak had entered the room, but bound by etiquette, he could not look at her. He felt her being seated and the exclamations of wonderment from the ladies at her beauty.

Hariyali came to take him for the arsi musaf.

A Hindustani ceremony adapted with Islamic touches, it had become hugely popular amongst Muslims in the past few years.

Arsi in Hindi means mirror, while the Arabic word musaf means a book and is used to referring to the Holy Quran.

When Qaiser went in, he saw Falak sitting with her head resting on her knees with only her hands visible as they were clasped around her knees.

He was made to sit there amidst much teasing. This would have been done in the bride's house with the bride's sisters and cousins having fun with their new brother-in-law. But considering the chaos in the palace, it was decided to be held in the relative peace of Mirza Aftab's house. As it was set near the Asad Burj, not many sawars or sepoys were around.

The bride and groom were covered by a dupatta and a copy of the Holy Quran was placed between them to seek divine blessings. A filigreed silver mirror was kept between them by Mahtab Ara Begum in such a way that if Falak lifted her ghoonghat, Qaiser could see her face in it. She then asked Qaiser to write the *Surah Ikhlas* with his finger on his bride's forehead.

As soon as Qaiser's trembling fingers had traced the words on his bride's forehead, Chand Kanwarji said, 'I am going to be from the dulhan's side today. Qaiser, look in the mirror and say, "Wife, open your eyes, and I promise to be your slave." Say that if you want your bride to lift her ghoonghat and show you, her face.'

After much good-natured ribbing, Chand Kanwar lifted Falak's ghoonghat and a bemused bridegroom saw his wife's face. *Surely, no angel can be this beautiful,* were his thoughts.

The ceremonies over, Falak was taken back to her room.

The most anticipated night of her young life was about to come.

Qaiser waiting patiently outside for all his guests to go, was thinking of Momin Khan Momin's lines:

Chaara-e dil siwaye sabr nahin
So tumhare siwa nahin hota

The heart's cure is nothing but patience
And without you, that will never come to me.

30

Henna or Blood: The Colour of Both Is Red

Mehndi ke dhoke mat rah zalim nigah kar tu
khoon mera dast-o-paa se tere lipat raha hai

Don't be fooled, oh tormentor that this is henna, see you
It's the blood from my hand and feet embracing you

—Mushafi

Falak Ara had waited for this night since eternity. She had felt herself melting every time she imagined him reaching out for her. She was no longer the girl who had left the mahal shyly in her doli. These few hours of anticipation of their union, with his smell and presence enveloping her, had made her into a woman of flesh and desire.

The longing was becoming unbearable as she sat with her head bent down under the weight of the heavy dupatta and jewellery, waiting for him to enter. All she wanted to do was throw off the veil and be one with him.

Good God, what was she thinking, what had happened to all the decorum she had been taught? She wasn't this wanton creature, whose very existence was this slow burning desire. She didn't even understand it, for she had led such a sheltered existence. To distract herself she turned towards Mubarak, but Mubarak was busy adding more flowers to the bridal bed, which as it is was looking like a flower garden. The heavy fragrance of the jasmine strings that hung from the canopy of the four-poster bed and the incense was intoxicating.

To steady her nerves, she reached out to rearrange the masnads and cushions, touch the cool water of the crystal bowl in which rose petals were floating. She was just patting some water on her forehead when she felt him enter and wish Mubarak. She froze.

As if in a dream she heard Mubarak present her salam and then heard retreating footsteps and the sound of a door closing.

Oh! She was alone with him.

Her heart was pounding and she felt like a caged bird about to jump out.

She felt him come towards her and sit down.

He sat down and gently put his fingers under her chin. Lifting her face, he recited Mir Taqi Mir's immortal verse.

Khilna kam kam kali ne sikha hai
us ki aankhon ki nim-khwabi se

The bud has learned to slowly unfold
from her drooping eyes.

He then followed it up by saying with a quiet intensity, 'How I have longed to see your face, feel your breath on mine and sweep you into my arms.'

Falak felt her breasts tauten, her body tense and a flush covering her body. She involuntarily looked up and seeing the loving look and passion on his face, mingled with his innate gentleness, felt herself dissolve.

They were one in each other's arms, savouring each other's contours, trying to become familiar with each other's bodies when an urgency swept over both. The exploration of the body was now urgent, and as his fingers went over her face, down to her neck then bosom, she felt that she would explode. To steady herself, she caught his shoulders, and now it was his turn to burn in that touch. His fingers were now travelling lower and feeling her moist desire he threw away her veil and helped her undress. There was no time for taking off their complicated clothing and with just the lower halves undone, he helped her lie down and spread her legs gently.

It seemed to Falak that she was the candle burning in the niche, and he was the moth, she was melting, and he was getting sucked into her.

They were one, with the ferociousness of a storm that rages, the gentleness of the morning breeze that caresses and the sweetness of the rosebud that gives out a fragrance when held tightly in the palm.

They were finally one. The flame that had burnt in each other's hearts for so long was not so easily doused and they kept exploring each other's bodies, growing bolder till it was time for azan.

Getting up, they both had their ritual bath, necessary after sexual intimacy, so that they could make the vow to fast that day.

When Mubarak, who had stayed just outside the door in case her darling needed help, sensed that they were ready, she knocked with sehri on trays. She found them both reciting prayers of thanksgiving.

A new morning had dawned; a new life had begun.

The next few days passed in prayers and devotion, fasting and remembrance of Allah but the nights were the fumbling and taking off, of red and green clothes, the fragrant henna on the bride's hands and roses on the bed, smiles and passion.

On the morning of 16 May, they had dozed off late after sehri and prayers when shouts woke them up. It was twenty-first Ramzan, the day of Hazrat Ali's martyrdom and they had stayed up doing the special prayers for that day.

Their house was between Asad Burj and the naqqarkhana.

Qaiser quickly put on his jama and went out.

'Ababjan, what is happening? Why these screams?'

'I don't know son. I was just going to find out. Come with me.'

They both walked towards Mirza Mughal's house, which had two storeys so they could see all over the Fort from it. The screams were coming from the naqqarkhana area.

They found Mirza Mughal and his courtiers in a state of agitation.

'Sahib-e Alam, what is the matter? Why these screams?' asked Mirza Qaiser.

'Qaiser, these accursed purbias and tilingas don't listen to me. Despite Huzur Alampanah's pleas that Islam does not sanction the blood of an innocent, they have forcibly taken all the firangi men, women and children to the tank outside naqqarkhana. I was just going up to the roof. Come with me.'

'Sahib-e Alam, can we not stop them?' asked Qaiser.

Just then the tutor of Mirza Mughal's daughter, Maulana Ainullah sahib said, 'Sahib-e Alam this is an act of great cruelty. No religion approves of the murder of women and children, and Islam has especially forbidden it in very strict terms. *Lillah*, for God's sake, ask these soldiers to spare the women and children.'

Mirza Mughal replied, 'Undoubtedly, this is an act of oppression and tyranny. However, it is not easy to control the ignorant soldiers and the angry officers. They are totally out of control and have lost their sense of decency. Ever since they rebelled against the angrez, they have become so wilful and wild that they do whatever they want and refuse to listen to anyone's orders.'

Maulana Ainullah sahib replied, 'They have appointed Sahib-e Alam as their commander-in-chief, and they have accepted Jahanpanah Zill-e Subhani Aala Hazrat Badshah Salamat. Why won't they listen to your orders or your father's? You should try to make them obey you. Can't you see that the wails and cries of these British women and children are shaking the skies?'

Mirza Mughal replied, 'Maulana, my father and I are mere puppets. The truth is that they listen to neither me nor the Hazrat Badshah Salamat. When these angrez men and women were arrested, I had sent them to the Lal Qila to be under the protection of the Hazrat Badshah Salamat so that their lives could be spared. But even inside the Qila, these cruel rebels kept the angrez men and women under their control and did not listen to any intervention by the Emperor. So much so that when he sent food from the royal kitchens for the prisoners, they resisted, and it was with great difficulty that they agreed to let them eat. They think that the Badshah Salamat and his progeny are conspiring with the angrez against them.'

Seeing the shocked look on Qaiser's face he continued, 'As a result, their sepoys have often confronted me and Jahanpanah saying, "We have jeopardized our families and ourselves, yet you don't appreciate what we are doing. In fact, you keep taking their side on every issue. If this continues, then we will first kill you with our swords."

'Qaiser, Maulana sahib,' continued Mirza Mughal, 'I ask you in all fairness to tell me how can I negotiate with such a murderous and rebellious group? If I try to prevent them from killing these angrez men and women, they will take me and my family to this same spot where these prisoners have been rounded up and murder us first.'

Hearing this, Mirza Aftab left for the Khan Samani building, where he found Hakim Ahsanullah sitting. They found that Zahir Dehlvi had reached before them and was pleading with the Hakim sahib.

'Khan sahib, are you aware of what is happening?' asked Zahir.

'What?' asked Hakim Ahsanullah.

'Those ruffians are taking the prisoners away. I am afraid that they will murder them. Please make arrangements for their safety,' pleaded Zahir.

Ahsanullah Khan retorted, 'What can I do?'

'Khan sahib,' said Zahir, 'this is a test of our loyalty. If you want to save the Badshah Salamat, please reason with the rebels and save the prisoners. Or remember that the British will raze Dilli to the ground.'

Ahsanullah Khan replied, 'Miyan, you are very young. How would you know that man does not listen to reason when caught up in circumstances such as these? He does not think of the result of his actions. If we remonstrate with them now, they will kill us first, and then murder the prisoners.'

'It is better that a few of us are killed,' Zahir said. 'At least the Badshah's empire will be saved.'

Seeing that he was unmoved, Mirza Aftab, Qaiser and Zahir left from there and came back to the deorhi.

They sent a message to the Huzur Alampanah through the khwajasara stating that the purbias had taken the prisoners whom Huzur had kept in his special protection. The Badshah Salamat gave immediate orders to call Hakim Ahsanullah Khan so that he could make arrangements to save the prisoners.

The khwajasara came outside the palace and sent a messenger to get Hakim Ahsanullah Khan post-haste. Two more messengers were sent one after the other, but though time was passing, Hakimji did not move from his place. After some time, Hakim Ahsanullah Khan came to the tasbihkhana and entered the presence of Huzur.

Alampanah gave orders: 'Call the officers and reason with them and save the prisoners.'

Hakim Ahsanullah Khan said, 'Huzur Salamat, as you wish.'

He came out to the Diwan-e Khas and sat down against the arch in the middle enclosure. Zahir, Mirza Aftab, Qaiser and a few other courtiers were with him, waiting helplessly. Perhaps he had sent a few people to call the rebel officers.

Suddenly they saw that two companies of purbias, bearing loaded guns on their shoulders, were coming from the door of the Lal Purdah. As soon as they came into the Diwan-e Khas, they surrounded the group of courtiers and stood in front of them with guns pointed at them. All of them were praying to God and reciting the kalima, anticipating that the sawars and sepoys would blow them up at any moment. For a few moments, they kept standing there like that. After that, two sawars lofted a red flag outside the Lal Purdah, which was an indication to the other sawars to put their guns back on their shoulders and leave.

A messenger came after a few minutes and gave them the news: 'The prisoners have been murdered.'

Qaiser stumbled home in shock at the turn of events. The past few days, he had been living in his own little world and had forgotten about the ghadar, purbias and tilingas.

He went crying into his room and into the shelter of Falak's arms.

'What has happened, Mirza sahib, to make you cry so? Who was screaming?' she asked.

Qaiser, with tears rolling down his cheeks, described the turn of events, 'I cannot describe my distress at hearing the words that the prisoners have been killed. These monsters had blood on their mind and were unwilling to listen to anyone in their frenzied state. I am just as sorrowful at the killing of these children as I would be, God forbid, at the death of my own children. I am astonished at how stone-hearted these villains could be to lift their hands to kill those innocent children and helpless women.'

Falak comforted him as well as she could, holding him tight and rocking him instinctively as a mother would. Married amidst unfolding tragedies and challenges, Falak quickly found herself taking on the roles of a lover, friend, confidante and mother. She gave of herself freely, whether it was physical comfort, emotional support or mental engagement. The bond between the two was growing stronger and stronger. The incipient trust they had begun to place in each other over the course of their frenzied correspondence now took root more deeply. It was a bond that made them truly one.

Meanwhile, Zahir Dehlvi left for his home, walking past the naqqarkhana. He wanted to mourn in peace. He lived in Maliwara and had to go through the Ajmeri Darwaza.

When he reached the darwaza of the naqqarkhana, he saw that the hacked corpses of the prisoners had been strewn to the right of the darwaza. He could not bear to see this scene of death and destruction, and covering his face with his handkerchief, he went away from there.

After this event, the purbias began to rule the city and their writ ran large: Knaves rule in the kingdom of fools.

All that was heard was the thunder of cannons and screams of innocents and sounds of falling tears. The poetry and songs for which the city was famous had now been silenced.

31

Knaves in a Kingdom of Fools

The next day, as Naseeban and Mubarak were walking to the Qila, they heard the dhobis of Kucha Mir Ashiq engaged in a loud discussion. The two friends stopped to talk to them and hear the news. The dhobis went everywhere, to every area, and so knew the latest news.

They were discussing the massacre.

'Two carts were brought in and loaded up with bodies. The palace sweepers took the carts towards the Salimgarh Fort, where the corpses were thrown into the river. There were fifty-two bodies in total—all but five or six were women and children.'

'How do you know the exact number, Mani Ram?' asked a dhobi sitting next to him.

'The sweeper, Chuni Lal, told me. And we will soon know how many were involved in the murder, for their clothes will come to us for washing,' replied Mani Ram.

The two women shook their heads and walked towards the Fort. This was turning out disastrously.

The residents of the city were miserable, as they had no recourse to justice. They were praying to God to help them get rid of this unforeseen, unexpected evil. All they wanted was to find peace so that the city could go back to normal, and the oppressors left it and went away.

In the palace, there was gossip that the mutineers wanted to elect Mirza Abu Bakr as their Badshah in place of the Badshah Salamat, whom they declared to be too old and infirm.

Qaiser was considering his options now that Mufti Azurda had joined the Hindustani cause.

Mufti Sadruddin Azurda had been employed by the Company bahadur, drawing a salary of twelve hundred rupees per month from the Company and getting a stipend of two rupees fifty paisa from the Badshah Salamat. His love for the Badshah was such that he always valued those two and a half rupees more than the twelve hundred. Now he was happy to throw the salary away and serve the cause of the Hindustanis under Shahenshah-e Hind Abu Zafar Sirajuddin Mohammad Bahadur Shah Badshah Ghazi.

Qaiser took permission from his father and wife and presented himself before Mirza Mughal.

He was made the commander of one regiment.

Money and resources were becoming a huge problem. At the Diwan-e Khas where Qaiser was present, he heard orders given that a salary of thirty rupees was to be given to the sawars and infantry sepoys would get ten rupees per month to carry out their functions. Troops were coming from Jalandhar to Firozpur Sikandra, Hansi to support the Shahenshah-e Hind; money from the treasury such as Palwal, Hansi and Mathura.

A Rebel Constitution was formed, as well as a council.

All efforts were being made to control the soldiers, for while the residents of Shahjahanabad had welcomed the soldiers, their brutish ways, loot and plunder had turned the people against them.

Thakur sahib, Mir sahib, Imam sahib were using Bhooray Khan's network to try and reach out to them and make them understand the importance of the task at hand and their erroneous way, which were antagonizing everyone.

Even the courtesans who had helped the rebels were turning against them as they would arrive unannounced and take whichever girl they liked and behave roughly with them.

Mirza Qaiser came home from Salimgarh, where he was training with the other princes and soldiers, to see his father reading *Dehli Urdu Akhbar*.

'Does it give news of any other city, Abbajan?'

'God bless Maulvi Mohammad Baqar,' replied Mirza Aftab, 'Yes it does. Let me read and tell you.'

'Does it talk of the behaviour of the soldiers?'

Maulvi Baqar was acquiring information from various sources to present an authentic account of the events from other newspapers and had sent correspondents to different parts of the area. He himself was collecting information about events in Delhi. On 11 May he had come out of his house near Kashmiri Darwaza after hearing the chaos. On 17 May, in the first publication, after the ghadar had started, he reported the news of Europeans being chased and often killed by the purbias and telingas, and the looting and plunder.

'Yes, my son. Maulvi Baqar is urging them to behave with discipline and is exhorting them. He writes that everyone should see the larger picture and that they are liberators of the people, who have smashed the pride of the angrez. For him, this uncivil behaviour is simply an aberration. He is calling the purbias and telingas lions and the *fauj-e* Zafar, or victorious forces.'

On the twenty-third Ramzan, one of the auspicious days of the month, Huzur Purnur held a durbar in the Diwan-e Khas which was attended by the Executive Council and army officers. Mirza Aftab attended along with Mirza Qaiser.

Huzur Alampanah sat on the Takht-e Huma and conferred khilats on his sons. The next day coins were issued in his name.

'Allah be praised!' said Mirza Aftab, 'Huzur's sovereign status so long denied by the angrez has been reinforced today.'

Qaiser's days were spent in training and strategizing with the soldiers and his nights in passionate lovemaking.

Falak was learning to handle and run her house under the guidance of Mirza Aftab, who had declared that she was his daughter, not daughter-in-law, and was guiding her as she navigated her new role. There was so much to learn as the mistress of her own house—and assuming these responsibilities in the midst of the pandemonium and violence all around was even more daunting. She was anxious not to disappoint her new household. There was so much to do and so much to worry about—and it was inevitable that the pigments and material that Mubarak had brought were neglected since there was no time to paint now. Maybe when things calmed down, she would take out her painting and complete it.

It was in the midst of this unrest that Falak celebrated her first Eid with her husband.

Since the Hindustani soldiers were training or resting in this period, Qaiser had free time.

Mubarak had taken Naseeban's help to stitch a new jamdani dress for her darling. This material was so fine that Hazrat Amir Khusrau had said that it looked like one had smeared pure water on the body. It was a textured weave where extra wefts were used to create patterns on a body of fine mulmul.

The material had belonged to Dil Ruba, but she died before it could be stitched for her. It was extremely costly and just as sensuous, so Mubarak had waited for her precious darling to be married before using it for her. Mubarak had heard the story that Badshah Shah Jahan had once asked Shahzadi Jahanara Begum about the appropriateness of the jamdani dress she was wearing, and she showed him she was wearing seven layers of fine gossamer material.

It was just apt for this humid weather, and to create closeness between the new couple, now that the ghadar wars were dulling.

Over the dress was a heavy dupatta, so that Falak's purdah was maintained in front of Mirza Aftab, for she would go to pay her respects to him and claim her *Eidi*, the gift given by elders.

The crescent moon had been sighted the night before, and Mubarak had stayed on at night. The cooks had prepared a delicious feast. But first, the namaz.

Mirza Aftab and Qaiser joined the Badshah Salamat's procession as it went to the Jama Masjid for Eid namaz. Usually, he went to the Paharganj Eidgah, but considering the attacks from the ridge, Paharganj was deemed unsafe this year. They reached the Jama Masjid and offered prayers. The darogha of the department of armoury tied a sword to the imam and the imam then went to read the khutba.

Everyone greeted one another with embraces, and guns were set off in celebration of the moment.

The Badshah returned in his *negdambar* to the royal apartments in the Qila and sat in the Baithak to take everyone's nazar and salam. This marble monument was the heart of the Qila, with its delicate decoration, breathtaking elegance and the verses of Wazir Sa'dullah Khan written in gold ink on its northern and southern arches.

Agar firdaus bar ru-ye zamin ast
Hamin ast-o hamin ast-o hamin ast

If there is Paradise on earth
It is this, it is this, it is this

Mirza Aftab and Qaiser came home. Mubarak led Falak Ara, with her head bent by the heavy dupatta, to present her salam to Mirza Aftab.

'Abbajan, salam.'

He blessed her and gave her a pair of diamond and pearl bracelets that had belonged to his wife and said, 'May you live in your husband's protection forever.'

Since Qaiser was at home, Mirza Aftab went off towards the Diwan-e Khas to get a grip on the current happenings.

In their room, alone in the day, without the restrictions placed by Ramzan, Qaiser was looking at his wife's exquisite beauty, showcased in that jamdani dress.

Spontaneously the words of the poet Mushafi came to his lips:

Saath us ḥusn ke deta tha dikhai voh badan
jaise jhamke hai paṛa gauhar-e tar paani mein

Her body glimmers through the dewy fabric
As if the moon's reflection is playing mischievously in the water

Soon he and she were mischievously playing with each other, discovering their moistness and tender spots.

Eid provided an interlude, but not for long, for the next day, Qaiser came running from Salimgarh. 'Abbajan Abbajan, calamity has struck!'

'Take a deep breath and tell me slowly,' said Mirza Aftab.

'Abbajan, Badshah Salamat is feeling so angry and frustrated with the behaviour of the rebels that he has threatened that he would leave the palace and move to the shrine of Qutub Sahib or go to Kaaba.'

'Calm down, my son,' said Mirza Aftab, 'tell me the details.'

'Abbajan, Alampanah says the soldiers are making the life of the residents of Shahjahanabad miserable and are harassing both the population and the loyal servants of the state, and making it impossible for them to continue. Huzur has issued an edict saying earlier, the firangis issued orders as they pleased and now, the tilingas are causing even more grief and trouble. If this continues, he has given notice that he will proceed into retirement towards Qutub Sahib, and all his loyal subjects will accompany him. That he plans to migrate to Mecca, to the Kaaba, and spend the rest of his days in prayer, and remembering the Almighty.'

The Badshah Salamat wasn't the only one feeling the heat, the residents of the city were just as unhappy. Eid had failed to provide any solace for the residents of the city, who were reeling under shortages and price rises. The Muslims had barely managed to procure some milk and sugar to cook siwain, the sweet vermicelli made on Eid. Hariyali passed by a group bemoaning the hardships that the people were enduring. 'Two *ser* of ghee is available for a rupee, and wheat flour, maida and semolina have become almost impossible to find,' her neighbour was lamenting. 'In earlier times, the rate of wheat was about forty sers to the rupee and that of ghee, four sers to the rupee.'

'Behen, think of it this way. Once we are rid of these firangis, everything will become cheaper. I am not an educated woman, but I go to the houses of all the rich and educated. I have heard Maulvi Baqar sahib talking, saying that the angrez have reserved all the high offices for themselves—after all, the blind distributes sweets only to his own. They take large salaries which they took out of our country, and we get no benefit from our own money. They loot our rulers and don't give them respect. We are left with famines and diseases and our industries are suffering.'

'Hariyali, I am sure what you are saying is correct, but what does a poor man's stomach understand of all this talk? I only know what my hungry stomach growls into my ear,' replied the lady.

'Let the purbias and tilingas prove themselves,' said another city resident. 'All they do is eat at the sweet shops and harass us.'

'I am sure they will,' said Hariyali as she moved away. Her son's death was still burning in her heart, and she would do whatever was needed to see the angrez bite the dust.

The opportunity to prove themselves came a few days later.

On 30 May, they engaged with the angrez in the battle of Hindon River, the village of Ghaziuddin Nagar. The Company bahadur along with troops from Meerut were advancing towards Delhi, knowing full well that Delhi was the centre of the ghadar and the Badshah Salamat was the magnet for more rebellious sepoys to join in. The aged Emperor had been urging his sons to take the troops and squash those soldiers in and around Meerut who were still loyal to the Company before they could harm their cause. His warnings went unheeded.

They had now arrived at the Hindon River, near Ghaziuddin Nagar, and the sound of bugles could be heard everywhere. This news had already reached the officers in the Qila via their outriders, and they were ready for battle. Eventually, the troops led by the inexperienced Mirza Abu Bakr met the enemy. The topkhana was ready and the wooden carts were standing loaded with cannons in the magazine. At 10 a.m., the platoons were standing at attention and the regiments were standing on either side of the river when the call was given to attack. The sawars and sepoys immediately left through the bridge door, below Salimgarh, crossing the bridge, over the Jamuna, along the road to Shahdara. Mirza Qaiser was with them on his horse.

Falak and Mirza Aftab were getting ready at home for *zohr* or noon prayers when they heard the distant sounds of cannons firing. Hindon River was twelve miles away, but the sounds were loud. Both of them lifted their hands to beseech Allah for the safety of Qaiser and the other Hindustani troops. They could hear a volley of shots from the cannons as well as guns. This continued for two hours and was then replaced by intermittent fire.

It was now 3 p.m. It seemed that the British Army had not only reached the city at double speed but had also engaged the rebels within two hours of getting there.

Within three hours, the outcome had been decided. But inside the city, everyone was still waiting to learn who the victor was, and who was the loser.

Mirza Qaiser returned with his troops in time for asr prayers. They entered the *chatta* of the Lahori Darwaza, their wooden carts, bearing artillery, leading the way.

Though many of the soldiers were celebrating and blowing trumpets at what they thought was their victory, Qaiser was more cautious.

Seeing him safely home and having read thanksgiving prayers, Mirza Aftab asked him about the battle.

'What kind of battle did you fight?'

Qaiser replied, 'We were on either side of the embankment. There was artillery fire from both sides, Abbajan. Mirza Abu Bakr had climbed on top of a house to oversee operations. He had placed a battery near the bridge and the exchange of fire with the angrezi fauj was like a question being asked and an answer given. We fought bravely but had to retreat in front of their fire power. We used the 18-pounders we had captured and wounded a few of their forces. Then the angrez soldiers crossed the river and we had to retreat.'

'You were wise, my son. It is better to retreat and go and fight the next day,' said Mirza Aftab.

'That is not all Abbajan. We were robbed by Gujjar villagers on our way back to the city. They even robbed the firearms from some men and some took clothes from them.'

It was only at night in the comfort of Falak's arms that Qaiser gave voice to his fears and hopes. 'Mirza Abu Bakr is very inexperienced, I am scared for the future of our mission. None of us have any military experience or exposure. You know, Falak, when a shell burst near the battery and the gunner was covered with dust and it seemed like a scene from doomsday, Mirza Abu Bakr descended from the rooftop and galloped off with his escort sawars. That created confusion.'

'But didn't Abbajan say that it is wise to retreat so that one can live to fight another day?' asked Falak.

'God forgive me if I am wrong, and I wish my tongue had been cut off before I voiced such suspicions, but for a moment I felt that Mirza Abu Bakr ran away because he was scared,' said a disconsolate Qaiser.

'God knows how much you care for the khandan-e Timuriya so you are not being disloyal, my beloved,' said Falak, intuitively understanding his fear, rocking him into an uneasy sleep.

Meanwhile, Mirza Mughal and the other princes held a meeting with the soldiers and decided to go back and attack the next day. Badshah Salamat had reproached the soldiers for retreating in what he said was cowardice, resulting in the loss of the heavy guns. He urged them to return to the Hindon river the next day to put things right.

The next day again, Qaiser left with the fauj. This time there was fierce fighting from both sides and Qaiser's training as part of the Bachera Paltan came in good use. But despite the bravery shown by the sepoys, there was no breakthrough and the *Badshahi Fauj* had to retreat once again. There was despondence in the camps in the Qila and Shahjahanabad. Some of the sepoys deserted their posts and left the city that day.

At home, Mirza Aftab, hearing the continuous firing of shots kept praying, 'May God keep us safe from cannonballs. When one bursts and its pieces fly in the air, it can destroy entire buildings, however high they may be. If it falls on the ground, it can make a ten-yard crater and blow all the houses in the area in its wake. It is the wrath of God.' He had started staying at home with loaded firearms because of Falak. Even though Mubarak came every day at dawn and stayed with her till night, he had heard of the chaos that some badmash were creating in the guise of the sepoys. There were also random cannon balls falling on the Qila, and he didn't want to take chances. Falak was the pride and treasure of his house, and he would guard her with his life.

Ten days later, the angrez troops attacked again in Badli ka Sarai. Their numbers having been reinforced with a battalion of the Gurkhas commanded by Major Reid, the angrez fauj crossed the Jamuna and reached Delhi. The Hindustani soldiers put up a gallant fight but were routed by a bayonet charge by the 75th Regiment of Foot, who captured the rebel battery that was raining fire on them. They lost the ridge from where they were firing upon the angrez. The angrez promptly set up their camp on this high vantage point. From here they could fire directly at the Salimgarh Fort.

That night, when Mirza Qaiser reached home, he was wounded. A gunshot had grazed his firing arm, and one of the other officers with him had tied a makeshift bandage around the wound. Seeing the blood-soaked fabric, Falak started weeping; but Mirza Aftab, keeping his calm, called out for warm water, bandages and balms. He cleaned the wound and tied it up with fresh bandages using balms procured from Hakim sahib in case of just such a calamity. Sending thanks to Allah for having spared his son any major injury, he ensured that Qaiser was fed and then asked him to rest. Knowing how traumatic that day must have been, Falak did not question him further and just held him as he slept.

The next morning, seeing him recovered, Mirza Aftab asked his son about the battle.

'They had advance information that we would be attacking them,' said Qaiser. 'God curse the spies who are betraying our Huzur's cause. Abbajan, they had ensconced themselves in a very strong position in the Badli ki Sarai, having crossed the canal at night. They placed their heavy guns on the elevation in front of the Sarai Gate. Their infantry was able to take the cover of the village next to it. Even then our fauj fought back valiantly. However, because of their better location, they were able to push us back. I got injured in the artillery fire, but I am proud to say, I injured quite a few of them. My training proved advantageous for me.'

Mirza Aftab and Falak listened quietly, knowing there must be more. Sure enough, with a shake of his head, Mirza Qaiser continued. 'Abbajan, we had to retreat and left behind some of our guns. I am afraid that we have lost the ridge to them in the process.'

With the capture of the ridge, the Hindustani soldiers were restricted to the walled city and the Fort. There was no more fighting on the open battlefield. Instead, there was entrenchment and fortification. Guns were being fired day and night. The British were entrenched on the ridge, from Frazer sahib's kothi to the Flagstaff tower. There was firing all day on the city.

Skirmishes continued after that for the next few days. Mirza Qaiser was nursing his injury, unable to join the sepoys. Nonetheless, he kept himself abreast with the news.

A few days after the Badli ki Sarai battle, Falak noticed that Qaiser was more distressed than usual. He was engulfed in a worrying silence and had not even touched the food prepared for him. At first, Falak said nothing and only urged him to eat so that he did not go to bed on an empty stomach. Later that night, Falak held him in her arms and, stroking his hair gently, asked him what the matter was.

'Meri jaan, you are my life, and I can't hide anything from you,' he said at last. 'Yes, indeed I am worried for I have heard that the Maharaja of Patiala and Jind have pledged their forces with the angrez. Not only that, but their forces are also attacking the Hindustani soldiers who want to come and join the Badshahi fauj. How can these rulers be so short-sighted? Don't they know that we are fighting for our Badshah Salamat's right to rule this land and overthrow the firangis? I have heard that Begum Hazrat Mahal in Lucknow and Nana sahib in Kanpur have joined the fight against the firangis.'

Falak, comforted him as well as she could but knew that his fears were well-founded.

'Not just that,' continued Qaiser, 'The Maharaja of Jaipur is also supporting the angrez. Mirza Abu Bakr told me that Huzur Alampanah had written to Maharaja Narendra Singh of Patiala, Sawai Raja Ram Singh of Jaipur, the Raja of Alwar, the rajas of Jodhpur, Bundi and Kota, asking them all to attend the durbar with their armies but it seems they only care for temporary gains.'

'It is a difficult time, my love,' said Falak, 'But you are on the side of truth, of *haq*, and I am sure victory will be yours. We are all praying.'

'O Falak, I pray that your prayers are accepted. It is just such a difficult time. Huzur Alampanah is trying to raise money for the troops, but the city residents are all so angry with the sepoys who indulge in looting in the city that they are unsympathetic. You know our treasuries are empty. The daily expense of the Badshahi fauj is twenty-five thousand rupees per day, and Huzur had commanded each of the traders to pay five lakh each but Mirza Khizr Sultan told me, they have refused. If only Mirza Mughal had heeded our Jahanpanah and attacked the angrez fauj in Meerut before they could recoup and attack us it would be a different story. Our inexperience and lack of a unified command worries me.

'Meri jaan, I can only express all my doubts to you, for you are my soulmate and complete me. I don't want to worry Abbajan, and the two of you are the only ones I can call my own.'

'Of course, my love, you can,' said Falak. 'I am there for you, with you always and forever.'

Even as this conversation was taking place, another was well under way.

The three familiar conspirators—now no longer worried about being found out—were meeting with Bhooray Khan in Thakur sahib's haveli.

'What news do you bring Bhooray?' asked Thakur sahib.

'Not very good, sarkar. The accursed sepoys are behaving as if they are on some kind of picnic. They have become very lazy since there are no daily military exercises or parade. They loot the shops and stand about eating halwa puri in the bazaar. Huzur Jahanpanah has expressed his displeasure at the way things are turning out. I heard that he has written a long letter to Sahib-e Alam Mirza Mughal about this.'

'God have mercy on us,' cried Imam sahib.

'Yes, may God have mercy on us, Imam sahib, for these sepoys are getting out of control. I heard from one of my sources in the Qila that Huzur Jahanpanah has written to Mirza Mughal saying that the sepoys must give up their excesses and also their indulgence in oppression and high-handedness. They must stop this disgraceful behaviour. He has ordered Mirza Mughal to send a regiment to the countryside to end all the disorder and disruption, and to take control and maintain peace. I pray to Allah that his words have their effect on these purbias and tilingas.'

Meanwhile, adding to all the other woes, Mahbub Ali Khan, the wazir, passed away from dropsy. Hakim Ahsanullah Khan was appointed the new wazir.

A durbar was held on 24 June and a council of war, consisting of Makhan Lai, Hakim Ahsanullah Khan and Nawab Ahmed Quli Khan was appointed. Huzur Alampanah addressed the officers of the Hindustani troops. He pointed out that they were destroying the kingdom that had lasted for more than 300 years, and remarked sarcastically that when they went out to fight the angrez fauj they returned 'topsy-turvy'.

*

32

Bakht Khan Arrives

It was in the midst of this gloom and doom that news came about Bakht Khan's arrival.

Bakht Khan had served loyally in the angrez fauj but was now throwing his lot with Badshah Salamat. He arrived with three thousand soldiers from the Bareilly brigade—composed of the 8th Irregular Cavalry and the 18th, 28th, 29th from Moradabad and the 68th infantry brigade, along with No. 15 horse battery and two 6-pounder guns. More importantly, he also brought four lakh rupees.

Bakht Khan had rebelled against the Company bahadur and joined the Rohilla Chief, Khan Bahadur Khan, the rebel leader in Bareilly and the grandson of Hafiz Rahmat Khan, the Rohilla chief of Bareilly. Khan Bahadur Khan had advised Bakht Khan to go to Delhi and defend it against the approaching British Delhi Field Force.

Bakht Khan was a much-decorated officer in the British Army, who spoke many languages, including English. He had reached the rank of subedar major, which was the highest position an Indian could reach in the British Army at that time.

He had already sent a message to Huzur Badshah of his arrival, and orders had been given for his accommodation to be readied near the Delhi Gate.

He was made the commander-in-chief of the Indian forces by Shahenshah Bahadur Shah Zafar and given the title of *Sahib-i-*

Alam Bahadur, or Lord Governor-General. Huzur gave orders for the Kalan Mahal to be vacated for General Bakht Khan and his troops. All the troops swore allegiance to him, including Qaiser.

Mirza Mughal, much to his displeasure was made second-in-command and given the title of Adjutant General.

In the city, when the news of the arrival of Bakht Khan spread, there were varied reactions, but mostly relief. The shahzadas had been creating havoc, and the general had promised to come down heavily on any prince who tried to loot and plunder.

Just the night before, Naseeban and Rahim had been discussing the plunder and looting of the city.

Rahim had said sadly, 'I was mistaken in my assessment of Hira. He is now one of those leading the badmashes with Gami.'

'But wasn't that accursed Gami working and spying for the angrez?' asked Naseeban.

'Gami is one of those ungrateful wretches who will fill his coffers by any means necessary,' replied Rahim. 'He has no notion of loyalty and will change sides to the one that's winning.'

The arrival of Bakht Khan put some joy into the despondent hearts of the three conspirators, Thakur sahib, Mir sahib and Imam sahib. They met in Thakur sahib's haveli and sent for Bhooray Khan. Bhooray Khan had joined the soldiers and was participating in all the skirmishes. He had been present at the court when Bakht Khan had come and was able to come from there and relay the news.

'Sarkar, now we may have some respite from the mismanagement and exploitation of the shahzadas and greed of the badmashes, who were oppressing and looting the city. General Bakht Khan sahib informed the kotwal of the city that if any more plundering took place, he would be hanged. Any soldier found plundering was to be arrested and his arm severed. He has even warned the shahzadas that if they are caught looting, they will be severely punished,' reported Bhooray Khan.

'And sarkar, that is not all, the General sahib has made a proclamation, by the beat of drum, in the city that all shopkeepers were to keep arms, and that no one should leave his house unarmed. Persons having no arms are to apply to headquarters for them, and they would be given them free of charge. Any soldier caught plundering was to have his arm severed from his body. All persons having ammunition are to give it over to the magazine, under pain of severe punishment. The police officers were ordered to protect all the respectable inhabitants.'

'This is an excellent news, Bhooray,' said Mir sahib. 'We were getting despondent.'

Thakur sahib joined in, 'I feel sorry for our Alampanah. He is being imposed upon by the shahzadas and the soldiers. Hopefully, the arrival of Bakht Khan will help. Bhooray, please keep us updated.'

Meanwhile, Mirza Aftab, happy that help had come, was also worried about the behaviour of the shahzadas and soldiers. He had invited his friend, Sikandar, to his house and was discussing matters with him.

'Sikandar, thank you for acquiescing to my request. I don't like leaving my daughter-in-law alone in the house. Had my wife been alive, it would have been a different matter. But now that Qaiser goes to fight with the soldiers, I have to stay home.

'Just yesterday I heard that Farkhunda Zamani Begum, wife of Mirza Bulaqi, Huzur Salamat's late son, had to come to the Badshah Huzur's court to complain that Mirza Abu Bakr, in a state of intoxication, had come to her house with several sawars to forcibly abduct her and fired several shots with rifles and pistols, and beat several people of the mohalla. The police arrived, but the shahzada resisted and attacked the kotwal with a sword, had him seized and taken away to custody, insulted him and finally plundered Zamani Begum's house.'

A shocked Mirza Sikandar looked at him, 'What are you saying, Aftab? This is terrible!'

'Now you know why I am worried. When Farkhunda Zamani Begum came to complain to Huzur Alampanah, he tried to bring in some discipline and ordered that Mirza Abu Bakr be stripped of all military rank. Though Huzur ordered his arrest, he escaped and took shelter with Mirza Mughal. However, Badshah Salamat has ordered all other shahzadas to maintain distance from him.'

Mirza Sikandar added, 'There are also daily rumours flying that Hakim Ahsanullah Khan is in the pay of the angrez. There have been so many attempts to arrest him, but for the intervention of Huzur Alampanah himself, the Hakim sahib would have been killed. I hope that ingrate Hakim sahib keeps this in mind when he conspires with the Malika and the angrez.'

'Shhh Sikandar, don't cast aspersions on our Malika,' remonstrated Mirza Aftab.

'Aftab, don't you realize that it is not in the Malika's best interests that the shahzadas succeed? If Mirza Mughal succeeds in throwing out the angrez, then his succession to the throne is assured. Her son will not stand a chance. All her careful plotting and planning will go down the drain.'

Before Mirza Aftab could counter this argument, a summons arrived: Huzur Alampanah had ordered Mirza Aftab's presence in the Diwan-e Khas.

He quickly put on his turban, adjusted his clothes and got ready. There were only a few people there, Shahzada Mirza Qaiser, Hameed Khan *jamadar khas biradaran*, Mir Fateh Ali *jamadar kaharaan*, and Hussain Baksh, the *arz begi* and Zahir Dehlvi, when the Badshah came out of the palace.

They made their salutations and the Badshah sat on the marble throne in front of the tasbihkhana.

Huzur addressed them. 'Do you know what the outcome of the events unfolding before us will be?'

Hameed Khan replied with folded hands. 'Huzur, your glory has been revived after a hundred and fifty years. The empire which had been taken away has been returned.'

Badshah Salamat replied, 'You are all ignorant of the facts that I know. Hear me out. I had nothing to lose. The foundation of strife is wealth, treasures, land and kingdoms, and I had none of them. I was already living the life of a mendicant. Why would anyone have any enmity with me?

Why would anyone be envious of a faqir? I was spending my life like a faqir living in his takiya along with a few of my close people, and I had nothing to lose.

Now a fire was started in Meerut by God's will and is raging in Delhi at present. Trouble has begun and I have realized that the rebellious sky and wicked world want to see my family destroyed. The family of Chagatai Sultans had been reigning thus far, but now no traces of this name will be left.

These ingrates who have rebelled against their masters and appeared here—they will go off soon. When they couldn't stay loyal to their masters, how can I expect any loyalty from them? These rogues came to ruin my dynasty, and now they have destroyed it. After they leave, the British are going to cut my head off, along with that of my children, and hang it on the Qila merlons. None of you will escape their wrath.

If any of you are still alive, then mark my words: you will never be able to eat in peace, and the nobles of Hind will fall lower than village peasants.'

After these words, he went back into the khwaabgah.

These painful words made a deep impact on Mirza Aftab.

He would take daily reports from Qaiser after his son returned from each battle, but he was losing heart.

33

The Ishtihar and the Last Battle

Bhooray had come early morning to meet Thakur sahib.

'Sarkar,' he said, addressing Mir sahib, 'please find out from Maulvi Baqar about an ishtihar that was put up on Jama Masjid?'

Thakur sahib immediately sent his servant to get that day's newspaper for him as well as for his friends. It should have come by now, but if what Bhooray was saying was correct, then the distribution may take time and regular subscribers like him may be getting it a little late.

The paper, which was now called *Akhbar al-Zafar* as a tribute to the soldiers fighting under Shahenshah of Hindustan Bahadur Shah Zafar, and to the aged monarch himself, came at the same time as his friends'. He updated them.

Sure enough, the lead story of 5 July was the *ishtihar*, or public notice, that had been pasted on the Jama Masjid, allegedly by angrez spies and agents. They were trying to mislead and threaten the residents and called upon Muslims to wage a jihad or holy war against the Hindus, for as per the shariah, the Christians were their friends as *sahib-e kitab*, or people of the book. The advertisement also said that no pig fat was used in the cartridge, implying that cow's fat had been used. In his editorial, Maulvi Baqar denounced it as a conspiracy, the handiwork of enemies of both '*Dharm*' and '*Iman*'— the faith of Hindus and Muslims.

Reading from the newspaper, the three friends kept exclaiming at the wisdom and sagacity of Maulvi Baqar, for not only did he denounce the notice but also provided a point-by-point rebuttal of the pamphlet, saying sarcastically that the English should not try to deceive anyone by invoking the shariah.

'Maulvi Baqar rightly says that Hindus and Muslims are fighting side by side and that they should stay united as Hindustanis, and stop the British from playing with their religious sentiments,' said Thakur sahib.

'And we are a living example of that,' replied Imam sahib. 'If the angrez really wanted to look after our interests, they should have been more sensitive and not forced people to switch their religion, or to fight one another.'

Another Eid, that of Eid al-Azha or the Eid of sacrifice, came and went.

There were once again attempts to stir trouble over the sacrifice but as Bhooray Khan reported to Thakur sahib, 'Sarkar, Huzur Alampanah has given orders that anyone caught cow-killing would be blown away by a gun, and that anybody who was found objecting to the killing of a goat would be punished. These accursed firangis are going on trying to sow the seed of discord between Hindus and Muslims.'

Mushtari bai had also celebrated Eid but in a subdued fashion. Her balakhana had been closed since the soldiers had become rowdy and had started harassing her girls, but tonight she had opened it. She was firmly invested in the cause of the Hindustani forces, but being practical, wanted to get a sense of what was happening, and her guests would be the ideal ones for her to gauge which way the wind was blowing. One of her girls, Hoornut bai, had joined the rebels. Mushtari bai wished she could go too, but then she had to perform other services for them.

Bhooray Khan sat at the edge of the room. Now there was no need to hide.

Only a few select people were invited.

Miyan Nabbu was one of them. He had remained unaffected by the ghadar raging around him, waiting to see which side won, before casting his anchor there. Though Gulab Jan was now a regular in his house to ease his loneliness, he missed his friends. Mirza Qaiser and Kunwar Ibrahim were fighting with the Hindustani troops and so were busy. Zoravar Singh had returned to Rajasthan with his parents after Qaiser's wedding, and Brijnath Zutshi had gone with his family to Agra. Most of the Kashmiri Pandits had gone to Agra, Gwalior, Jaipur or Alwar. Mirza Abu Bakr was staying at home, guarding it against plunder. Santosh Lal was stuck in his house studying. He didn't have the means to escape. Also, he was related to Munshi Jeewan Lal, who was an angrez spy, and now that angrez victory seemed imminent, he would be saved by his uncle.

Nabbu had sent word to Santosh that this evening would be on him and hoped he would turn up. To his delight, Santosh Lal did.

Mushtari bai was sitting on her masnad, her huqqah by her side, paandan in front and the musicians on her other side.

The instruments were strung, and she started singing Mirza Rafi Sauda's *shahr ashob*, lament for a city, written after Nadir Shah's sack of Delhi:

Jahanabad tu kab iss sitam ke qabil tha
Magar kabho kisi aashiq ka yeh nagar dil tha
Ke yun mita diya goya ke naqsh-e-batil tha
Ajab tarah se yeh bahr-e-jahan mein sahil tha
Ke jis ki khaak se leti thi khalq moti roll

Jahanabad you were never deserving of such tyranny
You were once the heart of lovers, many
It was erased like a wrong letter by destiny
T'was a one such shore in the ocean of the world
From whose dust people used to pick pearls.
The mood was set, everyone was sombre.

The always effervescent Nabbu asked Santosh about his uncle.

'Arre Miyan, he is living a dangerous life. The other day he was captured by Mirza Mughal's men, who wanted to kill him for spying on them and relaying information to the angrez bahadur on the ridge.'

'Oh! Does he really? And what happened?' asked Nabbu.

'Well, of course he does. He is employed by them. Nazir Ali, the kotwal, came to arrest him with a hundred men. He was arrested and placed in a palki and taken under a guard of soldiers with drawn swords to the Kotwali. There the chief kotwal, Mubarak Shah, treated him with respect. In fact, Mubarak Shah told my uncle not to be afraid, as he too was a servant of the angrez.

My uncle isn't the only one under suspicion, there are constant demands to arrest Hakim Ahsanullah Khan, the wazir. Just a few nights ago, the sepoys surrounded the palace and demanded Hakim Ahsanullah to be handed over to them. For hours Huzur Alampanah resisted their demands. My uncle told me that at last, finding himself helpless, he agreed, on the condition that the wazir's life was spared. This was agreed to, and the Hakim sahib was handed over to the soldiers, and confined by them in the *tosha khana,* where the royal jewels are kept. In fact, the Badshah Salamat even feared for his own life because it is said his Malika is conspiring with the firangis and asked the shahzadas to protect him. Miyan, no one is safe here. It's chaos and everyone for themselves.'

Bhooray Khan was listening with interest, though he was pretending to be disinterested. No wonder the Hindustani forces were losing. The city was riddled with spies.

'Even Ilahi Baksh, Badshah Salamat's father-in-law, is in with the angrez and sends all news to the ridge,' continued Santosh.

'Yes, I have heard that too,' said Nabbu. 'I don't know why this Bakht Khan thinks they can win when they are so undisciplined, and the city is full of spies.'

There were muted conversations going on in the salon and Bhooray Khan soon had enough information to relay to Bakht Khan and Thakur sahib. The reason for the mehfil had been fulfilled.

Bhooray Khan got news that the British troops had been joined by the Punjab Moveable Column, consisting of British, Sikh and Punjabi units under General Nicholson. While waiting for Nicholson to arrive, Major Hodson had avoided pitched battles and had been raiding the neighbouring cities of Hansi and Jind.

The soldiers training in Salimgarh or feasting in Shajahanabad were now getting restive. Though there were daily skirmishes, they were longing for a proper battle.

The much-lauded Bakht Khan had arrived and was appointed general, but there was no action.

'You have put the war in abeyance! What is the reason for that?'

General Bakht Khan decided to besiege the angrez fauj and cut off their supplies and possibly stop the siege train that was reportedly being sent from Punjab. He led his troops to the Najafgarh Lake on 25 August. Qaiser was with the Badshahi fauj, along with some other members of the royal family. The Bareilly forces stayed on the eastern side, while the Nasirabad and Neemuch paltans were forced to cross the canal near the village of Najafgarh before making camp there.

When the officers asked Bakht Khan why his men were not crossing with the rest of the army, Bakht Khan replied, 'If the British blow up this bridge, we will be cut off and stranded.'

They both crossed the bridge and set up camp on the other side. *Luck isn't favouring us*, thought Qaiser as it started raining when the camp was yet to be set properly, and the area was flooded. Sidhari Singh, the commander of the Neemuch regiment, had set his camp up near a hollow and a lake. The cannons and big guns were drowned in the water, which rose to waist level. The magazine boxes that held the ammunition got stuck in the mud and slush.

The British forces began firing continuously from their cannons and artillery. They blew up barrels of gunpowder in the river, which in turn blew up the bridge and cut off the escape of the encamped forces.

Bakht Khan's Army opened fire on the British forces from the other side. Sidhari Singh and Ghaus Mohammad Khan, another commander, were caught in the crossfire and had no place to run.

Somehow, Sidhari Singh, Ghaus Mohammad Khan and Mirza Qaiser managed to take the few men that they had left and bring them to Shahjahanabad in the morning. The camp was abandoned; the tents, magazine and artillery were simply left there, deserted. Thousands of lives were lost in this battle.

Meanwhile, news of this rout had reached the Badshah Salamat.

Mirza Sikandar came to visit Mirza Aftab. He knew Aftab was not leaving his house because of Falak.

'Ama, Aftab, I have just come from the Diwan-e Khas where Huzur Jahanpanah was holding court. Due to a lack of unity, there has been a grave loss of life today. Bakht Khan and Sidhari Singh couldn't coordinate or unite with each other and the Neemuch troops have been routed. Some princes have also been injured in the fight. I came to enquire about Qaiser's welfare. I know he is participating in the war. I heard a sepoy named Ashraf Khan report to the Badshah Salamat that over a thousand men had been killed and all ammunition lost. The angrez attacked when the men were putting up their camps in the heavy rain on the bank of the Najafgarh canal and were taken by surprise. Mahabali Badshah summoned and commanded Mirza Mughal, Mirza Quwaish, Mirza Khizr Sultan and Mirza Abu Bakr to send reinforcements and attack the angrez paltan.'

In the face of this news, there was nothing to do but endure the agonizing wait in the hope for news of Qaiser's safety.

By the time the wounded Qaiser reached home, Mirza Aftab and Falak were frantic and sitting on their prayer mats, pleading Allah for the safe return of their loved one. Seeing a limping Qaiser helped home by some sepoys, with blood staining his right leg, gave them some moments of joy before they started clucking around him, tending to his wounds.

'What happened, my son?' asked Mirza Aftab, after he had dressed his son's wounds.

'Abbajan, the Company bahadur had sent reinforcements, and the Maharaja of Patiala has given his forces to the angrez. We went there unprepared, and there was disarray immediately as we were exposed to the rain and the angrez attack. They have been busy building batteries and pickets all over the ridge and outside the city gates.'

That night, as Falak kept sending gratitude to Allah for saving her beloved's life, Qaiser wept in her arms.

'*Meri jaan*,' she whispered to him. 'Sleep for a while, things will appear better in the morning; they always do.'

Her soothing voice soon quietened his tears. '*Meri jaan o jigar*,' he said with a tremor in his voice, 'May Allah keep us safe, but I am very disappointed at the way things went today. When we were returning, the heavy rain pelted on us, and I could feel that the Badshahi fauj is very disillusioned that their lives had been endangered by the quarrels amongst the top three commanders. I don't think we have a chance in the face of the discipline and unity of command that the angrez fauj is displaying.

'Falak, when will we learn to be united?' he continued in an anguished voice. 'Three of our different infantry units fought separately and exhausted their ammunition. Bakht Khan refused to support Sidhari Singh. By the time the *Khas bardars* (imperial bodyguards), Bachera Paltan reached us, the forces were also in rout. I was injured too. There weren't enough dolis to bring the injured back. The sepoys carried their comrades on a makeshift bed made with their carbines.'

Falak could never have imagined how dramatically her life would change—it seemed that she had been flung from the strict protection of the Mughal haram into the chaos and violence of her current life. Her experiences had compelled her to grow up faster than she might have done otherwise; her anchor through all this tumult was her love for Qaiser and her belief that she needed to be strong because he depended on her now for comfort and solace just as she needed him for love and support.

Now, she said softly, 'Sleep, just now, meri jaan; tomorrow your mind will be clearer, and I am sure Badshah Salamat will find a solution. I know that the people are loyal and committed to him.'

Qaiser, groaning from his injuries replied, 'Falak, today I saw the emotion of the ordinary people. Villagers of Nangloi near Najafgarh came out to fight, even their women. It is a people's war now and it would have been a people's victory if only we had been united.'

'Shhh,' said Falak softly, 'You are wounded, if you stress yourself, it will start bleeding again. Is it paining you too much?'

'It is nothing, just a graze,' Qaiser dismissed the seriousness of his injury with a shrug and a shake of his head. He even managed a weak smile but his fear at what the future held for them made him clutch her tightly as he fell into an uneasy sleep.

'Ya Allah, *shukr hai tera*, thank you for saving my suhag. I can't live without him,' she sent up a silent prayer, as she sat cradling him, rocking him like a baby every time he became restless.

After the battle at Najafgarh, the purbias lost steam and their enthusiasm and desire to fight was dampened. This was the last big battle that they fought.

The Badshah Salamat held a durbar in the Diwan-e Khas. It was attended by Hakim Ahsanullah Kahn, Mirza Aminullah Khan, Mirza Ziauddin Khan, and five hundred officers and nobles. Once again there were complaints of lack of money, because of which soldiers weren't getting salaries, and the issue of extortion by the shahzadas was raised. Mirza Mughal and Mirza Khizr Sultan were summoned. They admitted to taking forty thousand rupees, but not three lacs that was alleged. The officers urged Badshah Salamat to make arrangements, failing which they threatened to plunder the city.

Now that Qaiser was at home till his wounds were healed, Mirza Aftab had attended and was standing quietly in the durbar. He wanted the earth to open up and swallow him when he heard Alampanah say, 'There is no need to plunder. I will sell my horses, elephants, silver and the gold ornaments of state, and pay the fauj. If I do not do so, you can all leave and abandon the city, the more so as I never summoned you. If you intend to plunder the city, kill me first. Afterwards, you can do as you please.'

Saying this, Badshah Salamat, rose and walked out of the Diwan-e Khas into his own private apartments.

Hakim Ahsanullah Khan brought a message that Nawab Zeenat Mahal Begum sahiba would pay the soldiers from her own resources within fifteen days and disburse the balance due. Mirza Aftab heaved a sigh of relief. Now, he could tell Sikandar that his fears of the Malika's loyalty were unfounded.

Mirza Aftab had gone to the court again, the next day. A letter by Mirza Mughal was the subject of discussion. The Mirza had assured the Emperor that he would fight to the end and gave assurance on behalf of his brothers and nephews.

When Mirza Aftab came home, he discussed the letter with his son. Qaiser's leg was in bandages which Falak had just changed a while ago, and he managed to limp into the baithak.

'Abbajan, what news from the court?'

On hearing about the letter, he replied. 'Abbajan, I am not very experienced, but I do feel that the apparent tension between Mirza Mughal and Bakht Khan is costing us dearly. The fauj is divided into many groups. Bakht Khan and the Bareilly regiments are only loyal to the Emperor and regard Mirza Mughal as a necessary evil, while the Neemuch and Nasirabad regiments are loyal to Mirza Mughal. I regret to say this, and I wish my tongue had been cut before I uttered these words, but Mirza Mughal is also not as far-sighted. He doesn't realize that the residents of our Shahr Panah are dispirited and feel there's no hope left, while the angrez are in very high spirits after this battle. They are building batteries and making preparations for a big attack, I feel.'

He continued, 'This is a terrible state of affairs, Abbajan. And I wouldn't be surprised if the angrez have sent their spies to create discord amongst us. They have been trying to do this for quite a long time. Who knows, they might have succeeded now.'

Getting up to hug his disconsolate son, Mirza Aftab said, 'Don't be so pessimistic, my son. I am sure Huzur Alampanah will sort all this out. Huzur holds daily court to sort these daily squabbles and demands.'

In another part of the city, Hariyali and Bhooray had brought news for the three conspirators.

'Sarkar, there were once again demands for money from the Huzur Badshah,' said Bhooray. 'He gave the quarrelsome men and officers forty thousand rupees including hundred and one gold mohars that the subedar of Bareilly had given to him as nazar.'

'That's not all,' reported Hariyali, 'Huzur came into the mahalsara, I was there when he came. He took jewellery from there and gave it to them. He was so angry that he threw the gold cushion he was sitting on and told them to assuage their hunger. Seeing him so distressed, Malika Zeenat Mahal sahiba has pledged to pay the soldiers from her personal money but even that can't last for long. My heart is sinking, Sarkar, it doesn't look good.'

The Badshah Salamat held durbar almost every day, and councils of war with his nobles and Bakht Khan, but due to a lack of resources, these were fruitless.

On 14 September, Hariyali, walking towards Bhawani Singh's *chatta,* saw many purbias running away. After the Najafgarh rout and loss of lives, they had become very demoralized.

There were many people in the bazar at that time. They stopped the purbias and asked, 'Where are you running after having forced the battle on us?'

The purbias threw down their weapons and said, 'Brothers, we are done fighting; now you fight yourselves. The angrezi fauj has breached Kashmiri Darwaza and is coming in.' And leaving their guns, they ran away.

Hariyali quickly ran back home and locked herself in, as did most of the others who were standing there.

Zahir Dehlvi, passing by, saw something that he felt compelled to go to Qaiser's house and inform him about, for he knew Qaiser was taking part in the battles.

On reaching the Qila, he headed straight for their house and told Mirza Aftab and Qaiser, who was also at home, 'A volley of firing came towards me from the front of the kotwali. The bullets began hitting the stone of the drains, as if they were hailstones. I saw that there was a party of angrez standing outside the kotwali. They have breached the Shahr Panah walls. Most probably at the Kashmiri Darwaza as I saw some Angrez soldiers coming that way. The purbias were running away.'

Mirza Aftab exclaimed in a worried voice, 'You have seen with your own eyes that the angrez fauj has entered the city and purbias have run away. Now the angrez fauj is going to enter houses and slaughter the inhabitants. Death is at our doorsteps! Whatever is Allah's will, will come to fruition now.'

Leaving the father and son in a state of extreme anxiety, Zahir headed home, for he had a newly wedded wife too and aged parents.

He sat down to pray to Allah for deliverance. Around an hour later he heard the firing of a cannon. It seemed very close, as though it were in his own mohalla.

When it was repeated, he went out to investigate. At the end of his mohalla in Maliwara, he found a lot of people.

He asked them, 'What happened? Where has the angrez army gone?'

They told him, 'The people have chased them away. There are riots in the city now.'

Zahir went to Chawri Bazar to find thousands of people roaming the streets carrying sticks, clubs, cudgels, swords and poleaxes.

He ventured further to be met with a horrific sight. The bazaar in front of Jama Masjid was piled with corpses.

He went ahead and saw more dead bodies. When he asked the people of the bazar how this had happened, they said, 'One party of the angrez army reached the steps of the Jama Masjid, and some people were looting the houses of the common folks. The angrez fauj wanted to enter the Masjid. The Muslims gathered inside saw this and feared that they would now kill inside God's house. They thought it would be better to go down and fight the soldiers. The Muslims came out of the Masjid Darwaza and down the steps. The angrez forces aimed their guns at them. The ones who survived kept moving forward and a terrible fight ensued.

People ran out of their houses with whatever they could lay their hands on—wooden sticks, rods from their beds, swords and so on. Some of the angrez party were killed—they are the ones whose bodies are lying here. The rest ran off to join their army.'

It was the same scene wherever he went; bodies were piled up everywhere.

Bhooray Khan was also out with Rahim Baksh. They relayed this information to Thakur sahib.

'Sarkar, there are riots all over the city, all the way to Hamid Ali Khan's kothi near Kashmiri Darwaza. Please secure your house. The angrez have put up cannons near Hamid Ali Khan's kothi. We are going to help.'

Naseeban also went to the Qila and saw the begums in turmoil. Sikandar Ara Begum had gone into a state of shock. In her hands was the book of Shahzadi Zebunnisa's verses that Falak had left behind in the confusion that had surrounded her nikah. She had the page open on the drawing, and all the memories of Rohilla intrusions into the Qila were playing on her mind. The memories came tumbling out. She had been a young girl when that evil Ghulam Qadir had ransacked the Qila. Caught up in the sweep of her memories, the frightened begum subconsciously began humming Shahzadi Zebunnisa's verse:

Within my bosom stirs once more tonight
A voice of song. Love, erewhile slumbering,
Intones his mystery, and the flowers of spring
Relive and bloom. Winter, forbear to smite
My heart's late flowers. Listen! From left and right
Through the green boughs the bulbul's note is heard,

And, wing-clipt and imprisoned, my heart's bird
Flutters against his barriers, wild for flight.

She was once again a young girl playing with her toys in a corner of her grandmother's apartment on the day that Shah Alam sani Badshah's eyes had been gouged out by that villain. At the time, she had picked up the diwan, because it had been with the painter-princess, and thus served as a last link to the grandmother she had lost in that traumatic time. She kept both with her and would fixate on the verse which the princess had been reading before her tragic death. For Sikandar Ara Begum, this verse became her connection to her dear departed grandmother. Obsessing over this verse also enabled the young girl to block the traumatic memories of those violent days and instead focus on the days of innocence that preceded that brutal time. She copied the verse in her childish handwriting and put it inside a mango-shaped locket that she had been wearing. Having learnt the poem by heart, she would hum it to herself often. That was how she could keep the memory of her own grandmother alive and cope with the immeasurable loss of her loved ones without conjuring its violent memories.

And that was how, many years later, Mirza Salim's wife, Sultan uz-Zamani, came to hear that poem during one of her visits to Sikandar Ara Begum. Sultan uz-Zamani liked the tune and wanted to learn the verse. Sikandar Ara was happy to oblige, having found someone to share this poem with. She taught Sultan uz-Zamani the poem and then, coming close to her, whispered in a conspiratorial tone that this was a verse to be treasured carefully and not forgotten. For Sikandar Ara Begum, the memories of that happier time which the poem conjured were indeed more precious than any treasure.

On an impulse she also gave a locket to her granddaughter-in-law and told her to keep it safe. Sultan uz-Zamani Begum did not know quite what to make of the locket. She was charmed by the poem she had just been taught, which she found very soulful, but the locket seemed a childish trinket from a lady who everyone said was senile. And so, Sultan uz-Zamani had casually given the locket to her attendant Hira bai for safekeeping.

Sikandar Ara Begum would not have known any of this. And now, all these years later, she was wondering how the locket came to Falak Ara but just then Rashid Ara Begum's voice was pulled back into the present.

'Naseeban, you have just come from the city. What news do you have?' asked Rashid Ara Begum.

'Begum sahiba, I wish my tongue had been cut off before I had to give this news. There are rioters all over the city, looting and killing at will. Dead bodies are piling up and a rotting stench hovers over the scene. I have just come to warn you all. I am sure Huzur Alampanah will make arrangements but be prepared.' Saying so, she left the Qila.

As the frightened begums and salatin waited in the Qila, and the residents and nobles waited in their houses and havelis, the angrezi soldiers started the slaughter at midnight.

They entered houses and began killing those sleeping inside, climbing onto the roofs to get at those sleeping there too.

In the morning, people living near and in Kashmiri Darwaza, Badar-Roo Darwaza and Kabuli Darwaza, as well as those in the Subhan Phatak, started running towards Chandni Chowk and Fatehpuri Masjid.

Mirza Khizr Sultan brought news to the Badshah Salamat that angrezi forces had advanced towards Kashmiri Darwaza, and finding the Siyah Burj unmanned, with no one there to stop the assault, they descended into the ditch and scaled the Burj with a ladder. After they had climbed the Siyah Burj, the purbia army standing on the nearby parapets jumped down and ran away. Thus, from the Kabuli Darwaza to the Kashmiri Darwaza to Baggapur Ghat, there was no one to man the parapets of the Shahr Panah. Even the soldiers on the parapet of the Lahori Darwaza and the bombardiers on the Burj ran away.

Mirza Mughal came within an hour with the news that the angrezi fauj had entered the city. It was the 14 September.

This news spread like wildfire in the Qila, and everyone waited for the Badshah Salamat's orders.

The night of the 14 September was the longest Falak had spent in her young life. It seemed endless, from having to improvise ways to manage the household with meagre resources to providing comfort and reassurance to a disconsolate Qaiser. He was weeping in her arms like a child. 'Falak, this is the beginning of the end. I am not afraid for myself for when the bugle for battle was blown, I had committed my life to my emperor and my mulk. I am worried about you and Abbajan. What will you do?'

A startled Falak put her palm on his mouth, 'Shh Mirza, don't even utter these words. I have prayed for your life all these days. I have prayed that I never outlive you and die a suhagan.' Continuing in a stronger voice she said, 'Nothing, absolutely nothing is going to happen to you.'

The morning of the 15 September brought stories of the mayhem, murder and pillage that the angrezi fauj was committing in the city. Mirza Aftab, sitting in his haveli, waiting for instructions from Alampanah, received information from Mubarak, who had got it from Hariyali.

Mubarak came with the news that the angrezi fauj had killed Miyan Mohammad Amir Panjakash, the matchless calligrapher. He had been sitting in his haveli when the angrezi fauj arrived. They had attempted to enter the zenana. He came out with his sword, ready to defend the honour of his women, and was shot down.

Qaiser sat down with a thud. 'Ya Allah, what a calamity is this!'

The next day, Bhooray Khan ran towards Thakur sahib's house to tell him to send his family away. 'Sarkar, all the city people found within the walls when the angrez troops entered are being killed by them. They are piercing them with their bayonets on the spot, and the number was considerable, as you may know. The angrez officer Major Hodson has shot our Maulvi Mohammad Baqar. They are killing not just mutineers but also residents. I am taking Mushtari bai and her people to the Paharganj barfkhana, just now, for I believe they will be safe there. Nawab Hamid Ali Khan has taken it on hire for those fleeing the city. Sarkar, I urge you to leave or at least send Thakurain sahiba and Radha bitia with us.'

Thakur sahib, sensing the urgency, immediately called for transport and sent his wife, children and servants with Bhooray. He was willing to meet his fate.

In the city, Mir sahib was crying in his haveli, waiting for his death, when Hariyali came.

'Mir sahib, doomsday has come.'

'I know it has, Hariyali, but what new calamity has struck us now?' he asked.

'The angrezi fauj entered Kucha Chelan and martyred the pride of Shahjahanabad, unique in their talents. I wish I had been struck down before I said these words, but they have killed Imam Baksh Sehbai sahib along with his sons. I have heard that fourteen hundred men from this mohalla were arrested and taken to the river from the Rajghat Darwaza. They were shot down and their corpses were thrown into the Jamuna. The women ran out of their houses with their children and jumped into wells. The wells of Kucha Chelan were full of dead bodies. Even Maulvi Baqar sahib has been shot dead.'

'Ya Allah raham,' said Mir sahib before collapsing. Imam Baksh Sehbai and Maulvi Baqar were his friends.

34

The Beginning of the End

Zeenat Mahal Begum sahiba came to the khwaabgah on the morning of 19 September to find Huzur Alampanah wracked with anxiety. The angrez cannons were pounding on the Qila from all sides.

'May I be sacrificed over you, my Huzur, my life, my all,' she said. 'What is it that worries you?'

'Zeenat, these angrez are after our blood. We are getting reports from everywhere that they are looting and killing our beloved people. They will not rest till they capture us and the Qila.'

'Why are you saying this, Alampanah? I am sure this is not true,' said Zeenat Mahal. Just then Hakim Ahsanullah Khan entered, having been given permission. He had been released by the purbias a few weeks ago and was justly very bitter and angry with them.

'Huzur Alampanah, may I be sacrificed over you, and may I be struck dead, but it is this servant's unfortunate duty to tell you that Bakht Khan and Sidhari Singh have packed their bags and left for Gwalior. We have three regiments here waiting to defend Huzur and the Qila till death. We await your orders.'

'Leave us alone, we need time to think and pray,' said the aged Badshah.

In the evening as the maghrib azan sounded, an extremely worried Kulsum Zamani Begum, the Badshah's daughter, entered along with a few other relatives. It seemed to her that the very walls of the Qila were weeping. The pearly white marble palaces had been blackened by soot from the gunfire and cannon shots in the past four months. No one had eaten for a day and a half. Her daughter, Zainab, was a year-and-a-half old and crying for milk. Neither she nor any of the foster mothers were lactating because of the hunger and trouble all around them. They sat disconsolately. A few of the other ladies in the mahalsara had joined them.

At midnight, she was summoned to the khwaabgah by Huzur-e Purnoor's khwajasara along with his other daughters and granddaughters who were in the Qila. The silence of the dark night was broken intermittently by cannon fire.

Huzur was sitting on his prayer mat with a rosary in his hands. They stood before him and presented three salutations. Though he addressed his eldest daughter it was meant for all his progeny in that room. 'Kulsum, I entrust you to the care of Khuda. If fate permits, we will meet again. Go away immediately with your husband. I am also leaving. I don't want to separate myself from my beloved children at this stage, but I don't want to embroil you in my problems. If you are with me, destruction is certain. Maybe if you are alone, God will open a path of escape for you.'

As she was leaving, Kulsum saw him raise his hands in prayer and say, 'Ya Khuda, please protect the honour of these princesses of the Timurid dynasty. Preserve their honour. The entire Hindu and Muslim population of Hindustan are my children and trouble surrounds them all. Don't let them suffer because of my actions. Give them relief from all troubles.'

Thus began an exodus from the Qila at midnight.

At dawn, Naseeban came rushing into Mirza Aftab's house. Mirza Aftab, seeing her panic asked, 'Naseeban, what is the matter?'

'Sarkar, the day of reckoning is here. May Khuda have mercy on us. I have just heard that Badshah Salamat has left the Qila. He has gone to Badshah Humayun's maqbara. Woe is me, why did I live to see this day!'

Mirza Aftab called out to Qaiser and Falak. Qaiser had been sitting up the whole night with his father and immediately joined him. Falak was inside and came out with Mubarak.

'Son, we have to leave from here immediately. Zill-e Subhani, Mirza Mughal, all other shahzadas and the begums have either already left or are getting ready to leave because it is suspected that today the British forces will enter the Qila. It's no longer safe for us here. I will arrange a bullock cart. We can escape in that. Dulhan, wear Mubarak's clothes as disguise. Cover yourself with her dupatta. Qaiser, you and I will wear Rahim's clothes. Ask him to get them. Tell the servants to meet us at the ice factory in Paharganj. I will go and check.'

'Sarkar,' said Naseeban, 'everyone is going from Delhi Darwaza towards Paharganj and Ghaziuddin Nagar. Let us try to make it to Paharganj and wait for news.'

'Abbajan,' said Qaiser, 'it is not safe for you to go to check or to arrange transport. Either you let me go or ask Naseeban to get us a bullock cart.'

'Jee Huzur,' replied Naseeban, 'you stay here while I go out and find a cart.'

Meanwhile, Falak, took out a few heavy gold pieces and put them inside the strip of the drawstring, *izarband*, in her pajamas. They were going into uncharted territory and jewellery, which could be converted into money, would be handy. They were ready and waiting for the cart to come. Qaiser was frothing at the bit, so to speak—impatient and frustrated at not being a part of the action and realizing that he had a wife and father to protect, and so had to avoid undue risks.

Naseeban came out of the Qila. When she reached Jama Masjid to cross into Matia Mahal, its gateways were bustling not with the dastango storyteller, the kebab sellers or the regular flocks of pigeons, but with angrez soldiers and officers in red uniforms. A few angrez officers were escorting some dignified-looking Indian gentlemen up the steps of the masjid. By the looks of it, it was not to exchange pleasantries.

Some young men, too, were being dragged, screaming, up those steps. The angrez seemed to have made Jama Masjid their headquarters.

Just as she approached the masjid she became aware of a group of men who, enraged by the angrez presence in the mosque, attacked the British picket at the bottom of the mosque steps with sticks. The British soldiers on duty were provoked into action and a volley of gunshots silenced the rebels.

Unnerved by this incident but refusing to fall to pieces, she continued towards Chawri Bazar to find a bullock cart. But there were none to be found. Everywhere there were scenes of panic-stricken people trying to escape. She found one cart driver standing under Mushtari bai's balakhana and asked him for help, but he refused saying that he was already contracted to Mushtari bai and her companions.

'Bai,' he said in a very sad voice, 'you are too late. All the carts have been booked.'

A disappointed Naseeban reached her home to see Rahim cowering in their hut, trying to shut out the wails and screams from the street. She told him of her failed endeavour.

'We will both look for one tomorrow,' said Rahim. 'Just now it is late and dangerous to be out.'

He asked her what was happening to the begums in the Qila.

Hariyali was also wondering the same. She went to the Qila to check and hid in the Khurd Jahan Bagh.

As the news spread that the Qila was being vacated, the little goldsmith boy came running to save his begum sahiba.

'Begum sahiba, come with me,' said Badri. 'I will take you to my house in Kinari Bazar. My Bapu will protect you.'

A weeping and wailing Sikandar Ara Begum said, 'I can't leave my house. I can't leave my grandmother.'

Sikandar Ara Begum had refused to leave. Her maid was with her. Zohrun Nisa was reluctant to leave without her and was pleading with Sikandar Ara Begum to accompany her on the waiting cart, All the other ladies had left in bullock carts at dawn once news had spread that the angrezi fauj had entered the city and were about to enter the Qila. The Badshah Salamat had left the Qila, the Timurid princes were on the run. She had no idea if any of them had survived or escaped to safety. She was determined not to leave the palace of her ancestors. Zohrun Nisa was trying to persuade her to leave.

'Begum sahiba, come, I can hear the goras coming,' beseeched the boy, pulling her by the hand.

The sound of thundering shoes brought back more memories of Ghulam Qadir Rohilla and she whimpered. Her frightened mind went back to 1788, when she had witnessed another tragedy.

She remembered the petrified khwajasara coming and telling her grandmother, 'The day of resurrection is upon us. Even God can't save us now!' as he collapsed at the feet of the begum in the palace.

'God have mercy on us. What new misery has that ungrateful devil Ghulam Qadir inflicted on us?' asked his mistress.

'I wish I had died before I had to utter these words, but Your Eminence, it is my misfortune to say them. That devil has blinded our beloved Badshah. Snuffed out the light from those very eyes that read the Holy Quran daily for sixty years. He is looting the palace, digging up the floor of the Diwan-e Khas. I have brought this bag which my Emperor gave me for safekeeping before Ghulam Qadir—may he rot in hell and insects eat his body—entered the Fort. I was told to give it to you if anything happened to my master, the Emperor. I have been whipped, tortured and should have died but I have stayed to keep my word to my master. I now hand over this amanat to your safekeeping.'

He took out a leather bag from inside his jama. The Begum took it in her hands. It was heavy.

'Hide it, my lady. Hide it before that madman, that demon, reaches here. It is only a matter of time,' gasped the khwajasara as he lost consciousness, never to regain it. The khwajasara was her personal servant and would bring her news daily. He would be granted a private audience with her each time.

No one noticed the child sitting in a corner who quietly followed them:

Quickly hiding the bag under her garments, the Begum then clapped her hands to summon her serving maids and armed women guards who had been sent out to grant her and the khwajasara privacy.

She sent them all away except her two trusted personal maids, telling one, 'Take care of Agha Jan.' To the other she said, 'Hurry. I have to go to Khurd Jahan.'

This was a small palace with a garden in the seraglio, also called Khurd Jahan or Small World, and the Begum's apartments adjoined it.

Normally, the Begum would have been carried even that short distance on her sedan chair, escorted by her guards and attendants, but today she reached it on foot, covered in a black cloak like her serving maid to make it seem as if they were both attendants scurrying to obey royal commands. The garden originally had flowering plants, shrubs and trees, fountains, waterfalls, a baradari, benches for sitting and bowers—perhaps it was meant to create a small piece of heaven on earth and thus the name Chhoti Duniya. Even today, it was far cooler than the rest of the palace in summers due to the strategic use of sprinklers. It provided a scented green haven when the hot months turned Delhi into an oven.

The Begum then sent the maid away. After an hour she called out to her maid again and returned to her apartments. No one knew why she had come to the garden and what she had done.

In one corner of the garden, unknown and ignored, sat a young girl with a piece of paper. She was making a drawing of the garden on a piece of charbi, or animal skin, which she would then transfer onto polished paper. She had been totally immersed in her drawing and now realized that she had drawn something unusual. There was a figure of a woman hunched in a corner, apparently digging the earth. A bag lay by her side. She shook her head, wondering what the significance of this scene near the flowering bush she had been sketching was. She went back to her apartment and put the charbi among a loose sheaf of papers containing poems by Makhfi, the Concealed One, as Zebunnisa Begum was known, that she had borrowed from the royal library.

No one knows whether the completed painting would have had that begum or if the shahzadi intended to even place her there, for before she could complete the drawing, she was dragged out of the apartment along with the begums and other royal princesses, paraded naked before the Rohilla chief, Ghulam Qadir and his men, and violated.

The ten-year-old Sikandar Ara had watched traumatized as she heard screams of the royal ladies being handed over to the soldiers. The artist–princess escaped and jumped into the well in front of their apartment where the little one was still hiding in her corner.

The apartments of the Emperor and begums in the palace was dug up a few days later to hunt for treasure, but nothing was found: neither the khwajasara, nor the Begum or the princess were alive.

However, in the confusion of the preceding days, nobody had noticed that the little girl had returned to that place in the garden the next day. Nobody had seen her digging in the undergrowth and retrieving a mud-encrusted leather bag which she clutched to herself. Had she been asked, she herself might not have been able to coherently explain her actions, acting as she was out of impulse and childish curiosity.

In any case, no one had bothered to ask her if she knew about any treasure or to inquire what was in that old bag which she kept in her box with her toys. That bag stayed with her but the memory of how it came to her was forgotten, erased by the nightmarish chaos that ensued. After her rescue, the overwhelming trauma of the experience had suppressed this memory altogether.

It all came back as Badri pulled her hand once again. She looked at him. In fact, Badri was the only living being who had actually seen what was inside the leather bag, as she would open it to give him a piece to work on every day.

Sikandar Ara was drawn back to the present in a flash.

How had this come to pass? She thought.

A long sigh and 'Astaghfirullah, Allah forgive my sins,' on her lips, and she had left this world for a better place.

Once again today, the palace was filled with screams as boots came marching in and royal feet ran hither and thither to escape.

A shocked Badri ran from there as fast as he could.

When the goras came they saw her lying on a bed covered with her own dupatta, a weeping Zohrun Nisa sitting by her.

Zohrun Nisa had now given up the idea of escaping herself, for all she could think of was how to procure a shroud or make arrangements for the burial. She had no idea what to do, for it was customary for the professionals to take care of the shroud and perform funeral rites before royal burials. The servant girl crying in the corner had no idea either. She was still whimpering and wondering what to do, when the goras and a few Hindustani sepoys entered.

Not caring about the dead begum sahiba or the crying old lady, they caught the servant girl by her hair and dragged her out, asking her to reveal the location of any hidden jewellery and money. The loot continued in the palace for some hours till each royal apartment had been stripped clean of its precious possessions.

Hariyali, watching from afar, saw the goras escorting Zohrun Nisa and Sikandar Ara Begum under her dupatta on a bed. She recognized the bed and feared the worst, for there was no movement in the shrouded body.

She knew it was dangerous to make her presence known and went furtively towards Mirza Qaiser's house to check on them.

For a few hours after Naseeban's departure, Mirza Aftab, Qaiser and Falak had been consumed by anxiety and fear. There had been no signs of Naseeban even as the situation outside worsened. A shout and a knock had spurred Mirza Aftab and Qaiser to answer the door hesitantly, only to find that a cart with driver was standing outside.

'Sarkar,' said the driver, 'I have been sent by Thakur Sangram Singh. Here is his letter. I have managed to come here with great difficulty. Please get into my cart and I will take you to safety.'

'Where is safety today?' asked Mirza Aftab, disconsolately.

'Huzur, for the moment in Paharganj in the barfkhana where many nobles are hiding and then Thakur sahib will arrange for you to go to Rajasthan.'

The three of them decided to leave as they were. There was no time to wait for the disguises that Naseeban and Rahim would bring; there was no knowing whether Naseeban had fallen prey to the continuing violence either. Faced with impending doom, Mubarak told them to go ahead in the *rath* and she would follow.

Qaiser was just going inside when some angrez officers and fifty soldiers from the angrezi fauj appeared on the scene along with Gami and Hira, who were coming out of the mahalsara. The soldiers rushed towards Qaiser.

Hira recognized Qaiser. He was sure Falak would be with him.

He led the looters towards the house. Qaiser had seen them too. He thought there was a possibility of rushing indoors and barring the door against the attackers, but they proved too quick for him. Before he could secure the door's latch, the soldiers deployed their collective strength to barge in.

Hira's eyes immediately looked for Falak and recognized her as she attempted to rush to Qaiser's side. But before she could reach him, Hira intercepted her. His hand immediately went for her throat to snatch the locket. It had been haunting him for months.

'How dare you?' said Qaiser and Mirza Aftab in one voice.

'You have lost your authority, but not your arrogance,' said Hira.

'Please let it be, don't say anything, I will give it to them,' said Falak, hoping to prevent a worse calamity, but it was too late.

One of the bloodthirsty badmashes picked up his gun and smashed his bayonet through Mirza Aftab, sending him to the next world. Another attacked Qaiser. Falak lunged to protect her suhag. But the oppressors had no pity. They struck him hard, and he fell to the ground beside his father. Falak bent over Qaiser. Meanwhile, fearing the worst, the frightened rath driver drove off.

Seeing her husband bleeding, Falak cried out to Mubarak. 'Mubarak, help me, someone please help me.'

But it was too late.

'Aah, Falak,' Qaiser uttered the name dying on his lips even as he writhed in the blood before passing away.

By now, Mubarak who had been packing for her precious shahzadi in the deep recesses of the house had heard the sounds of the attack. Determined to protect Falak, she had picked up Mirza Aftab's pistols and ventured to the scene of the tumult. She didn't know how to use the pistols, but she was sure she could frighten the soldiers with the weapons.

She arrived to hear Falak crying piteously and saying, 'Khuda hafiz, Mirza. But before going, tell me in whose care are you leaving me? You were my life and now you have also left me. The world will be hard pressed to find any girl as unlucky as I am; I was married a couple of months ago and now I am widowed.'

Hira, seeing his chance, pushed her over her husband's corpse and snatched the locket.

Another badmash leered, 'Let us relieve you of your miserable life,' and struck her fatally with his bayonet. She fell with a sigh on her husband's body, her arms clutching him in a tight embrace. This world had been unforgiving to them, but somewhere, they were together again.

Mubarak waved the pistol at them and screamed, 'What are you doing? How dare you touch my shahzadi?' But her cries fell on deaf ears.

One badmash had started stripping the corpses and Mubarak—whose initial shock at the appearance of the goons had been replaced with horror at the murder and mayhem unleashed—now rushed forward to protect what was left of her beloved Falak and Qaiser and even Mirza Aftab. But the villain pushed her away with brute force. Mubarak fell to the ground in a faint, her head cut and bleeding. Taking her for dead, the man left her alone to finish looting the rest of the house with the other thugs. Ironically, Mubarak had already made their work easy for them by having carefully wrapped the household's valuables in a cloth, ready to be taken at a moment's notice when escape seemed possible.

Hira ran from there and when alone, smashed open the locket. This was such an opportune time. He could search for the treasure undisturbed while the angrez were bringing back peace in the city.

The locket snapped open. In it was a standard amulet with a verse written on it. He was literate enough to recognize it as Shahzadi Zebunnisa's verse:

Within my bosom stirs once more tonight
A voice of song. Love, erewhile slumbering,
Intones his mystery, and the flowers of spring
Relive and bloom. Winter, forbear to smite
My heart's late flowers. Listen! From left and right
Through the green boughs, the bulbul's note is heard,
And, wing-clipped and imprisoned, my heart's bird
Flutters against his barriers, wild for flight.

If Hira was hoping for a clue to a vanished treasure, this was certainly not it.

'God curse these Timurids!' Hira spat. 'They deserve this pitiable end. Their empire has ended but not their love for song and verse. She's been leading me a merry chase just for this!'

He came back to throw the locket on her body just as Hariyali reached the miserable scene. Naseeban also arrived, huffing and puffing and saw three blood-stained corpses lying in the middle of the room, stripped of their valuables by the looters. Hariyali's wail was blood-curdling and set Hariyali and Naseeban off, shrieking and crying.

Naseeban saw Hira with shock in her eyes.

Hira spat at her and walked off. The others had already taken away all the jewellery the three had been wearing.

While Mubarak and Naseeban sat wailing with the three corpses, begging the angrez fauj for *kafans* to bury them in, Hariyali left in a daze.

In the city, seeing rivers of blood flowing everywhere, Hariyali staggered to her humble hut.

Once again, she walked through the streets of her beloved city, but this time there was no ektara, no song on her lips or basket of bangles at her waist, only blood stains and screams. Even the temple bells and masjid minarets were silent.

The only sound coming was from the *kotwali chabutra,* where thousands were lined up before the three gallows erected there.

As one Hindustani was hanged, the others waiting in line were privy to that man's death throes. They cried and screamed to no avail. Their pleas of mercy bounced off the ears of the sahib bahadurs sitting on the chabutra.

She returned home, picked up her basket of bangles and smashed its contents to the ground. They weren't needed now.

Shahjahanabad had been widowed.

Epilogue

21 September 1857

The residents of Shahr Panah, or the City of Refuge, as Shahjahanabad was called then, had become refugees. They wanted to escape the walled city before the angrez locked its gateways. In the few days since the British had breached the Kashmiri Darwaza, the air was thick with the wails of forlorn denizens and the innumerable stories of the summary executions of notable residents.

Those who were old, infirm or had no means to escape had hidden in the taikhanas of houses in the city. The angrezi fauj found them huddled together—hungry, miserable, crying—and relieved them of the burden of this world. It was not an exaggeration to say that blood ran through the streets.

Mir sahib, Imam sahib and Thakur sahib had chosen to remain in the Shahr Panah, for true to its name it would offer the protection of death. They had all gathered in Thakur sahib's haveli to await their inevitable end.

On 20 September, Bhooray Khan brought news to the three that Major Hodson had come to Badshah Humayun's maqbara and arrested the Emperor, Nawab Zeenat Mahal Begum and Shahzada Jawan Bakht, and had taken them to the Lal Qila.

A wave of shock ran through them.

'What are you saying, Bhooray? Did no one stop the accursed Major?'

399

'Sarkar,' said Bhooray Khan, his voice thick with anguish, 'General Bakht Khan had tried to advise the Emperor. He had said to the Badshah: "Although the angrez fauj have taken the city, militarily it is not a big blow to the Hindustani fauj as the whole of Hindustan is up in arms against the firangi and everyone is looking up to you for guidance. Travel with me to the mountains from where the fight can be continued in such a way that the angrez would not be able to break through." He went on to explain to the Badshah Salamat that Shahjahanabad was vulnerable as it wasn't built like a fortress, wasn't suitable for a war, and that the few months that the rebels have managed to defend it was in itself no mean achievement. The angrez were on a hill and even an untrained army would have succeeded from such a favourable position.'

'Why didn't Huzur Purnur listen to him, Bhooray?' asked Thakur sahib.

'Sarkar, when our own turn against us then what can anyone do? Mirza Ilahi Baksh and Hakim Ahsanullah Khan sahib convinced the Badshah Salamat not to listen to Bakht Khan.'

'Mirza Ilahi Baksh said to the Emperor, "I agree with every word that Lord Governor Bakht Khan said, however, I would ask the question whether this fight is between you and the angrez or is it between the angrez and the rebel fauj. The angrez know that you are not at fault and were pushed into this by those accursed purbias. You were helpless and did not have the force to stop them. They know that the rebel fauj issued orders in your name; Huzur Alampanah, there is no need for you to worry unless you go with the rebel fauj because then the Company bahadur will be convinced you are with them. In this hot weather, with heavy rains and in your feeble condition, how will you put up with all the trials and tribulations that will come with an army on the run? You have begums and children.'

Mir sahib and Imam sahib clutched their heads at this news.

'Sarkar, that's not all,' continued Bhooray Khan. 'Agha Jan khwajasara told the Badshah Salamat that Mirza Ilahi Baksh has joined up with the angrez and he should not listen to him and should go with General Bakht Khan. But just then Hakim Ahsanullah Khan came to intervene, and as you know, he was corresponding with the angrez throughout.

'Hakim sahib had already made a promise to the angrez, Sarkar, that he would not let Badshah Salamat go with General Bakht Khan. In the preceding months, the soldiers and princes had cautioned and warned and protested that Hakim sahib was not loyal to the Huzur but to the angrez. However, Huzur Alampanah was old and feeble— and despite all these protestations, he continued to trust Hakim sahib who had saved his life so many times previously. God alone knows whether Hakim sahib is loyal to the Badshah Salamat or not, but his words had a great effect on Huzur. Even Zeenat Mahal Begum sahiba who has great courage and determination, was neutralized by Hakim sahib's words. Badshah Salamat eventually agreed, and he was taken to the Qila-e Mubarak as a prisoner.'

They were silent after Bhooray Khan left. Now it was clear that death was ordained for them. The next day brought even more chilling news.

Once again, it was Bhooray Khan who brought these ominous tidings. He said that Munshi Rajab Ali and Mirza Ilahi Baksh had reported the whereabouts of Mirza Mughal, Mirza Khizr Sultan and Mirza Abu Bakr to Hodson. Taking a hundred riders with him, the Major had gone to Badshah Humayun's maqbara accompanied by Munshi Rajab Ali and Mirza Ilahi Baksh.

'The shahzadas knew it was their end, but I am told they said, "We have to die today or tomorrow, so why not meet death bravely?" They were arrested and taken by Major Hodson. On the way, the Major ordered them to descend from their carriage and disrobe. He then shot them dead at Khooni Darwaza near Firoz Shah Kotla.'

The three were sobbing by now.

'Sarkar,' implored Bhooray, 'harden your hearts for this is not all. I was told that after killing them, Major Hodson even drank their blood. If the rumours are to be believed, then it follows that he had said that if he did not taste their blood, he would go mad as these were the shahzadas responsible for the murder of helpless women and children from his country.

'He then cut off the princes' heads and presented them to the Badshah, saying, "This is your nazar, which had closed, and to renew it you had taken part in the rebellion." The Badshah Salamat looked on at his sons' heads and with surprising composure said, "Praise be to Allah, the descendants of Timur always come in front of their fathers in this brave way."'

'Hey Bhagwan,' said Thakur sahib while the other two people in front of Bhooray could say nothing else except rock themselves in grief.

Bhooray continued, 'Sarkar, the bodies of the shahzadas are hung out in front of the kotwali and the heads are hung on the Khooni Darwaza. The angrez are mad with bloodlust and want a thousand-fold revenge for every angrez life lost.'

Wracked with grief, the three men hung their heads in silence, mourning the end of an entire way of life that had sustained them as well as their ancestors for centuries. That once magnificent culture, rich and sophisticated, was now burned to ashes. Paradise had been plundered, its destiny rewritten.

And Shahjahanabad—once the beating heart of a vast and varied civilization—was now but a dream that had flickered and faded with the dawn.

Acknowledgements

As a scholar and translator, stepping into the world of fiction for the first time was a huge step for me.

This book has been possible only because of Ambar Sahil Chatterjee with whom I first discussed the possibility of writing a historical novel. Ambar not only guided me through this unfamiliar terrain carefully, but his edits have, as they say, *'char chand laga diye'*—made the novel resplendent.

I am further indebted to Hena Kausar who helped me in framing the romantic interludes of the protagonist.

Vaibhav Kaul unlocked for me the world of Kashmiri Pandits living in the nineteenth century Shahjahanabad, and I have incorporated many of those anecdotes into the book. I am extremely grateful to him and all our various conversations on the syncretic culture of those days.

I am very grateful to Maaz Bin Bilal who translated three verses for me; Mustansir Dalvi for translating a verse for me; and Mehran Qureshi for allowing me to use his English translation of a Persian verse. He has been credited in the endnotes. Conversations on Farsi verses with Faiza Zaidi and Prashant Keshavmurthy have enriched the book and translations.

The poetry website of Rekhta Foundation has been my source for many of the verses that I have used. It was possible to translate many of these verses because of their dictionary and meanings. I am extremely grateful for making verse selections easy and informing my translations.

The website of Prof. Frances Pritchett, A Desertful of Roses, has been extremely helpful in translating Mirza Ghalib's verses.

My sisters, Farzana and Farah, as well as my niece Alvia were my first readers, and their feedback helped me flesh out the novel.

I owe a debt of gratitude to Anjum Hasan, Ira Mukhoty, Navina Najat Haidar, Muzaffar Ali, Raza Mir and Swapna Liddle for their generous endorsement of the novel and support throughout the writing process.

Like all writers, I can't do without my editors, and I would like to thank Moutushi Mukherjee and Yash Daiv for polishing and pruning my work. Left to myself my self-indulgence would have made me extremely verbose!

Thank you A Suitable Agency for finding my work suitable enough to represent, believing in me and for going much beyond the duties of a literary agency.

And above all, a big note of gratitude to each and every reader of mine: your appreciation has given me the inspiration to write and continually keep challenging myself.

Bibliography

The Urdu books I read and consulted for this novel that helped me recreate the city and its life are:

1. Zahir Dehlvi's
   - *Dastan-e Ghadar*, Academy Punjab Trust, Lahore, 1955
2. Nasir Nazir Firaq's
   - *Lal Qilaey ki ek jhalak,* Urdu Academy, Delhi, 2013
3. Mirza Farhatullah Beg Dehlvi's
   - *Dilli ki Aakhri Shama*, Anjuman Taraqqi Urdu (Hind), New Delhi, 2015
   - *Phool Waalon ki Sair*, Mahboobul Matabe, Delhi, 1943
4. Khwaja Mohd Shafi Dehlvi's
   - *Dilli ka Sambhala*, Maktaba Jamia Limited, New Delhi, 2006
5. Syed Yusuf Bukhari's
   - *Yeh Dilli Hai*, Saeed Company, Karachi, 1963
6. Ashraf Subuhi Dehlvi's
   - *Dilli ki Chand Ajeeb Hastiyan*, Director Qaumi Council Bara-e- Farogh-e-Urdu Zaban, New Delhi, 2011
7. Khwaja Hasan Sani Nizami's
   - *Ghadar ki Subh o Shaam, 1857,* Shamsul Ulema Khwaja Hasan Nizami ki Barah Qadeem Yaadgar Kitabein, New Delhi, 2008
8. Lala Shri Ram's
   - *Dilli Ghadar se Pahle*, Arkaan-e Majlis-e Adbiyat-e Aliya Urdu Mehfil, 2002

9. Sir Syed Ahmad's
    • Both editions: *Asar us Sanadid*, Tulika Books, New Delhi, 2017
10. Wazir Hasan Dehlvi's
    • Dilli ka Aakhri Deedar, Urdu Academy, Delhi, 2006
11. Arsh Taimuri's
    • *Qila Moalla ki Jhalkiyan*, Urdu Academy, Delhi, 2009
12. Khwaja Hasan Nizami
    • *Begumat ke Aansoo, 1857,* Shamsul Ulema Khwaja Hasan Nizami ki Barah Qadeem Yaadgar Kitabein, New Delhi, 2008
    • *Dilli ki an Kuni*, 1857, Shamsul Ulema Khwaja Hasan Nizami ki Barah Qadeem Yaadgar Kitabein, New Delhi, 2008
13. Munshi Faizuddin's
    • *Bazm e Aakhir*, Urdu Academy, Delhi, 2009
14. Maheshwar Dayal's
    • *1857 Ki Dilli*, radio play, episode 1 and 2, published in 1957 and broadcast by Prasar Bharati in 2007
15. Khwaja Hasan Nizami's
    • *Bahadur Shah ka Roznamcha*, 1857, Shamsul Ulema Khwaja Hasan Nizami ki Barah Qadeem Yaadgar Kitabein, New Delhi, 2008
16. Charles Metcalfe's
    • *Two Native Narratives of the Mutiny in Delhi*, Aryan Books International, Delhi, 2016

Readers may also wish to consult my published translations of some of the works listed above. They are as follows:

1. *Dastan-e-Ghadar* by Zahir Dehlvi; published by Penguin Random House India in 2017

2. *City of My Heart* (a collection of writings by Munshi Faizuddin, Wazir Hasan Dehlvi, Arsh Taimuri and Khwaja Hasan Nizami); published by Hachette India in 2018

3. *Tears of the Begums* by Khawaja Hasan Nizami; published by Hachette India in 2022

Glossary

aab-e dast – to wash/clean oneself after easing nature

afreen – encore

ama – an abbreviated version of Ai Miyan

andrasa – sesame-covered rice balls

angarkha – a long robe

angethi – *wood stove*

ashrafi – *gold coin*

aspkhana – *horse stables*

attar – perfume

balakhana – salons of courtesans which were usually on the first floor, leading to the common term for it: *kotha*

batua – cloth purse

bazuband – armlet

chand baliyan – crescent shaped earrings

chanewala – vendors selling cooked chickpeas

chhati – ceremony held six days after birth of a baby

chilgoza – pine nut

chobdar – mace bearer

chougoshia – four-cornered cap

darogha – superintendent

dastar – turban

dohai – help

falak – sky, firmament fate, heaven, fortune

falooda – sweet dish consisting of long noodle-like thin strands

faqir – mendicant

filban – mahout

filkhana – elephant stables/house

gajak – sweet made from sesame seeds, sugar or honey pressed into
    small flat circles

garika – Indian red

ghaddar – traitor

ghoonghat – veil

gilori – a quid made of chopped areca nuts mixed with spices enclosed
    by an edible leaf

gulaal – dry colour

gular – glomerous fig-tree

gulqand – crushed and sweetened rose petals

halwa puri wala – vendors selling halwa with fried puffed bread

haq-e meher – a dower given by the bridegroom to the bride as per
    the Quranic injunction in Chapter 4 Surah Nisa verse 4: 'And
    give the women (on marriage) their dower (mehr) as a free gift;
    but if they of their own good pleasure remit any part of it to you,
    take it and enjoy it with right good cheer.'

haramsara – seraglio

hawadar – sedan chair

iftar – meal after sunset during Ramzan

inqilab – revolution

inqilabis – revolutionaries

jama – outer robe

jashn-e sehatyabi – celebration of recovery from illness

jasolini – female attendants

kamdani/ mukaish – embroidery with gold/silver metallic thread

khaka – tracing

khali – oil cake

khayal, thumri and *tappa* – various genres of Hindustani classical
    music

khwaabgah – bedroom

khwajasara – eunuchs

kornish – salutation (with an inclination of the body and head), obeisance; prostration; adoration

kutubkhana – library

lekhni – pencil

luqme – bite-sized tidbits

maaiy'on – a marriage ritual which took place a few days before the wedding day, after which the bride and bridegroom would give up all their outdoor activities, wear yellow clothes, and stay at home till the nikah

mahaldar – female superintendent of the palace

mahalsara – palace where women resided

maqbara – mausoleum

marhum – late departed

mirasan – singing-girls (of a caste who sing only before women)

morchal – flywhisk

muhnal – mouthpiece for a huqqah

mulk – country/land

mulmul – muslin

murabba – preserves

murid – a follower who has taken an oath of allegiance

mushaira – poetic soiree

nafiri – clarinet

namaz – daily Muslim prayer

nath – nose ring

naubat khana – drum house

nazar/nazr – offering

nigodi – wretch

nijam – Hazrat Nizamuddin Auliya

nuqtis – sweet tidbits

pahar – an ancient unit of time under which the twenty-four-hour day was divided into eight watches of three hours each. Night and day have four *pahar* each with specific names. The first *pahar* of the morning starts at dawn, the second *pahar* or *dopahar*

is afternoon and evening is *seh pahar*. *Dedh pahar* that is 7.30
p.m., is the point between evening and the last *pahar* of the day.
palki – palanquin
panja kashi – arm-wrestling
phansi ghar – gallows
pir o murshid – spiritual preceptor
qaba – cloak
qahwakhana – coffee house
qaliya – meat and vegetable preparation using turmeric
qaum – community
qirat – loud recitation of the Holy Quran
qorma – a meat preparation using curds and fried onions
rakabdar – chief chef
rasik – patrons
raushan chawki – a musical ensemble
rewri – sweet made from sesame seeds, sugar or honey pressed into
small flat cakes or moulded into laddoos.
sadqa – a propitiatory offering
sahnak – an offering or oblation to Fatima, daughter of the Prophet
sehri – pre-dawn meal during Ramzan
shagird – disciple
shahnasheen – royal seat
sharbati, mulmul, doriya, jamdani, nainsukh – names of cotton
materials
siyahi – black pigment
suhaagan – a married woman
suhag – sign of a married woman
suhag ka joda – bridal clothes
suhag pora – a packet with items used by a bride during the wedding
such as itr, sandal paste, etc.
sumran – bracelet
takhliya – leave us alone
tarahi mushaira – a poetic soiree where the first line of a verse has
been fixed beforehand and every poet has to expand on it

taveez – amulet

telingas – term for European-trained Indian soldiers.

tukhm – sweet basil seeds

ubtan – a scrub for the body

ulash – custom of offering a morsel of food by the Emperor to his
    family

zardozi – gold/silver embroidery

Notes

1   *The Diwan of Zeb-Un-Nissa: The First Fifty Ghazals*, Rendered From The Persian By Magan Lal And Jessie Duncan Westbrook
2   Translation by Pasha Mohammed Khan
3   Translation by Mustansir Dalvi
4   Qutub Sahib was called Qutub Sahib after the dargah of the saint Khwaja Qutbuddin Bakhtiyar Kaki
5   Terminalia Chebula and Phyllanthus Emblica
6   *The Diwan of Zeb-Un-Nissa: The First Fifty Ghazals*, Rendered From The Persian By Magan Lal And Jessie Duncan Westbrook
7   Translation by Maaz bin Bilal
8   Translation by Maaz bin Bilal
9   Translation and analysis that follows is by Suzanne Pinckney Stetkevych, *The Poetics of Islamic Legitimacy, Myth, Gender, and Ceremony in the Classical Arabic Ode*, Indiana University Press, USA, 2002
10 Translation by Prashant Keshavmurthy
11 Translation based on one provided by Rekhta.org
12 a euphemism to avoid taking the sick person's name due to superstition
13 Translation of original Persian verse by Mehran Qureshi
14 Mirza Muhammad Abdul Hasan Bahadur
15 Mirza Sultan Muhammad Sohrab Hindi Bahadur
16 Mirza Ulugh Tahir Bahadur
17 Mirza Muhammad Sultan Bahadur
18 Akbar Shah II

19 Saiyed Ahmad Khan's theory has been refuted. The Iron Pillar was forged in C.India and brought to Delhi by Sultan Iltutmish.

20 Translation in Urdu and English from the original Persian by Hammad H Rind

21 The Tears Of Zebunnisa, Being Excerpts From The Divan-I Makhfi, Metrically Rendered Into English By Paul Whalley, M.A. London, W. Thacker & Co. 2 Creed Lane E.C. Calcutta & Simla Thacker Spink & Co., 1913

22 The Diwan Of Zeb-Un-Nissa : The First Fifty Ghazals, Rendered From The Persian By Magan Lal And Jessie Duncan Westbrook

23 Translation Faiza Zaidi

24 *Radical Love: Teachings from The Islamic mystical Tradition*, Translated and Edited by Omid Safi, Yale University Press

25 Ekhtiar, Maryam, 'Practice Makes Perfect: The Art of Calligraphy Exercises (Siyāh Mashq) in Iran', Muqarnas, vol. 23, 2006, pp. 107–130. JSTOR

26 Translation by Maaz bin Bilal

27 Translation by Maaz bin Bilal

28 Various genres of Hindustani classical music

29 Translation from Rekhta.org

30 Present-day Jorbagh area

31 The monthly subscription rate of the *Dehli Urdu Akhbar* was two rupees, and advance subscription rate was eleven rupees half yearly and twenty rupees annually.

32 This is a story my mother would often tell us

33 From *Omid Safi, Radical Love: Teachings from the Islamic Mystical Tradition*, Yale: Yale University Press, 2018.

34 Mirza Ghalib, Dastanbuy, *A Diary of the Indian Revolt of 1857*, English translation by Khwaja Ahmad Faruqi, Asia Publishing Hoiuse, 1970